BELLE
STARR

*Belle Starr lives
in the West of
the imagination*

BELLE STARR

A Novel of the Old West
by Deborah Camp

Harmony Books / New York

Published by Harmony Books, a division of Crown Publishers,
Inc., 225 Park Avenue South, New York, New York 10003
and represented in Canada by the Canadian MANDA Group

HARMONY and colophon are trademarks of Crown
Publishers, Inc.

Manufactured in the United States of America

Book design by Ron McCutchan

Map by True Sims

Library of Congress Cataloging-in-Publication Data

Camp, Deborah.
   Belle Starr : a novel of the old West.

   1. Starr, Belle, 1848–1889—Fiction. 2. West
(U.S.)—History—1848–1950—Fiction. I. Title.
PS3553.A4375B4 1987   813'.54   86-29473
ISBN 0-517-56522-6

10 9 8 7 6 5 4 3 2 1

First Edition

"Belle Starr was less than a man,
but more than a woman."
Jesse James

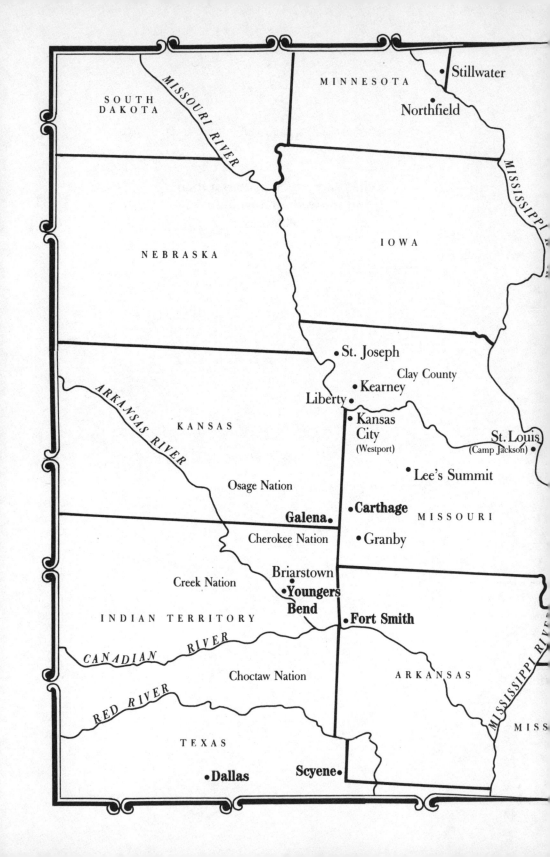

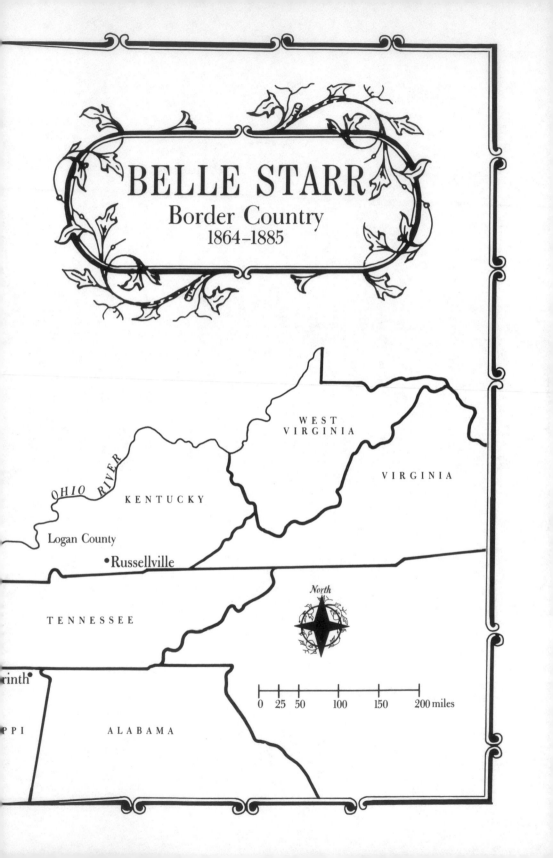

BELLE STARR
Border Country
1864–1885

WEST VIRGINIA

VIRGINIA

OHIO RIVER

KENTUCKY

Logan County

•Russellville

TENNESSEE

North

rinth•

PPI

ALABAMA

0   25 50   100   150   200 miles

PART ONE

Missouri
1864

Chapter One

BEDROLL TUCKED under her arm, Belle crept toward the back door on cat's feet. Her fingers curved around the ornate doorknob, inches from a clean escape, when her brother Edwin's voice reverberated through the hotel lobby.

"Where you going, Maybelle?" He grinned with spite, showing off buck teeth and licorice-stained gums.

A wild urge to slap Eddie's face swamped Belle, but she knew the little wimp would wail and sob as if he were dying and then she'd be stuck at home for sure.

"Shush up," she hissed, "or I'll pin back your floppy ears! Where I'm going is none of—" Holding her breath, Belle was poised by the door, ready to swing it open and sprint for freedom.

"Myra Maybelle, where are you off to without permission?" John Shirley stepped around the registration desk to confront his daughter.

Removing his half-moon spectacles, he peered down the dark corridor. He was in shirtsleeves rolled up to his elbows. His legs were braced apart and his knuckles were planted at his waist. He looked formidable to Belle as he glared at her from beneath black, bushy brows.

Edwin snickered behind his sticky hands. Belle pinned her brother with a scathing glare, sending him scurrying for cover. He bolted for the stairs, making a wide arc around Belle—not fast enough. Belle managed to reach behind her and pinch a plug out of his left side. Eddie yelped and raced to find his mama and tattle.

Belle composed herself, cleared her throat, and attempted the resonant, unbesmirched tone of a church bell. "I have permission from Mama. Mama told me I could go visit the Richeys out Newtonia way."

John pulled on his beard thoughtfully.

A dust-covered older man approached the desk and asked for a room and bath. John handed him a pen and the registration book.

"Welcome to Carthage, Missouri. Looks like you've ridden a ways." The man wrapped stubby, dirt-caked fingers around the pen and made his mark in the book.

Belle heaved an exaggerated sigh and slouched to her father's side behind the desk. She looked longingly at the staircase, wishing she'd wrapped her hands around Edwin's scrawny neck.

"Drove some cattle up from Texas. Gonna have 'em slaughtered to feed the boys in gray."

"Bless you, sir," John said with heartfelt sentiment. "Do you bring any news of the war?"

"Just that it's still going on. Things could be better for us," he admitted, beating his hat against his leg. Dust billowed from it, covering the threadbare Persian rug. "Still fighting on the border?"

"It never stops," John said with a hint of sadness. "Those Kansas do-gooders won't let us be."

"Jayhawkers," the man said through gritted teeth. "Slimy bunch, ain't they?" He included Belle with a glance and a

4

grin as she nodded in complete agreement. "There's a good Rebel lady," he said, winking at her.

"The room's at the top of these stairs and the bath is at the end of the hall." John cordially sent the man on his way.

Belle took a backward step and tried to look innocent, "Papa, Mama said I could . . . ," she began.

"You know your mama isn't half herself these days," he interrupted. "She's living in her own world where there are no wars or battles or border scrimmages." He closed the registration book with an authoritative snap. "Do I know these folks? The Richeys? Aren't they Union sympathizers?"

"I don't know," Belle said on a long sigh. She dropped the heavy bedroll and her tapestry purse onto the rug. She'd packed a few provisions in case her plans were foiled and necessity forced her to spend the night under the stars instead of with the Richeys. "I used to see them in church all the time. Their daughter and I attended the academy together, so why can't I visit them? They're not going to shoot me or take me prisoner, I can assure you."

John held his daughter's dark, unfathomable gaze and lowered his voice so that the man and woman seated in the lobby couldn't hear him. "And I can assure you that if I find out you're lying to me I'll horsewhip you, young lady!"

"Lying to you?" Belle widened her eyes in mock horror and her full lips formed a perfect O. "Why would I lie, Pa?"

"I think you're sneaking off to meet Jimmy Reed, that's what I think!" John's short fingers gripped one of her wrists and held it against the polished desktop. "Look here, missy, lately you've come up with all kinds of friends outside Carthage to visit. I'm more 'n a little suspicious since you never were a social butterfly before brother Bud introduced

you to that Reed boy." He wagged a finger in her face.
"Mark my words, Myra Maybelle, if I discover that you're
meeting that brash bushwhacker or *any* bushwhacker for
that matter, I'll take a switch to you."

Belle sniffed the air with contempt. "Papa, do you truly
believe that?" She threw him a wheedling sweet look, sure-
fire to convince Papa of her innocence. "You know better,
don't you?"

John considered this for a moment before he let go of
Belle's wrist and pulled at his beard again. He gave her a
sheepish grin. "I sit around here day after day and listen to
these harebrained war stories and I can't tell the truth from
the tall tales." He ran a forefinger down one side of his
daughter's face and smiled warmly at her. "You're a pretty
thing, Maybelle. Just like your mother."

"Mama seems better today," Belle said, glancing upstairs
where her mother was changing the linens in the guest
rooms. "I think she's coming around to accepting the war,
don't you?"

"Eliza won't ever accept her son riding off to fight his
neighbors and friends. She comes from a bad-tempered
family and she can't tolerate any kind of feuding. Just sends
her into a stupor when she's around it." John ran a hand
over his thinning hair and sighed wearily. "I worry so about
her, but there's nothing any of us can do."

"Poor Mama." Belle cast another glance at the ceiling,
then straightened. "May I go visit my friend now, Papa? It's
quite a ways so I'll be staying the night with her family and
come home tomorrow."

"Be careful, May." He knitted his brows in a thoughtful
scowl. "Perhaps I should send Edwin with you."

"No!" Belle clutched her father's forearm in a death grip.
"Please, Papa. Not Eddie," she pleaded. "I'm saddled with

him and the other little 'uns too much as it is. Let me go on my visit alone. I'll be fine, Papa."

"Very well." He patted her hands before she removed them from his arm. "We'll be looking for you tomorrow. Stay on the main road, you hear me?"

"I hear. 'Bye, Papa!" Belle stopped at the foot of the stairs and looked up at the sunlit landing. " 'Bye, Mama! See you tomorrow afternoon!" She ducked out the back door, making good her escape, and hurried next door to the Shirleys' livery. The stable boy came running to greet her. "Simon, do you have my horse saddled?"

"Yes, Miss Maybelle." Simon brought Queenie forward and helped Belle up into the saddle, then tied her bedroll behind her. "You off visiting again?"

"Yes, I am." She glanced down at his brown face and waved him away. "I'm heading toward Newtonia so I won't be back until tomorrow."

"Be careful, Miss Maybelle. Yankees is crawling all over these here hills."

She tipped up her chin and laughed. "Yankees don't scare me, Simon. *I* scare the Yankees!" When the slave boy cackled wildly, Belle lifted a haughty brow at him. "I hope you're laughing with me and not at me, Simon."

"I'd never laugh at you, ma'am." He backed away, ducking his woolly head and lowering his brown eyes in deference. "I knows you'd shoot any Yankee that gots in your way."

"Right between his beady little eyes." Belle set her heels into Queenie and set off at a gallop.

She skillfully guided Queenie around the cannonball holes in the main street of Carthage. Was there any Southern town that hadn't felt the angry fist of war? Carthage had been kept safe for a long while thanks to guerrilla fighters like her brother, but the Kansas border fighters had penetrated several times during the past months and wreaked havoc. It was hard to remember Carthage before the war. It was hard to remember life before there were Yankees and Rebels and border warriors.

When the War Between the States had finally reached Carthage, lots of folks headed for less troubled lands, her eldest brother being one of them. Preston had packed up his family and hightailed it to Texas. The coward! He was most surely his mother's son.

A bittersweetness stole through her as she looked—*really looked*—at her hometown and what the fighting had done to it. The streets were rutted by the wheels of artillery and supply wagons. The buildings were scorched by fire, some completely burned to the ground except for broken brick chimneys. Where there had been smooth tree-lined streets and charming buildings, now there were only the sad vestiges of bloody conflict. Border guards from Kansas raided Missouri cities and towns, leaving smoldering ashes and dead bodies in their wake. The homegrown Missouri guerrilla soldiers were left no choice but to retaliate on Kansas soil. It was one raid after another.

The town's male population was reduced to men who were either too old or too young to be soldiers. All the others had taken to the hills, banding together, or roving deeper into the South to join the Confederate regiments—or being killed dead.

Belle could feel the panic in the air that made everybody in town jumpy and quick to accuse neighbors and friends of all kinds of lowdown desperate deeds. Every Sunday the congregation at the Baptist church grew smaller as more and more families either moved to the Union's Kansas or the Confederacy's Texas and Arkansas.

Ducking under tree branches that spread across the road, Belle sent Queenie at a gallop out of Carthage and on toward Newtonia. She kept her eyes peeled for any sign of movement as the brush got thicker and the roadway narrowed. Quantrill's encampment was somewhere near if Jimmy's directions had been accurate. The fall foliage—reds and greens and golds—became a brilliant blur before her eyes. Her nose pointing into the wind, she careened down the highway. The first chill of winter sharpened the air. Snow was on the way.

Belle's sixth sense tingled and she tightened the lead she'd given Queenie. The pony slowed to a walk. Belle glanced over her shoulder, making sure she hadn't been followed. Her father's warning rang in her head.

"Maybelle?"

Belle's heart rose in her throat as her head snapped around in the direction of the familiar voice.

"Yes. Where are you, Jimmy?" she whispered.

He stepped out from behind a brambly thicket of denuded bushes. Jimmy was irresistible, all white teeth and rakish freckles.

"Here I am." He held out his arms. "Hop down and give me a kiss."

"Not out here in the open!" She glanced around again, urging Queenie to the side of the road. "Take me to Quantrill's camp like you promised."

"Not until I get my kiss."

"Oh, hell's bells and peanut shells!" Belle slipped out of the sidesaddle, wrapped her arms around Jimmy's strong neck, and kissed him soundly on the mouth. "There! Now which way?" She released him and stared over his shoulder into the underbrush.

Jimmy was tickled to see her. Ever since Bud had introduced them months earlier, Jimmy had been her willing slave. He'd fallen in love with her at first sight, which flattered Belle, but also exasperated her. She loved a good chase and she secretly wished that Jimmy wasn't so obviously smitten. However, she wasn't one to complain. Most girls her age didn't have boyfriends as brave as Jimmy. He was one of Quantrill's Raiders and that was as close to heroism as a man could get.

Jimmy placed the back of his hand against his mouth and laughed shortly. "That wasn't much of a kiss. I wasn't ready."

"Well, next time pucker up quicker."

"One more," Jimmy begged sweetly, holding out his arms to her.

"No." Belle sidestepped him, glanced at his teasing smile, and caved in. "Oh, why not? One more can't hurt." She tilted her head back, lifting her mouth to his and sighing as his lips sucked warmly on hers. When his hands slid down her sides to rest intimately on her hips, she pushed him away. "That's enough. Take me to Quantrill. Now, Jimmy!"

"Ah, Maybelle," he sighed, taking her hand and grabbing Queenie's dangling reins. "They're camped about a quarter mile back in these woods, but they'll be moving on before nightfall. Bud's not going to be happy to see you."

"He'll get over his mad soon enough," she assured Jimmy. "He worships me."

"I know the feeling," Jimmy mumbled.

"James Reed!" Belle widened her eyes with coquettish appeal. "Do you mean that?"

"You know I do. Why else would I be taking you to meet with Quantrill? It's only going to bring me a heap of trouble."

"Not when I tell him what I know about the Richeys and who's visiting them."

"Won't make any difference. Charley Quantrill doesn't need a girl to spy for him."

"Balderdash! You just leave him to me."

They trampled through the thick undergrowth until Belle could hear the faint rumble of masculine voices. She squeezed Jimmy's hand and felt her skin flush with excitement. She'd waited for this meeting for weeks, dreamed of it and planned for it. It had taken a goodly amount of sweet-talking to get Jimmy to agree to take her inside the sacred circle. Now that the meeting was only a few footsteps away, Belle experienced a momentary qualm. She stopped dead in her tracks and stared wide-eyed at Jimmy.

"What's wrong?" Jimmy asked, giving her hand a gentle tug. "We're almost there. They're just right through these trees."

"I . . . I know." Belle swallowed the lump in her throat and took a deep breath, releasing it slowly. "I'm okay. Let's go."

They stepped into the clearing surrounded by a stand of oak and pine. It was crowded with horses, wagons, and small artillery. The woodland hideout was a beehive of activity.

Bud spotted her first. He dropped the rifle he was cleaning and turned a peculiar shade of raspberry. "What in the hell are you doing here?" he roared, striding toward her and Jimmy. "Are you crazy, Jim?" he yelled, reaching out and grabbing Belle by the wrist. "What do you mean by bringing my sister here?" He yanked Belle to his side, away from Jim Reed.

"Sh-she wanted to come," Jim stammered. "Sh-she wanted to see you."

"Do you do *everything* she wants you to do? You're in big trouble, boy. Big trouble." Bud gave Jim an angry shove and grabbed Queenie's reins from his hand. "Maybelle, you get back on your horse and head for town. No backtalk or

I'll tell Papa all about this and you won't be able to sit down for a week after he gets through with you."

"I'm not leaving!"

Bud whisked her off her feet and deposited her painfully in the saddle.

"Sit up there, little sister," he warned in a deadly tone Belle had never heard him use before. "Take these reins. *Take them!*"

She obeyed, stunned by her brother's spurt of rage. But she coolly regained her composure, adjusting her hat and smoothing the wrinkles from her riding gloves.

"Who's this, Lieutenant Shirley?"

Bud turned. "Uh, Captain Quantrill . . ."

"Quantrill?" Belle whispered to herself in shock.

The great William Clarke Quantrill was a couple of inches shorter than her brother and had a quirky voice that warbled like an adolescent boy's. She'd expected him to be bullish with a booming voice and tough demeanor. Instead, Charley Quantrill was no more than five feet six inches, slight of build, and ferret-faced with bulbous, green gray eyes.

Quantrill sauntered forward, thumbs hooked in his gun belt and his gray hat tipped down low on his forehead.

"Is this your little mama?" Quantrill asked with an oily chuckle.

Bud blushed crimson. "No, sir. This is my sister Myra Maybelle."

Belle removed her black velvet riding hat with a flourish and looked down upon the little man. "How is it that you can command a band of brave men when your eyesight is so pitifully poor, sir?" she asked archly.

The men within earshot snickered and tried to hide their grins behind their hands. Even Bud turned aside to cover his smile.

"Come close and have a good look," Belle taunted as Quantrill's jawline hardened. "Do I actually look old enough to be Bud's mother? If so, you're as blind as a bat."

"Lieutenant Reed!" Quantrill shouted, his voice rising to a screech as he spun on his heel to lambaste his junior. "Why have you brought this child into camp?"

Belle let out a throaty laugh and propped one gloved hand on her hip. "Now I'm a child! Is there any among you who can see beyond his nose?" She loved being the center of attention and the only female among so many young men.

The men moved closer for a better look at their fair visitor. A squinty-eyed man swaggered forward and spit tobacco juice at Queenie's front hooves.

"I say we should shoot her. She might be a Yankee spy," he drawled, and he wasn't kidding.

"Brother Frank, you don't mean that. What a waste of female flesh." A loose-jointed man with a dangerous smirk broke rank and strode arrogantly right up to Belle's horse. He ran a suntanned hand down Queenie's blazed face and shot a cocky grin at Belle. "What do you think, Cole?" he asked, glancing back at a tall man with robin's-egg-blue eyes. "Should we send Bud's little sister packing or play some poke-in-the-bush if she's willing?"

"You son-of-a-bitch!" Bud sprang, going for the man's throat. They fell to the ground punching and grunting; a cloud of dust and dried leaves rose around them.

"Stop it! Get off him, Bud." The blue-eyed man pulled Bud off the other and flung him aside as if he were weightless. "Jesse, get up and keep your filthy mouth shut for a change."

Belle stiffened when the pastel-blue eyes focused on her.

"Miss Shirley, I believe you've caused enough trouble for one day," he said in a voice that was husky and even-timbered. He moved with a natural grace, taking three strides to reach her and pulling the reins from her unresisting fingers. He turned Queenie around so that she now faced the direction of the road. "Jim was wrong to have brought you here."

"I have news that will further your cause," Belle said, remembering her mission.

"Be on your way," he said.

"Who are you to give me orders?"

"Cole Younger's the name." He placed the reins in her gloved hands and curled her fingers around them with extreme patience. "Good day, Miss Shirley."

"No, I can't leave until I tell you what I know. Don't you see?" she implored, looking over his head to Bud, Jesse, Jimmy, and Quantrill, none of them returning her glance with the slightest hint of encouragement.

"*I see* that you are a young lady who has no business among us ruffians." Cole applied the flat of his hand to Queenie's rump, and before Belle could say another word, the pinto surged forth at a breakneck gallop. It was all Belle could do to hold on and find her proper seat in the saddle.

Damn them! Damn them all, she fumed, reining in Queenie with iron hands. She'd be back. They hadn't seen the last of her. Not by a long shot!

Chapter Two

"Easy, Queenie," Belle cautioned her pinto when the mare quivered with anticipation. "You smell other horses, don't you?"

Belle stroked Queenie's mane as she surveyed the heavily wooded area. Quantrill's camp had to be around here. Bud had taught her how to track animals, and the same applied to humans. Belle knew she was close to her quarry. She could feel it in her bones.

For the tenth time, she rehearsed what she'd say to Quantrill. He wouldn't dismiss her—no way! He'd hear her out. She'd risked too much in coming here to be turned away as if she were a bothersome child. If Cole Younger laid a hand on her horse this time, he'd pull back a stump! Belle touched the sheathed knife strapped around her waist, but somehow it failed to comfort her. Common sense told her she was crazy to barge in on these men again. She shuddered to think how Bud would react. He'd been kidded so much about his little sister tagging along that this might be the straw to break the camel's back.

Well, she wasn't a little girl anymore. She was a woman

with a mission. She wouldn't sit by and watch. Belle had to get involved. Her mother and eldest brother had deserted the Confederacy in their own ways, but she was determined to embrace it passionately.

Rocks and pebbles came dancing down the hillside above her. Startled, Belle looked up to see a horse and rider burst through the underbrush, bearing down the rise toward her. It wasn't Jimmy and it wasn't Bud. Belle frowned. The man's face was concealed beneath the brim of a slouch hat.

Jesse James, she groaned inwardly. Why him? He made her edgy and Belle was instantly on her guard. Of course, it could be worse. It could be Jesse's surly brother Frank, who would rather shoot her on sight than speak to her.

She stiffened and threw Jesse a supercilious glance as he pulled his horse up alongside hers.

"Where's your brother?" she asked, trying to sound flippant, although her heart was racing. "I thought that you and Frank were joined at the hip."

"Frank's out on patrol with your brother and your sweetheart," Jesse shot back with a rakish curl of his thin upper lip. "Have you brought more town gossip?"

"What I have to say I will say to Charley Quantrill," Belle informed him icily, then felt her face flush with anger when Jesse laughed at her. "My gossip might save your ugly hide, so I wouldn't laugh too hard."

"Ugly?" he repeated, his hand darting out to rein her horse to a prancing halt. "Look at me, missy." He grabbed her chin and pulled her face around to his. "Do you really think I'm ugly?"

Forced to confront the proof of his good looks, Belle pursed her lips to keep from smiling. His high cheekbones, deeply socketed eyes, wide mouth, and silky chestnut hair were made to order for a girl's fondest dreams. Without a doubt, Jesse was a good-looking man, but something told Belle to keep her distance.

"I think you're a pain in the backside," she said, hedging and hoping he'd accept her teasing and not press the point. But his smile waned. "Are you going to take me to Quantrill or do I have to find the camp myself?"

His hand fell from her chin to rest lightly on his thigh. He eyed her intensely. A bar of sunlight slanted through the tree branches and was caught in the circle of gold around Jesse's pinkie finger. Belle wondered if he had taken a wife or had a sweetheart back home—wherever that was. What kind of woman could trust Jesse enough to love him? She began to grow uncomfortable as he continued to scrutinize her.

"I think we should bury the hatchet. Let's be friends. What do you think?"

A warning bell rang in her head. "Why would you want to be friends with a female you hold in contempt?"

He smiled warmly. "Bud says that you'd die before giving up any information about us. Is that true?"

"It's true," she said without hesitation. "I wouldn't turn you or your pug-nosed brother over to a Yankee." Her smile took the edge off her words. "Even though you've been nothing but mean to me."

"Mean?" He chuckled and shook his head. "Little girl, you haven't seen 'mean' from me." He placed both hands on top of the saddle horn and hunched his shoulders. "You want to be friends or not?"

"Why are you so interested in friendship all of a sudden?" she insisted, unsure of his motive.

"Oh, I figure you'd make a better friend than an enemy."

She nodded, sliding her eyes away from his. All she could see were trees and tall grass, all brown and dead from winter. "I could say the same thing about you. I wouldn't want to be your worst enemy, but then I don't want to be your best friend either." She peeked at him from the corner of her eye. "Too much trouble. Know what I mean?"

He chuckled again, low in his throat and sounding more like a purr. "There you go," he agreed with a jerky nod. "So let's be pals, Maybelle." He held out his hand to her. "Put her there, little lady."

She slipped her gloved hand into his and winced slightly when his grip tightened.

"Friends for life," Jesse said, deadly serious.

"Yes," Belle agreed. "Whenever you cross my path, you'll be welcome. I'll never turn you away."

"Same goes for me." He let go of her hand and faced front down the trail. "Charley won't be happy to see you again. You insulted him. Made him look foolish in front of us."

"It wasn't hard."

Jesse lifted a hand to wipe the grin off his face. "Yeah, well . . . you'll have to do some fast talking to make him listen. Jimmy Reed says you're a cut above the normal female. He might be right."

Belle laughed inwardly at such an absurd statement. The trouble with Jesse and the other Raiders was their low opinion of women. To begin with, they saw women as decorations, brainless and pretty, good for feeding their male egos and continuing their bloodlines.

"The fighting is fierce up in these hills and you're courting danger by hanging around us. Even Charley is thinking that it might be the end of the road. We've all been considering disbanding and joining the regular army." Jesse continued, softly, almost to himself, "Bud doesn't want you around us, but I guess you know that already."

"I know." Belle shrugged and kneed her mount into a walk. "Let's go, Jesse. I need to warm myself by the campfire."

He glanced at the pinto and frowned. "Why don't you get yourself a horse worthy of you? That little pony is meant for a child."

"Queenie's fast and brave," Belle informed him. "She's all I need."

"She's a woman's horse."

"So?" Belle asked with a short laugh. "What am I? A man?"

"You're less than a man, but more than a woman." One corner of Jesse's mouth tipped up. Then he reached out to tug on Queenie's bridle. Leaning sideways until his lips brushed Belle's cheek, he planted a soft kiss on her mouth.

"Be careful, little sister," he whispered against her parted lips. "I'd hate to see you killed over the likes of us."

For a moment Belle stared into his eyes, mesmerized and intrigued. He was the first to break the spell. Throwing back his head, he laughed uproariously and applied his heels to his chestnut gelding. The horse reared in surprise, then settled on all fours and leaped forward.

"Try to keep up with me, Belle Shirley!" Jesse called over his shoulder, his white teeth flashing.

Baffled by his quicksilver moods, Belle rolled her eyes in exasperation but she gave Queenie her head. The pinto set off, eagerly pursuing the larger horse. Belle shifted her weight in an unconscious effort to keep balanced in the sidesaddle. She hooked one leg more firmly around the saddle horn and inched her hands up on the reins until her fingertips touched the bridle and metal rings. Trees whipped past her and the thunder of Queenie's hooves sounded like gunfire in the quiet woods. Jesse's voice lingered in her mind. She kept hearing him call her "Belle" and she decided she liked the name. It fit her like a glove, she thought. Short and sweet. Belle. Yes, she liked it fine.

She spotted the clearing ahead and yanked on the bridle,

breaking Queenie's stride and forcing the excited pinto to cut her speed in half and then stop altogether.

A score of men sat around the fire and several raised their hands in greeting to Jesse, turning slack-jawed when they saw the woman with him. Belle slid off Queenie's back to the hard, frozen ground. Jesse came toward her, leading his horse and reaching for Queenie's dangling reins.

"I'll tie her up and give her some water," he offered, winking as he passed in front of her. "Good luck, Belle."

She studied his long-legged stride for a few moments, mulling over Jesse's sudden decision to be her friend instead of her foe. It made her proud to think that she'd won him over. She looked around, searching for gold-dust hair and pale blue eyes. Now if only she could convince Cole Younger that she was a woman he could trust . . .

Charley Quantrill marched toward her, smoking with fury. His clenched fists pumped at his sides and his black boots pounded the hard ground.

"Madam, you aren't welcome here," he screeched, pointing a finger at the path she'd taken. "Turn your mount around and go back to your kitchen!"

Belle squared her shoulders, refusing to be intimidated by Quantrill. If she could handle Jesse, she could handle this pipsqueak.

"I've come to tell you what's cooking in Carthage's kitchen," she announced. "A Yankee troop is holed up at the Richey farm. They're planning to attack you and your men by the end of the week."

Quantrill lowered his shaking finger and cocked his small head to one side. "Says who?" he asked.

"Says Millie Richey, who happens to be a friend of mine. I'm on my way there now to get more information from her. She thinks we're best friends and she doesn't know that I'm spying for you."

"Spying for me?" Quantrill asked, laughing as he glanced around at his men. "Since when?"

"Since right now. If you'll offer me a cup of hot coffee and let me sit by the fire, I'll give you the rest of my recipe."

Cole Younger shouldered his way past several onlookers and stood beside Quantrill, dwarfing the commander. He examined Belle's flushed face with eyes that seemed to see through her. Belle held her breath, knowing that his opinion would carry a lot of weight with Quantrill.

"Who commands the Union troop you're speaking of?" Cole asked after a tense silence.

"Major Eno," Belle answered, and she could tell by the minute widening of Cole's eyes that she'd made an impression.

"I've heard he was around here somewhere," Cole admitted, then shrugged as if he couldn't care less. "We might as well hear her out, Charley."

Charley nodded decisively as if he'd come to the notion all by himself. He motioned toward the campfire with a sweeping flourish.

"Welcome, Miss Shirley." Charley came toward her, hands outstretched, taking Belle by surprise. "Come warm yourself by the fire and have a cup of coffee." He curved an arm at her waist and bundled her toward the dancing flames. "It's getting colder by the minute. Wouldn't be surprised if it didn't snow a foot by nightfall."

Belle sat down near the fire, surprised and excited by the sudden acceptance. After a few moments, she realized that the others had formed a circle around the fire and were waiting for her to say something. She looked at each face in turn, but let her gaze linger longer on Cole. There was something about him. Something special.

She glanced at the boy sitting next to him, then gasped when she realized the trembling bundle wasn't a boy at all.

The girl was young, undeniably younger than Belle. She was huddled between Cole and another one of Quantrill's lieutenants. The girl stared sullenly at Belle. Her blond hair fell in tangles to her shoulders and her dark eyes smoldered with a stinging hatred. She looked from Belle to Charley then back to Belle before she pursed her lips and spit into the fire. Belle blinked, amazed at the crude gesture. Cole stood up and moved away from the circle of bushwhackers.

"Since when have you allowed children to ride with you?" she asked, looking up at Charley, who was still standing.

"Uh . . . oh, you mean Kate?" He laughed and dropped to his haunches beside Belle. "She's my gal."

"I'd heard that you'd kidnapped a girl from Jasper County, but I didn't believe it. I marked it up to Yankee slandering."

"I didn't kidnap her!" Charley's voice climbed to its upper registers. "Did I snatch you, Kate?" he asked of the girl, and she shook her head but spoke not a word. "See? She wants to be out here with us."

Belle stared into the firelight and held her hands out to it. "She's no more than fourteen. She should be with her mama."

"What about you? You've just turned sixteen yourself, according to your brother," Charley said, his voice cutting and shrill. "Maybe you should be with your mama. I've a good mind to send you packing."

"You want to hear my news or do you want me to go back to Carthage?" Belle asked, knowing the answer before Charley could make it.

Charley sat back on his rump and circled his arms around his knees. "Go on. I'm listening," he said in a resigned way that tickled Belle.

"Eno is headquartered at the Richey place. He's here to clear out these hills of bushwhackers. You're at the top of his list. I think he's got a good idea of where you're camped. It wasn't hard for me to find."

"You didn't find us. Jesse brought you in."

"I tracked you down. Jesse made the last leg easier is all. Do you know the Richey place near Newtonia?"

"No. Are they Union?"

"They are. They make no bones about it." Belle lost her train of thought as Cole Younger moved into her vision. Her heart climbed into her throat and became lodged there, beating furiously and painfully. What was there about Cole that made her so light-headed? She wondered as her eyes followed his lithe movement around the circle of men across the fire from her. He held a tin cup in his hand and steam rose from it. Stopping behind Kate, Cole extended the cup of coffee to the girl, who took it eagerly and looked up into his face with a timid smile of gratitude. The solicitation touched Belle and her esteem for Cole bloomed. He held out another cup, and Belle knew it was for her.

"Belle, go on," Charley urged beside her. "What makes you think Eno is planning to raid us?"

Belle tore her gaze away from Cole, forcing herself to pay attention to Charley. "I've put two and two together is all. I've got a plan."

"Let's hear it." He looked toward Cole and motioned for him. "Come here. This little girl is going to tell us how to catch the big, bad Union major!"

Belle forced control, furious at Quantrill's placating tone. He was joshing her! Treating her as if she were a half-crazy child.

"I'm disappointed in you, Quantrill," she spit back between gritted teeth. "I was expecting to meet a man with a brain in his head. Hell, you'd be as dead as a drowned rat by now if it weren't for these good men surrounding you!" She made a wide gesture, encompassing the others and her hand smacked into the tin cup Cole had lowered toward her. Coffee splashed across his shirt and he stepped back in alarm.

"Land sakes!" Belle's temper gave way to mortification. I'm sorry. I didn't see . . . I didn't mean . . ."

"It's nothing," he said, running a hand across the damp spots. He crouched down on his haunches next to her. "I'm already filthy. We're short on bathtubs out here."

He rested his elbows on his bent knees and his hands hung loosely between them. He wore soft buckskin trousers and a blue overblouse. The guerrillas had adopted the collarless style with its triangular front that ended in a fancy rosette. It was called a raider shirt. Cole looked mighty good to Belle. He didn't look filthy at all.

"I think you should drink that coffee and be off," Charley said, clearly incensed by her opinion of him. "We don't need your information. We know all we need to know about Yankees and Jayhawkers in these parts."

"You don't know how many men are with Eno, do you?" Belle asked, smiling to herself when Charley grew quiet. "I could find out for certain."

"Do tell," Cole's raspy baritone intervened. "He's set all kinds of traps for us, hasn't he?"

Belle nodded. She cleared her throat, took a drink of the strong coffee, and felt more herself.

"It's us who'll set a trap for him and his soldiers," Belle assured Charley and Cole. "I want to visit the Richeys before you move in on their place."

"Why do that?" Charley asked.

"Because I know their daughter. She talks a lot. If it weren't for me she would've failed Latin and Greek mythology at school. This war has caused tension in my friendship with her, but she won't turn me out. Her folks will let me stay the night."

24

"Do you use all your friends in such a manner?" Cole asked in a deceptively innocent tone that didn't fool Belle for a minute.

"You disapprove of my motive and method, Lieutenant Younger?" she asked, arching a winged brow at him. "Because if you do, I can—"

"No, missy. Pay no mind to Cole's holier-than-thou talk," Charley interrupted, placing a soothing hand on her shoulder. "He means nothing by it."

"You can call me Belle."

"Belle it is." Charley smiled, obviously offering a reserved kind of friendship. "So you'll spend the night and ferret it out. Is that it?"

"That's about the size of it," Belle said, slowly sweeping her gaze from Cole's chiseled profile to Charley's sharp features. "I'll cut switches before I leave. Have a man posted to watch for the sign. I'll cut one switch for every twenty men I find stationed at the Richey place so you'll know what you're up against. I won't stop at camp on the way back in case I'm followed. I'll head straight for Carthage, leaving the rest up to you and the boys."

The two men fell silent for a moment and exchanged long glances before both nodded in unison.

"It's a good plan," Charley said for Belle's benefit. "I'll send Cole to watch for your sign. That okay with you, Younger?"

"Fine with me." Cole nodded in the direction of a pot of stew simmering over the fire. "Maybe you should eat something before you ride."

"Coffee will do me. The Richeys will insist on my eating dinner with them, I'm sure."

"Northern hospitality?" Cole jested, drawing an admiring smile from Belle. He straightened to his full height and strode toward the tethered horses standing in the deep shadows.

"It's good of you to want to help us, Belle," Charley assured her, but his gaze had drifted to a shivering Kate. "I know the chance you take in coming here and the boys are all beholden to you. Your bravery is—"

"Go to her," Belle said, cutting into Charley's half-hearted speech. "She's scared as a rabbit and needs a gentle hand."

Charley laughed under his breath. "I didn't steal her away. She wanted to come."

"She's too young to know what she wants."

"What about you? Folks could say the same about you."

Belle shook her head. "I'm different. I've always known what I want and how to get it. That girl is letting everyone else think for her."

Charley didn't leave immediately; mildly confused and definitely intrigued, he took a few moments to study the certainty that seemed to shimmer like an aura around Belle Shirley.

"You've got a mean tongue in your head, but I guess we can get along all right." He squeezed her shoulder affectionately before rising to his feet and going around to the girl. He offered her his hand and she practically sprang at him, going eagerly into the shadows with him and away from the others.

Belle shook her head, pitying the girl and wrestling with her disappointment in Quantrill. He was a good leader of men, but a weak chord ran through him that bothered Belle. She wished she wasn't so critical. These were dangerous times and even heroes couldn't be all things to all people.

Belle's eyes searched the outer edges of the encampment for Cole. She was glad that Jimmy and Bud were on patrol, leaving her to her own devices for the time being. Cole stood near the horses with Jesse. She waited a discreet minute or two, hanging back to listen to their low voices, punctuated by an occasional chuckle or bark of laughter. Cole was an inch taller than Jesse, broader and more muscular. He had missed being a redhead by only a shade. His hair was thick and a burnished blond, parted on the side and falling naturally across his lined brow. The hair on his arms was tipped with auburn. Belle imagined that all of his body hair was as coppery colored. His hands were large and square fingered. Freckles were sprinkled across the back of them. He wore a turquoise-and-silver ring on the third finger of his left hand, but it was commonly known that he wasn't married.

The way Cole used his hands held Belle in complete fascination. While most would hold their coffee cups by hooking a forefinger through the handle, he used his middle finger and splayed the others against the sides of the tin cup. Cole's every movement had a stamp of individuality about it.

Jesse moved off toward the fire and Belle forced herself to approach Cole, mentally patting herself on the back for showing such courage. As she expected, Cole paid no attention to her.

"This coffee is strong enough to stand up and walk on its own," she said, lifting the cup and smiling over its rim at Cole.

He didn't seem the least bit surprised to see that she'd followed him, but he made no attempt at conversation. The setting sun streamed through naked branches and backlit Cole's broad shoulders and limned his proud profile with pale gold. Without realizing it, Belle released a wishful sigh that brought his pastel blue eyes to hers. She felt her skin grow warm and a blush paint her cheeks.

"Bud will be sorry he missed you," Cole said, turning

aside to examine the stamping horses. "Not to mention Jimmy Reed. He's lost his head over you, but I guess you already know that."

Belle sashayed closer, swaying her hips and making her skirt swirl around her slim legs. "You got a girl back home, Cole Younger?"

"A sweetheart, you mean?" He glanced at her nodding head, then shook his. "No, not me."

"Why not?"

He went around a roan mare, putting the animal between them, and crossed his arm across the horse's broad back. Resting his square chin on his arms, he scrutinized Belle. She quivered.

"I've got enough family to worry about without adding a girlfriend or wife to my list," he said, after a charged minute. "Loving someone is a big responsibility and one I can't afford right now."

"Why not now?"

"There's a war on, if you hadn't noticed," he said with pointed sarcasm.

"Yes, but that doesn't stop people from loving each other."

"It puts a crimp in the social scene," he countered with cool logic. "The country is being torn apart and the worst is right around the corner."

"What's the worst?" Belle asked, wondering what could be more horrible than to hear cannons blasting in the distance and reading daily body counts in the newspapers.

"The worst will come after the war ends. Somebody will have to lose and I've got a feeling it's going to be us."

"Hush up!" Belle placed a finger to her lips, feeling a sense of betrayal. "Don't say things like that. The South can't lose."

"The South *is* losing." He gave a short, mirthless laugh. "We've been so caught up in keeping the Kansas Jayhawkers out of Missouri that we haven't paid all that much attention to the movement of the regular armies." He smoothed his hand across the horse's swayed back. "The Yanks are knocking at our back door. Hell, most of our soldiers are boys!" He shook his head in a jerky movement of anger. "Our job is done here. It's time to join up with the boys in gray and make a last stand for dear old Dixie."

"How come you know so much?"

"I read between the lines in the newspaper," he told her with a secretive smile. "I keep my ears and eyes open. It doesn't take a genius to see that we're getting our asses handed to us."

"I don't believe it," Belle insisted. "We've got a lot of fight left in us. We'll never surrender!"

His smile was melancholy. "You're so young."

"I'm not! I'm old enough to hold my own in this war."

"You haven't lost anyone yet, have you?"

"You mean, buried anyone?" she asked, then shook her head when he nodded. "No. Have you?"

"Yes, my father."

She ducked her head. "I'm sorry."

"No, you're not," he said, matter-of-factly and unmindful of her gasp of annoyance. "You can't be sorry until you've felt the grief. My father was a staunch Union supporter."

"You're joshing!" Belle charged.

"No, it's true." He looked to one side and chuckled softly. "He was quite a character. He thought Lincoln was a sign of the second coming. Federal soldiers raided our livery stable in Harrisonville. They helped themselves to thousands of dollars worth of wagons and buggies and took forty of our best horses." He paused and his skin flushed with renewed outrage. "I was so mad I couldn't see straight and I took off to join the bushwhackers. Lincoln's militiamen paid Pa another visit. They robbed him of his money that time and then shot him right through the heart." Cole's throat flexed as he swallowed and his eyes grew hard and cold. "Capt. James Walley," he said in a dull voice. "No matter what, I'll see that man dead for murdering my pa."

"We'll kill all those Union troublemakers," Belle said, desperate to show Cole she was on his side.

Cole blinked as he came back to the present. "Kill? You say that as if it were nothing. Have you ever killed anyone in cold blood?"

"No, but I'd be happy to send a Yankee to hell!"

"Belle, Belle, Belle," he chanted, shaking his head with each repetition. "You should be at some barn dance flirting with boys your age instead of out here among us ruffians talking of killing and going to hell and back. It's not right."

"Why not? Why can't a woman do her share?"

"Do you feel like Lady Marion in the Robin Hood tales?"

"Do you feel like Robin Hood?" Belle asked, surprised by her boldness. She stepped around the horse until she was at Cole's side. "You don't approve of me, do you?"

"I don't want to have your blood on my hands," he said, ignoring her coy flirting. "A woman has no business on the battlefield. If you were my sister, I'd—"

"I'm not your sister," she interrupted pertly and set the tin cup on a tree stump. "We are of no relation." She ordered her heart to settle down to a normal pace and met Cole's quizzical smirk. "So you may kiss me, if you're a mind to."

"I may *what*?" Amazement widened his blue eyes and slackened his iron jaw. The corners of his wide mouth twitched, but he managed to keep from laughing in her face. He set his hands at his waist and inched back his head to examine her stormy glare. "Whatever gave you the idea that I wanted to kiss you?"

Belle mirrored his cocky stance and jutted her chin forward at a stubborn angle.

"You saying you never entertained the notion?" she asked, then tacked on, " 'cause if that's what you're saying, then I say you're a damned liar!"

"Well, well, well." Cole reached out blindly to run the fingers of one hand through the roan's chestnut mane, drawing Belle's attention for a moment and diffusing her anger. "Miss Maybelle Shirley has a wicked temper and can cuss with the best of them, can't she? What happened to the simpering Southern lady you're so keen on portraying?"

"I am a Southern lady through and through, sir. A rogue like yourself wouldn't be expected to recognize one."

His eyes crinkled at the corners as he continued to take in her flushed face, clenched fists, and jutting breasts. A strand of her ebony hair fell from its pinnings. It curled along the side of her face and tempted him. Cole stopped stroking the roan's mane and tucked the wayward strand behind Belle's small ear. He saw her anger subside immediately at his touch and stepped back as she swayed toward him.

"I thought you were Jimmy's girl," he reminded her, and she had the good grace to blush and duck her head. "Am I wrong?"

"I like Jimmy," she murmured, turning away to grab up her cup and sip from it.

"You think he'd like it if he knew you'd asked me to kiss you?"

"I didn't ask!" She spun around to face him again, the cup clutched between her hands. "I offered and you threw the offer back in my face!"

Cole started to walk past her, but stopped when he was shoulder to shoulder with her.

"Listen here, girl. You're safe playing your little courting games with Jimmy Reed, but don't try to play with me. I'm no boy. I'm a man. When I want to kiss you, I won't wait for your permission."

She shivered, trying to hide how unsettled she was by his gravelly voice. "Is that so?" she challenged, unable to think of a better comeback.

His light blue eyes narrowed. "That's so, sugar britches."

Belle shut her eyes and listened to his departing footfalls. For a moment she thought she might swoon, but then she brought herself up sharply. She looked around to make sure no one had observed her humiliation and pressed the back of her hand against her forehead, amused at herself for perspiring when the air was so cold. Jimmy never made her feel like this.

"Damnation!" Belle threw the tin cup aside. She reached for Queenie's reins, suddenly eager to saddle the pinto and be on her way.

Chapter Three

MAJ. EDWIN ENO was short and stocky with thinning dirty blond hair and thick muttonchop whiskers that gave him the look of a squirrel whose cheeks were full of stored pecans. His bright brown eyes were beady and closely set. Belle had the feeling that nothing much escaped the major's attention.

Sitting at one end of the dinnertable, he held court while at the other end sat Judge Richey, the host, proud as a peacock, all white hair, beard, and mustache, and dressed in a white suit. The judge never spoke below a mild roar and he had the air of a man who considered his every word a precious jewel to be savored and admired.

The major was softspoken with a decidedly Yankee accent that grated on Belle's nerves. Perversely she began to speak in a more pronounced drawl to counteract the major's rapid-fire delivery.

Mrs. Richey, a round-faced blonde, sat to the left of her husband. Millie was at the judge's right. Belle had been seated beside her school chum. At her other elbow was the major and across the table from her was a young captain named Cartwright from the major's regiment.

"Is it true that you shook hands with President Lincoln, Captain Cartwright?" Mrs. Richey asked after everyone had paid lavish compliments to her for the roasted pork, yams, white beans, and cornbread muffins.

"It's true, ma'am," the captain said, throwing out his chest in a proud boast. "He's a striking individual. A born leader. You can see that in his eyes."

"And so handsome," Mrs. Richey added, glancing coquettishly at her husband. "But not as handsome as you, dear."

The judge chuckled and Millie giggled. Belle poked at the bland Yankee beans on her plate. Mrs. Richey had set the table with guests in mind, using her best china in the red willow pattern. The crystal goblets sparkled, the silver was of a flower design, and the tablecloth was off-white damask linen.

The voices around her droned on, but Belle paid them little heed since the conversation was kept on a socially acceptable level for the sake of the ladies. So far there'd been no talk of military strategy, but Belle had decided she could pry that information from Millie later when they were alone.

Unexpectantly, her conscience rose up to ridicule her, killing her appetite. To feel like a cheat was ridiculous. Yet she *was* partaking of the Richeys' food and accepting their hospitality while planning a surprise attack on their uniformed guests. Belle shrugged off the conflict, reminding herself that the Richeys shouldn't let troops bunk down on their property unless they were ready and willing to face the consequences.

"We're ignoring our other guest," Mrs. Richey said, interrupting Belle's wandering thoughts. "Maybelle, didn't you say that you were visiting kinfolk in Newtonia?"

"Yes, ma'am. Distant cousins on my mother's side," Belle

lied with a sweet smile. "I got lost on the way back. Guess I took the wrong road. Anyway, by the time I came up on your place and realized where I was, it was getting dark and I was scared to go on until morning."

"I don't blame you, child," Mrs. Richey assured her. "We're pleased to have you as our guest. Millie tells me that your father owns the guesthouse in Carthage."

"Yes, ma'am."

"I'm surprised your folks would allow you to visit relatives alone," Judge Richey proclaimed in a voice that made the crystal tremble. "I wouldn't hear of Millie traveling these roads alone, what with all the bushwhackers roaming these hills and valleys."

Major Eno cleared his throat and all eyes focused on him as he dabbed at the corners of his mouth with a linen napkin. His brown button eyes moved from one to another before coming to rest on Belle. "I don't imagine Miss Shirley is the least bit concerned with bushwhackers, seeing as how her brother is one of them."

Belle placed her knife and fork aside and squared her shoulders. The major was way ahead of her and she'd better watch her step, an inner voice cautioned. Major Eno had a far-reaching reputation as a shrewd, fearless Yankee officer and Belle was beginning to see how he'd earned that tag. She glanced out of the corners of her eyes at him and stiffened.

"Come again, Major Eno?" Judge Richey asked when Belle failed to speak up and defend herself or her family name. He jutted his head forward and tipped it to one side, making Belle wonder if the judge might be a hair's breadth away from being deaf. Was that why he never spoke below a bellow?

"Your brother *is* Bud Shirley, is he not?" Major Eno asked, then looked down the table at the judge and raised his voice to be heard by the man who was straining to catch each syllable. "One of the bushwhackers on my 'most wanted' list, I might add. Bud Shirley."

Comprehension dawned on the judge's face and his mouth dropped open as his watery eyes moved to take in Belle's taciturn demeanor.

"Is this true?" Judge Richey asked, his eyes widening with the knowledge that he had a bushwhacker's sister under his own roof. "I'd heard that John Shirley was talking against the Union, but I had no idea that his son was one of those cutthroats hiding in the hills!"

"Oh, dear me," Mrs. Richey wailed, her hand plucking at the collar of her teal-blue dress. "Your parents must be brokenhearted!"

Belle folded her hands in her lap and turned away from the major to address her hosts. "My folks are—"

"Yes," Major Eno interrupted Belle as if she hadn't spoken, "they should be at their wit's end. Their son is out murdering innocent people and their daughter is roaming the countryside—"

"Sir!" Belle's voice sliced through the major's smooth denouncement and her sharp glare cut to the bone. "Excuse me, but I was not roaming the countryside. I was visiting relatives. As for my brother, we hear only rumors spread by hotheaded military men like yourself." She took a deep, steadying breath and met the major's bemused expression. "Murder is a strong word, sir. The boys in gray and their families would look upon *you* as a murderer." Sensing the uneasiness around her, Belle tried to lessen the tension with a ladylike sweep of her hand. "But why should we speak to each other like this? I'm most grateful for your hospitality, Mr. and Mrs. Richey, and for the opportunity to spend time with my dear friend Millie. Can't we enjoy this evening of good, old-fashioned Missouri hospitality without resorting to petty name calling?"

"Yes, I agree," Mrs. Richey said, eagerly grasping the olive branch Belle was offering. "Let's not speak of such vile things. I'm so tired of hearing nothing but war talk."

"Maybelle's my friend," Millie said, touching Belle's arm in a show of comradeship. "Her folks have always been nice to me. I'm sure they don't approve of what Bud's doing."

Belle remained prudently silent, but she felt the major's intense regard and she knew that her silence had not fooled him. Major Eno dipped his head in a salute to Belle's own brand of fast talking before addressing the others.

"Yes, it must be unsettling to the Shirleys to know that their son has thrown in with the likes of Quantrill, the James boys, and Cole Younger."

At the mention of Cole's name, Belle bowed her head so that the others wouldn't see the blush on her cheeks. A trembling gripped her as Cole's face appeared in her mind's eye. Where was he? He had to be close by, waiting to receive her sign tomorrow morning. Was he supine under the stars? Was he thinking of her?

"I've heard about them!" Millie's voice squeaked with excitement and broke into Belle's pleasurable musings. "I heard that Quantrill kidnapped a girl and took her into the brush with him. Nobody's seen or heard from her since! I wonder if he killed her?"

"Mildred Lucille, please!" Mrs. Richey begged. "This talk is bringing on one of my fainting spells." She fanned her pale face with her napkin and closed her eyes.

"I'm sorry, Mama. Don't faint. I'll hush up," Millie promised, cringing from her father's thunderous glare. "Sorry, Papa. I was only repeating what—"

"Don't repeat it again!" Judge Richey warned, throwing a worried glance at his chalky-faced wife. "Once is enough. I don't want those renegades mentioned in this house again. Do I make myself clear?"

"Of course, of course," Major Eno agreed. "The captain and I will mind our manners and speak of pleasant things." He swirled wine in his crystal goblet and looked through it at Belle. "I understand from Millie that you are an accomplished pianist, Miss Shirley."

"Yes, I play," she allowed, wondering what else Millie had blabbed about her.

"Perhaps you might reward us with a selection this evening after supper?" he suggested.

"Oh, yes, Maybelle. Please do!" Millie squealed encouragement, then turned to her mother, who was recovering quickly now that she'd gotten her way. "She's very good. Teacher says that May has a natural ability as a musician."

"Will you play for us later?" Mrs. Richey asked, color sweeping up into her face again and giving her a youthful gleam.

"I'd be most honored to do so," Belle replied, seizing on the new topic. "I hope no one objects to Mozart."

"I dare say that even graybellies and bushwhackers would be forced to admire the works of a master such as Mozart," Major Eno said, and everyone laughed.

Everyone except for Belle.

All she could manage was a strained smile as she told herself that she'd get the last laugh tomorrow when Quantrill's fighters fell upon the smug Major Eno and his bluebellies like a swarm of angry wasps.

Standing at the bedroom window, Belle watched shadows weave among the trees. Voices drifted up from the barn where light spilled out the windows and open doors. The

Richey place was alive with activity and Belle was taking it all in, committing the scene to memory.

"What are you looking at?" Millie asked from behind her.

"Your corral. How many horses does your papa own?"

"Only a few. Those belong to the major and his men."

Satisfaction washed over Belle. Millie always had a loose tongue and Belle was ever so glad that she hadn't changed.

"How many horses did they bring with them?"

"Oh, at least forty. One for each man, I guess."

"Do you usually have so many soldiers on the place?"

"No, no." Millie laughed girlishly. "Major Eno is using our place as headquarters for just a little while. Papa's so proud to be able to accommodate him."

"It must be nice having all these young men on the premises." Belle turned around to share a teasing grin with Millie. "That Captain Cartwright could hardly keep his eyes off you during supper."

"Oh, Maybelle!" Millie waved a dismissing hand and laughed. "How you go on!"

"Does the captain stay in this house at night?"

"No, only the major. The others bunk in the millhouse across the road and in the barn. Most of them are married or have sweethearts. Mama says they're all too old for me. She keeps me penned up inside all the time like she's scared I might speak to one of them and he'll jump on me." She laughed again and fell back on the bed. "I like older boys. The ones our age are so . . . so . . ."

"Young," Belle finished for her.

"Yes." Millie propped her head in one hand and tugged at her blond curls with the other. "Do you have a sweetheart in Carthage?"

"Not really."

"That's not what I've heard," Millie said in a singsong

voice. "I heard that you were sweet on a Border Guard named Reed."

Belle concentrated on buttoning the cuffs of her night dress. What other gossip was floating around about her and Jimmy? Didn't folks have anything better to do than spread stories about her and who she was seeing?

"Don't believe everything you hear." Belle cautioned herself not to reveal one tidbit of truth to Mildred Richey. She was the type of girl who'd run and tattle everything to her papa and mama. "My pa is just as strict with me as yours is with you. He won't allow any boy near our place unless he's there to see one of my brothers."

Millie rolled onto her stomach and propped her chin in her hands to gaze wide-eyed at Belle. "Is it true about Bud being a bushwhacker? Major Eno is here to clean them out of these parts. Aren't you scared for Bud?"

"I'm scared for everyone, including Bud." Belle faced the window again, feeling more comfortable with the shadows than with Millie's bright eagerness for gossip and girlish secrets. "Bud's only doing what he's been forced to do."

"Forced? Who forced him to hide in the brush and attack people?"

"Not people," Belle corrected. "Yankees. Jayhawkers. Anyone who tries to kill him or endanger his family or friends."

"Would he shoot me?"

"Why are we talking about this kind of thing?" Belle asked, laughing uneasily. "We were talking about beaus and now we're talking about bushwhackers. It's silly." Belle examined Millie's reflection in the dark windowpane. She was a pretty, chubby-cheeked blonde. The kind of girl who made the boys in school act plumb stupid when they were within six feet of her. "Who are you sweet on these days?"

"Oh, I don't know." Millie glanced down at the muslin

sheet beneath her, then her gaze bounced back up to Belle. "Maybelle . . ."

"Belle. I'd prefer to be called Belle."

"Okay. Belle." Millie smiled and her cheeks dimpled. "I heard something else about you. Something terribly exciting!" Millie's eyes shone as she scrambled off the bed and came to stand beside Belle at the window. "You want to know what I heard?"

"What?" Belle asked in a dull tone, resigned to passing gossip back and forth, an activity she found increasingly tawdry.

"I heard that you're a spy for Quantrill's Raiders! Is it true? Are you a Rebel spy?"

Alarm bolted through Belle and she turned on Millie with the finesse of a striking rattler.

"Hush, you silly ninny!" Belle hissed at her, making Millie jerk backward in alarm. "What do you mean spreading rumors like that? You want to get me thrown in jail?"

"No!" Millie's hands covered her flushed cheeks. "I-I was j-just talking. May . . . I-I mean, Belle, don't look at me like that. You scare me when you look at me like that."

"You make me so mad I could spit!" Belle paced in front of the bed, walking off her nerves. "You've got Major Eno under the roof and you're talking about me being part of Quantrill's gang! How am I supposed to look at you?"

"I only meant to—"

"I don't care what you meant." Belle stopped, fists clenched at her sides, black eyes fixed on Millie's white face. "You're going to get me in trouble talking like that. Is that what you want?"

"No. You know I don't want that. We're friends, aren't we?"

"I don't know when you talk crazy like this. Did you really

believe those tall tales? A true friend wouldn't even listen to them!"

"I am your friend," Millie insisted. "It's just that Major Eno has heard the same stories about you spying for your brother and he told Papa about it. Then you showed up on our doorstep and, well, Major Eno is real suspicious. I bet he thinks you'll lead him to your brother. What do you think?"

Belle sat on the bed beside Millie, thankful the other girl didn't have the good sense to keep her mouth shut. In fact, Millie wasn't the dumb stump Belle had her figured for. Little pitchers have big ears, Belle recalled with an inner smile that quickly gave way to worry. What if she did lead Major Eno right to Bud and the others? Oh, she'd never forgive herself if such a thing should happen! If Eno suspected her, then it was a sure bet that other Yankee officers had gotten wind of the gossip as well.

As much as she hated the thought, Belle knew that it was too risky to continue her report to Quantrill if it meant she might be followed and bring harm to Bud, Charley, Jimmy, or—heaven forbid!—Cole.

"Belle, what are you thinking?" Millie asked with a nasal whine. "You thinking about how much you hate me?"

"I think I was an awful old thing to yell at you a minute ago. I don't know what got into me. I guess I'm all nervous about these soldiers being here. I've never supped with the military before or played the piano for them." Belle placed a hand over her steadily beating heart and rolled her eyes in a convincing imitation of a flighty Southern lady. "I hope I played well. I was so nervous that my fingers kept jumping over the keys like rabbits through a field."

"You played beautifully," Millie said, giving Belle's hand a squeeze. "I don't blame you for being edgy. I'm used to the soldiers being here, but it must be unsettling for you. Especially with your folks being against the Union and all."

"My folks aren't against the Union," Belle corrected patiently. "The Union is against my folks, that's all. We don't take kindly to strangers telling us how to live our lives." Belle shook her head when Millie seemed perplexed. "Let's not talk politics. Tell me about Captain Cartwright. He's not married, is he?"

"I don't think so." Millie laughed, then blushed. "But, really, Belle! He doesn't even know I exist."

"Mildred Richey, don't tell me that you didn't notice him flirting with you all during supper! Are you blind, girl?"

Millie giggled and snuggled under the covers. "Do you think he's handsome?"

"I sure do." Belle slipped into bed beside her. The feather mattress curved around her and the quilts were piled so high that Belle couldn't see over them. She turned down the lamp, turned over on her side to face Millie, and told the girl what she wanted to hear since Millie had been gracious enough to do the same for Belle. "I think he's the best-looking Union soldier I ever did see."

"Do tell!" Millie's eyes sparkled in the semidarkness. "And he was flirting with me? Are you sure?"

"Why you could have poured the look he gave you over a waffle. I can't believe you didn't notice."

"Well," Millie said, drawing out the word, "I did catch him looking at me a time or two."

Belle smiled and closed her eyes. Millie had taken the bait and began reciting the virtues of Captain Cartwright, lulling Belle to sleep.

"Won't you take breakfast with us?" Mrs. Richey asked, following behind Belle as she prepared for her journey back to Carthage.

"No, I mustn't waste another minute. Mama and Papa

will be looking for me and I should be on my way immediately. I don't want them to worry, you understand." Belle stopped in the foyer and propped her bedroll on top of the banister while she secured it with two strips of leather. "I should have been gone before sunup but I overslept. Thank heavens that old rooster of yours hollered good and early and woke me up."

"I hate to send you off with an empty stomach," Mrs. Richey fretted. "What will your mother think when you arrive home half starved?"

Belle laid a hand on Mrs. Richey's arm. "She'll think that you're a kind soul to have taken her daughter in and kept her safe from harm."

"You're a sweet girl."

"It was good of you to let me stay, especially since you already have guests."

Mrs. Richey looked puzzled for a moment, then she lifted her hands to her face in a gesture of surprise. "You mean the troop?" She laughed at her own short-sightedness. "I clean forgot about them. I don't view them as guests . . . well, Major Eno is our guest. He's staying in the house, but I hardly notice the others since they stay outside." She shrugged helplessly. "We must do what we can for the war effort."

Belle didn't respond immediately, taken aback by the ways in which the war had twisted friendships and neighborly gestures. Mrs. Richey was a sweet woman, part of Belle argued, while another pointed out that this sweet woman was harboring the very men who were set on killing the men Belle admired and loved.

"Yes," Belle agreed when the silence became oppressive, "we all must do what is asked of us."

"Leaving so early?" Major Eno's boots tapped out a military strut on the marble floor. His blue uniform served to reinstate Belle's convictions. Damn Yankee, she thought with an acidity that put a sour taste in her mouth.

"Yes, I'm heading out," she replied crisply, turning on her heel and striding through the foyer and outside into the misty morning.

Queenie stamped impatiently as Belle tied the bedroll behind the saddle. Mrs. Richey and Major Eno watched her every move from the half-moon porch. Mrs. Richey wore a slight frown of worry. Major Eno was studying Belle with a calculating squint that made Belle's skin tingle. She pulled on her riding gloves and looked around for a bush in clear view to fulfill her final mission.

"Have a pleasant journey home," the major called to her.

"I shall. I'm so glad to have met you, Major Eno." Dark humor moved through her like a shadow passing across her soul. "How long will you and your troop be staying here with the Richeys?"

"As long as it takes," he said, his cheeks puffing out and reminding her of a squirrel's again. "Be careful out there. Bushwhackers might mistake you for an enemy instead of a friend."

Belle's head snapped up and her gaze sharpened as it fixed upon the little major.

"I am a schoolgirl," Belle said, her voice curiously flat and lifeless as the lie fell easily from her lips. "I take no part in this war you men have concocted. If you doubt this, why not abandon your polite sham and arrest me for treason?"

"Oh, no!" Mrs. Richey rushed to Belle's side and placed a protective arm around her shoulders. "Major Eno, I believe you've offended our guest. Maybelle is a school friend of my daughter's and I won't have her treated as a criminal! She's right about this terrible war. Brothers fighting against brothers. Sons against fathers. It's a nightmare, I tell you."

"Mama, is everything all right?" Millie asked, emerging

from the house and giving the major a suspicious glance as she passed him. "You're not having another fainting spell, are you?"

"No, but I do feel weak," Mrs. Richey said, placing her other arm around her daughter's waist. "Myra Maybelle is leaving us, dear."

"Already, Belle?" Millie protested. "You're not even staying for breakfast?" She turned and delivered a scathing frown to the major. "Did you say something bad about Belle and make her want to leave?"

The major bowed at the waist in a stiff, military salute. "Forgive me for any offense I might have afforded you, Miss Shirley," he said, and his manner was as phony as his apology.

Belle arched a condescending brow and turned away from him to embrace Millie.

"See you soon," Belle said, bussing Millie's rosy cheek. "I'd stay longer but my folks will be frantic."

"I understand. I'm ever so glad you stopped over." Millie's smile was as sweet as honey. "It was fun having you to talk with about . . . things."

"Stay on the main road," Mrs. Richey cautioned as she walked toward the house and went inside with the major.

"Did that old major say something mean to you?" Millie persisted as Belle looked around for a suitable shrub.

Millie followed along when Belle went to a young cherry tree. Taking her knife from her pocket, Belle reached up and cut one branch and then another with slow deliberation.

"What are you going to do with those?" Millie asked.

"Use them as quirts. Queenie is sluggish in the mornings. She won't be in the mood to race home unless I put her in the mood with these switches." Belle glanced over her shoulder at Millie's high color. "No, Millie. I'm not leaving because of anything the major said. I've just got to get home before my pa cuts some switches to use on me!"

A conflict of emotions swept over Belle as she looked into Millie's innocent eyes. She reached out and hugged her naïve friend. "Go inside," Belle whispered, afraid that she might cry if Millie didn't get out of her sight. "I'll see you again soon."

"Promise? I had a good time with you being here. I never had such a good girlfriend."

"Oh, hush up, Millie!" Belle vaulted into the sidesaddle.

"Are you mad at me?" Millie asked.

"No, I'm not mad." Belle sighed and her hand closed tightly on the switches she'd cut. "I've got to go is all." She chanced one more glance at Millie's trusting expression and then looked away sharply. "Take care!" Belle laid the switches across Queenie's rump and the pinto bolted forward, racing along the dirt path toward the main road.

Belle leaned close to Queenie's neck and willed the horse to sprout wings and fly. How lovely it would be to fly away to some peaceful place where no one knew fear or hatred, where there were no politics or politicians, where men like Lincoln and Eno weren't allowed entry. How lovely it would be!

But Queenie was just a horse, not Pegasus, and Belle was anchored to Missouri and all its strife and contradictions. The Richeys weren't the enemy, but they were harboring the enemy. Judge Richey had put his family in danger by allowing Eno's troops to camp on his land, so Judge Richey would have to take the blame when Quantrill's Raiders swooped down from the hills and laid to waste the Richey property. Belle shut her eyes tightly and prayed that Millie and Mrs. Richey would suffer no harm. They were good women caught up in a bad situation.

Belle reined Queenie off the main road and through the

underbrush, across the rolling country. Her sixth sense told her that one of Eno's soldiers had been sent to follow her and she had no intention of making it an easy mission. Queenie forded a stream, then followed Belle's firm hand and doubled back in the direction of the Richey place. Riding like the wind, Belle narrowed her watering eyes against the wicked breeze and buried her cold nose in Queenie's silky mane. Her plan was simple; double back to the Richey farm and then take the main road again so that she would be following the soldier instead of the other way around.

She directed Queenie closer to the road and was about to send the horse through the bordering trees and back onto the thoroughfare when a disturbance up ahead made her jerk violently on the reins. Queenie reared, then danced sideways as Belle tried to settle the horse with soothing hands while she examined the thicket ahead for any movement or sign of life.

"Who goes there?" she whispered, knowing for certain that someone was just ahead and waiting for her. She reached for her knife, preparing to defend herself against her unseen enemy. "I know you're there, so show yourself."

The horse stepped into view, hidden partly by shadow and mist. The rider flicked the reins and the horse surged forward, heading right for Belle and Queenie. The pinto sidestepped and strained against Belle's command to remain stationary. Queenie flung her head from side to side, jerking on the reins and chewing on the metal bit.

"Hold up," Belle commanded softly, for she'd recognized the rider by the way he sat in the saddle—erect, broad-shouldered, and ever so graceful. Like he was born to it. Her hand fell from the knife strapped at her waist and she smiled, feeling one side of her mouth tip up almost against her will. "Cole Younger, are you trying to scare the life out of me? Why didn't you answer me when I called out to you?"

He said nothing and gave nothing away in his expression. When his horse was parallel to hers, but facing the opposite direction, he reined hard and the buff-colored gelding dug its hooves into the soft earth. Mist rose up and curled around his knees. Cole tapped the brim of his hat so that it fell back off his head and swung from his neck by the chin strap. Then he straightened his legs, lifting his rump from the saddle. He reached for her, one hand curving at the back of her neck, gently pulling her to him. Cole swooped down upon Belle like a hawk claiming a small prize.

She went willingly, melting into submission. Was this happening? Was he really going to kiss her? Why now? What had changed between them?

His lips were cool and relaxed upon hers, sending a thrill from her mouth to the tips of her toes. His fingers gentled the soft hairs at the nape of her neck. Cole's lips parted, took in more of hers, sucking her sweet juice, and then ever so slowly, lifted away. Belle opened her eyes and felt herself drowning in the blue depths of his. Moments ticked by before she remembered to breathe again.

"You did good," he said in a voice that reminded Belle of nappy suede, seasoned and a little scratchy. "So why are you going back to the farm?"

"I'm not. I'm pulling a fast one. I doubled back to get the drop on a soldier who's following me."

Cole's eyes sharpened and he tracked the path ahead of him. "You're being followed? The major suspects you of aiding and abetting the enemy, does he?"

"He does, and I'm afraid I'll lead him or some other bluebelly right into your camp. I can't do that, Cole. I can't take that chance. Tell Charley . . . tell Bud." She swallowed against the tightness in her throat. To think she wouldn't see Cole or any of them again for . . . how long? A month? Longer? "Tell them they're in my thoughts and in my heart, but I can't see them for a spell."

"I'll tell them. You'd better get going."

"Cole?" When he started to remove his hand from the back of her neck, she hooked her fingers in the crook of his arm. "Why did you kiss me? I thought you didn't want to."

"I didn't want to . . . at first." He seemed to memorize her every feature and his smile clung to her like morning dew. "You're so young, Belle, and so pretty. I hope you find yourself a good man."

"I have."

A wariness tensed his mouth and he looked ahead at the path. "You mean Jimmy Reed."

"No, I mean—"

"No." His hand moved from the back of her neck to cover her lips and stop her words. "Don't say it. I don't want to hear it. Now, go on before someone sees us. I've got to get back to the others, and you've got to get back to your pappy." His hard fingertips slipped from her mouth to her chin and then ever so lightly down her throat. "Bless you, Myra Maybelle Shirley. I'll give Jimmy and Bud your love." He pulled his gelding off to one side and nodded toward the road in a silent command.

"Good-bye, Cole. Take care of yourself."

Belle turned Queenie in a tight semicircle and headed back toward Carthage. Bittersweet tears filled her eyes and she wiped them away with her free hand. She forced Queenie into a jarring trot, then a more comfortable gallop until she figured she wasn't far from the soldier sent to tail her. She left the road again and let Queenie pick her way through the underbrush. Around the next bend Belle spotted the soldier. She guided the pinto back onto the road as quietly as possible. With a sly grin, she kept Queenie on a tight rein and shouted to the Yankee soldier, who was searching frantically for his quarry.

"Yoo-hoo, sir! Are you one of Major Eno's men?"

The soldier twisted around in his saddle and pulled his horse up short. His mouth opened in surprise, then snapped shut in annoyance. He was young, self-righteous, and thoroughly humiliated. His face flushed bright red and he stammered mindlessly before making any sense. "I . . . it . . . how . . . it's you!"

"Me?" Belle laughed lightly. "I'm Belle Shirley. Are you one of Eno's men or not?"

"Yes, but—" He waited for her to ride up to him, eying her suspiciously all the while. "How'd you get back there?"

"Back where?" Belle asked, looking behind her with feigned confusion. "I've come from the Richey farm."

"You left . . . I was right behind . . . never mind." He heaved a choppy sigh and stared ahead with stony belligerence.

"I was wondering if you might be headed for Carthage," Belle said, enjoying the soldier's slow burn.

"I am," he snapped, still not looking at her.

"Wonderful! So am I. I was thinking that we might ride together and then I won't be afraid of being ambushed by bushwhackers." When the soldier didn't make a sound, Belle leaned forward to peer into his beet-red face. "Sir, would that be acceptable?"

The muscles in his jaw flexed and his hands were fisted around the reins so tightly that his knuckles showed white beneath his skin. He gathered in a deep breath, then dug his heels into his horse's sides. "Fine," he said. "Come along."

"Good. I feel ever so much safer with you along for the ride. Aren't I the lucky one to run up on you like I did?" Belle sat tall in the saddle and smiled with supreme satisfaction all the way home.

Chapter Four

"SON, YOU'RE LOOKING POORLY. Have you been getting enough to eat?" John Shirley asked, examining Bud with open concern.

Belle paused in clearing the table, agreeing with her father's assessment. Bud's chalky complexion and sunken eyes made him look ever so much older than his twenty-two years. His skin was drawn tight across his cheekbones, and he had bluish smudges underneath his brown eyes. A network of wrinkles spread across his forehead and from the corners of his eyes. His black hair was dusty and dull like horsehair. Seeing him in such poor health made Belle ache inside.

It's only been two months since I saw him last, she thought with alarm. Only two months since he'd bristled with energy and lifted her up into her saddle as if she weighed ounces. The war had sucked the life out of him.

She thought of her younger brothers sleeping upstairs—Eddie, Mannie, and Shug—and wondered if they'd be riding off someday only to return beaten and bedraggled. Old men in young men's bodies.

The damned war, Belle thought with a burst of vengeance. It was ruining everything: the men, the women, the fabric of life. When would it end and how would they survive when it did?

"I'm eating good, Papa," Bud said as he shoved another half of a biscuit into his mouth. "I've been taking meals over at the Stewart place in Sarcoxie. You remember Mrs. Stewart, don't you?"

"Yes, I believe I do."

"God bless Mrs. Stewart," Eliza Shirley chimed in. John, Bud, and Belle looked at her in shocked surprise. Eliza hardly ever spoke these days or took interest in any conversation other than the silent one going on in her own head.

"Mama?" Belle asked hopefully. She rested her hand on one of her mother's, which was frail and blue-veined. "Are you with us tonight?"

Eliza's expression grew wistful as she stared at Bud. Rising from her chair with the weightlessness of a ghost, she sighed sweetly and acted as if she hadn't heard Belle's voice.

"Bud's here," she said simply.

"Yes, Mama." Belle smiled at Bud, thrilled to have Eliza lucid after all this time. "Bud sure loves your cooking. He ate a dozen biscuits all by himself."

"I'll make some more," Eliza said, drifting over to the floured sideboard.

"No, Mama. I'm all full up," Bud assured her. He leaned back and patted his stomach as if to prove it.

"I'll make some for you to take along." Eliza glanced over her shoulder at him. Her smile was so tenderly beautiful that it brought tears to Belle's eyes.

Bud stood up and went to his mother. He dropped a kiss on her cheek and gave her shoulders a squeeze. "Mama, you should rest more and take better care of yourself."

"You won't be staying. You never stay for long."

Bud bowed his head for a moment in heartsick sadness. "Mama, I want to stay, but it's not safe. I've got to keep moving."

"We understand, Bud," John assured him. "You do what you think is best. We understand."

"Mama, do you understand why I can't stay?" Bud asked, turning her around to face him. "You know I love you, don't you? If I could stay with you, I'd do it. It's the war . . . the Yankees are looking for me."

Eliza's gaze wandered over Bud's face and then beyond it as her mind sent her back to that other place. "We'll plant cotton and soybeans. We should have a good crop this year." She shrugged off Bud's hands and began kneading the dough before her. "I'll bake these biscuits, and you and your father can take them out to the field with you in the morning. They'll taste awful good should you get the hungries before dinnertime."

"Oh, Mama." Bud's head fell forward until his chin scraped across his collar. He drew a trembling breath and ran his hands through his hair. "I hate to see her like this. I feel . . . well, it's my fault, I guess."

"Come and sit down, son," John said in a voice that rolled from his chest and held a note of authority. "No one's to blame. The war's made her unstable. It's got nothing to do with you. Sit down and have another biscuit and cup of coffee."

"Don't mind if I do." Bud looked at Belle and patted the chair next to him. "Sit down and quit fussing with those dishes."

Belle was aching to talk to him alone, but she knew that her father was just as anxious to spend time with Bud. Time was in short supply lately. Nobody had time for nothing except surviving from day to day.

"How's it in the brush?" John asked as he leaned back in

his chair and touched a flaming match to the bowl of his pipe. "We've heard that you boys are making it uncomfortable for the Yankee troops coming through here." John chuckled and winked at Bud. "I guess those Yankees think you're as slippery as a snake."

"There's not a bluebelly around here who hasn't heard my name," Bud boasted. "And they just keep coming. More and more every week." Bud reached for another biscuit and finished it off before continuing. "Papa, it's getting bad out there. Real bad." He glanced at his mother, making sure she was still in her world of crops and biscuit dough. "Did you hear about Quantrill leaving? I think he's in Indian Territory."

"We heard," John said between puffs on his pipe that sent smoke curling around his head like a crown. "What happened to the others in your outfit?"

"Most of them left to join the regular army. There's only a handful of us left in the brush. I started to leave, but I just couldn't. I figure I can fight just as well here as I can somewhere else, but ..." He paused to glance over his shoulder at Eliza. "I'm worried about Mama and the rest of you. The Union burned the Younger place to the ground just to get back at Cole."

"Younger's mama is a poor old widow," John protested.

"Yes, but that didn't stop the troopers from burning and looting her place. She's staying with relatives in Harrisonville. Cole and one of his brothers joined up with the regular Confederacy."

"Damn Yankees!" John ran a hand down his face in abject frustration. "Can't they fight clean and leave the women and children out of this?"

"Guess not." Bud peeked up through his lashes at Belle, who had fallen back in her chair and was staring blindly at the pile of soiled dishes.

"There's talk of a surrender," John mused aloud. "The Yankees are spilling over every border and—"

"We'll never surrender!" Bud brought one fist down on the table and set the plates and flatware to dancing. "They can send army after army and we'll stand and fight them until we're all struck down."

"Son, son," John said, patting the air with placating hands. "Settle down. No need to fly off the handle about it. I'm just telling you that the news is bad. We've lost one major battle after another and the newspapers are saying that we can't hold on much longer. The Union has claimed the whole Mississippi valley, and there seems to be no stopping Sherman's troops." John ran a hand through his thinning hair. "I don't know what President Davis is thinking of . . . what he thinks we can accomplish now that our armies are reduced to eighteen-year-old boys. People are saying that Sherman is going to take Atlanta before the year is out."

"They're wrong." Bud dropped into a sullen silence, staring moodily at a knothole in the kitchen table. "They might win the war, but they'll never beat us. We'll make sure there's no spoils for them after this one is over."

Belle caught her father's worried scowl and sent it back. She squeezed one of Bud's big, square hands. He looked into Belle's bright eyes and her smile almost chased away his black mood. "Want to go outside and sit a spell in the porch swing?" she asked.

"Sounds nice." Bud stood up and held out a hand to his father. "Good to see you again, Papa. I'm sorry to hear that the hotel and livery are doing so bad. Guess business is sorry all over Missouri."

"All over everywhere," John amended, then patted Bud's hand before letting go of it. "Go on. I know you and Maybelle want some time alone. Go before your mother realizes you've lit out again."

Bud and Belle left the kitchen and sat side by side on the porch swing for a few minutes, swinging back and forth and listening to the distant sound of cannons and the crack of gunshot.

Spring was in the air. A breeze came up laden with the scent of rain. Bud took Belle's hand and pulled her up from the swing. They walked side by side to the end of the block where the shadows had gathered in the space between the hotel and the livery.

"I've missed you," Bud said after a few moments.

"I heard that you and the others ruined Major Eno's plans."

Bud laughed and stuffed his hands in his trouser pockets. "We kicked his ass. Turned out to be our last big victory before things started falling apart." He cocked his head to one side. "Seems like that happened years ago."

"Right after my sixteenth birthday," Belle reminded him. "February, and this is May."

"Time gets away from me out in the bush," he admitted, kicking absently at pebbles underfoot. "Everything's getting away from me . . . I just wish that—"

"What?" Belle asked when his voice melted into a whisper she could barely hear. "You wish what?"

Pinpoints of light glimmered in his brown eyes, but the rest of his face was as dark and somber as the shadows that concealed him. Apprehension trailed a finger down Belle's spine, making her stiffen. She reached out, needing to touch him, and her fingers curved in the crook of his arm and stayed to pleat his shirtsleeve.

"I'd rather die than see the Yankees win." His voice was toneless; a death knell that brought tears to his eyes.

"Don't say it. Saying it will make it so!"

"I heard that Charley Quantrill is dead."

"No!" Belle snatched her hand from him and pressed her knuckles against her lips.

"That's what I've heard. I believe it."

"And Cole? What of Cole?"

"Cole?" Bud tilted his head at a curious angle. "He either joined the regiment or he went back to Lee's Summit to see about his mother. I thought you'd be interested in knowing about Jimmy Reed."

"I am!" Belle grasped his forearms. He felt ropy; not strong, just tough. "Where's Jimmy? He's riding with you, isn't he?"

"No. He hasn't been with us for weeks. Haven't you missed him?"

"Of course I've missed him," she said irritably. "I've missed all of you. You, especially. I've been as restless as the wind since I stopped riding out and reporting to you. I hate sitting around and doing nothing. I don't know how women stand it!"

"Most women aren't like you," Bud said with a lopsided grin that was so like his sister's. "They don't have the courage to spy and run around with a bunch of tough-talking men." Bud pulled her against him and hugged her hard and fast. "I was so proud of the way you handled yourself. There wasn't a man among us who didn't respect you. I think most of them had eyes for you."

"No," Belle objected with a scoffing laugh. "Most of them just put up with me because they respected you so much." She closed her eyes and rubbed her cheek against Bud's downy soft shirt. "I thought it was a game back then . . . the war and all," she added to explain. "It was fun and exciting and I was a part of it all."

A cannon blast shredded the moment and Belle jumped involuntarily. She placed a hand to her thudding heart.

"It's coming from Sarcoxie," Bud said. "I should saddle up and join the action."

"It's not a game," Belle said, her eyes stinging with tears, "and it sure isn't any fun." She glanced toward the street. "Some Kansas boys set fire to the church last week."

"I heard."

Belle shut her eyes for a minute. "I'm tired of it all. I wish they'd leave us alone."

"They won't until we're all dead and buried."

"Don't talk about dying." She reached out and took his hand, pulling him into the moonlight. "Papa's right. You look dreadful." She curved her other hand along his chin and cheek where his whiskers were stubbly and pricked like dull pins. "I'm worried about you. Why don't you stay with us a week or two? You can keep low and no one will know you're hiding out here. It's been a hard winter and it's taken its toll on you. You've got to get some rest and some homecooking in your belly."

"No, Belle." He flattened his hand against hers and rubbed his whiskers against her palm. "I'm doing fine. I won't bring any hardship down on you. I couldn't stand it if any of you were hurt or—or killed."

"My sweet Bud," she said, taking his hands in hers. "You'll always be my hero. You taught me to shoot straight, ride like the wind, and stand up to friend and foe. You taught me how to survive." She sighed and leaned her forehead against his. "Everything's changing so fast, isn't it? Nothing will ever be the same again."

"I can't imagine what it will be like if the war ends. What'll I do if I'm not fighting? It's all I'm good for."

"Don't say things like that. You can do lots of things." Belle returned his smile, glad to see his mood lighten. "Where did you say Jimmy was hiding out these days?"

"I'm not sure." Bud lifted his forehead from hers and

swung her arms back and forth between them. "He might have joined the regular army or headed for Texas. Lots of the boys have hightailed it to Texas."

"Guess it must be safe there or Preston sure as hell wouldn't have stayed."

"Myra Maybelle," Bud scolded, but laughter lit his eyes and lifted his voice. "You're a wicked-tongued girl."

"I learned it from being around my ornery brother." Thinking on better days, Belle sighed and stepped up onto the sidewalk in front of the hotel. She looked up at a sliver of yellow moon. "Lordy, I miss all of them, don't you? Cole and Jesse and Jimmy. I even miss Charley and Frank a little. I wonder if we'll ever see any of them again?"

"If fate is kind, we will." Bud pulled his gloves from his back pocket and thrust his hands into them. "I've got to ride."

A breeze encircled Belle and she crossed her arms and rubbed her hands up and down. "Lord! That wind is coming right out of the north, isn't it?"

Bud shook his head. "What wind? It feels nice out here to me. Feels like spring."

"Are you wearing armor under your clothes? Didn't you feel that wind kick up just now?"

"Nope." He soaked up beads of perspiration from his forehead and upper lip with his shirtsleeve. Fever lit his eyes, making them glisten in the semidarkness. He dropped a kiss onto her cheek and his lips felt like dry autumn leaves. "Take care, little sister. Do you think Mama will be okay?"

"Sure. She's better off where she is." Belle's fingers trailed up his sunken cheeks, then she adjusted his slouch hat at an angle. "I wish I was going with you. Be careful. I'm worried about you. You seem weaker this time. I can't help but think you're ill."

"I'm fine. I've just got battle fever is all."

"Battle fever?" Belle grabbed his forearm when he started to turn away from her. "What in tarnation is that?"

One corner of his mouth tipped up into a grin that wasn't at all pleasant.

"Don't worry, Belle. It's a good kind of fever. Keeps me warm at night. Keeps my hatred burning."

Belle watched, dumbfounded, as he darted into the livery and then emerged astride his battle-scarred chestnut mare. Bud blew a kiss to Belle and chuckled.

"If I see Jimmy I'll tell him that you're pining away for him."

"You do that, you rascal," Belle called out to him.

A sadness weighed upon her heart, but Belle smiled and waved happily to Bud. She wanted him to remember her smile and take that memory with him until they met again.

"What's become of you out there?" she wondered aloud as he was swallowed by the night. He lives in another world just like Mama. Only Mama's is a pretty, clean world and Bud's is a private inferno that fires him with a fool's bravery. He's no longer fighting to preserve a way of life. Fighting *is* his way of life.

Belle felt the chill in her bones again and she started to cry. The war was a lost cause, pretty Carthage was pocked with battle scars, Quantrill's Raiders were scattered to the four winds, and Bud, sweet Bud, was crazy with a gunpowder fever he'd caught somewhere in the brush.

The cotton sheet floated above the bed like a stiff cloud and then drifted down in a billowing sigh. Belle tucked in the corners with practiced efficiency and sent an apologetic glance toward the elderly man standing on the threshold of the room.

"Sorry to keep you waiting, sir. I'll be finished here in a snap." She eyed the black bag beside him. "Are you a doctor?"

"I am. I'm headed for an army post to offer my services to our wounded Confederates."

"Bless you, sir." Belle plumped up the pillows and stood back to admire her handiwork. "There's water in the pitcher and we can send up a cold dinner to you, if you want." She opened the windows wider and pushed back the thin curtains. "It's hot at midday, but it cools off come sundown. We're having a humid June."

"Thank you kindly." He shuffled into the room and stood to one side to let Belle out into the corridor. "Do you have family fighting on the front lines?"

"No, but most of the boys I grew up with are there." A thought struck her and she placed a hand against the door when the doctor moved to close it. "Excuse me, sir. In your travels and doctoring have you run into Cole Younger or James Reed?"

"Reed, no." The doctor stroked his white whiskers and screwed up one eye in contemplation. "Younger . . . that's familiar."

Belle's heart kicked against her ribs and she placed a hand just below it. "Thomas Coleman Younger. He's about twenty. Tall, blond, blue-eyed. He's got a nice voice . . . sort of whispery and scratchy."

"Is he your sweetheart?" the doctor asked with an understanding smile.

"He's a friend. I heard that he'd joined the regular army, but I don't know where he went or what regiment he's with."

"I can't place him, but I'll think on it. Might come to me before I leave tomorrow."

Her hope shriveled and her heart thudded listlessly as she left the doctor to his thoughts.

Belle was at the foot of the stairs when her mother's scream ripped through the hotel's still air. Belle flew down the stairs. A young man slumped against the registration desk.

Milt Norris stared hollow-eyed at Eliza Shirley's prostrate form on the Persian rug before him. John cradled his wife's head in his lap and fanned her white face with a newspaper.

"Mannie, get the smelling salts," John ordered, and the youngster ran past Belle and up the stairs to his parents' room.

"Papa?" Belle said, forcing one foot in front of the other as she kept her gaze stubbornly averted from the young bushwhacker. His rasping breathing was uncommonly noisy in the quiet front foyer. Edwin stood beside him, but he was hardly breathing at all. "What made Mama faint?"

"Maybelle, go get that doctor," John said briskly. "Young Milt's wounded and needs tending to."

"I'm already here," the doctor said, shouldering past Belle and helping Milt to sit in a chair. "How's your wife?"

"Fainted. She'll come around," John said.

Blood seeped from a wound on Milt's thigh and soaked the leg of his pants. He held his hand over the bullet hole and looked from Belle to the doctor, who knelt before him. He seemed more afraid than in pain.

Mannie returned and John took the smelling salts from him and waved the bottle under Eliza's nose. She coughed and her lashes lifted. She moaned and closed her eyes again.

"Papa, is it Bud?" Belle asked, knowing it was. She gripped the banister with both hands, afraid she might fall to her knees.

John Shirley stood and gathered his wife up into his

arms. He swallowed hard, making his Adam's apple bob up and down slowly as he moved with long, measured strides to the staircase.

"I'll take your mother upstairs," he said, but he paused when he was shoulder to shoulder with Belle. His woeful eyes met Belle's fearful ones. "Bud's dead, Maybelle. He was shot by Yankee soldiers last night."

"He's in Sarcoxie at the Stewart place," Milt spoke up. "You need to claim the body before the Yankees do something with it."

Grief blinded Belle's eyes for a few moments; then her vision cleared and she realized that the others were staring at her, waiting for her to drop like a stone as her mother had done before her. She'd expected it of herself, but her knees didn't give out and her heart didn't break in two. The news was an anticlimax. Belle had been preparing herself for six weeks . . . ever since Bud had ridden into the night. Hearing the news of his death was merely the last nail hammered into a coffin her mind had been building.

"Daughter," John said close to her ear, "are you all right?"

"Yes, Papa." Something tugged on her skirt and she looked down at Shug, who was hugging her legs and staring up at her with teary eyes. "Poor baby," Belle crooned, leaning down and gathering the toddler into her arms. He pressed his hot, wet face into the curve of her neck. "See to Mama. I'll take care of the others." She reached out her arm and gathered Mannie to her side. Eddie came forward, slump-shouldered and sniffling softly.

"Belle, it ain't true," Eddie said, stopping in front of her as he ran a palm up his nose. "Milt's lying, ain't he?"

"It's true, Eddie. Our Bud is gone." Belle looked at her father and shared his tired, heavy burden of grief. "I'm coming with you to Sarcoxie, Papa."

"If you wish. I think—" John's voice broke and he turned

his head sharply aside as his face contorted with grief. He shifted his wife in his arms and took the stairs two at a time. "We should leave here soon, Maybelle. I don't want Yankee trash touching my boy's body." His voice drifted down to Belle as he carried Eliza to their room at the opposite end of the landing.

Belle hugged her brothers tightly, possessively, and prayed that Bud would be the last one she'd have to collect like so much dirty laundry.

War is blasphemy, destroying every beautiful thing in its path. Youth, hope, dreams, and faith all vanish in the smoke of battle and betrayal. War is pointless. When it's over, what will have been accomplished? Cemeteries will be full. Families will be torn apart.

"The Yankees wanted this war," Belle said, speaking her thoughts to her father seated beside her on the springboard seat. "I hope every last one of them dies in it."

John glanced at her, troubled by her words but too full of grief to comment.

"If they'd left well enough alone," Belle continued, "if they'd just let us live our lives in peace, we wouldn't be burying our future . . . our Buds. Oh, Papa, how will we go on without our Bud?"

"We'll go on because we must." John stared at a point between the horse's ears. "Don't fall to pieces in front of the Yankees. Don't give them that satisfaction."

Belle nodded, but she had no idea how she'd react to seeing Bud's body. She tried preparing herself for the reality of Bud's demise as the horse and wagon pulled up in front of the Stewart place in Sarcoxie. The house was small and weather-beaten. It sat on the end of a short, residential street. The Walton place was to the south and open fields were on the north and west of it. A shed and outhouse squatted along the east side. Usually this area was quiet and secluded with nothing much to break the monotony other than squawking chickens and barking dogs.

Not so today, Belle thought as she took in the activity around her. It was like some revival meeting without the tent. Yankee soldiers milled around the house. Horses and wagons were tied to every post and scrub brush. Children climbed trees and played at ambushing each other, using cocked thumbs and stiff forefingers to intimidate young and old alike. Everyone, including the youngsters, gave blue uniforms a wide berth and dagger glances. Blue uniforms were everywhere. Sarcoxie had become Yankee territory, making Belle wonder if Carthage wouldn't fall too. Their dreams of glory had died at Vicksburg and Gettysburg. Surrender was a mere formality.

Before John got down from the wagon, Mrs. Stewart and a neighbor, Mrs. Walton, came running from the house toward him.

"Oh, Mr. Shirley!" Mrs. Stewart dabbed at her red, swollen eyes with a lacy handkerchief. "I'm as grief-stricken as you. To think! Yankees killing sweet Bud right under my nose!" She buried her face in her hands and turned to sob uncontrollably upon Mrs. Walton's shoulder.

"She's beside herself." Mrs. Walton comforted her neighbor with helpless pats on the back and shoulders. "She was giving the boys supper when the Yankees burst right into the house. The boys bolted and ran. The Yankees shot poor Bud as he jumped over the back fence. He was dead before he hit the ground. The Norris boy was mighty lucky to get away alive, I'm here to tell you. Six Yankee soldiers against only two of our boys! Those Yankees never heard of chivalry. Bud wasn't even armed. His gun belt is still hanging on the back of the kitchen chair inside."

"Where's my son?" John asked woodenly.

"Inside, sir." Mrs. Walton and Mrs. Stewart started back along the path to the house and John followed behind them. "We laid him out on the dining-room table."

Belle made no move to join them. She closed her eyes and swayed slightly back and forth in a rocking motion. She willed herself not to faint or cry while the Yankee soldiers looked on. Papa was right about not giving them the satisfaction of witnessing her grief. The last thing Bud would want was for her to collapse in front of Yankee filth.

"Are you all right, ma'am?" a deep voice inquired of her. Belle's eyes flew open to take in the blue-uniformed man standing beside the wagon. He was no more than seventeen or eighteen, but he had the swagger of one who had been given too much authority too soon. He brimmed with self-importance.

"Go away," Belle said, looking him up and down with surly contempt. "If I was drawing my last breath, I wouldn't ask you for help."

"It's hot in the sun," he told her with the persistence of a horsefly. "It'd be better if you'd wait in the shade for your father."

Belle snatched up the riding crop and cocked her arm menacingly. "It'd be better if you'd get away from me before I lay open the side of your face with this!"

He held up a placating hand. "I'm only thinking of your welfare, lady."

"You should've thought of my welfare before you shot my brother." She half-rose off the seat and brandished the whip. The young soldier almost tripped over his feet in a backward scramble.

Two other Yankee soldiers watched the proceedings. Both touched the guns swinging at their sides when Belle popped the whip high over their comrade's head. Belle choked back bitter laughter. Such brave men, she thought with an inner scoff. Can't even handle a woman without going for their guns.

"Your brother was a murdering, good-for-nothing bush-whacker," the Yankee in retreat charged, his voice piping up to an adolescent shrillness.

"And you're a white-livered, pompous little bastard!" She straightened to her full height, making the horse look back at her curiously.

"Maybelle!" John Shirley shouted in warning.

Belle frowned at her father, who was coming down the walk. But her irritation quickly melted when she realized that the stiff bundle of blankets he carried was all that remained of Bud. Her heart swelled and pride tightened her throat as her brave, proud papa swept past the young Yankees to deposit the body of his son in the back of the wagon.

"Need help, sir?" one of the soldiers offered.

"Not from the likes of you," John said, never even looking toward the others. He scowled at Belle, silently berating her for losing her temper. "I'll collect Bud's horse and tie it to the back of the wagon, then we'll be on our way."

Belle sat down and faced front again, her back to the bundle of plaid blankets. Mrs. Walton approached the wagon and laid Bud's slouch hat and gun belt in Belle's lap.

"Poor, dear girl," Mrs. Walton crooned, squeezing Belle's cold, trembling hands before placing them on top of the hat and belt. "These were your brother's. We all thought he was a fine young man. May he rest in peace. How's Mrs. Shirley?"

"She's taken to her bed," Belle answered by rote. Un-flinchingly aware of the Yankee soldier who stood within her field of vision, wearing a cocky smirk, Belle felt the rage pumping through her veins. The other two Yankees whispered to each other and laughed softly as they glanced in her direction.

"Poor thing. I know what it's like to lose a child. My own son was cut down at Vicksburg." Mrs. Walton's voice broke. She placed an arthritic hand to her eyes, hoping to compose herself sufficiently to make her way back to the Stewart house.

Belle stared at her hands resting upon Bud's dusty, sweat-stained hat and scuffed gun belt. She ran her fingers across the cold metal of the revolver tucked into the holster and it comforted her in an odd way. The sun beat down on the top of her head, burning into her bonnet and spreading through her until she began to feel Bud's battle fever. It felt good. It made her feel alive. Her fingers curled around the gun butt and she felt powerful, able to do something about the senseless war instead of merely enduring it. Her bones ached, longing for action.

The rumble of the Yankee soldiers' voices drummed in her ears like a yellow jacket caught in a bell jar with no hope of escape. No escape. No . . . hope. No escape.

She pulled the revolver from the holster ever so slowly as the voices became a roar in her head. The fever intensified, shooting through her like harnessed lightning. She was hardly aware of standing. Her whole being was focused on clutching the revolver in both hands and raising it up, up, up. Arms stiff, elbows locked, hands gripping the gun butt to keep it steady, she aimed the weapon at the cocky Yankee soldier. She let the fever take her, lift her, carry her away.

"What do you think you're doing?" the young Yankee barked with the blind audacity of one who expects answers even from mad girls with guns. "Are you planning on shooting someone?"

Belle curled her finger around the trigger and pulled.

"Maybelle! No!"

Her father's scream was so sharp and wrenching that Belle thought at first it was the retort of the gun in her hands, but she felt no accompanying jolt and realized that the gun hadn't fired. She flexed her trigger finger and tried again. Click. The hammer fell on another empty chamber.

The Yankee soldiers burst into wild laughter, doubling over and slapping each other on the back. Their raucous laughter broke the fever and Belle collapsed onto the seat, dropped the gun in her lap, and covered her face with her hands.

John tied Bud's chestnut mare to the tailgate then climbed into the wagon beside Belle and took up the reins. He made a clucking sound and the horse set off, turning in a semicircle and then moving at a sedate clip down the road. As they passed the Yankees, John delivered a flinty-eyed glare.

"Uncover your face, girl," he said under his breath. "Don't hide yourself from them. No Shirley hides from Yankee scum."

Belle wiped the tears from her cheeks and tipped up her chin. Head high, she stared straight ahead as the wagon jostled through Sarcoxie.

Belle thought of the gawking, laughing soldiers and her face flamed. "I made a fool of myself," she said, glancing at her father's sweat-beaded face. A drop of perspiration formed on the tip of his nose and dropped off onto the front of his shirt.

"You've always had a terrible temper. It'll be the death of you some day."

She lifted her face to the weak breeze sailing in from the north. "Sometimes I'm so full of hatred I don't know what I'm doing."

John scratched at his beard and flicked the reins to urge the horse into a trot. "It's time we left before the hatred consumes all of us and destroys what's left of our family."

71

"Left for where?" she asked, looking sideways at him.

"Texas."

"You mean, sell the hotel and everything? What would we do in Texas?"

"I'll find something. Preston says there's plenty of good land to be had in Texas. He's doing well for himself. The war hasn't ruined that part of the country yet."

"Preston," Belle repeated, making the name sound as bored as she felt when she thought of her oldest brother. She looked off the road at a field where a chimney stuck up amid the charred remains of someone's home. "We'll be running out when the South needs us the most, Papa."

"The South doesn't need us. The South needs factories, a shipping fleet, and fifty thousand more men to fight off the Yankees."

"Are you surrendering for us, Papa?" Belle challenged.

"Somebody's got to," John countered. "If we don't leave soon, we'll lose your mother for good." He glanced over his shoulder at the bundle of blankets. "This will about do her in, but if we can get her out of Carthage and to Preston, I think she'll pull through."

"Her and Preston are cut from the same cloth," Belle said, resenting the weak members in her family tree.

"Preston will work like a tonic on her. You'll see. If anybody can bring Eliza back to us, it's Preston. His wife's had another baby and Eliza will make herself useful tending to it while the rest of us make a new home."

"We'll bury Bud in Carthage."

"Of course. We'll bury him here, dispose of our property, and set out for Texas."

It sounded so cut-and-dried that it was repulsive. Belle examined her father's icy control and rejected it.

"Papa, I'm staying here with Bud. I can't leave him. He's

part of us, Papa. He needs one of us to stay and see to him and—"

"Maybelle, stop it!" John reined the horse and seized Belle by the shoulders. He ducked his head to catch her downward gaze. "Bud is dead. No use fooling yourself about it."

"No, we can't leave him. You might be able to forget, but I—"

"Look at this."

John reached back and tore the blanket away to reveal a face that held little resemblance to Bud's. Belle moaned and shut her eyes tightly against her brother's death grimace.

"That's what's left of Bud, and *that* doesn't need anyone to stay behind and tend to it." John stared at her white, tearstained face and a sob worked up his long throat. "Oh, Maybelle, I know how you loved him." He pulled her head down to his chest and flicked the edge of the blanket back over his son's head. "I know he was your favorite, but he's gone. The war took him from us months ago . . . long time before the bullet finished him off. There's nothing left for us here in Missouri. It's best if we pack up and find a better life. Someplace where we all can heal. Not just your mother, but all of us."

Belle wrapped her arms around her father's middle and rested her head on his shoulder. The horse started off again, rocking the wagon through the heat of the day. John hummed softly and Belle closed her eyes, drifting back to her childhood where Bud still lived and the South still thrived.

"Texas will be good for us," John said when they were almost to Carthage. "Preston says it's pretty there. He lives near Dallas."

"Dallas," Belle repeated, but the name held no magic for her. "I won't like it there."

73

"Don't be a Missouri mule," her father begged. "I need your strength now, not your dag-burned stubbornness!"

His honesty stirred her. Belle lifted herself from her father's protective embrace. She straightened her bonnet and retied the bow under her chin.

"It'd be nice to live on a farm again," Belle said, laying Bud's gun and hat to one side. "Crop prices ought to go sky high after the war."

John looked admiringly at Belle and wished his wife possessed one-tenth of his daughter's mettle.

PART TWO

Texas
1866

Chapter Five

I SWEAR THE SUN IS HOTTER in Texas than it was in Missouri," Belle complained. Sweat trickled down her spine and under her arms, making her feel sticky and itchy all over. She stacked soiled dinner dishes and moved listlessly along the wood table where the Shirleys took most of their meals when weather permitted.

An April breeze sailed across the flat land and teased the raven curls that framed Belle's face. She paused to appreciate the caress, then picked up a stack of plates and started for the clapboard house.

"I luff Texas," Shug said, grinning to show his two missing front teeth. "I luff it better than Carthage."

"You would," Belle said with a playful scowl. "If I hate something, you're sure to love it just to be contrary."

"I love not having to work in the fields on Sundays," Mannie piped up. He was settled in the swing suspended from an oak branch. He pushed off and went sailing on a sea of blue sky.

"I agree with that last part," Belle said. "But *I* still have to work. You boys have it made in the shade. Wish I'd been born male so I could relax after dinner."

"Poor, poor Belle," Edwin crooned as she passed him. He leaned a shoulder against the side of the house and his smirk made Belle itch to slap his face. "She works so awful hard," he taunted.

"I work a hell of a lot harder than you do, Edwin Benton."

He really knew how to get under her skin. Edwin was ferret-faced with slanty eyes and sharp little teeth. The older Ed got, the more dangerous he looked.

"I'm gonna tell Mama that you're cussing," he threatened.

"Go ahead, then I'll tell her about how you're running around with a pack of horse thieves, and we'll see who gets whipped first."

Ed narrowed his light brown eyes and chewed on a long blade of spring grass. When Belle failed to flinch under his assessment, he shrugged nonchalantly. Belle jerked up her chin in superior contempt and went on into the house where her mother and sister-in-law were elbow-deep in suds and hot water.

Eliza and Mary looked up from the tubs of dishwater. Their faces glistened with perspiration. Mary pressed a wet hand to the small of her back and bowed over it. She was a pale blonde in poor health, following two miscarriages, and the premature birth and subsequent death of a baby boy a year ago.

"How many more dishes are out there?" Mary asked, pushing back a damp strand of her flaxen hair.

"Cups and glasses and some utensils," Belle answered, setting the stacks of plates on the table near her mother. "We're almost finished."

"Good." Mary sighed and reached for a dirty pot. "It's hot as blazes in here. I'm thinking of a glass of lemonade and the front porch swing. What about you, Mrs. Shirley?"

"Sounds like heaven to me," Eliza said, glancing toward

the back door. "It's such a pretty day that it's a sin to spend it indoors."

Belle went back outside for the last load of soiled dishes. Ed stood where she'd left him. Mannie and Shug were nowhere in sight. Gathering up the dishes, Belle gave Ed a sidelong glance and wondered why he was watching her so intently. She arched a brow in a silent question and Ed grinned.

"You're jealous," he said, chuckling.

"Of what?"

"Of me."

Belle rolled her eyes in ridicule. "Edwin, you're going through a strange stage. Why would I be jealous of a sixteen-year-old kid who's still wet behind the ears?"

"Because I'm the one who's running with the boys and living on excitement instead of you. You're jealous is all." He stood tall and squared his bony shoulders. "Did you think I was so stupid back in Carthage that I didn't know about you running off and meeting with Bud and the rest of Quantrill's men?"

"Ancient history, brother, and best forgotten."

"You're not denying it?" Ed asked, coming closer to breathe down the back of her neck.

"I'm not talking about it." She drew her arms back swiftly, sending her elbows into his ribs. He grunted in surprise and stumbled back from her. She wheeled around, smiling into his beet-red face and laughing when his lips drew back from his sharp teeth in a fearsome snarl. "Don't crowd a rattler unless you're looking to get bit," she cautioned. With a jolt, she realized that he was an inch or two taller than she. When had that happened? Overnight? "Eddie, you're growing up fast."

"I sure am, *little* sister."

"But you've got a lot to learn," she tacked on. "Quantrill's

Raiders were fighting for the Confederacy. Your pals are stealing from people for no good reason other than lining their pockets."

"We—they happen to be taking horses from Yankee supporters." He grabbed her elbow and jerked her roughly. "I don't need you preaching to me, Myra Maybelle. Your hands ain't clean."

Belle stomped the heel of her shoe down on Eddie's bare foot. He cursed under his breath and reached for her, but she whirled away, running for the house.

"Mama, Eddie is getting clean out of hand," Belle said, bursting in the kitchen door. She deposited the glasses on the table. "He's running around with a bunch of ornery, no-good—"

"Maybelle, they're just boys," Eliza cut in. "Boys his age have got to kick up their heels. It's only natural."

Belle stamped her foot in frustration. "Is that so? Well, is it natural for him to be ste—"

"Belle, why don't you pour us some of that lemonade?" Mary interrupted sharply. Her eyes widened in silent appeal then darted sideways at her mother-in-law. "We're almost done here and we're dying for a drink of it."

Surrendering to Mary's pantomime, Belle went to the sideboard and poured the lemonade. Everyone protected Eliza from anything unpleasant, fearing she might lapse into her "other" world again. She'd been in a trance when they'd arrived in Dallas. Frequent visits from Preston and Mary had eventually brought Eliza around, but no one mentioned Bud or the defeated Confederacy.

Belle played along, but she resented it. Pretending nothing bad happened wasn't Belle's way of dealing with life. She wished her mother would develop some backbone and learn to take life's punches. She was as frail as a rosebud in winter.

"Don't fret over Ed," Eliza said, taking one of the lemonade glasses. "He's a smart boy."

"If he's so smart, why isn't he in school?" Belle asked.

"Why aren't you?" her mother shot back. "You're hardly ever in the schoolhouse these days."

"Oh, Mama." Belle threw up her hands and turned her back to Eliza. "I hate that school. Everyone's younger than me and I know most of the things the teacher's teaching already. It's so boring that I think I'll go out of my head!"

"You could still learn a thing or two, I reckon." Eliza fitted her arm around Mary's waist and guided her toward the door. "Let's find us a place on that porch swing, honey. You want to sit with us, Maybelle?"

Belle shrugged and followed them outside to the swing. She sat between her mother and sister-in-law. They set the swing in motion and let out a collective sigh when the first breeze touched their hot faces.

"Have you met any nice boys in school?" Mary asked, plowing her shoulder into Belle's.

"I told you that they're all younger," Belle said with an exaggerated sigh. "And they're all as dull as dishwater. The only thing those boys have going for them is that they're from good Confederate families." Belle yelped when Mary's elbow rammed into her ribs. "That hurt, Mary!"

Mary shifted her gaze warningly to Eliza. Belle jumped up from the swing in frustration. She walked to the other end of the porch and hugged the support post, looking out over the flat land and tranquil sky. Her mind filled with sharp words, her body disturbed by an edgy restlessness.

It was foolish to pretend nothing had happened in their lives. She pressed her lips together to keep from giving Mary and her mama a piece of her mind. Even her father was becoming a mealy-mouthed pacifist! It was as if the entire family had buried the Confederate flag when they'd buried Bud.

Texas was the perfect place for such a farce, for nothing in Texas was what it seemed. It was a place of escape, whether it be from the war, the law, or both. Dallas was a town of runaways and deserters. Every desperado in the country had come to Texas to forget the loss of dreams and loved ones.

Looking out over the plains, Belle yearned for Carthage ... or rather for the Carthage she remembered. Word was that Rebel soldiers had burned the town to the ground to keep the Yankees from using it as a stronghold. The Shirley hotel, livery, and blacksmith shop were nothing but a pile of ashes, but Belle could close her eyes and see her former home and relive the good times. She could smell the green earth and dank forest as she rode Queenie out to Quantrill's hideout, delivering news and gossip. The heroes of Missouri hanging on her every word. Belle smiled and wanted to purr like a kitten. If only she could see one of them again, she'd throw herself on him and—

"Who's that, Belle? You know them?" Eliza asked. Belle shaded her eyes from the harsh sunlight with her hand, squinting into the bleak present.

A wagon, drawn by two mules, swayed and creaked along the rutted road leading to the house, but it was too far off for Belle to make out the people in it.

"I don't know. Don't recognize the wagon or the team," she said. "Looks like they're going to be our company, whoever they are."

Ed rode past the house on his flashy white stallion and made a beeline for the wagon. He circled it, doffed his hat, then came back to the front of the house.

"Who's that, Edwin?" Eliza called, standing up from the swing and patting her damp hair into place.

Ed grinned wickedly and looked at Belle. "It's Belle's one true love."

Belle's world grew brighter and better. She gripped the support post, her nails digging into the soft wood. She looked longingly toward the rickety wagon as her heart pumped joy through her veins.

"Cole?" she breathed, her joy taking wing and moving her from the porch to the beaten path in front of the house. "It's Cole?" she asked, looking back at Ed.

Edwin raised his heavy brows in answer to the question he hadn't expected. "Wrong true love," he said, still grinning. "My mistake, I reckon."

She whipped her head back around to face the wagon, wondering who was in it if not Cole.

"Who did you say it was?" Eliza asked, removing her apron and flinging it inside the house.

"The Reeds from Missouri. You remember them, Mama? Sol and Susan Reed and their army of brats?"

"Of course!" Eliza fairly flew off the porch, waving one arm over her head in a big Southern welcome. "Hi there y'all! Isn't this wonderful! It's the Reed family. It sure is good to see folks from home."

Belle stared at the barrel-chested man who drove the wagon. It wasn't Sol Reed, but one of his sons. Susan Reed sat next to him. The back of the wagon was packed with children and adults of all sizes and ages. The children scrambled off the wagon as it rolled to a stop. Belle stood on tiptoe to see over the man and woman seated in front.

A stocky young man vaulted over the side of the wagon and landed lightly on his feet. Sunlight poured over his sandy hair and bronze skin. His teeth sparkled when he smiled at her. Belle's vision blurred and she found she couldn't utter a sound, her throat was so swollen with emotion.

"Belle," Jim Reed whispered, his lips stretching into a grin that lengthened his full mustache. "Don't you remember your Carthage beau?"

She ran forward, her fingers touching and then clutching his shoulders. "Jimmy, it's you!"

Being in his arms again was like coming home. Belle pressed her face against the front of his coarse shirt, laughing and crying. Wiping the tears from her face, Belle laughed nervously and glanced at her father's shrewd appraisal and at Ed's sly grin. They were surrounded by spectators. To hell with them, she thought, winding her arm through one of Jimmy's and pulling him toward the porch swing. She had her Jimmy back! She delivered a challenging glare to her father, and to her surprise, he ducked his head, giving in so quickly that Belle was stunned.

Belle dropped onto the swing and pulled Jimmy with her. "Jimmy, I'm so glad to see you. Everybody around here has milk for blood and would rather go belly-up than stand their ground." She grasped his muscled forearms and looked straight into his brown eyes. "You're not like that, are you? *You* haven't changed, have you?"

Jimmy smoothed her hair back from her heart-shaped face in a gesture that made Belle want to smother him with kisses.

"I haven't changed in that way." He smiled and placed a kiss on the tip of her nose. "You bored, honey?"

"You betcha!"

"Not for long," he said, leaning his forehead against hers. "We've moved to McKinney."

"All of you?"

"Most of us. Pa died last year and there wasn't anything left for us at Rich Hill. We've bought some land and we're going to farm it. We heard that the Shirleys were near

Scyene, and I couldn't rest until I'd found you." His hands tightened at her waist. "Are you still my girl?"

Something delicious curled in her stomach and made her smile. "As long as you keep me interested, I'm your girl."

"That's a mighty tall order."

"But nothing you can't handle," Belle assured him. Then she wriggled away to sit primly at the other end of the swing. "I'm awful glad to see you," she whispered for his ears only. "I'm in sore need of some fun and frolic. How about you?"

Jim gave her a long, well-remembered look before he answered, "I'm your man, sweetheart."

A bumble bee hummed near Belle's ear, giving off a lethargic sound that mixed perfectly with Belle's mood—lazy, contemplative, slightly edgy. Lying in Jim's arms, she gazed at the eager moon that hung in the clear sky. It was still daylight, a good hour from twilight, but the moon couldn't wait and had taken its place early. She appreciated the smell of earthy, green things.

"Having a good time?" Jimmy asked.

"Sure. Any time I'm not waiting on kids or working in the field, I'm having a good time." She felt his low-timbred chuckle vibrate against her back. The tickle of his fingertips skimming along her forearm brought goose bumps. "I always have a good time with you, Jimmy. You know that." She glanced up at him with a worried frown. "You do know that, don't you?"

"I know it." He bent over her like a willow over the creek and his kisses felt like raindrops upon her lips. "Me and you are two of a kind, sweetheart."

"Yes," Belle said in a musing tone. "Yes, we are." She sat up, eager to share her thoughts with him.

A duck was startled by the movement and took wing. Belle looked over the duck blind at the gurgling creek. Edwin and Mannie had built the blind, but she and Jim used it as their trysting place. Tall grass grew on the creek bank and willows leaned over the lazy water. The Shirley house was around the bend, a quarter mile down a hunter's path.

"I was thinking about the preacher's sermon this morning," Belle said, returning her attention to Jim.

"I didn't listen. All I could see was you and all I could hear was my heart beating."

Belle loved it when he talked to her with such gentle devotion. It made her choke up. For two months he had courted her, chased her, teased her. He swore he loved her and no other. But Belle was confused about her feelings for him. She wondered if she loved him for himself. When she looked at Jim she saw Bud and Cole and Jesse, all rolled up into one handsome package. He was a former guerrilla soldier, a compatriot, a by-product of a war that had ended in surrender but was still being waged in city streets and back country roads.

"The preacher was calling for peace, telling everyone to forget the Southern cause and build new lives under the Union rule. He even went so far as to say that maybe it was fitting that our boys be jailed for their doings during the war!" Belle sat up as anger churned in her stomach. "I swear, I hate that kind of cowardly talk! Why should Rebels be jailed while Yankees go free? It's not fair. War is war, by gum."

She looked toward the creek where Jim's quarter horse grazed along the bank. "I keep thinking about the others, Jimmy. About Cole and Jesse and Frank. They're outlaws now!"

"Don't you worry about them. They're heroes. The only

heroes we got left. It does my heart good to hear news of their robberies. I wish I could—" His teeth clicked together when Belle's fingers bit into his forearm. "What? What did I say?"

"You've heard from them?" Her black eyes went wide with eagerness. "You told me you didn't know of their whereabouts."

"I don't know exactly where they are, but rumors are rife in Dallas about the Jameses and the Youngers. I heard-tell that they're robbing Union banks. You heard about the Liberty job, didn't you?"

"That bank was robbed by the Youngers and the Jameses?" Belle felt her mouth drop open as she struggled to take it in. Repercussions of that daring robbery in Missouri were still being felt and it was all anybody talked about in Dallas.

"They made off with thousands of dollars," Jim said, lying back on the boards and lacing his hands behind his head for a pillow. "I bet they're off somewhere like Mexico or the Territory, spending that money like it was water."

"A man was killed during that robbery!" Belle felt her mouth go dry. Cole and Jesse were murdering people? What was happening to them? Where would it all lead?

"Yes, I believe so."

"You say that like it was nothing," Belle charged, glancing her fist off Jim's shoulder.

"Well, hell, it wouldn't be the first man they killed. They fought in the war like everybody else."

"But that bank robbery wasn't war."

Jim squinted up at her and moved his mouth from side to side, making his mustache twitch. "It wasn't? The Union says they're criminals and should be shot dead or put behind bars, making it impossible for them to make an honest living. You don't think that's cause enough for them to strike back? Who's side are you on, Belle?"

"Well . . . I . . ."

"If Bud were still alive I can guaran-damn-tee-ya that he'd be riding with them, because the Yankees would never grant him clemency."

She turned her face away sharply to be alone with her thoughts. When she faced him again, he couldn't read her expression. She was a puzzle, and Jim liked that about her. Easy women were a dime a dozen, but tough-minded women like Belle were rare.

"You're right, Jimmy. The Jameses and Youngers are off fighting our battles for us and we're sitting here in the middle of dag-burned Texas like a couple of do-nothings. I *hate* doing nothing! It's not natural to me. I feel like I should be out there—" She gazed into the distance and felt the landscape pull at her. "Out there where people face up to the way things are instead of acting like nothing's changed, nothing's different, when the whole damned world is topsy-turvy."

Belle flung out her arms and flapped them before falling back against Jim. "Oh, Jimmy. Did Bud die for nothing? Did he give his life so people could wear blinders and grow yellow streaks down their backs?"

Jim took her into his arms and kissed her soft cheek. He tasted salt and realized she was crying.

"Honey, don't cry now." He kissed the side of her neck, letting his mouth linger there for a few extra moments. "I know it's hard for you to settle down. It's hard for me, too. But we can't all ride the range and play shoot-'em-up."

"Why can't we?"

" 'Cause we can't. That old preacher was right in a way. We've got to start building another life for ourselves and for our children to come. We can't be looking back and regretting all the time. We can beat those Yankees at their own game by becoming prosperous despite the odds."

Belle leaned sideways and looked at him. The years had added maturity to his face, but the light of youth was still in his eyes. Belle reached up and tousled his hair. In his eyes, she saw devotion and understanding. In his eyes, she liked herself. She looked away. Her shining reflection made her uneasy.

"We'll have to get back soon," Belle said, settling back into Jim's embrace. "Mama expects me to help her put the boys to bed."

"I'll be glad when you put this boy to bed," Jim said, holding her close and nuzzling the back of her neck with his ticklish mustache. "Let's set a date."

"A date for what?"

"To marry, of course."

She felt as if a noose were closing around her neck and she tried to shake it off.

"Well?" Jim persisted.

"Maybe Christmas . . ."

"Christmas!" He said it as if it were a century away instead of only six months. "Uh-uh, lady. I ain't no saint. I'm not waiting around and playing five-finger stud that long. A man has needs!"

Belle giggled, loving the thought of Jimmy pining and aching for her. She rolled over to look up into his frowning face.

"A woman has needs, too, but there's more to marriage than squeaking bed springs. Will we live at your mother's?"

"At first," he said, but added quickly, "but we'll move out as soon as I can afford it. Honest, honey."

"Promise?" she asked, teasing him with the brush of her mouth upon his.

"Promise. You know, honey, we don't have to wait until we're married. We could pleasure each other—"

"Nope!" She stood up and brushed grass from her forest-green skirt. "Nothing doing."

"Why not?"

"I'm not bedding down with you until we're married."

"Why are you being so stubborn about this?" Jim sprang to his feet in frustration. "You ain't a cold-blooded woman, are you? I mean, you *will* do it once we're married?"

She started to get angry, but she laughed at his sulky expression instead. Placing her hands on his shoulders, she stood on tiptoe to kiss his pouting lips.

"Why do I put up with you, James Reed?"

His frown became a grin. "Because you're crazy about me."

She laughed and raced toward the house with Jim in hot pursuit. He caught up with her at the bend and gathered her into his arms.

"You win," he whispered. "I'll save every penny and we'll be married before Christmas. Before Thanksgiving. Please, Belle. Please?"

"Before Thanksgiving, Jimmy love. Will I see you tomorrow?"

He grinned and kissed her soundly, his hands moving up her back and around to her breasts. She sensed his urgency, his restlessness, and she felt sorry for him. He'd been so patient with her, so sweet throughout the courtship. If any man deserved her, James Reed did.

"I can't see you tomorrow," he said, breathless from the kiss. "I've got to work in the fields all week. I'll come around on Sunday and take you to church again. Oh, Belle, I do love you."

"I know." She planted kisses along the long bridge of his nose. "I'll be thinking about you . . . about us."

He blew her a kiss and rode off toward the Reed place.

Belle walked slowly toward the Shirley home and wondered what it would be like to have a place of her own.

It was twilight by the time the clapboard frame came into view, and Belle's interest perked when she saw the unfamiliar horses tethered outside the barn. Company, she thought, hurrying forward. Traveling preachers? Salesmen? Carpetbaggers? Who? She broke into a trot, hopped up onto the porch, and swung around the doorframe and into the kitchen.

Two men sat with her papa at the table. All three men looked up at her sudden entrance and Belle felt her curious smile freeze solid.

"Ah, here's my Maybelle," John Shirley said, reaching back for her hand and pulling her to the edge of the table. "May, this here is Jesse James and Cole Younger. I know you've heard of them, but I don't think you ever met them."

Cole stood up and nodded politely. "Glad to make your acquaintance, Miss Shirley. The pleasure is ours." He stared at Jesse until Jesse remembered his manners and stood to receive Belle. "Me and Jesse knew your brother Bud."

Belle gradually became aware of the others in the room. Her mother was at the stove where something simmered and gave off a hearty aroma. Three young men stood near her, each sipping coffee from tin cups. Something about them was familiar. Something in their eyes, in the way they stood, all lanky and at ease in their bodies.

"My brothers," Cole said. "Jim, Bob, and John. Boys, this is Mr. Shirley's daughter Maybelle."

"They're on their way to Missouri and stopped here for a spell," John Shirley said, patting Belle's hand. "Help your mother, girl. She's fixing them a little something before they bed down in the barn."

"Yes, Papa." Belle moved woodenly to her mother's side at the stove.

"What's wrong with you?" Eliza asked.

"N-nothing. Why?"

"Are you going to peel those potatoes or just stand there cutting air with that knife?" Eliza asked.

"Oh." Belle stared at the knife in her hand and the potatoes piled in front of them. "I'll peel them."

"Good." Eliza threw her another baffled glance. "You can think about James Reed and peel taters at the same time, I reckon."

Belle nodded, but James Reed was a distant memory and had nothing to do with the smile she felt in her heart.

Chapter Six

THE NEXT TWO DAYS were heaven for Belle as the Youngers and Jesse endeared themselves to the Shirley family. They were headed back to Missouri after spending several months south of the border. Why they'd been in Mexico was a mystery, although Jesse had mentioned something about working cattle.

Eager to please, the visitors helped around the place by building a better chicken coop and repairing broken farm equipment. Bob and John Younger worked in the fields while Jim and Cole put on a new tin roof over the house. Jesse and Cole spent long hours with John Shirley, admiring his extensive library, which had been packed into boxes for the move to Texas. They were particularly interested in the lawbooks and began calling their host "Judge Shirley," which delighted him no end.

They slept in the barn, and Belle spent a good deal of time gazing out the window at the boxy structure and yearning to be in it with her former compatriots. More than anything, she wanted to steal an hour or two alone with Cole.

"We'll be heading home this morning," Jesse said on the third morning of the visit.

Belle spun around from the stove, a pan of biscuits in her hands, and looked beseechingly at Cole. He ducked his head as if her wide-eyed appeal were too much to bear.

"All of you?" she asked, setting the biscuits on the table as her happiness shattered like glass.

Jesse nodded, his gaze sliding to Cole and then back to Belle. He lifted his fine brows as if to say, "Well, girl, what's it going to be? You going to let Cole ride off or you going to make your move?" Belle huffed out a sigh, miffed that Cole expected her to advance even as he retreated.

"All of us," Jesse said after a minute. "We couldn't go without filling our bellies with your fine cooking." The last was directed to Mrs. Shirley with appreciation. She blushed.

"We've enjoyed having you with us," John Shirley said, glancing toward his wife. "Haven't we, Eliza?"

"It's been our pleasure," Eliza agreed. "Sure is nice to have so many strong men on the place. I know your mother will be awful glad to see you boys again."

Belle continued to stare at Cole, but he was engrossed in shoving biscuits and gravy into his mouth. *I don't want you to leave. But I'll be damned if I'll come right out and beg for your company!*

Disgusted with herself and the situation she was caught up in, Belle whirled from the table and flounced toward the door. She untied her apron and flung it aside as she went.

"Where are you going, May?" her father asked.

"Out!"

"But we're not finished with—"

"I'm finished," she said, lengthening her stride. She jumped off the end of the porch and headed blindly down the path that meandered to the creek. It was misty, but the sun was rising and beginning to burn off the dew. The hem of her skirt dragged across the long grass and it was soaked before she reached the bend in the path.

"Damn him," she muttered, dire disappointment crackling through her and making her eyes tear. "I've made a fool of myself over him for the last time!"

Thinking of her moony-eyed behavior over the past two days—of the hours spent in a lonely vigil, watching and waiting and wanting—she wanted to scream with frustration. Who needed Coleman Younger anyway? She had a man who wanted to marry her, who was crazy in love with her. She sure as hell didn't need to throw herself at Cole's head like she was some ugly old maid. Why, she could go into Dallas and have any number of men at her beck and call!

Reaching the creek, Belle sat in the duck blind, hiding from the world and the humiliating sting of rejection. She sat cross-legged, letting her skirt billow over her legs. She let her hair down and braided it into one long pigtail, her hands working fretfully as her mind roiled with real and imagined insults.

Cole was leading her on—had been from the moment they'd met. Sure, he hadn't acted interested in her at first, but what about that kiss right before the Raiders had swept down on the Richey place to roust out Eno and those other Yankees? She hadn't asked for that kiss. Cole had given it freely. Maybe it had meant little to him, while it had meant the world to her.

Morning glories grew up and over one side of the blind, and Belle picked several of the pink and violet flowers to weave them into a necklace.

The ground trembled beneath Belle and she doubled over instinctively, hiding from the approaching horse and rider. She peeked over the side of the blind. Sweet Jesus. Cole hadn't left her high and dry after all.

She sat up straight to make sure he'd spot her. He reined the big black Morgan and swung out of the saddle with that liquid grace Belle had come to expect from him. He was dressed in travel clothes: rough cotton pants of dark gray, a faded red shirt, a striped Mexican poncho, and a straw sombrero hanging down his back. The morning sun fired his blond hair. It fell in golden curls around his collar. He moved toward her with a springy step and light-footed grace.

Belle had taken note of inconsequential things about Cole Younger such as the characteristic way he had of squinting his right eye and tipping his head to the left when he was baffled or bested. She loved to watch him do that. She also loved the way his hair swept down across his forehead in a silky curtain and her fingers itched to smooth it back into place so that she could watch it fall forward again.

Still, Belle remembered his rejection and she gathered her anger around her like a protective cloak.

"If I had a gun, I'd shoot you," she said, drawing a look of surprise from him. "You heard me. I'd kill you."

He reached to his side and withdrew one of his six-shooters, then extended it toward her, butt first. "Be my guest."

Belle started to take it, but batted it aside. "Get out of here."

"I was doing just that, but I decided to let the others ride ahead. I wanted to find you and say *adios*."

"Isn't that nice!" Belle said, sarcasm dripping from her words. "Well, you've said it, so now you can get."

He slipped the gun back into his holster. "You're mad."

"Damn right." She looked away from him because it was difficult to remain angry when he was so fine to gaze upon. The complexities of her feelings for him writhed in her like a nest of snakes. It had always been this way where he was concerned. I want to hold him and I want to slap his face. I want him to stay and I want him to go. I want to spend every moment with him and I never want to see him again. *Want* was the key word. With Cole, *she* wanted. With Jimmy, *he* wanted.

"You've changed."

Belle looked at him from the corner of her eye. "Is that good or bad?"

"Good. You're older and wiser. Of course, you always were a wise child."

"I'm not a child."

"No, not anymore. None of us are anymore. War leaves no room for childish things." He looked back at his horse and shifted his feet restlessly. "Well, if you don't want to talk with me, I guess I'll—"

"Why now? You didn't want to talk yesterday or the day before."

"Yes, that's true. There's a good reason for my behavior."

Belle crossed her arms at her waist. "I'd love to hear it."

His shining blue eyes bored into hers. "I'm too transparent around you. I was worried that your folks might see how I feel about you, and that wouldn't be right."

"Why not?"

He looked surprised. "Because you're practically engaged to Jim Reed, aren't you?"

"Oh." Belle averted her face, ashamed. "That's right. I am."

"I was sure surprised to hear that you and Jim still had a claim on each other."

"Why were you surprised?"

"I just didn't figure you two would find each other again after the war. I guess fate played a hand in it."

"Jimmy and you keep popping up in my life like bad habits." She smiled, taking the sting from her words. Then she stretched her legs out in front of her and demurely rearranged her skirt. "Don't you ever think of getting married?"

"I think of it often, but I never see my way clear to do it." He removed his sombrero and hung it over his saddle horn. "I'm a wanted man. I couldn't drag a woman into my life while it's still so unsettled and dangerous."

"That didn't stop Jesse from marrying."

His grin flashed like lightning. "I'm not Jesse."

She smiled back, then motioned for him to sit in front of her. He hesitated a moment before crossing his ankles and lowering himself to the platform.

"Is this a special place?" Cole asked, examining the secluded blind.

"A private place," Belle amended. "There's not much privacy around the Shirley clan. How's your mama?"

He took the morning glory necklace from her and fingered the fragile blossoms. "She's fading fast like these flowers."

"My mother lost her head. She pretended like the war wasn't going on. Now we can't mention it or anything connected with it. Not even Bud."

"Bud." His gaze was direct and went straight for the heart. "I was so grieved to hear about Bud. I know how you worshiped him. I was afraid his death would harden you."

She looked deeply inside herself and winced. "It did a little. I'm not so quick to care for people. I can feel myself holding back and I can't help it. I guess I'll never trust anyone as completely as I did Bud."

"Don't say that, Belle."

"You know it's true." She covered his hands with her own. "Sometimes I think you know me better than anyone."

"How can that be? We've hardly—"

"It doesn't matter how seldom we've seen each other," she

said, anticipating his objection. "I'm with Jimmy almost every day, but I don't know him near as well as I know you."

"You only think you know me."

"Look at me, Cole Younger." She tightened her grip on his hands and waited for his blue eyes to lock with her dark brown ones. "Now tell me that you don't know what's in my heart. Tell me you don't know me better than any woman you've been with. Tell me."

"I think you have a way of shaking me up, that's what I think." He cocked his head to one side. "I can talk to you in a way I can't with anyone else. I don't have to worry about you turning on me."

"Turning on you," she repeated. "Who's turned on you?"

"I'm a criminal. Anyone could—"

"You're a hero!" Belle asserted, and Cole smiled sadly. "You are. Everybody thinks so."

"Confederates think so. Yankees want me behind bars."

"Yankees," Belle said with a slur. "They've ruined the country."

Cole laughed softly, deep in his throat. He trailed his fingertips down the side of her face. "Still the brave little Rebel, aren't you?"

"Aren't you?" she shot back.

"Yes. I'm still a Southerner, through and through." He sighed and his hand dropped back to his thigh. "But we lost, and that makes me a murderer instead of a hero."

"Not to me. Never to me." Desperation filled her as she sensed his withdrawal. When he glanced back at his horse and shifted as if preparing to leave her, Belle gripped his wrist. "You're not leaving."

"I should."

"Don't go . . . yet."

He stared at her hand moving from his wrist and into his palm. His fingers closed around it automatically.

"Do me a favor," Belle said.

"What?"

"Make love to me before you leave." Wonder filled her. Where had she found the courage to ask that of him?

Cole shook his head in a gentle rebuke. "Belle, you always jump the gun. If you'd waited another minute or two, I would have asked that favor of you." He let go of Belle's hand and pulled the poncho off over his head. He spread it out beside her. "You could benefit from more patience."

"I'll make a deal with you," Belle said, pleased that he wasn't being obstinate. "I'll be more patient if you'll be more impatient." She spread her hands on top of his broad shoulders. "I've dreamed of you often, Cole."

He nodded solemnly. "You made me want you. I've fought these feelings for as long as I'm able."

His mouth claimed hers. Little moaning sounds came from deep within Belle. His arms crushed her against him and she could feel his heart beating wildly against her breasts. His lips became more demanding, nibbling and sucking until she felt her insides melt. He took her breath away, then gave it back, breathing hotly through her like a rogue wind.

A mockingbird lighted in the willow branches overhead, puffed out its chest, and began to sing its lovely song. Belle watched it from half-closed eyes as Cole cradled her in his strong arms. He kissed her eyes, her upturned nose, trailing his tongue in a fiery blaze down her neck and back up again to whisper words of passion in her ear. Cole's kisses were more and more searching as he pushed her down to lie flat on the fragrant moss. His large hands fumbled with the buttons on her blouse, parting the fabric with an urgency that alarmed her. Belle began to quiver uncontrollably. She'd no idea how fiercely he'd wanted her. She opened her eyes and saw the sapphire-flame burning in his. Cole's tender passion made her feel cherished, feminine, and fragile.

Belle wound her arms around Cole's strong neck, pulling his head down to her pounding heart. He took her budding nipple into his mouth and Belle arched up in an instinctive plea for fulfillment. Mindless desire overtook her and she was only vaguely aware of him removing the rest of her clothes. She had no idea when Cole peeled off his, she only knew that his skin felt glorious beneath her wandering hands and that his mustache was a soft brush upon her skin, leaving goose bumps in its wake. She combed her fingers through his golden hair, exploring its silky texture. The hair on his chest was plentiful, red tinted and coarse. Belle rocked forward to rain kisses across his breast bone and up the side of his strong neck. She pressed her breasts flat against him and moved up and down, rubbing her turgid nipples against him and quivering with the need that was racing through her.

Belle felt his hardness against her thigh, but she was too shy to look at him there. Of course she'd seen naked men before, but never one aroused for her. The thought made her dizzy and diffident. Cole was a man, but was she woman enough for him? Would she disappoint him? What did he expect of her? Wasn't this supposed to come naturally for a woman? Why did she feel so awkward all of a sudden?

When he lowered her onto her back again, Belle closed her eyes and prayed for divine intervention. Instinct seemed to have deserted her. She shivered, more from fear now than from desire. Cole's fingers danced to her waist and pulled her up hard against his aroused manhood. He murmured incoherent words of pleasure. Blood pounded in her ears, blocking out Cole's voice and then, quite suddenly, she was filled with fiery flesh and sinew as he entered her.

Belle arched and gasped, feeling her own resistance. Cole

gave a startled grunt, driving hard against her virgin's shield. Belle squeezed her eyes so tightly that tears rolled from the corners. When she opened them, she saw dismay on Cole's face and a strange sadness in his eyes.

"What's wrong?" she asked, touching his frown with trembling fingertips.

"Oh, Belle. Why didn't you tell me?"

He shook his head and moved his hips more carefully now. Cole mastered her body as if she were a spirited thoroughbred and he the only man who could tame her. She bucked beneath him, but he forced her to follow his rhythm. He measured each thrust of his body into hers, enjoying the look of pleasure and self-absorption on her face. She'd never been so consumed by her own responses. It was wonderful to be selfish, to revel in her emotions, to simmer in passion's juices, to cling damply to Cole as he hurtled her toward womanhood.

She quaked violently when she felt him pour into her and she bit into his shoulder to keep from crying out with joy. Cole was hers. She was his. They had joined together and nothing could ever sever their ties. Not war. Not danger. Not distance. Nothing.

He smoothed her hair back from her face and stared long and lovingly at her.

"You should have told me that you'd never been with a man," he said, kissing her left temple where her hair lay in damp tendrils. "I feel as if I've taken something from you that I can never return."

"Why would you think I'd been with a man? Who said I'd been bedded?" Belle demanded. "Who?"

Cole rolled off her and onto his back. "Jim Reed. He said he'd slept with you way back when we were with Quantrill."

"He *what*?" Belle propped herself on one elbow to look

down at Cole. "That lying, little—! He's never . . . I wouldn't let him!"

"Then why did you let me?"

She stroked his golden locks, pushing them back off his forehead. "Because it was fitting that you be the first. That's how I wanted it."

"Jim Reed should be horsewhipped."

Belle kissed Cole's tense lips. "You leave Jimmy to me."

"You're not going to marry him?"

"I *am* going to marry him."

His brows shot up. "But why?"

"Because *you* won't marry me." She laughed at his chagrin, rolling playfully onto his chest. His arms came up to hold her possessively and he kissed her long and hard.

"Don't look so guilt-ridden. You and me, we understand each other. I know you can't take on more family when you've already got a brood depending on you."

"But why marry Jim when you can do better?"

"I can't do better. Jimmy loves me, and I'm fond of him. Maybe I even love him, but not like I love you. Anyway, me and Jimmy will do just fine together."

"I shouldn't have told you about his bragging."

"I'm glad you did. Besides, now that I've been loved by the one man I wanted to love me, I can settle down to what's been offered instead of pining away for what I can't have."

Belle began putting on her clothes, aware of Cole's watchfulness.

"I respect you," he said after a while. "I'll never carry tales about you and me. Telling others about what we've shared would be . . ." He glanced up as if seeking the word in the clear sky. "The ultimate treachery."

"Will I ever see you again?"

"I wish I could answer that." He sat up to pull on his shirt and button his trousers.

"Where will you go from here?" Belle asked, picking up the necklace she'd made.

"Back to Missouri." He looked around him, smiling as he did so. "But I like Texas, and Texas likes me. We're all safer here than we are in Missouri. Me and the other boys are thinking of talking Mama into relocating here."

"I hope you do."

"And I hope you get on with your life and live in peace." He framed her face in his hands and seemed to memorize her every feature for future reference. "Forget the war and what it did to us. Jim's not wanted, so he can give you a solid foundation."

"But he can never give me what you give me." She swayed forward, opening her mouth eagerly to his tongue's caress. "Love," she whispered against his lips. "A heart full of it. No man will ever be able to fill me with it like you do, Cole."

"Belle, don't talk like that." He let go of her and sprang to his feet. "It makes me uneasy."

"The truth always makes you uneasy, but you need to hear it and accept it." She held out her hands to him, letting him help her to her feet. Belle put her arms around his neck before he could get away. "Thank you, Cole."

"No, you've got it wrong. I'm the one who should thank you, and I do. I'll live on this memory for a lifetime."

"You don't have to. Anytime you want me, I'm yours. Remember that. Promise me that you'll remember that I'm only a heartbeat away."

"Belle, don't say things like that. How can you talk about marrying Jim and then say that?"

"Because I'll always be married to you in a special way that has nothing to do with holy vows or wedding bands." She held him close, running her hands up and down his broad back before letting him go and stepping away from his temptation. "Go on while I'm still strong enough to let you."

He swung up in the saddle and she handed the poncho up to him. He poked his head through the single hole and the heavy cloth fell around his shoulders and concealed his gun and holster. Belle stood close to him and placed a hand on his thigh. He dipped his head down and she looped the chain of blossoms around his neck, arranging it under his collar.

"You're a handsome *hombre*," she said, smiling up at him. "Nobody sits a horse like you."

He reached down one hand to trace the peculiar slant of her smile. "Did anyone ever tell you that you've got the most mischievous grin this side of the border?"

"No. Does that mean you like it?"

"I hanker for it." His throat flexed as he swallowed with difficulty and tore his gaze from hers. "Take care of yourself."

"I will." Her hand drifted reluctantly down his thigh to his knee then away as she moved backward. "What kind of husband do you think Jimmy will make?"

Cole stared at the horizon and narrowed his expressive eyes. "If you can keep him in the fields, he'll be fine."

"You think that's a tall order?"

"I know it is for most of us." He rested both hands on the saddle horn and rounded his shoulders under the poncho. "Keep him on the farm and on a tight rein, Myra Maybelle."

Cole winked and clucked his horse into a slow walk. "I'll see you in my dreams, darlin'."

Chapter Seven

THE BUGGY CARRYING Preacher Thomas and Deacon Daniels jostled up the dirt road and stopped in the Shirleys' porch yard. Able Baumgartner, astride a bay pony, rode beside the buggy. Able owned a farm north of the Shirleys and Belle had met him once in church.

Belle nodded to the visitors as she stepped out onto the shadowy porch.

"Morning," she said, drying her dishwater hands on her apron. "What can I do for you?"

"Where's your father?" Preacher Thomas gave her an ingratiating smile. "Our business is with him, missy."

"Well . . ." Belle glanced toward the barn where her mother and father had gone to milk their six cows. "Pa? He's right out—"

"I'm here." John Shirley stepped around the side. "What brings you gentlemen out here? Church business?"

"In a way," Preacher Thomas said, chuckling a little as he glanced at the balding man sitting beside him in the buggy. "Me and the deacon hear-tell you haven't been listening to my sermons of late, John Shirley. We've come here to check into those rumors."

John Shirley laughed under his breath and pulled his dangling suspenders up over his shoulders. He moved back into the shadows and leaned against the outside wall.

"Checking out rumors must keep you awful busy," he said, still laughing. "Seems to me that you'd have better things to do with your time. I know I do."

Belle propped a shoulder against one of the porch supports and looked back at her father. His laughter had a false ring, and she wondered if he weren't wary of the visitors.

"Maybe you should send the girl away so's we can talk alone," Able Baumgartner said, glaring pointedly at Belle.

Belle looked to her father, hoping he wouldn't obey. They exchanged glances, and Belle knew that he had no intention of doing that.

"State your business and let's get on with it," John said, his hands hanging limply at his sides. In contrast his body was as taut as a bow string.

"We heard that you been harboring the likes of the Youngers and the Jameses under this here roof!" Able spoke up, everything about his string-bean body screaming accusations.

"If I did, it's none of *your* business," John asserted.

"It *is* his business," Preacher Thomas said. "If a neighbor is hiding criminals, it brings trouble for everyone. Don't you see that, John?"

"No, I don't see it. No trouble's befallen any of you."

Belle nodded, feeling smug and knowing that these men could never win a war of words against her father. John Shirley was book learned and he never stopped learning. Lawbooks, poetry, plays, novels—they were all inside in his coveted library—six shelves in the corner of the main room.

"The war is over," Preacher Thomas said. "Folks like you have just got to understand that. You can't hide outlaws just because they were born in the South. Isn't that right, Deacon Daniels?"

Daniels bobbed his head again but kept silent.

"We lost the war, John. We've got to accept that and get on with getting along. We can't protect lawless men like the Youngers and the Jameses. They're robbers!"

"Murderers!" Able contributed.

"Trash," Daniels said, finally finding his voice.

"You've delivered your sermon, now get," John said in a voice that made the tiny hairs on the back of Belle's neck stand on end. "I'm not listening to any more of your drivel."

"John, we have to have your word that you won't associate with those criminals again. We want peace here. We don't want that kind of filth hiding out amongst our flock."

"Why, you yellow-bellied, spineless Yankee lovers!"

John moved so deceptively that Belle didn't know who had fired the warning shot. She flung her arms over her head in a protective gesture, saw the shocked expressions on the visitors' faces, then looked back at her father, who was holding a smoking rifle and taking a bead on Preacher Thomas. Pride marched through her like a brass band. She wanted to whoop for joy. Seeing her father's stance against the mealy-mouthed Yankee converts, just seeing her father face them off, made her feel better about the world.

"John!" Preacher Thomas was the first to speak after the shock wore off. "You can go to hell for harming a man of the cloth!" The preacher looked to Daniels. "Isn't that right, Deacon?"

Daniels had lost his voice again. He just nodded and tried to hide behind the preacher in case John decided to squeeze off another shot.

"I'll chance it," John said, hitching the butt of the rifle to a more comfortable tilt against his shoulder. "Get off my land. All of you! And don't come back."

"Why do you insist on socializing with scum like them Youngers?" Able asked.

"That *scum* rode with my boy. My Bud!" John's voice shook with anger. "As long as I've breath in my body, they'll be welcomed at my table. Now get, or as God is my witness, I'll blow you from here to Scyene with one blast."

"Before we go, we must have your word that you'll harbor no more riffraff," Preacher Thomas persisted with a haughty lift of his pointed chin.

"To hell you say!" Deacon Daniels gathered up the reins before the preacher could utter a protest and laid them across the horse's back. "Yaha!"

The buggy circled wide, almost tipping over, then made a beeline away from the Shirley house and back toward town. Able Baumgartner's bay pony was close behind.

"Pa!" Belle swung toward him, hands clasped and eyes awash with bursting admiration. "I'm so proud of you! I'm—so relieved to hear that you haven't forsaken the South or the Confederacy."

"Forsaken the—?" He smiled wryly and replaced the rifle just inside the front door. "Daughter, whatever made you think I'd done that?"

"I don't know." She shrugged and closed the distance between them, slipping her arms around his middle and resting her cheek against the front of his flour-sack shirt. "When we moved from Carthage and came here, it seemed to me that we were deserting everything. Folks here in Texas didn't seem to be fired up about the war. They ignored it and hoped it would end. Nobody even seemed to care who won!"

"Nobody won," John said slowly and with great care, "but everybody lost. Come sit with me a spell on the swing and let's me and you have a little talk. We haven't done that in quite a while, have we?"

"No, sir." She let him draw her over to the swing and sat beside him. She relaxed in the cradle of his arm and waited for him to begin.

"Maybelle, I knew that you felt we were leaving Missouri at a bad time, but there was nothing I could do for the war effort. I'd given my son, and that was all I had to give. Besides, I was terribly afraid that if we didn't leave and find a peaceful place, I'd lose Eliza for good."

"You put her feelings above everyone else's, don't you?"

"Of course!"

"Why, 'of course'?" she asked, lifting her head from his shoulder and twisting around to look him in the eyes. "Why is she the most important member in this family?"

"Because she's the mother and the wife, pumpkin." He cupped Belle's chin in one of his calloused hands. "It's that way in a good marriage, don't you know?"

"Shouldn't the man make the decisions?"

"I did make the decision." He laughed to himself. "The man wears the pants in the family, but the woman wears the suspenders and keeps everything in its proper place. Maybelle, this family would be torn asunder without your mother. I believe that with all my heart. You'll understand when you're married yourself. A good husband always puts his wife above all else."

Belle moved away from his gentle touch and stood up from the swing. Looking across the flat land, she thought of her own place out there somewhere. Away from her mother and father. In a place where she would be worshiped and placed above everyone else.

"Pa, I'm going to marry Jimmy Reed." Relief poured through her once the words were out. "He loves me, Papa. He'll be good to me."

"That I know," John Shirley agreed, rising from the swing

to give his daughter a tight hug. "Jim's a bit headstrong, but his heart is in the right place. Have you told your mother?"

"I mentioned it. Mama said she thought I'd be driving my cattle to a bad market."

John laughed. "Well, she probably doesn't think anyone is good enough for you. She thinks the world of you."

"Papa!" Belle stood back, examining her father's sincerity. He was blind when it came to Eliza Shirley.

"Yes, Maybelle?" John asked, clearly confused by the surprise on her face.

"Oh, nothing." Belle looked away, preferring to keep her thoughts to herself. Let him think that Eliza loved her. Let him have his illusions. Belle knew different. She knew that when she moved off the Shirley property her mother wouldn't miss her—she'd only miss the extra pair of hands when chores needed to be done.

"Be happy, daughter," John said, taking her small shoulders in his big hands. "The Reeds are fine, hard-working people. It's a good match."

"Thank you, Papa." She stood on tiptoe and kissed his leathery cheek. "Your blessing means a great deal to me."

Jim Reed carried Belle over the threshold of the borrowed cabin and set her on her feet in a large room that contained the bare essentials. A bed, a bureau, a table, a fireplace, and three chairs.

"Here we are, honey," Jim said, indicating the inside of the hunting lodge with a wide sweep of his arm. "Our love nest for the night."

"Are you sure nobody will bust in on us?" Belle asked, feeling like an interloper.

"I'm sure. The old boy that uses this cabin is in Dallas for the next two weeks. I spoke to him personally and he offered the cabin to us for our wedding night. It'll be our only chance to be alone. Once we move in with Ma, there'll be no privacy for us. All us Reeds sleep in the same room. This place is right cozy, don't you think?"

Jim crossed to the bed and sat on it. He bounced up and down, making the ropes under the mattress creak. A mischievous grin overtook him.

"Right cozy," he repeated. "This bed is heaven, honey. Come sit by your new husband and see for yourself."

Belle looked down at the toes of her black shoes peeking out from under the hem of the cream-colored dress she'd made for her wedding day. She felt awkward and afraid. Was she being naïve? Could she fool Jim into thinking he was bedding a virgin?

"You ain't scared of me, are you?" Jim asked, concerned by her hesitancy. He sprang up from the bed and went to her, enfolding her in a sheltering embrace. "It won't hurt much, Belle. I'll be careful."

"I guess you've done this a bunch of times," Belle said, glancing up into his face. "Been with women during their first times, I mean."

"Well . . . not really." He shrugged and looked sheepish. "I've only been with one other woman that I didn't have to pay for and she was a young widow."

Praise be! Jim wasn't that much more experienced than she.

"Belle?"

"Yes, Jimmy?"

He framed her small face in his hands. "I want you to know that I was most proud standing beside you before that justice of the peace today. Most proud. I guess I've loved you since the first moment I ever laid eyes on your pretty face."

"Oh, Jimmy." She sighed and closed her eyes, feeling like

a cheat before his intense devotion and trust. Her love for him rose up, banishing the darker emotions. "Kiss me, sweet Jimmy."

His lips trembled, lingering on hers. She lifted her arms and draped them around his neck, laughing lightly as he gathered her up like a bouquet of flowers and took her over to the bed covered by a patchwork quilt.

He undressed her as if she were a china doll. His touch was so achingly tender that Belle's heart went out to him. She ran her fingers through his sandy hair. Their eyes locked; she imagined him staring right into her soul. She was grateful to have a man like Jimmy Reed in love with her. Most men would be intimidated by a woman with a past like hers—riding with Quantrill and spying for the Confederacy. Those weren't things ladies did, after all. But not her Jimmy. Jimmy loved her because of those things, not in spite of them.

The setting sun had left the room in long shadows. The dying day bathed Belle in orange light. It caressed her skin, fell softly over her hair, and set her eyes aglow. Belle was a golden night creature and the vision took Jimmy's breath away. He slipped under the muslin sheet beside her and laid a burning hand on her stomach.

"You're trembling, darling," he whispered. He kissed her softly on the eyes, then on her moist lips, his fingers gently pinching her rosy nipples.

"I don't want to disappoint you, Jimmy."

"You won't. Oh, Belle. I want you so much!"

Jimmy rolled on top of her. She could feel the fierce heat and hardness of his body. He pressed his mouth on hers, crushing her lips. His tongue invaded, and she felt panic shooting through her small body. He was moving too fast. She couldn't catch her breath. It seemed as though he had

completely lost control, consumed as he was by his unbri-
dled passion.

His hands roamed over her, squeezing and stroking. She
could feel him grow damp all over—and then he claimed
her, entering with such force that she cried out.

"Sorry, honey," he breathed heavily into her ear. "It always hurts at first."

She sucked in her breath as Jimmy moved in and out of
her, reaching her greatest depth. Flashing pleasure mixed
with sharp pain. One hand went beneath her, raising her
toward him, and he held her that way as the blows were
repeated until he gave a great moan. She could feel his
throbbing pulse burst, bathing her insides with his hot
fulfillment.

"Oh, honey, that was wonderful," he said, kissing her
cheek and then her lips. His tongue darted out and then he
touched her swollen lips with his fingertips. "Your lip is
bleeding."

"Is it?" She licked away the tangy droplets. "I guess I bit
through it."

"Poor darling." He kissed her again and slid off her,
letting her gather a decent breath without his weight crushing her.

Belle laid her limp hand along the side of his face. "Don't
fret. The important thing to me is that you're not disappointed in me. Are you?"

"Disappointed? Hell, no!" His hand curved around her
wrist, holding her hand firmly in place against his face.
"I'm the luckiest man around. I've got me a beautiful bride
with courage to boot! Belle, you're all I've ever wanted.
You're all I'll ever need."

"Jimmy, Jimmy." She brought his head down and kissed
him with genuine ardor. "I do love you, sweet Jimmy. God
knows you have your faults, but I love the me I see in your
eyes. I'm going to be a good wife to you, Jimmy."

"And I'll be a good husband," he promised in such an endearing way that Belle forgot his rough lovemaking and found herself wanting nothing more than to honor his trust in her.

The stallion was lathered. Sweat lined its neck like a necklace of lace and spotted its withers and hocks. Belle approached it, talking softly as she went. She ran a hand along its damp rump and felt the brand, reading it with her fingertips. *Rocking T.*

"Just what I figured," she murmured, rubbing the animal between its pointy ears. "Welcome to the Reed Ranch. I hope you don't bring trouble with you."

She lifted her skirts, stepping high over the horse droppings and sticky hay, as she let herself out of the corral. Rocking T was the name of the Tupperman ranch on the other side of Dallas. Mr. Tupperman was a big-bellied, loud-mouthed Yankee, so it was only fitting that he'd lose a couple of his horses to some well-bred Rebels, but Belle couldn't help but wonder if Jimmy and his brothers might have bitten off more trouble than they could chew this time.

Male voices rumbled from the outhouse and Belle waited until Jim emerged with two of his older brothers before she moved to where they could see her.

"Belle, what are you doing up?" Jim asked, stopping in his tracks with his brothers flanking him. "Hell, it's after midnight."

"Nearly three," Belle agreed, eying their dusty pants, shirts, and manure-caked boots. "Where have you boys been?"

Jim looked over his shoulder at Jasper, seeking guidance.

"Town," Jasper said, buttoning his trousers. "We rode into Scyene."

"What you been doing in town?" Belle asked, keeping her

voice light although her insides were turning to red-hot iron. When were Jimmy and his lame-brained brothers going to realize that she could see right through their pitiful lies?

"Playing cards," George Reed spoke up. "We won some money."

"Did y'all win that stallion in a card game?" Belle asked, glancing back at the corral where the stallion ran in nervous circles.

"St-stallion?" Jim stuttered.

"Ain't none of your business, little sister," Jasper growled and pushed Belle to one side on his way to the house.

"I'm not your sister, Bubba," Belle growled back, then curled her upper lip when Jasper swore under his breath at her.

"That's right," George said, following in Jasper's wake. "We don't owe you no explanations. Ain't none of your business."

"Pete and Repeat," Belle sassed, laughing at George's attempt at a fearsome scowl.

Jim started to follow them dutifully into the house, but Belle stiff-armed him.

"Hold on, buster," she said, keeping him in place. "I've never seen shiftier eyes in all my born days. Playing cards in town, my sweet ass! You've been stealing horses. You've stolen three this week. You think I'm blind? Do you think I'm as stupid as your mother and sisters and don't notice the new horses on the place?"

"I didn't figure you paid much attention to such things," Jim muttered.

"Jimmy, I pay attention to *everything*. That's why I was such a good spy for Quantrill." Belle moaned, glancing at the dark sky. "When are you going to understand that I'm not simpleminded? I've got eyes and a powerful brain and I use them." She pointed to the corral. "The Rocking T. Are you crazy, stealing horses from Kenneth Tupperman? Do you think an important man like him is going to look the other way when his prize stallion is snatched?"

"We're going to take them into the Territory. I know a family of Indians there who deal in this sort of thing."

"Who?"

"The Starrs."

"Let me get this straight. You're going to sell these stolen horses to a bunch of Indians in the Territory?"

"That's right." His teeth flashed in the dark.

"And then they're going to sell them?"

"Or trade them. Whatever they want."

"You trust these Indians?"

"Sure! They're good people."

"How long have you known them?"

"Oh, I don't know . . ."

"How long?" Belle persisted.

"I don't *know* them, but I've heard good things about them."

"Oh, Jimmy," Belle groaned. "When are you going to quit trusting everyone who—"

"The Starrs are friends of the Youngers."

Belle digested this information with a slow nod. "Okay, maybe these Indians are on the up and up, but what if you're caught and sent to jail or hanged? Where does that leave me?"

"I'm not going to get caught, honey." He ran his hand over her shining hair and pulled her closer to kiss her forehead. Belle punched him playfully in the stomach and he laughed. "With the money I make off these horses we can buy some land and build our own house."

"I thought your job at the saddle shop would bring in enough money for that."

"I quit that job."

"When did you quit?" When he didn't answer, Belle lifted her head from his shoulder to examine his grimace of guilt. "When did you quit your job, Jimmy?"

"Couple of weeks ago."

Belle wrenched from his arms. "That's just dandy. What in the hell have you been doing every day in Scyene when you've left here for work?" She read his expression and held up her hands. "No, wait. Don't tell me. Let me guess." She stood on tiptoe and thrust her face close to his, hoping her fury would singe his eyebrows. "Gambling, right?"

"What have you got against gambling?" he asked, anger pumping through his voice.

"Nothing, just against losing."

"Get outta my way." He pushed the back of his hand against her shoulder and sent her sideways a couple of steps. "I'm tired and I'm going to bed."

"When are you moving those horses out of here?" Belle asked, grabbing for his forearm and missing.

"You don't worry about them horses. I'm handling this. It's none of your business."

"It *is* my business. You're my husband." Belle trotted at his side, trying to keep him from going into the house where eavesdropping was rampant.

"You wanted me. You got me, so quit your whining. You nearly held a shotgun to my head to get into this family."

"Ha!" Belle grabbed his belt from behind and dug her heels into the ground. Jim stopped and sighed wearily as he propped his hands at his waist to wait her out. "I didn't hold a shotgun to your head. I only told you that I knew you'd soiled my name. You're the one who was jumping up and down to get married. You wanted me so bad, I had you running in circles. Don't go denying it."

He angled a glance over his shoulder and grinned at her. "I'm not denying anything and I'm not complaining." He turned to face her. "I'm crazy in love with you. Just don't worry your pretty head about them horses. I know what I'm doing."

Belle wrapped her arms around his waist and held on tight. "Jimmy, Jimmy," she sighed, kissing his generous mouth beneath his drooping mustache. "I won't worry if you'll do one little thing for me."

"What's that, baby?"

"Move the horses out of here by tomorrow night or there'll be hell to pay."

"What are you talking about?"

"The law will be out here looking for that stallion—the law or Tupperman himself. I can lie for you boys if those stolen horses aren't here, but there's nothing anybody can do if you're caught red-handed."

"You'd lie for me?"

Belle tipped back her head and laughed. "Honey, I've done it before. Why should this time be any different?" She kissed him again, smiling against his mouth when his hands cupped her hips and pulled her against him. "Just do as Belle says, okay? Get those horses out of here and head off the trouble coming this way."

"What makes you think Tupperman will send the law out here? He doesn't know it was us that took his horse."

"You covered your tracks all the way back here?" Belle asked, knowing the answer before she phrased the question.

"Well, we—uh, w-we—it was d-dark and—"

"That's what I thought. You didn't cover your tracks and you think Tupperman is so stupid he won't follow you?" She pressed four fingertips against his lips. "Jimmy, love, listen to Belle. Get the hell out of here and I'll handle Tupperman and the law. And next time you steal horses, you cover up your tracks. Got that?"

"Yes, honey." He grinned and lifted her up for a hard, lingering kiss. "I love you, Belle."

"And you need me."

He set her back on her feet. "You think this horse business is okay? We only take from damned Yankees."

"I think it's okay for the time being." She fitted one arm around his waist and moved with him toward the house. "If it'll get me out of this shackful of in-laws, then I'll tolerate it for a while." She kept him just short of the door. "Jimmy, the gambling's got to stop. I told you when I married you that I wouldn't live in your mama's house for more than a year and I meant it. You'd better have me a house built by the first of November or I'm moving back with my folks."

He nuzzled the side of her neck and chuckled with disbelief. "Awww, sugar, you'll miss me if you leave."

"Yes," Belle agreed, then nodded inside the house where the snoring was deafening, "but I sure as hell won't miss them."

Kenneth Tupperman and one of his sons rode behind two lawmen from Dallas. They approached the house at a slow gait, giving them time to assess the bleached wood structure with its rusty roof. Tupperman's belly rolled over his belt and strained the fabric of his black shirt. He sat astride a blaze-faced chestnut. His son rode a flaxen-maned roan. The horses were bred for strength and speed and were far superior to the common cow ponies ridden by the marshals.

Mother Reed started outside, but Belle caught her elbow and pulled her back.

"You let me do the talking," Belle said.

"I'm the missus here and I'll—"

"Do as I say!" Belle fired one of her withering glares that never failed to cower her mother-in-law. "Stay behind me and keep your trap shut. I'll handle this." Belle faced front again and fixed a pleasant smile on her face before stepping out onto the narrow porch.

One of the lawmen touched the brim of his hat and they all reined their horses.

"Good morning to you, ma'am. Are you Mrs. Reed?"

"I am. I'm Mrs. James Reed and this is my mother-in-law, the widow Reed."

The men nodded in turn and shifted uneasily in their saddles.

"And you are?" Belle asked after a moment.

"Pardon me, ma'am. I'm Marshal Callen out of Dallas and this is Deputy Fillmore." He twisted in the saddle to look back at the Tuppermans. "Ken Tupperman and his son Jake, ma'am."

Belle turned on her smile. "Howdy to all of you. Would you like to water your horses at our trough? Where y'all headed?"

Marshal Callen removed his hat and knocked sweat salt off its brim. "Well, ma'am, our business brings us here. We're looking for your husband and a couple of his older brothers."

Mother Reed sucked in her breath and moaned, drawing attention to herself and making Belle want to punch her in the gut.

"Why are you looking for my husband?" Belle asked sweetly. "Is he in danger?"

"I'll have you know that them no-count Reed boys stole my best stallion, young woman," Tupperman said, his voice booming like a cannon blast. "Where are they?"

"Some of the younger boys are on the place," Belle said, the smile slipping from her lips. She didn't like Tupperman one bit, but she decided that good manners were her best defense against an oaf like him. Kill him with kindness, gal, but don't overdo it. "They're in the fields and out in the corral. Jim, George, and Jasper are in Missouri visiting their sister. Talitha and her new husband are settling outside Carthage and Jim and his brothers are helping them build a house and barn." She turned aside to place an arm around Mother Reed's narrow shoulders and bring the shivering woman to her side. "We Reeds are close knit. We take care of our own."

"How long have they been in Missouri?" the marshal asked.

"About three weeks, isn't it, Mother Reed?"

Mother Reed nodded, keeping her gaze glued to her scuffed black shoes.

"Three weeks?"

"Yes, sir," Belle asserted. "Three weeks." She angled her chin up and met Tupperman's look of disgust. "My husband and his brothers couldn't have stolen your horse, sir. I'm sorry for your troubles, but they've nothing to do with me or mine."

"We've got an eyewitness who says he saw your husband stealing the horse," the marshal said.

"Your witness needs to get his eyes checked," Belle suggested with a convincing smile. "What time of day did this happen?"

"It was late in the evening," the marshal said.

"Dark?"

"Yes, ma'am."

"How could your witness be sure it was my husband? Had he met my husband before?"

"He's played cards with him. He says he's pretty sure it was James Reed he saw," the marshal said, glancing back at Tupperman.

"He's probably lost at cards and this is his way of getting back at Jim."

"That's not it at all," Tupperman argued. "Davis says the man had a big nose and—"

"And my husband is the only man on God's green earth with a prominent nose?" Belle asked, taking a bead on Tupperman's son's beak. "Are you sure it wasn't your son's nose he was seeing in the dark of night?"

Tupperman and his son turned beet red while the lawmen ducked their heads, their hats casting shadows over their simian grins.

"Don't get sassy with me," Tupperman warned. "My best stallion is gone and somebody's gonna swing for it!"

"Now, let's all calm down," Marshal Callen urged. "Mrs. Reed says her husband hasn't been here for three weeks and we've no cause to say she isn't telling the truth as she knows it."

"Thank you, sir," Belle said, hugging Mother Reed to her side. "I don't know why this Davis fella is lying about our men. They're off helping their sister and they'd never take anything that didn't belong to them, would they, Mother Reed?"

"No," Mother Reed said, her voice nothing more than a high-pitched wail. "I raised 'em up right."

" 'Course you did, ma'am." Marshal Callen touched the brim of his ten-gallon hat. "Sorry to bother you."

"Is that it? You're not going to take anybody in?" Tupperman asked incredulously. "I'm telling you that this Rebel trash is tweaking our noses like they're the ones who won the war, and you're going to ride off like they've done nothing wrong?"

"Which one should I take to jail, Ken?" the marshal asked, twisting around in the saddle to address Tupperman. "The young Reed boys or these two women? You heard them. The older ones aren't around."

"You didn't look for them!" Tupperman bellowed, swinging an arm to indicate the corral and fields.

"I'm taking these ladies at their word." Marshal Callen swung around to Belle. "Would you have your husband and his brothers come by my office in Dallas when they get back? I just want them to verify their whereabouts in person."

"Certainly, Marshal," Belle promised. "I hope you catch the men responsible."

Their business completed, the men turned their horses and headed back the way they'd come. Tupperman glared at Belle over his shoulder until the road obscured her from his smoldering eyes. Belle stepped away from Mother Reed and sat down on the edge of the porch.

"You're a cool one, aren't you?" Mother Reed asked from behind her. "I never saw a better liar than you."

"And I never saw a worse one than you."

"My boys ain't going to that marshal so he can put them in jail. No siree!"

"They'll go," Belle said, driving home her point with a sharp glare. "By heaven, they'll go and they'll tell the marshal all about how they helped their sister build a house and barn."

"But he'll arrest them!"

"No, he won't." Belle leaned back on stiffened arms and turned her face sideways to the gentle caress of a breeze. "But he'll come back here looking for them if they don't go into Dallas and face him."

"I'm afraid for them. I don't want them going to the marshal's office." Mother Reed wrung her hands and whimpered like a kicked dog.

Belle closed her eyes and frowned with impatience at her mother-in-law's spineless show. "If they've got the balls to steal horses, they've got the balls to walk into Callen's office and tell some little old stories."

"Did you talk them into this horse-stealing business? You did, didn't you? You weren't satisfied with this nice home and good life my Jimmy's given you and you've—"

"Come again?" Belle asked with a harsh laugh, then flung her arms out to embrace the tiny house and grassless yard. "Are you calling this a nice home? This pile of rotting lumber and rusty tin? And what good life are you talking about? I sure as hell haven't seen much good in it."

"It's as much as you deserve! You Shirleys are no better than the rest of us," Mother Reed asserted, then crouched back when Belle sprang to her feet to face her with black, snapping eyes and grimly set mouth. "Don't you hit me," she begged, her voice quivering with fear.

"I'm not going to hit you. I'm going to tell you once and for all to keep your nose out of my business and your wicked tongue off my family. I didn't tell Jimmy and his brothers to steal horses, but since they've decided to do it, I've decided to make sure they don't hang for it. You got a problem with that, old woman?"

"No," Mother Reed said in a tiny voice.

"Good. Now you go about your business and leave Jimmy to me."

"He was a good boy before he met you," Mother Reed mumbled as she turned and moved turtlelike into the house. Twelve children and countless days bent over a washtub or a cotton row had bowed her back and weakened her knees, making her creep instead of walk. She was fifty and afraid.

"He was a good boy after he met me and a better man after he married me!" Belle mumbled at her back.

Chapter Eight

YOU AND YOUR HUBBY are cutting in on my piece of the pie," brother Edwin said, grinning around the toothpick he'd fashioned from a sharp stick.

Belle mirrored his lopsided grin. "If you'll tell me what you're talking about, it'll make the conversation a hell of a lot more interesting to me."

"I'm talking about the horse-thieving ring the Reeds have formed. I hear-tell you're the brains behind the operation." Edwin hooked his thumbs under his suspenders. He leaned way back in the rocking chair, dragged out into the porch yard of the Shirley house. "Doesn't surprise me none. None of them Reeds is very bright. They got a lot of gumption and guts, but not a lick of sense."

Belle surveyed the crowd of kinfolk around her and shook her head in a bemused fashion. Once every month or two, weather permitting, the Reeds and Shirleys got together on a Sunday afternoon for supper and jawing. The men and boys gathered on one side of the porch yard and the women and girls on the other, but sometime during the course of the afternoon or evening Belle broke rank and joined the men. The women bored the stuffing out of her.

Ignoring Edwin's goading, she watched Jimmy, who was pitching horseshoes with three of his brothers and two of his brothers-in-law. He hung one shoe around the post and leaped up with joy, letting out an Indian whoop and shaking hands all around. Belle rolled her eyes. Lord, you'd think he'd lassoed the moon instead of only winning at horseshoes.

"Ain't you talking?" Edwin asked, peering at her as if he were trying to see through her skull.

"You get on a subject I like and I'll talk up a storm." Belle settled more comfortably in the tree swing, kicked off, and held tightly to the ropes. The sky rushed at her, then fell away, rushed, retreated, rushed and retreated.

"Your gang stole some horses night before last not more than an hour before me and my boys got there to steal them. We wasn't happy about it. We still ain't."

Belle laughed, picturing Eddie and his cohorts sneaking up on an empty corral.

"Quit that cackling and talk to me, girl!" Eddie barked.

Belle dug in her heels and locked her knees, standing upright in the swing. "Get one thing straight in that pea brain of yours, Edwin Benton Shirley," she said, her voice as icy as her eyes. "I'm not a girl, and you're not my boss man. Just don't you forget that I'm the one who changed your dirty didies and sat up nights with you when you cut your first teeth, so if I'm a girl, that makes you nothing but a pink-cheeked baby." She bent her knees, lifted her feet, and soared on in the creaking swing, her skirt billowing out behind her and then dragging along in the dirt. "I don't know anything about a horse-thieving ring, and I'd thank you kindly not to spread such vicious rumors about your own sister."

"Oh, hell!" He lunged forward, propelling himself out of the rocker. "There's no talking to you when you're trying to be sly. You'd better keep your thieving on the other side of Dallas. This side belongs to me."

"Where's your name written on the map?" Belle asked, then sucked in her breath when Edwin's hand closed over hers, stopping her in midair. "Let go, Eddie."

"Does Pa know you're helping your husband to steal horses?"

"I don't answer to Papa anymore, little brother."

"We know what route y'all take into the Territory and so does the law. One night you're gonna get ambushed. Who do you deal with over in the Indian lands? If you don't tell me, I'll find out and take over your trade."

"Eddie, if I was stealing horses you'd be the last one I'd confide in."

His dark brows shot up and he turned his head and spit out the toothpick. "But I'm your brother!"

"Yes, and you're standing here threatening me like I'm your enemy. Well, brother, if that's the way you want to play this hand, so be it. All's fair, Eddie. From now on, you stay out of my way or I'll run right over you. You follow?"

"You'll run me over, huh?" He chuckled and let go of the swing. "I'm shaking in my boots."

"I've cut down bigger boys than you. Hell, I learned how it's done from the likes of Jesse James and Cole Younger, so don't go threatening me unless you mean business." She held his cold gaze for a long, tension-filled minute and was ever so glad when he relented.

With a shrug of his shoulders and a nervous laugh, he kicked at a bunch of autumn leaves and spun away from her. "I was just funning you, sis," he said, moving off with his lanky, awkward gait. "Hell, can't you take a ribbing?"

Heavy hands landed on her shoulders from behind and Belle nearly jumped out of her skin.

"Whoa, honey," Jimmy said, easily lifting her out of the swing. He kissed the side of her neck. "What's wrong?"

"Eddie," she said, nodding toward her temperamental sibling. "He worries me. Doesn't he make you think of Charley?"

"Quantrill?" Jimmy mused. "No, not really."

"Well, I see more and more of Charley in Edwin every day."

"Is that so bad?"

"It's not good. I never thought Charley was near the man folks made him out to be. If he hadn't had a band of Missouri's best fighters, he wouldn't have lasted more than a month in the brush country."

"I keep hearing that Eddie is stealing horses with a bunch of other boys."

"That's right."

"Is that what you two were fussing about?"

"We weren't fussing. We were testing each other and I won," Belle said, then glanced over her shoulder so that Jim could see the worry on her face. "This time, I won. Next time . . . I don't know."

Jimmy looped his arms around her small waist and held her tightly against him. "Forget all that business. We're supposed to have some fun today." He ran his hands along the sleeves of her mint-green dress. "You sure look pretty in this new frock."

"I feel pretty in it, too. I probably shouldn't have dipped into our nest-egg money to buy it, but I just had to have a Sunday dress. My other one is fading. It used to be yellow, but I've washed it so many times that it's almost white."

"I'm glad you bought it. What's the point of having money, if you don't spend it?"

Belle turned in his arms and held his face in her hands. "Jimmy, the point of having the money is so that we can build our own house on our own land. Remember? We're not going to spend the money on anything else. We agreed to that. Remember?" When she spoke slowly as if to a young child, he tended to listen and realize that she meant every word.

"Sure, honey." He grinned, melting her heart. "Anything you say, baby. If a house and land is what you want, well then, that's what you'll get."

"Look, Belle," Jasper said, pointing through the foggy darkness to a full-bodied mare. "She'd be a good one to take along."

Belle was sorely tempted, but she shook off temptation. "No, no. We've got two of his best stallions and they'll bring a better price than that mare."

"But Old Man Fisher won't miss her," George whined. "If we snatch her that'll bring the number to ten we can take into the Territory."

"Even or odd, what's the difference?" Belle argued, looking to Jim for support. His brown eyes sparkled like they always did when he was doing something underhanded.

Jimmy loved living on the edge, and if she were honest, she loved it too—more than she cared to admit. Lord, he looked good enough to eat sitting astride his big bay with his eyes atwinkle and that black kerchief hiding the lower half of his face.

Belle forced her mind back to business with some effort. "Fisher might not miss one or two horses for a day or two, but three leaves a big hole, especially if one's a mare with foal."

"She's right," Jim agreed, coming through for her. He pulled his hat lower over his forehead and adjusted the scarf across his nose and mouth. "Let's ride while the moon's still behind cloud cover."

"Y'all go on and I'll hang back to cover your tracks. Take the north road back to the ranch."

"North road?" George asked. "Why? That'll take a good hour longer and we've still gotta set out for the Territory after that."

"I know, just do it. I've got a feeling that competition is tailing us tonight." She looked around at the unfamiliar land with its stands of pine and oak. Belle curled her arm around Jim's neck and pulled him sideways to buss his cheekbone. "God speed, sweet Jimmy."

"Who's following us?" Jim whispered for her ears only.

"Nobody I can't handle. Forget what I said about the north road," she whispered back to him. "Take the usual route." She let go of him and spoke normally. "Now get along. Y'all have a long ride ahead."

He touched a gloved fingertip to her pug nose. "Mrs. Reed, you be careful, y'hear? Don't do anything foolhardy. See you in a few days." Jim moved off with his two brothers, who were leading the two horses they'd winnowed from Abe Fisher's stock.

Belle gave them a head start, then followed at a painstakingly slow pace. That old feeling swamped her, making her feel sinful and intoxicated. Mostly, she felt alive and young.

You should be home baking bread and making babies, she told herself sternly. This is no business for a married lady. Oooo, but it was fun! She pulled her lower lip between her teeth to keep from smiling. There was nothing like slipping into the night, penetrating a fortress, and stealing off with loot in hand. Nothing like it! Especially when the loot belonged to high-and-mighty Yankees who thought they ruled the land and lorded over the Southerners.

She glanced up when the moon slipped from its cover to

spill accusatory light upon her. Could she help it if she was a natural-born thief? She was blessed with a sixth sense about following and being followed; a knack for staying one step ahead of trouble.

There was plenty of money in the flour canister back at Mother Reed's—more than enough to buy land and build a two- or three-room house. Best of all, Jim stayed home and by her side more often since she'd thrown in with him and his brothers. He no longer rode into Scyene or Dallas for a piece of action. He seemed content to be with Belle and talk of their next job or what they were going to do with the money they'd made off the horses. Life was good, but it would be better in her own home on her own land.

At the place where Jim and his brothers branched off across open country, Belle took the north road instead. Following it for a couple of miles, she spurred her quarter horse up a steep rise, to the crest where the trees grew thickest.

"Good boy," she murmured to her winded mount. "Easy there, Dazzle. Let's be real quiet from here on in." The gelding was a wedding present from her pa.

She leaned over his neck and spoke soothingly. The horse took comfort in her voice and settled into a slow, measured walk. Belle kept one hand firmly on the saddle horn and the other buried in Dazzle's mane. She tracked the area below her with eyes as sharp as an eagle's, looking for any hint of movement.

Halfway down the rise she saw dark shapes and heard the rustle of leaves crumbling under horses' hooves. She knew her quarry was among those shadows. Sure enough she found him no more than a dozen yards from his companions, hunkered behind a boulder, his back to her. Belle tugged Dazzle's mane, signaling him to stay put. Holding her breath, she dismounted and crept toward the crouched man, who was so immersed in his lookout over the north road that he wasn't paying any attention to his blind sides. He wore dark clothing and a floppy brimmed hat. A shotgun was propped against the boulder and two six-shooters hung from his tooled leather holster.

Damn fool, Belle thought as she inched closer to him. Doesn't even have a weapon ready in case somebody tries to get the drop on him. There's nothing worse than a young idiot who thinks he can beat death to the draw.

When she was at arm's length, she paused to mentally rehearse her plan of attack. She had it down pat. Before her victim could draw a decent breath, Belle had swiped both of his six-shooters. His hands slapped against his empty holsters, seconds too late. He spun around with a startled gasp and stared down his own gun barrels. Belle laughed in the face of his humiliation.

"Boo, brother!" she said, using the back of her wrist to knock her hat back off her head. It swung from the chin strap and her ebony hair tumbled to her shoulders. "Isn't it a bitch when you're captured during your own ambush attempt? It's enough to spoil a fella's day."

Edwin's upper lip rose in a dangerous snarl; his eyes darted frantically sideways at the shotgun.

"Are you going to grab up that thing and shoot me?" Belle asked, amazed at Ed's bloodthirsty streak. She spun the guns in her hands so that the butts were held out to him. "Here. Take them. I was only showing you how silly it is for you to try to outfox me."

"You're lucky I didn't blow your head off," Ed said, taking the guns and sliding them back into his holster.

"With what? Your bad breath?" Belle laughed at his rage, but inside she cowered from it. She reminded herself that Edwin had inherited the blinding Shirley temper.

"I've known you were following me ever since I left the

ranch. I just wanted you to know that I knew, so you'd stop being an idiot and mind your own damned business."

"This is my business. You're taking horses that I've staked out to steal!"

Belle laughed again, although she didn't find Edwin the least bit amusing. "Eddie, listen to yourself. We're talking about breaking the law here. There's no rules and regulations among outlaws. If you want to steal horses, fine, but don't go thinking you've got the market cornered or territory staked off. It's every man for himself out here."

"You're taking too many and you're going to bring the law down on all of us," he said, shaking a finger in her face.

Belle caught his finger and lowered it with a strength that made Ed grimace with a sharp intake of breath. Surprise and then respect flitted across his features.

"Don't wave that finger at me, little brother. If the law is biting at your ass it's because you're a sloppy amateur and not because we're stealing more than our fair share—whatever *that* is." She let go of him and glanced off to the right where the rest of his bunch was making enough noise to wake the dead. "Listen to them. Hell, it's a wonder y'all haven't been thrown in jail by now. Sounds like a herd of mules coming this way." She shook her head at the commotion before looking at her younger brother again. "This isn't a game, Ed. This is the kind of stuff that sends you up the river for a good portion of your life."

"I know that. I don't need no woman telling me anything."

"I'm not just any woman. I'm your sister, and you're going to listen to me."

Hearing raised voices, the others broke through the underbrush, stumbling over their own feet. Belle held out a hand and all movement ceased. They stared at her in open-mouthed amazement.

"What the hell is she doing here?" one of them asked, his voice squeaking with youth.

"I'm having a private talk with my brother, greenhorn," Belle answered, disturbed to see how very young they were—no more than sixteen. They had no business out here among thieves and cutthroats. They should be home tending to their mamas and little sisters and brothers. "Vamoose," Belle ordered and the boys jerked, her voice galvanizing them.

"Stay where you are," Ed commanded. "We don't want to listen to what she's saying."

"Fine, don't listen," Belle said, spinning around and heading back up the rise to where she'd left her horse. "But if you won't respect your elders, then at least acknowledge your betters," she called over her shoulder. "And watch your back, for pity's sake. I've buried one brother and I sure as hell don't want to bury another one."

Belle stepped out on the porch and shaded her eyes with one hand as she looked at the approaching riders. "It's Jimmy," she said, glancing back at Mother Reed, peeling potatoes. "I hope he's got a good excuse for dragging in here a week late."

"Don't nag him. A man's gotta do what a man's—"

"Don't feed me that chicken shit," Belle snapped, slicing through Mother Reed's mindless recitation.

"You talk like trash!" Mother Reed accused.

"And you smell like it," Belle shot back. She hopped off the porch and waved at Jim.

"H'lo, sweet pea!" Jimmy reined his horse and leaned down, flinging an arm around Belle's shoulders and giving her a smacking kiss on the lips. "We're home from the hills! Glad to see me?"

"Where in the hell have you been?" she demanded, hating him for being in such a jubilant mood.

"In Missouri." He dropped from the saddle and handed the reins over to George. Oblivious to her tone, he draped an arm around Belle's stiff shoulders. "Did you miss me? Owww!" He drew away from her sharp elbow. "What's that for?"

"That's for worrying me half to death, you jackass. What have you been doing in Missouri? We expected you back days ago."

"Boys! Boys!" Mother Reed stood on the porch, her eyes full of tears, a dopy smile on her lips. "Praise the Lord!" She hugged Jasper and Jim, looking like an elf clutching giants.

"Did we worry you, Ma?" Jim asked.

"No, I knew you'd be home today."

"Jesus," Belle said, matching Mother Reed frown for frown. "Her hair's gone completely white these past few days. You had us worried sick."

"It ain't right for a woman to cuss," Mother Reed grumbled. "Tell her, Jim."

Jim laughed, but kept prudently silent on the subject. "Ma, we've got a surprise for you that'll put everything right."

"What? What is it, son?"

"We're moving back to Rich Hill." Jim stood back to take in his mother's look of disbelief. "No fooling. We bought our land back. The house still stands and we'll all be in it by Thanksgiving."

Mother Reed clasped her hands to her bosom and her mouth worked before words came out. "Praise be! Is it true? I've so wanted to go back home."

"We're going," Jasper assured her. "That's where we've

137

been. The land is ours and no Yankee's ever gonna drive us off it again."

Belle felt her hopes dashed. It was like a kick in the stomach. She looked toward the house, envisioning the flour canister gaping empty like a well with no water ... like a heart with no love, a mind with no sense, a marriage with no trust.

She felt the bile rising in her throat. Her head pounded with repressed anger as Jimmy wrapped his arms around her. Belle stiffened against the unwanted comfort. Jimmy's fingers drew aside the curtain of her raven hair.

"Aren't you happy about my news?"

"Why should I be?"

"We're going back to Missouri, Belle. We're going home."

"That's funny," she said, wriggling from his arms. "I thought we were home."

"Honey, don't be like that." He reached out to her, but she slapped away his hands.

"You spent the money. I ought to cut your heart out," she spat.

"You don't mean that."

"You cut *my* heart out when you took that money and spent it like I had no claim to it. You had no right."

"I had every right. I'm the man in the family, ain't I? That money was mine to do with what I wanted, and that's exactly what I did."

"Why, you backwater bumpkin, where do you get off talking to me like that? Who planned the jobs? Who picked the horses? Who covered up for you when your tail got caught in a crack?"

"I could've done right nicely without you. Me and my brothers are the ones who pulled off the jobs. We let you in with us just because you had your heart set on helping."

"Come again?" She stepped up to face him off, unmindful of the others who were watching the confrontation. "James Reed, you and your brothers would be swinging from ropes if it weren't for me. The three of you put together don't have enough sense to pour whiskey out of a boot with the instructions printed on its heel."

"Watch your mouth," Jim warned, cutting his eyes sideways to indicate the others. His pride was on the line and he didn't want her stepping on it in front of his family. "What's done is done. We're moving to Rich Hill."

"I'm spending Christmas in Texas."

"You don't mean that. You'll come with me."

"Not this time." She laid the back of her hand against his shoulder and brushed him off, walking past him with long, pounding strides.

"You've gotta come with me. You're my wife, damn it!" Jim shouted at her back.

"Much to my everlasting regret," Belle said between gritted teeth.

Chapter Nine

WALKING ALONG THE BUCKLED BOARDWALK of Scyene's main street, Belle Reed cut a pretty figure against the gray, rainy sky. The mud-splashed cowboys, lounging in doorways or sauntering down the street, couldn't resist a second look at the petite curvaceous brunette. She wore a gaily printed dress of powder blue and yellow, its neckline close-fitting and edged in lace. Her hat was blue satin with clusters of golden flowers at its crown. She wore buckskin gloves that matched her high-button shoes.

Her figure was hour-glass, dipping and swelling in all the right places. Belle filled out a dress in a way that made a man's heart pound. She wasn't beautiful, but she had a womanly essence, a confident sensuality that no male could ignore. There was something about the catlike slant of her eyes—a wise gleam that was rare in a woman. Her smile, being off-centered but utterly attractive, bewitched and dazzled even the most hard-hearted of men. She was a temptress.

On this blustery afternoon, she clutched her parasol and paid no mind to the admiring glances. Christmas, she thought, and a scowl deepened the lines on her forehead. Thanksgiving had been a day of gloomy contemplation, surrounded as she had been by the Shirleys while the Reeds were in Missouri at their beloved Rich Hill farm. Belle had felt like a fifth wheel, not belonging anywhere or to anyone.

My, how things had changed. Strangely enough, Eddie was her only comfort these days. She and Eddie huddled together and laughed over botched horse-stealing jobs, gloated over successful ones, and boasted of future accomplishments.

Thank heavens for Edwin. He was the only bright spot in her own winter of discontent. She lifted her skirts, stepped daintly off the boardwalk and across a muddy alleyway. What a mess! Christmas was two weeks away and her spirits were as droopy as a mule's ears at the end of a day in the fields. She was wrapped in a blanket of depression, making her feel old and useless. Where had the golden days gone? Lifting her gaze skyward in search of a sparkle or a glimmer of what had been—if only she could find a reason to—

Belle pulled herself up short. Was it possible? Bright golden hair. Pastel blue eyes. A smile, slow and warming like the sunrise.

"Good afternoon, Mrs. Reed. You're looking mighty pretty today." Cole Younger brought one arm across his silver vest and bowed over it. He looked for all the world like a fancy gambler standing in the doorway of the Scyene hotel. Black, close-fitting trousers, snowy white shirt, silver vest, black leather jacket and boots. He wore no hat. His blond hair seemed to brighten the gray day.

Her knees buckled and she reached out blindly. Her parasol dropped from her numb hand, her beaded purse from the other. Cole caught her by the elbows and held her upright, concern giving way to relieved amusement.

"Myra Maybelle Shirley swooning?" he scoffed at the notion. Holding tightly to one of her arms, he reached down to retrieve her parasol and purse. "Unthinkable! I must be mistaken. You're not Belle Shirley from Carthage, are you?"

"I am." Feeling flustered and girlish, she gained her balance and proudly squared her shoulders. "Are you a riverboat gambler or merely a rakehell?" she quipped, looking him up and down. Something was different about him . . . "You've grown quite a beard there, Mr. Younger. You had a mustache last time I saw you, but this makes you look . . ." She smiled and glanced away shyly. "It hides your dimples, and I so love your dimples."

He stroked the reddish gold beard and laughed. "Where have you been this morning all dressed up?"

She folded her parasol and tapped its point against the boards at her feet. "In church, praying for a bit of sunshine. Looks like somebody up there was listening." She grinned when he checked the cloudy sky and then her teasing expression. "You. You're my sunshine. Oh, Cole, it's good to see you."

He chucked her under her chin. "Why the long face? Has life been kicking you in the gut lately?"

"You said it." She looked past him into the hotel. "Are you staying here?"

"Sure am."

"Buy me a cup of coffee."

She brushed past, making sure that her body pressed against his for a few heavenly moments before she moved ahead into the hotel. Cole was right on her heels. She gloried in the feel of his hand at the small of her back. They made their way to a secluded table for two. Cole held out one of the chairs and she made herself comfortable in it. A waiter took their order for tea and toast. Belle removed her gloves and let her eyes feast hungrily on Cole.

"You look as if you've been living well," she commented after the refreshments had been brought. "Where are you hanging your hat these days? Are you still thinking of moving to Texas?"

"I'm looking at some land and a house right here in Scyene." He sensed her remorse and leaned forward with blatant concern. "What's wrong? What did I say to upset you?"

"Nothing. I've got a decision to make and you're not making it any easier."

"What decision? And what do I have to do with it?"

She sipped the sweet tea before answering. "Jimmy and the others moved back to Rich Hill and he wants me to join him. I can either go and be his wife again or stay here and be near you. What should I do, Cole?" She sighed, knowing he wouldn't take a stand where she was concerned.

"Stay here."

Belle gasped, her eyes growing enormous with hope. "W-what did you say?" she asked, afraid that she'd heard him wrong. She'd waited so long for encouragement from him . . . a lifetime, it seemed.

"Stay," he repeated succinctly as he reached for her hand and held it between both of his. "I've no right to ask you to do this, but I want you to stay with me."

"I can't believe you're saying this," Belle admitted, her breathing coming in short gasps as if she'd run a far distance.

"I can't offer you anything except my undivided attention." His hands closed more tightly upon hers. "Oh, Belle," he said, sighing her name, "there's some kind of magic between us. I guess what I'm saying is that I need magic in my life right now, and I think you need it too."

"Yes." Belle smiled through her tears. "Oh, yes, yes, yes!"

Belle felt delightfully sinful, lying naked on top of the only man who could move her physically and spiritually.

She bestowed carefully staged kisses across his furred chest and tangled her bare legs with his. His eyes were closed and Belle ran the tip of her tongue across his lids, wetting his stubby, dark blond lashes and making him chuckle deep in his throat. She nuzzled his beard playfully.

"I miss my dimples," she said, pouting.

"They missed you. You make me happy," he murmured, his arms closing on her waist. "It was better this time, wasn't it?"

"Yes, it's better when I know what I'm doing." She sighed and nestled her cheek against his downy chest. "It's so different with you. I feel more. With Jimmy it's over too fast. He's pleasured, but I ... well, I'm left feeling all jumpy inside like a fish washed up on the bank."

"And with me?"

"With you I'm exhausted when we're done with each other, but it's a good kind of exhaustion. I glow inside and out. We're good for each other."

His arms rode up to her shoulders, crisscrossing and keeping her solidly against him.

"Maybe we'll produce a few pearls from all of this," he said after a while.

"A few pearls?" She laughed softly. "What are you talking about?"

"Pearls. Have you ever heard about how they're made?"

"No, can't say that I have. All I know is that they're mighty pretty."

"Oysters make pearls. It all starts with a grain of sand. A tiny grain of sand." His voice took on a wondrous tone. Belle was struck with a sense of awe. "The sand irritates the oyster, causes conflict and turmoil. Like the war did with us. Don't you see?"

"Yes," Belle said, rubbing her cheek against his chest. "I do see. Go on."

"The war grated on us. Our most important years were interrupted by the horror of it all. It changed us forever, made us tougher and resilient and crafty. Those aren't pretty things to be, are they?"

"But if we weren't those things we'd be trampled. We had to be tough to get through it."

"True," he agreed, "but the timing was rotten."

"What's this got to do with that oyster?"

"Well, that grain of sand irritates that old oyster and makes its life miserable and then one day—poof!—like magic there's this beautiful, perfect pearl, making all that misery worth it. Maybe us being together like this is our pearl, Belle. Maybe it's our reward for getting through the war in one piece and with sound minds."

Belle was quiet, thinking of what he'd said and the beauty in it. Cole was so special. Most men wouldn't talk poetry like he did. They'd be too embarrassed to open their hearts to a woman and let her see the sentimental workings within.

After a while he let go of her and sat up in the bed to light a thin cigar. When he had it going and a halo of aromatic smoke hovered above his head, he cleared his throat and stared pointedly at the tip of the cigar.

"Why did you let Jim go without you?"

Belle sat up beside him, fitting the sheet up under her arms and arranging it just so around her body. "I'm mad as hell at him, that's why. He bought that property without asking me anything about it. He expects me to pack up and go, no questions asked. Well, I'm not his shadow. I've got a mind of my own."

"Y'all been mighty busy lately. Tom Starr says y'all were supplying all the horses he can sell up until around Thanksgiving. Were you saving the money for your own place?"

"Yes." Belle glanced sideways at him, wondering just how much he knew. She noted the cagy squint of one of his eyes and remembered how he did that when he was figuring something out. Had he figured her out?

"But Jimmy took it all and bought the Rich Hill place back from a Yankee family. Personally, I would've had more respect for him if he'd gone in and made those Yankees sign over the deed to him at gunpoint. Damn Yankees, buying up Rebel land for a song and then making us buy it back from them for twice what it's worth. Makes me so mad I could . . . could—"

"Steal 'em blind? Or, at the very least, steal their best horseflesh out from under their blueblood noses?" Cole finished for her with a wide grin.

"Look who's talking," Belle admonished. "Don't you think we've heard about you and Jesse raising hell all over the place?"

"Don't believe everything you hear. I'm as clean as a hound's tooth."

"No fooling?" she asked, examining his expression closely and seeing the truth in his eyes. "You are! But all I ever hear is about this robbery or that robbery. You and Jesse are legends."

"Despite the stories, me and Jesse hardly see each other. He's busy with his family and I'm busy with mine. Me and my brothers want to settle Ma down in a milder climate. She's getting up there in years and she's never been strong since the war."

"Who's pulling off the robberies?"

"I don't know for sure, but I think it's some of our old friends from Quantrill's band. If I'm a legend then it's through no effort of my own." His glance was sharp and accusing. "You, on the other hand, are a different story. I've been worried about you. I don't like thinking of you riding through the night with the law at your heels."

"It's not like that."

"What's it like then? I know you're the one who planned all the jobs. I told Tom Starr as much and he thought I was plumb loco. Old Tom thinks that women are good for one thing and it's got nothing to do with anything from the neck up."

"I've got to meet that old coot someday," Belle said, stalling for time. "How well do you know those Indians?"

"Well enough for them to name their land after me and my brothers."

"That right?" she asked, arching her thin brows in respect.

"Youngers Bend," he explained. "That's what Tom calls his spread. He says that me and my kin have been there so much that we've got a stake in it. It's Tom's idea of a joke, but it stuck. Everybody calls it Youngers Bend. Nobody knows it as the Starr land anymore."

"Youngers Bend," Belle repeated. "I'd like to see it someday."

"You keep stealing horses and you probably will. Tom likes to meet his business partners."

Belle sighed and rolled her eyes. "Jimmy and his brothers did take a few horses, but I—"

"Uh-uh-uh," Cole said, wagging a finger at her, then laughing when she snapped at it like a turtle. "Don't you lie to me after you've just made love to me. Tell the truth. You're the brains behind the operation, aren't you?"

"What makes you think that?"

"Because Jim Reed isn't too smart. He can't plan a walk to the outhouse without help."

"Coleman Younger!" Belle popped him in the shoulder with her fist. "Jim's a friend of yours and you're talking about him like that!"

"He's your husband and you're lying naked in bed with his *friend*," Cole reminded her. He gave her a tender hug when she winced and struggled to get out of bed. "Stay put, sugar britches. I'm glad you're here and I'm glad Jim's in Missouri. I'd just as soon you'd stay away from him so long as he's flirting with the wrong side of the law. I couldn't stand it if you ended up behind bars. I think I'd go crazy if that happened."

"Don't talk foolish. I'm not going to jail." She rested her head back against his shoulder and felt loved. "Jim's going to farm, or so he says."

"What do you think?" he asked, stubbing out his cigar in the cut-glass ashtray on the nightstand.

"I think he's got good intentions. You know, those things that the road to hell is paved with?"

"Yes, I surely do know about them. When I came here I told myself I was going to stay away from you."

Belle twisted around to face him, a smile tugging at the corners of her mouth.

"And here I am," Cole said. He pressed his mouth against her neck and moaned. "Thank God, I listened to my heart instead of to my head."

The hotel ballroom was packed with Dallas merrymakers, intent on bringing in 1868 in style. Only thirty minutes away from the new year, the crowd was rowdy. Most of the well-dressed men were as drunk as skunks. The women, wearing the latest fashions, pretended not to notice.

A couple of the musicians had passed out, one being the piano player, but Belle had taken his place at the upright. She played by ear while she searched the crowd for Cole. She spotted him standing by the bar, drink in hand. Their eyes met, and he raised his glass in a silent toast to her. Incredibly, she blushed. When was the last time she'd done that? A lifetime ago.

Did he feel hot all over when he looked at her? Did she

look as good to him in her gown of champagne satin and lace as he did to her in his black suit and ivory brocade vest?

Their eyes locked in mutual admiration.

The ballroom was festooned with streamers that fluttered from the ornately carved ceiling. The crush of bodies warmed the room, although a bitter wind blew outside and folks were predicting snow. Good thing they'd planned to stay the night. Traveling back to Scyene would be treacherous with snow on the way.

Cole wove through the couples, standing head and shoulders above most of the men and women. He made a beeline for her, stalking like a sure-footed bobcat.

He'd shaved for her as a Christmas present. His dimples were showing even though he wasn't smiling. His expression was intent. He was a man with a mission. She shivered uncontrollably. She'd been with him since before Christmas, but she still felt like she was dreaming. It was all too good to be real.

He stopped beside the stage and held out a hand to her. Belle realized that her hands were folded in her lap. When had she removed them from the keyboard?

"You've played that thing enough," he said. "Play me for a while, why don't you?"

She smiled, liking the mischief in him. She put her hand in his and let him help her down the stage steps and into his waiting arms. The fiddles and guitars played a waltz, and Belle followed Cole's lead as if she were born to it.

"I want to be holding you when the new year arrives," he said, brushing a wayward curl back from her temple. "We'll welcome it together."

"Together." Belle sighed with pleasure. "That sounds nice. I hope we can keep it that way."

"Can't you be happy with right here and now without

bringing tomorrow into it?" He rolled his blue eyes in exasperation.

"Why are you scared of tomorrow?"

"I'm not."

"Happy New Year, *Mrs.* Reed."

Belle stiffened and turned toward the honey-dipped voice. Lilah Sewell, one of Scyene's busiest busy bodies, lifted haughty brows at Belle and the man who held her like he owned her.

"Same to you, Mrs. Sewell," Belle answered over her shoulder, glad when Cole danced her away.

"That was one of the reasons why I can't help but think about tomorrow," Belle said, frowning. "The whole town of Scyene is talking about us."

"Let them talk. Why let it bother you?"

"It bothers me because I *am* Mrs. Reed."

Cole leaned back a little to see her face. "Feeling guilty? For what? You don't love him, do you?"

"Not like I love you. I'm his wife, but I feel married to you."

"Oh, Belle!" He stopped dancing and framed her face in his hands. Every sweet emotion he felt for her was reflected on his face. "Don't you know that you're the only woman I've ever loved?"

He kissed her, his lips capturing hers, his tongue sliding into her mouth. She tore her mouth from his and pressed her cheek against his chest where his heart beat furiously.

"I don't want you to go back to him. I want us to keep on loving each other. I don't want anything to change. Everything's so perfect the way it is."

"That's just it. It can't stay this way."

The old year ticked away and a raucous din welcomed the new year in, drowning out Belle's voice. Cole brought her lips to his again, making her forget tomorrow's uncertainty.

"Happy New Year, darlin'," he whispered against her lips. "This year will be ours. Our pearl."

Belle blinked back her tears. She stood on tiptoe to meet his descending mouth, unmindful of the noise around her or the popping gunfire outside. He gathered her to his side and made his way from the ballroom to the staircase that led to their room. They closed the door on the rest of the world.

Belle pushed Cole's topcoat off his broad shoulders. She laughed from simple happiness.

"What's got you giggling?" he asked, beaming at her.

"I'm such a softie around you," she said. "All you've got to do is touch me and I turn to mush."

Cole dropped to his knees before her. He embraced her hips, moving his hands to cup and squeeze her buttocks through her skirt. He buried his face in the folds of her dress and his breath was hot on her skin. Belle combed his golden hair with her fingers, pushing it back from his weather-worn forehead.

"I swear, you're the best-looking man God ever made." She arched her back as his hands moved up her spine, and laughing huskily at first as his fingers released one button at a time, she soon was groaning with pleasure.

She tipped back her head, loving the warmth of his big hands as they moved inside her dress to caress her breasts. She looked down at the top of his head, loving his kneeling posture of vulnerability. She couldn't imagine him being this trusting, this tender, this happy with anyone else.

"You love me, don't you?"

He nodded, then looked up at her. "Completely. Shamelessly."

She backed away, pushing her dress down her body and stepping out of it. She removed her petticoats and undergarments, smiling all the while as she watched Cole's eyes dilate with desire.

"Show me," she challenged, lying on her side upon the white bedspread. "Show me how much." Her pretty toes curled in expectation.

Cole grinned and slowly, teasingly unbuttoned his trousers, revealing the unmistakable evidence of his desire. He kicked off his boots, then undressed to his skin. He stood before her, proudly offering himself to the woman he adored. The air in the room was cool, but he was perspiring from the heat growing inside him. He felt himself swell and pulsate with longing. Belle was so beautiful to his eyes. Moonlight streamed in from the windows beside the bed, painting her skin with ivory and blue light. Her hair, as black as a raven's wing, spilled over her shoulders and framed her small face. She smiled at him and his heart tripped over itself as it always did when her lips slanted into that wicked, tantalizing grin.

She crooked a finger at him in a seductive, silent order and he went to her, lying beside her and running one hand over her delicate ribs and down to press her swelling mound.

"Who taught you how to make love?" Belle asked, draping her arm over his sinewy shoulder.

"Who taught me?" he repeated with a chuckle. He dropped soft, sipping kisses on her parted lips. "I don't rightly know. I don't think anybody taught me. I just knew how."

"You taught me," Belle said, rocking her head to one side so that he could rain swift kisses down the side of her neck. "You spoiled me, you rascal. I expect every man to be as good at it as you, but few are."

"You've tried quite a few, have you?"

"Well, no." Her lashes swept down to dust her cheeks. She rolled onto her back. Cole's fingertips trailed between her breasts. "Just you and Jimmy, but I've heard women talking. They talk as if they don't enjoy it. They lie back and take it like a beating." She gave him a long, measuring look. "And nobody taught you? You just come by it natural?"

"When you love somebody," he said slowly, "it comes natural."

"Cole, you fill my heart." She brought his head down to her breasts and his lips toyed with a full, hard nipple.

Cole felt like he was a brushfire, burning out of control. He began to kiss her, taste her, smell her—possess her totally. He shuddered uncontrollably as he moved in and out of her.

Belle thought of her past and could only remember it in terms of Cole. It was as if she'd been born on the day she'd met him. "If you leave me . . ."

"I'm not going anywhere," he promised. "I'm going to love you right into tomorrow. Nothing can change that. Nothing."

"I'm going to have a baby."

Cole was standing by the window and the sunlight clearly illuminated his face as it drained of all color. His eyes grew large and dread darkened them to a cobalt blue as he brought his gaze to Belle's. His lips parted, but he had to swallow hard before he could speak.

"Are you sure about that?"

"Pretty sure," Belle said, trying to keep her spirits up. He's not disgusted, she argued with herself. He's just shocked, surprised. In a minute he'll be whooping with joy and making plans to marry. "I haven't seen a doctor, but I know my body, and it's telling me that I've got a baby growing inside of me."

She pressed a hand to her midsection, feeling queasy because Cole was still staring at her as if she had horns and a forked tail. She smoothed her hands down her satin dress, a dress Cole had bought her only days ago for her twentieth birthday.

"Oh, Belle." He sat down heavily in the nearest chair. He ran his hands up and down his face in a washing motion. "What have we done?"

A sense of betrayal washed over her. "What do you mean by that? I'll tell you what we've done. We've made love and now we've made a baby. Have you got a problem with that?"

"Of course, it's a problem." He sat back, his hands hanging limply over the ends of the chair arms as he stared morosely out the window. "You're married to an old friend of mine. I'm a drifter with responsibilities I've been running from, and now you've added another. Lord, I feel as if I'm carrying around a ball and chain."

Belle laughed harshly. "A minute ago I was your blessing and now I'm your curse. Funny how things can change in the blink of an eye." She gave him a long, hard look. "Forgive me for not laughing."

He roused himself from his misery. "Don't get me wrong. I take part of the blame for this."

"I'm not blaming anyone," Belle corrected. "No blame and no shame. I'm glad I'm going to have a baby."

Her confession jarred him and he stared at her, dumbfounded, for a few moments.

"Glad?" he repeated stupidly. "A baby is a big responsibility. You need a stable home and a loving family and—"

"You don't have to tell me how to raise babies. I've raised my share." She went to the bureau mirror and released some of her anger by bundling her dark hair into a twist at the back of her neck. God, how she'd like to slap his face! She should have known that this couldn't last. It was too good. She'd been too happy. It had been a fairy tale and not all fairy tales have happy endings.

"Belle, I'm sorry for acting so—"

"You don't have to worry about this *ball and chain* because I'll carry it, give birth to it, and raise it," she said, choking on her disappointment.

"Belle, I'm sorry for saying what I did." He rose from the chair and came to stand behind her. His gaze met hers in the mirror as he rested his hands on her shoulders. "You caught me off guard."

"In other words, you spoke the truth before you could think of a lie."

"No, that's not what I meant." He kissed the side of her neck. "This complicates things."

"I thought it cleared things up."

His look was puzzled. "How?"

"We've made a baby. I think that's wonderful. It connects us for all time. I thought you'd be happy about it, but I can see that you aren't."

"I'm not ready to be a father." His hands slipped down her arms and then away. "I'm not ready to be a husband either."

The mirror reflected his imposing back and her devastating pain.

"I see." She picked up her bonnet and placed it over the waves of her hair. "Well, that's that then."

He glanced over his shoulder at her. She was tying the bow under her chin and pulling on her gloves. The firm set of her lips told him that she had built a dam to keep the fury of her emotions from him.

"You're going home? It's still early."

"It's too late for us."

"Belle, don't." He grabbed her arm as she moved past him toward the door. "Let's talk about this."

"We have. We've said too much already."

"I want you to understand why I'm acting this way. You

see in me what you want to see. I'm full of contradictions
and puzzles even I can't solve. I want to settle down, but
then I want to move on. I'm as unpredictable as the weather
and that's what makes me dangerous."

"Dangerous?" she repeated, smiling. "Not to me."

"No, maybe not, but I'm not husband or father material.
Not yet. Not now."

"Well, I don't have the luxury of time. I'm carrying a
child, so that makes me mother material whether I like it or
not." She jerked her elbow from his grasp. "I was hoping
that you'd be happy for us. I was wishing that you'd smile
and tell me that you love me."

"I do love you. I'll always love you. That's the one thing
in my life that is constant."

"Cole." Her throat tightened and she laid a hand against
his cheek. "Why do you say things like that when I'm trying
my best to hate you?"

He turned his head and kissed the palm of her hand.

"What you need is an anchor. Why can't you understand
that? I'd be good for you. This baby—our baby—would be
good for us."

He backed up a step. "I've got too many people depending on me already. When it was just me and you, it was fine.
But a baby?" He combed his fingers through his hair. "A
baby I can't handle. Hell, I don't have honest work or a
place to live, and you're asking me to father a child? Belle, I
can't—"

"I didn't ask you!" Belle shouted, angry and offended by
his rejection of her love offering. "I didn't ask you to do
anything. I'll raise the baby, so you're off the hook."

"Are you going back to Jim?"

"That's my business, not yours." She opened the door,
but couldn't leave without wounding him as he'd wounded
her. "Cheer up, Cole," she said with an evil smile. "Maybe

the baby will be born dead." She closed the door on his grimace of pain.

Belle sat huddled before the fire with her mother. A log split in two, sending sparks flying from the grate to the floor. Both women pulled their feet back, waited for the embers to die, then placed their stockinged feet near the flames again.

"You going back to your husband?" Eliza asked, never looking up from the shirt she was mending.

"I guess." Belle examined her mother's face, which was less lined by time than Mother Reed's. Eliza's hair was streaked with gray while Mother Reed's was snow white. "You getting tired of me hanging around? I suppose you think I should be making my own way or living with my husband's family instead of being piled up in your house."

"I think you should be either here or there, but not in a hotel room with Cole Younger."

Belle sighed.

"I know you don't like to have the truth flung in your face," Eliza persisted, "but somebody's got to look after your reputation."

"I'm pregnant with his baby."

Eliza's hands fell still in her lap and the crushing disappointment evident on her face unnerved Belle to such an extent that she had to look away.

"What has become of you, daughter?" Eliza asked. "You weren't raised as an alley cat, so how come you're acting like one?"

"I'm not!" Belle wished she was a cat so that she could hiss at her mother and scratch and claw in a wild rage. "I love Cole, Mama. I've loved him since I was a girl."

"Your husband—"

"I don't love Jimmy like that. I married Jimmy because I couldn't marry Cole. Jimmy's always been second fiddle to me."

"How could you love Cole for so long when you didn't even know him until he rode up a year or so ago?"

"I knew him before that. Way before that." Belle pressed her hands against her stomach and closed her eyes. "Cole doesn't want to claim this child, but I don't care. This baby is his . . . ours, and it's special. If I can't have Cole, then I'll at least have his child."

"Are you going to raise it by yourself or make Jim help you? You going to tell him it's Cole's?"

"I don't know." Belle rested her elbows on her knees and peered beseechingly into her mother's face. She hadn't come to her mother for advice since before the war, but she needed another opinion. She needed a woman's thoughts on this maternal dilemma. "What should I do, Mama? Should I come clean with Jimmy or should I keep my mouth shut and hope that he thinks the baby is his? It'll come early, you know. Too early to be Jimmy's. Do you think he'd believe me if I told him it was an early bloomer? Can you fool a man like that? Maybe I should just admit that I slept with Cole. What do you think I should do?"

Eliza rocked back and forth, her attention arrested by her shaking hands as she tried to thread a needle.

"Mama, what do you think?" Belle asked again after Eliza had the needle threaded.

Eliza shrugged and screwed up her face in concentration as she bent over the loose button on the shirt. "It's your baby and you've got to rock it."

Irony bubbled in Belle and burst forth in a bark of laughter. She mimicked her mother's look of shock, then let her resentment pour out.

"Why am I asking you for advice? You didn't want me to

marry Jimmy, and you gloated when I came back home, broken and disappointed by him. You don't want me to be with Jimmy and you don't want me to be with Cole. You don't want me to be happy at all, do you, Mama?"

"That's not true!" Eliza put aside the shirt and the needle and thread, finally giving her daughter the attention she'd begged for earlier.

"I think it is. You tell me to rock my own baby, but who rocked yours? Who looked after your children while you lived in a dream world? *Me!*"

Belle jabbed a thumb into her own chest and shot up from the rocker, sending it into a crazy motion. "But don't you worry none. I'm going to raise my own child and not drop it into someone else's lap."

"It wasn't like that. The oldest girl is supposed to help her mother with the young 'uns."

"Says who? I didn't mind doing my part, but I resented the hell out of raising your children because you were too weak to face life's bumps and ruts. You were damned lucky to have me around, weren't you? Most women had to confront the war and deal with it. You had me, so you could go off in your other world and leave the reality for me to wrestle. Mama, I was a child, too! You robbed me of my childhood. Not the war—*you!*" Belle pointed a trembling finger at her ashen-faced mother.

"That's not right. I did my share." Eliza's lips quivered and her eyes filled with tears. "I was ill. Bud was killed and I had to bury him."

"You had to bury him? *You* buried him? You weren't even around! You were in your bedroom with the door closed. *I* went with Papa to collect the body, not you. We buried him, Mama. You think it was easy on any of us? Bud was my—" Tears choked off her voice.

Belle turned away from her mother's pained expression,

knowing that she'd opened a Pandora's box of poisoned memories. In a way, she was glad to have lifted the lid, but she felt sorry for her mother. Facing the truth was tough, and Eliza Shirley was anything but tough. Oh well, Belle thought with a deep breath that cleared her mind. What was done was done.

She stumbled toward the door that led outside, sensing that her relationship to her mother had been changed forever and the rents couldn't be mended with a needle and thread. Time and distance might mend them ... maybe, possibly.

"Forget it," Belle said, her voice a monotone reflecting the emptiness she felt. "I'm going back to the Reeds. I'll leave tomorrow at first light."

Belle went outside where the wind was wickedly cold, but it was the slap in the face she needed to bring her back to the present. She wiped tears from her cheeks and eyes and gathered her composure. *No need in feeling sorry for yourself. You took a chance in loving Cole and now you've got to pay the piper. It's not so bad. You're going to have his baby. You'll always have a part of him. Always.*

"Belle?"

She jerked out of her reverie and turned startled eyes on the tall bundle of dark clothing lounging at the end of the porch. Ed stepped closer. He hugged himself and shivered.

"I've been standing out here listening to you and Ma," he confessed with a half-smile. "I'm going to be an uncle, huh?"

Belle turned aside, irritated by his snooping. "Looks that way. You ought to go inside before you catch cold." She pulled her shawl more tightly around her, then stiffened with wariness when Edwin placed an arm about her shoulders. Glancing sideways, she was surprised to see tenderness in his brown eyes.

"Don't worry, Sis. Everything will work out."

She smiled and relaxed. "You think so, Eddie?"

"Sure. Don't tell Jim about it being Cole's baby. He's thick-headed enough not to know the difference, and what he don't know won't hurt him. You can handle Old Lady Reed if she suspects anything."

"Why, Eddie, you're smarter than you look," Belle teased, but she was grateful for his advice.

"I'll ride with you to the Reeds."

"You don't have to—"

"I want to. A woman in your condition shouldn't journey alone."

Belle closed her eyes, fighting off a wave of self-pity. She turned in to her brother's arms and wept as he held her close and rocked her like a baby.

Chapter Ten

BELLE HAD BEEN SETTLED at Rich Hill less than a month when Cole Younger came riding up, accompanied by Jesse and Frank James and a couple of others from the old gang. Jim welcomed them with open arms, but Belle hung back, waiting for the other shoe to fall. She knew that Cole was up to something besides good ol' boy reunions.

Later that afternoon the men went outside with Jim, but Belle remained inside the white frame house and observed them from the window. They sat under a spreading oak, laughing and talking and slapping one another on the back. All, except for Cole. He kept staring at the window where Belle stood.

"How long will they be staying?" Mother Reed asked from behind Belle.

"How should I know? I'm not a mind reader," Belle retorted, falling into the short-tempered dialogue she used with her mother-in-law since moving back under the Reed roof. She wanted to get Mother Reed's goat and keep it. Once she announced her pregnancy, Belle didn't want Mother Reed to ruin everything by thinking too much and flapping her gums when she should keep her mouth shut.

"Jim don't need that kind of riffraff around him. He'll get in trouble."

"Jimmy doesn't need help to get into trouble. He looks for it." Belle laughed as she untied the apron from around her waist and neck, her attention momentarily caught by her husband, who was pointing his finger as if it were a Smith & Wesson. He's telling another windy tale, she thought. If he was half as rough and tough as he said he was, he'd be made out of metal instead of bone.

"He's a good boy."

"Yeah, sure." Belle rolled her eyes, thinking that Mother Reed was as bad as her own mother about wearing blinders. Thoughts of her husband were swept from her mind as Cole Younger finally broke rank and headed for the house. "Oh, Lord," Belle moaned, throwing aside the apron.

"What?" Mother Reed asked.

"Nothing." Belle grabbed her bonnet off its peg by the door and tugged it over her raven hair. "You just mind your business and let me mind mine."

"How come you're so tacky with me?"

" 'Cause you ask for it." Belle wrinkled her nose in a hateful expression before meeting Cole on the porch. "What can I do for you?"

"Take a walk with me," he said, cupping her elbow in his hand and manhandling her off the porch and around to the back of the house. Freshly plowed fields stretched to the horizon. They stepped over patches of last week's snow and tried to avoid the muddiest parts of the back yard.

"You haven't told Jim about the baby yet, have you?" Cole asked, letting her go and standing off to one side of her.

Her wicked tongue tingled and Belle delivered a sideswiping glare that made his eyes widen.

"Why are you looking at me like that?" he asked, inching

his chin back as if he were afraid she was going to use it for target practice. "You look like a she-devil."

"That's how I'm feeling these days. I've been used, refused, and ignored, but no more." She shook her head in a rock-ribbed denial. "You're looking at a new Myra Maybelle, and this one isn't going to lay out her feelings so that somebody in cowboy boots can trample all over them." She dropped her gaze to his rattlesnake-skin boots. "That goes double for you, cowboy."

"Did I do this to you?"

"No, you did *this* to me," she said, illustrating herself by placing her hands on her belly. "And *this* did this to me. I've got another life to plan besides my own now. I can't live one day at a time anymore, thinking of no one but myself. I haven't been a good daughter or a good sister or a good wife, but by damn, I'm going to be a good mother, come hell or high water."

His hands rode his waist and he studied the tips of his boots for a full minute before he could find anything to say.

"I've been thinking—"

"Uh-oh." Belle crossed her arms at her waist and frowned at a distant spot where the frozen fields met the pale gray sky. "Here we go. I knew you'd come here for something besides trading stories about the old days."

"I came here for several reasons, and one of them has to do with us."

"Us?" Belle laughed harshly. "There is no 'us.' "

"There could be."

She eyed him again from the side and it seemed to irritate him so that he came to stand in front of her so that she'd have to look at him, face to face.

"I reacted from the gut back in Scyene," he said, taking hold of her shoulders. "Now that I've had time to mull this over, I think I might have been too hasty. We could go back to Scyene and give it a try, couldn't we? If I can settle down with any woman, it'll be you."

"Where in Scyene?"

"At the place I bought."

"I thought that your brothers and mother were living there with you."

"They are."

She nodded sagely and a bitter smile tipped up one side of her mouth. "Just what I need. Another family to intrude on. If that's all you've got to offer, then forget it. Hell, I've got that here!" She flung her arms wide to take in the rolling land, then let them flap against her sides in a display of frustration.

"What do you want, Belle?" he asked with a weary note.

"I want to be queen bee somewhere," she answered before twisting away from him when he reached for her again.

"Okay, I'll buy us our own place."

His simple offer knocked the wind out of her. For a few moments she fantasized about telling him that she'd go off with him, let him buy her a place, give him a trial period of being a husband and a father before he made the final decision to stay with her or to leave her forever. Such a lovely dream, she thought with her eyes closed and her heart full of it and of him. But dreams were a fool's gold.

Cole came up behind her and his arms closed around her waist. His lips brushed the side of her neck and then moved up to her ear as he bent over her like a rangy willow tree.

"I wish I could promise you a beautiful life. God knows, you deserve it. All I can promise is that I'll try. I told you about this restlessness I've got inside me, almost like there's unfinished business I've got to see to. The feeling haunts me, but you haunt me too. I close my eyes and think of you, and when I think of you I want you, and when I want you I can't think of anything else but of being inside you . . . deep, deep inside."

"Oh, Cole." Her knees liquefied and she was glad for his arms around her. Heat built between her legs and in her stomach—in her stomach where his child grew. "I can resist almost anything but you and your sweet talking. Sometimes I wish we'd never met. Life wouldn't be as rich without you, but it'd be a hell of a lot less complicated."

"Give me a year to get used to being one of two . . . uh, three." His mouth slipped to her cheek and he turned her face until their lips could meet. "How about it?"

Belle shut the door on her dreams and escaped from his arms. She turned, drawing a deep breath. She summoned her inner strength.

His smile was sweetly hopeful, yanking at her heartstrings.

"Cole, I can't. Jim Reed might be lame-brained, weak-willed, and self-indulgent, but he did something that you wouldn't do. He married me." She glanced around sadly. "This isn't a castle, but it's not a ditch by the side of the road either. Jimmy's no great lover, but he'll accept this baby. I know he will. I've got to go with the sure things now that I've got another being to look after. You and me aren't a sure thing, and I doubt if we ever could be. You're as unpredictable as a rogue wind." She laughed, winning a smile from him as she reached out shyly and plucked at the front of his chambray shirt. "I guess that's one of the main reasons why I love you like I do. You're the best lover I'll ever know, but you're not cut out to be a good husband or father. I know that. You know that."

"But we could try," he suggested, catching her hand in his.

"No." She looked away from his pleading expression and jerked her hand away. Her heart was breaking. "I want to be beautiful things to you. I saw that cornered look that came over your face when I told you I was carrying a baby. I don't want to be a burden to you."

"You won't. I swear it! I think we can be good for each other."

"No, Cole." She smiled in a wistful, wishing way. "We're good for each other in spurts, but not for the long haul. Let's be satisfied with what we've had and what we've been to each other. Let's not ruin it by trying something we both know we'll fail at."

He chewed on the inside of his lip and walked in a tight, agitated circle before stopping before her.

"I don't like the idea of Jim raising my child."

"He won't," Belle said with certainty. "I will. Jim will just be around. That's what he's good for—being around."

"The way you talk about him . . ." Cole laughed under his breath and rubbed the back of his neck in a distracted way. "It sounds as if you don't give a damn for him."

"Oh, but I do. I know his limitations, and I've accepted them."

"What about me?" Cole asked, holding her in place when she started to walk away.

"You'll survive, and so will I." She stared at his hand on her upper arm until he let go. Then she went briskly back to the house to deal with her nosy mother-in-law, who had been watching them from one of the back windows.

The other Reeds, except for Jim and Sol, had gone discreetly to bed, but Belle had not followed suit. Ignoring Frank James's pointed glare, savoring Jesse's mischievous smirk, acknowledging Cole's hesitant smile, and mirroring Jim's pleased grin, Belle sat down at the "men only" kitchen table.

"We've got business to discuss," Frank said, throwing Belle a black look. "Skedaddle."

Belle looked behind her in feigned confusion. "Are you talking to me? Because if you are, you're wasting your breath. I'm not going anywhere."

"This is man talk," Frank insisted, flinging off Jesse's warning hand on his arm. "Jim, see to your wife before I do."

"Why don't you simmer down before I have to take you outside and beat the shit out of you," Cole said, surprising everyone at the table. Frank's mouth dropped open, surprised at being threatened by a normally cool-headed Cole Younger. "You've got a short memory, Frank. Belle's one of us from way back, and that gives her the right to be here." Cole held Frank's angry glare, matching it with a fire all his own. "You got something to say to me, Frank?" Cole challenged when the silence seemed unending.

Jesse laughed nervously, breaking the tension by slapping his brother on the back. "Hell, yes! Belle's as honest as the day is long. You remember that, Frank. We don't mind one bit that she sits in on this powwow."

Cole would always be her champion. He's become an outlaw, she thought with a tiny smile. She'd never seen him as such until this moment, facing the madness of Frank James without flinching. Heavenly days! Cole Younger and the James Brothers were as tough as beef jerky, as brassy as spittoons, and as dangerous as desert rattlers.

"What've y'all got up your sleeves?" Sol asked, eager to commence. With George and Jasper married and living lives as straight as arrows, Solomon had thrown in with his younger brother Jim.

"We're planning a robbery, not a crooked card game," Jesse said with dry humor. "And we're willing to cut you in, Solly. You and Jimmy, of course."

Belle's temper flared and her glance at Cole was rapier sharp. So, Cole had come here for Jimmy and not for her after all. The weasel! Coming on to her with all that honeyed talk, just to sweeten her up so that she'd let Jim ride off with him on some harebrained scheme. Well, she'd fix his wagon!

"Jim, I'll understand if you'd rather hold off this time," Cole spoke up. His partners looked at him as if he'd come unwrapped. "I told Jesse that you had responsibilities here and that it'd be foolish of you to leave Belle and—"

"Belle can take care of herself," Jim cut in. "Tell me about this job. Where is it?"

"That's the spirit!" Jesse slapped Jim on the back, all the while skinning his teeth at Belle. He knew she was doing a slow burn and he loved it. Jesse loved to watch Belle's eyes smoke like a brushfire. "I told Cole, 'Don't you worry about old Slim Jim. He's got an outlaw heart and he won't be able to pass up this little jewel. Hell, it'll be like taking candy from a baby.' "

Belle pressed her hands flat against her stomach and warred with Cole, eyeball to eyeball, across the table.

His eyes told her that she had it all wrong. Her eyes said that he was a damned liar. His eyes spoke to her of trust, regret, and respect. Her eyes stubbornly rejected his tributes. His were softly blue and begging for understanding.

Her eyes smarted with sentimental tears and damned him for finding her weak spots and driving his love into them. She lowered her lashes in a grudging surrender, letting the curtain fall on the play of tense, turbulent emotions.

". . . since Missouri has become such a hotbed of law enforcement," Jesse was saying, trapping Belle's wandering attention. "We've set our sights on Kentucky."

"Kentucky? Where in Kentucky?"

"Russellville," Frank answered. "What difference does that make anyways?"

Belle heaved a sigh and delivered a worried frown in Frank's direction. "Well, if you don't know, then it won't do me any good to explain it to you."

"I never liked your attitude," Frank said with a snarl.

"Oh yeah? Well, I never liked your face, so what's that got to do with the price of beans? I thought we were talking business, not likes and dislikes."

Frank began easing up from his chair like a snake from its hole. "You listen here, you little—"

"Hey, hey!" Jim slammed a fist down on the table. "Don't forget that this is my house and that there is my wife."

Belle settled back, folding into herself like a pampered cat. Frank settled back, coiling again and ready to strike if Belle or anybody else gave him the chance.

"What's so special about Russellville?" Sol asked.

"Nothing's special about it," Cole said. "There's a bank there that looks promising. An old Yankee fart by the name of Nimrod Long owns it."

"Right," Jesse joined in, his eyes sparkling with devil-may-care. "Easy pickings. I figure we can make off with ten thousand as easy as making an apple pie."

"Right, right," Belle said, nodding. "And you've made so many pies, haven't you?" She exchanged wicked, grimacing grins with Jesse. "How well do you know that territory? How long have you had this bank staked out?"

A lantern sat in the center of the table and its light flickered over the faces around the table. Belle studied each one in turn, catching the uncertainty and flicker of panic. Jim and Sol were already sold on the deal. Belle could tell by the way they were licking their lips and trying to keep from grinning like a couple of jackasses. The Reed boys were adept at going off half-cocked.

"Nobody's staked it out, as such," Jesse admitted. "Donny Pence has been there and he's the one who told me about it."

"Nobody at this table has eyeballed the place?" Jim asked, and Belle was relieved to discover that Jim wasn't so far gone that he'd shut down his brain entirely.

"No, but we're agonna," Frank said. "We haven't gone over every little detail yet. We're getting the men for the job and then we'll plan it."

"I heard that you boys were making hay by robbing banks and the like," Solly said, spittle flying. He always spit when he was excited. Belle pitied the Carthage girl he was seeing of late. "I never thought you'd ask me and Jim along on one of your jobs. What do you say, Jimbo? We could use some extra cash."

Jim glanced at Belle and shrugged. "I need to hear more before I fall in line."

"Well, there ain't no more," Frank said, glaring at Belle as if she were the one holding out instead of Jim. "Like we told you, we're getting the men together and then we'll hammer out the details later. Me and Jesse know what we're doing, so don't worry none about pulling off the job. When we rob a bank, it gets robbed and we get away with no trouble a'tall. Right, brother?"

"Right." Jesse grinned like a monkey at Belle. "What say, little sister?"

"What do you care what she thinks?" Frank asked, clearly exasperated with Jesse. "We came here to listen to Jim, not his woman."

"Wife," Belle corrected. "There's a big difference among civilized people. I don't expect you to know about that, so you're excused."

Frank pounded the table with one fist, almost overturn-ing the lamp. "I'll not have you speaking to me like that!"

He reached for his gun, but didn't even get it out of his holster before Cole's pearl-handled Colt revolver was in his face. Frank had to cross his eyes to see the tip of the barrel.

"Take your hand away from your gun belt," Cole said, his voice deadly and steady like his gun hand. "I don't want to kill you, but I will if you don't sit down and act like you've got some sense."

"She provokes me," Frank said, almost whining with irritation.

"When you leave the door ajar, she can't help but walk in," Cole said. "Just put your hands on top of the table and apply your butt to the chair again. That's right." Cole holstered his own gun and addressed Belle, although he didn't look at her. "How about keeping a rein on that runaway tongue of yours, just to be on the safe side, okay?"

"Okay." Belle folded her arms against her breasts and pushed out her lower lip in a pout. She felt thoroughly scolded and she didn't like it.

"You in or out?" Jesse asked, staring holes through Jim, who squirmed in his seat. "Well?"

"I don't know," Jim said, slapping at the back of his neck as if ants were marching down it.

"Sounds like a honey to me," Sol said, his voice inching upward along with his blood pressure. Saliva gathered in one corner of his mouth, making him resemble a mad dog.

"Does it?" Jim asked, glancing at Sol and catching the fever in his eyes. "It does sound mighty tempting at that! So tempting that I couldn't pass up a—"

"Jimmy," Belle said, stopping him just short of his deci-sion to ride. "I've got to talk to you alone for a minute."

"Not now," Frank said. "We're talking to him now."

"Right this instant," Belle said, standing up and feeling

no fear. Frank had never scared her. He had the scare in on everybody but her and Cole. "Come outside with me, Jimmy. This can't wait."

"But, Belle—"

"Outside!" Belle strode from the room and out to the porch, her skirts twisting around her legs.

"Belle, what in God's name couldn't wait until my business in there was finished?" Jim asked, slamming the door behind him. "Sometimes you make me so damned mad that I—"

"You can't go with them," Belle interrupted, placing her hands against his shirtfront and rising up on tiptoe to be eye level with him.

"And why not?"

"Because I'm not taking the chance of having this baby alone, that's why. I want my child to have a father and I want that father to be you."

"B-baby?" He stared at her, his face as void of expression as that of a dead coon's, then he grinned ear-to-ear. "You're ribbing me."

"I'm not." She smiled back at him. "So you can't leave now, Jimmy. I need you here with me."

"Well, hell yes!" Jim wrapped his arms around her waist and lifted her high, whirling around in a circle as she threw back her head and laughed with him. "Nobody could take me away from you, honey bunch! I'm staying right here until you put that babe in my arms."

Belle kissed him hard, then sighed when the kiss softened and lingered, causing a simmering in her heart.

"Oh, Jimmy, when you kiss me like that I want to cry," she confessed, wishing it could always be so. "I think I love you more now than I've ever loved you before." She pressed her face into the curve of his neck and hoped the child would cement their union, which had always seemed doomed, temporary, in flux.

"When's it due?"

"I-I don't know for certain. In about eight months, I reckon."

"Eight months," he said, closing his eyes to count.

"November," Belle supplied, then wondered if she hadn't slipknotted her own noose. "Maybe earlier. First babies sometimes come two or three months early." She held her breath, wondering if he'd cut the rope or let her swing.

"Really? So it could be here by the end of summer?"

"Maybe," Belle said, breathing again. "September, perhaps."

"That's great. I hope we don't have to wait until November. I've always wanted a son."

"Or daughter."

"Oh, sure. I guess it could be a girl."

"Would that upset you?" Belle asked, disturbed by the wilting pitch of his voice.

"Not if she looks like you," Jimmy said, laughing again. "I'd spoil her, but it'd be fun."

"A baby is what we need," Belle said, lounging back in the circle of his arms. "We can do without bank robbery." She glanced at the door, thinking of the plotting men on the other side of it. "You want to tell them or do you want me to?"

"I'll tell them." Jim released her, puffed out his chest, and opened the door. "Boys, count me out."

"Aw hell!" Jesse applied the flat of his hand to the table top. "What did you say to him, Belle? You've got him so pussy-whipped that he can't take a sh—"

"Not that it's any of your damned business," Belle said, glaring spitefully at Jesse and raising her voice to a near shout, "but I happen to be with child." She linked her arm in Jimmy's and tipped up her chin in triumph.

"Congratulations, you two." Jesse hung his head, subdued and sheepish.

Belle brought her gaze around to Cole and her gladness was instantly dissipated by his visible regret. His mouth curved into an upside-down smile that wasn't quite a frown, more like a restrained grimace. He didn't shrug, but Belle felt it nonetheless. It was as if he'd said, "That's that. You've made your choice, selected your lie, and that's what we've both got to live with from here on in."

"Well, hey!" Jimmy hugged Belle to his side and laughed nervously. "Is that all y'all have to say about my news? It sure is quiet around this here table."

Sol jumped up and pumped his brother's hand.

"I'm tickled pink for you," Sol said, chuckling and spitting and turning red. "Ma will sure be glad to hear it." His gaze bounced to and from Belle. "It oughta be a fine-looking boy. Yessiree, bob."

Cole stood up and offered Jim his hand. "Put her there, Pops," he said, managing a heartfelt grin. "I don't blame you one bit for staying behind. If it were my decision, I wouldn't leave Belle either."

Jim shook Cole's hand and the other men rose and submitted their rowdy congratulations to the father-to-be. The mother-to-be left the room, unnoticed and unquestioned. For the first time in her life, she felt like a sinner.

The baby girl was born on a bright, breezy September day in 1868. Mother Reed was on hand during the eight-hour labor, assisted by a neighborly midwife. The child had cobalt-blue eyes, uptilted like her mother's, and her father's dimples. The babe was a strawberry blond. Mother Reed found this extremely fascinating.

"Heavens to Betsy, where did this child get her red-tinted

hair?" Mother Reed exclaimed minutes after handing the babe over to her son. "None of us Reeds ever had red hair. Don't recall seeing any carrot-topped Shirleys neither."

"You haven't met the entire Shirley brood," Belle told her. "We're either blackheaded or redheaded. My grandmother was red-haired."

"That so?" Mother Reed asked, arching a brow at Belle.

"That's so!"

"She's mighty pretty," Jim cooed. "I like her hair. I think it's the prettiest hair I ever did see."

Belle smiled saucily at Mother Reed, then screwed up her face in an overt comeuppance smirk.

"Her hair makes me think of roses," Jim said in a whispery voice that new fathers often adopt. "Let's call her Rosie. Rosie . . . Lee!"

"Lee?" Mother Reed and Belle echoed in unison.

"Yes, after General Robert E. Lee," Jim proclaimed, making his arms a rocking cradle.

"Shouldn't you wait and name one of your sons after Lee?" Mother Reed ventured.

"No, it's a good name for a girl. A courageous name. Right, Belle?"

"Right. Rosie Lee is a fine name." Belle held out her arms and took the baby from her husband. "Time to feed this pretty thing," she said, fitting one of her taut nipples into the babe's rosebud mouth. Rosie Lee tugged hungrily, making Belle think of the baby's father and how he loved her generous breasts.

Where was Cole now? she wondered. She'd heard that the Russellville robbery had gone off without a hitch. Solly said he'd heard that the James Brothers and a couple of the Youngers had hightailed it into California because things were heating up for them in Missouri and Texas. Jesse had an uncle in California who ran a sanitarium. A perfect place for outlaws to rest and heal up from any wounds they might have suffered. Had Cole been wounded? Was he laid up in some loony bin in California? Oh, to have word from him! Not knowing for sure was driving her to distraction.

She looked at her baby, wondering what Thomas Coleman Younger would think of this pink-cheeked, sleepy-eyed stranger. Her wispy, pale red hair curled like a woolly cap, and Belle ran a careful hand over the baby's damp head.

"Rosie Lee," Jim said, leaning down to kiss the baby's forehead and then Belle's. "Get some rest, both of you."

"We'll do that," Belle promised, smiling as Jim and his mother left her alone with her child. The baby closed her eyes and drifted off.

"Rosie Lee." Belle shook her head, frowning at the name. "I guess it's good enough to put on a birth certificate, but it doesn't seem quite right."

Belle shifted slightly in the bed, rousing the baby in her arms, who started suckling again. A memory floated back to Belle. A memory of a burnished blond man who spoke like a poet.

"You're my pearl," Belle whispered, kissing her child's satiny button nose. "That's what you are to me. Mama's pearl."

Chapter Eleven

BELLE FOUGHT BACK TEARS as the minister completed his eulogy and the first shovelful of dirt clattered on the pine coffin containing the remains of Edwin Benton Shirley. Sensing her mother's misery, Pearl began to whimper fretfully in Belle's arms.

Tall and stern-faced Scott Reed, one of Jim's older brothers, stood beside Belle, making her feel small and frail. Jim hadn't been home when the news of Edwin's murder reached them, so Mother Reed insisted that Scott accompany Belle back to Texas for the funeral. Jim was hardly ever home lately.

Belle let Scott guide her from the gravesite to the wagon. He handed her and Pearl up to the seat and took his place beside her.

"Who shot Edwin?" he asked when they were on their way back to the Shirley house.

"I don't know . . . some lawman," Belle said, dabbing at her burning eyes with a handkerchief. "He got shot for stealing horses." She shivered, realizing that Jim could be next. "The law is cracking down on horse thieves. It's not safe anywhere anymore."

"It's safe at Youngers Bend," Scott said. "The law stays away from Tom Starr and his bunch."

"Why?"

"Because Tom is one mean son-of-a-bitch, that's why." Scott chuckled and switched the wad of tobacco from one cheek to the other.

"You've met him?" Belle asked, draping her handkerchief across Pearl's face to keep the sun off the babe's delicate complexion.

"Yeah, I've met him." Scott shook all over like he was trying to shake off a bad omen. "He's a strange old guy. He's dark-skinned, but he's got light-colored eyes that don't hardly ever blink. Makes him look like some kind of spook."

"I don't like the thought of Jimmy hanging around someone like that."

"He's a good friend to have," Scott said, turning his face away from Belle for a moment to spit tobacco juice. "If you make the Starrs your friends, they'll put their lives down for you. Can't say that about many folks these days."

"Let's quit talking about dying. I've had enough of it for a spell. This is the second brother I've buried in the past five years."

"Was you two close?" Scott asked, looking along the long bridge of his nose at her.

Belle nodded, grateful that Pearl couldn't inherit the Reed Roman nose.

"He was young, wasn't he?"

"Not yet twenty." Belle's eyes filled with tears of futility. "It makes me mad, you know. Me and Eddie got to be good friends last Christmas when I was here with the folks. We used to fuss and fight, but we got close last year. He had so many big dreams. He wanted to make something of himself. I guess he got sidetracked some."

"It's a damn shame. You find out who shot him, and me and Jim will come back and take care of business."

"No." Belle held Pearl closer. "Jimmy takes enough stupid risks as it is. What's done is done. Another killing won't bring Edwin back to us."

"But it'll set things square."

"It'll just add another tombstone to the cemetery." She pointed to the turnoff road up ahead. "There's the road that leads to the house. Not that you could miss it. Looks like the whole town of Scyene showed up. Ed would be fit to be tied if he could see this. Hell, he didn't know half of these people."

She grinned, laughing a little as a thought struck her. "I'd bet money that he's stolen horses from most of these people. He wasn't particular like Jim. Ed took from Rebels and Yankees alike."

"That ain't right," Scott mumbled, shaking his bull's head. "We Rebs got to stick together."

Belle sighed. "You know how some of the young boys are, Scott. They have short memories."

"Yeah, but it ain't right. Damn Yankees. I'll never forget!"

"Me neither," Belle intoned. "And I'll never forgive."

Several buggies and wagons sat in the porch yard, and neighbor women were spreading oilcloths on two long tables set in the shade of towering ancient oaks. Others carried bowls and platters of food. Every funeral in the South was followed by covered-dish feasts as if a full stomach made death easier to swallow.

Belle joined her mother in the two-seater swing hung from a hefty oak limb in the side yard. Eliza and John Shirley had aged five years in the past one. Belle placed Pearl into her mother's arms.

Another Christmas was bearing down on them, less than two weeks away, but the weather was uncommonly mild as autumn clung to the countryside in a stubborn last stand. Shawls were all the women needed and most of the men were in their shirtsleeves this solemn day.

"One life ends and another takes hold," Mrs. Shirley said as she rocked the baby. "Does Jim accept this child as his?"

"Yes." Belle pulled her black shawl closer around her shoulders. "Jim is her father."

"My first redheaded grandchild," Mrs. Shirley mused, touching the strawberry-blond curls on the babe's head. "Her skin is mighty fair. Kind of like porcelain."

"She's ivory-skinned and delicate like the strand of pearls Grandma Hatfield gave you on your wedding day," Belle said.

Pearl grew fretful and Eliza handed her back to Belle. Glancing around at the milling people, Belle pulled a cloth from her belt and draped it over her shoulder and Pearl's head. She reached underneath it, unfastened her dress's bodice, and let the baby nurse.

"I buried *this* son," Mrs. Shirley said without preamble. "I'll thank you to remember it."

Belle turned wide eyes upon her mother. She hadn't forgotten their bitter argument last Christmas. So, her mother was also nursing. Not a babe, but hurt feelings.

"Mama, I'm sorry I yelled at you about that. . . . I never was one to beat around the bush, and I sure didn't think a buttoned lip was the way to deal with your unstable mind."

"I wasn't unstable."

"Wh-what?" Belle asked with a startled chuckle. "Mama, you acted like nothing bad was happening. When Bud visited, you hardly acknowledged him. Most of the time you pretended we were farming when we were running a hotel!"

"I drifted, that's all. I wasn't crazy." Eliza Shirley's chin jutted out, rock hard and pointy. "But I buried Edwin today and I didn't fall to pieces. My boy was shot off his horse, dead before he hit the ground. But I didn't sh-shed a t-tear . . ."

"Mama, Mama," Belle crooned, fitting her free arm around her mother's shaking shoulders. Eliza pressed her face into the curve of Belle's neck and sobbed. "You've got a right to drift, Mama. If I'd buried two strapping sons, I'd be driftier than a hand-fashioned compass. I shouldn't have said anything to you about it. Now that I've got my own baby . . . now that I'm a mother, well, it scares me silly to think that something bad might happen to my Pearl. If I had to bury her, I'd just as soon lie down with her and let them put dirt over both of us because I'd be dead too."

"I didn't do right by you," Mrs. Shirley said against Belle's neck, "but I so love my boys. My beautiful, brave boys."

Belle grew cold inside as her mother killed whatever pity Belle had been feeling for her. It was one thing to know in her heart that her mother favored her sons, but to hear her say it aloud was almost unbearable. She took her arm from around her mother, plucked her nipple from Pearl's lax mouth, and buttoned her dress. Since coming back to Texas, she'd placed Pearl in Mrs. Shirley's arms a dozen times and she hadn't held the baby more than a minute before giving her back to Belle. Daughters were dirt, sons were gold.

Not in *my* family, Belle swore to herself as she gazed down at her carrot-topped wonder. No matter how many sons or daughters she had, she'd love them equally and wholly. She looked up to spot long-legged Mannie and gawky Shug.

"Boys," she called, "get over here and tend to your mama. She's prostrate with grief over Ed. This isn't a picnic, you know!"

They scowled and dragged their feet over to her. Eliza Shirley wiped her eyes and seemed to come back to the living.

"No, no. You boys go on and have a good time," she said.

"A good time?" Belle echoed. "They just buried their brother!"

"Go on, boys." Eliza hugged each, sending them off to mingle with the other boys who'd come with their parents.

Belle stood up, baby in arms, and gave a cursory glance at her sister-in-law Mary.

"Mother Shirley," Mary said in a honey-dripping voice, "you poor dear! Let me sit a spell with you. Put your head on my shoulder, dear heart. That's right . . . that's right . . . I'm here now."

Belle gritted her teeth, grinding them to keep from screaming. *That's right, that's right,* she mimicked in her mind. Eliza Shirley loved Mary better than her own daughter because Mary was Preston's wife and Preston had always been the favorite son.

"Scott, let's set off for home," Belle said, stopping beside the other stranger in the crowd.

"Now?" Scott asked, bewildered by her sudden request. "We haven't ate nothing yet and—"

"Now. I'll say my farewells to my father and then we'll be off. I want to get home."

Home, she thought, bittersweetly. Rich Hill was the only home she had left. It was where she belonged.

Mother Reed fingered the French lace bordering Pearl's pinafore and suspicion made her eyes gleam.

"Where do you get the money for such fine clothes for this here baby?" she asked after a few moments of silent speculation.

"Where do you think?" Belle lay back and stared up at the blue sky. Winter had passed, a mild winter that brought snow only once to Missouri. On this March day, the trees were trying to bud and patches of soft grass dotted the countryside.

"It ain't coming from this place. We haven't had a decent foal born here in more than a year, and our crops barely keep us in food. Is Jim stealing horses for you?"

"He isn't doing anything for me. If he's stealing, he's doing it for himself."

"But you're buying pretty clothes for you and the baby with that ill-gotten money."

"And I'm keeping the tax man away from our door with that money, too," Belle pointed out. "Mother Reed, do yourself a favor and just quit wondering about things and asking a bunch of stupid questions that you don't want answered with the truth."

"You're used to finer things, and Jimmy works day and night trying to keep you and that baby in style."

"If you believe that, then I could sell you a stick with one end," Belle said, cackling at the thought of James Reed working day and night at anything other than a winning poker hand. "You want the truth? He and his brothers are stealing horses and running them into Youngers Bend. The Starrs sort through them, sell most of them, and take some of them into Arkansas to enter in races. There's the truth. It isn't pretty, is it?"

"And you're letting my boys do such things?"

Belle propped herself up on her elbows and delivered a bewildered glare to her white-haired mother-in-law. "And how the hell am I supposed to keep them down on the farm? Do you think I want Jimmy galloping all over the country while I sit here with nothing to do but worry and pray for him every Sunday in church?"

"What do you do of a evening when you slip out under the cover of night and stay gone an hour or two?" Mother Reed squinted her eyes as if she'd caught Belle in a torrid affair. "You didn't think I knew about them nights, did you? I know you snuck out a week ago around midnight and didn't come back till almost daylight."

A devilish thought struck Belle. It was so easy to get her mother-in-law's goat. "What do you think I was doing? Do you think I was meeting a man out there in the bushes?"

"I wouldn't be surprised," Mother Reed said with a little sniff as she flipped Pearl over on her tummy so that the baby could kick and practice crawling. "Maybe you're seeing Rosie's real daddy. Maybe you're thinking of getting Rosie Lee a brother off him, hmmm?"

"Maybe so," Belle agreed with a catlike purr. "Jimmy wants a son."

"His *own* son," Mother Reed amended. "I know who it is . . . I know who fathered Rosie Lee. It was that scoundrel Cole Younger. He's the one you sneak off to see, ain't he?"

Belle tired of the cat-and-mouse game and lay down on her back to contemplate the fluffy clouds above her again. "It's Jimmy I've been meeting."

"Jim? Why for would you sneak off to see your own husband?"

"Because he doesn't want to be tracked here and he doesn't want nosy neighbors and family to mess up his plans. He brings money and we divide the cash, then he heads out for Youngers Bend." She smiled and stretched lazily. " 'Course sometimes we peck and coo out there in the bushes before he rides off. You got to get your loving while the getting's good, you know."

"I don't want to hear such talk!"

Belle laughed at Mother Reed's flustered state. "Lord above, woman. You got yourself a dozen children, and you can't convince me that you got all twelve while you weren't looking! You and old Sol must have hit the feather bed every chance you got."

"Hush up that filthy talk!" Mother Reed gathered Pearl in her arms in a protective embrace. "And in front of your own baby, too! You should be ashamed!"

"Oh, lawdy, I am! I am!" Belle giggled and rolled side to side in the grass, to the horror of her straitlaced mother-in-law.

"Grab a hold of yourself, girlie," Mother Reed said, looking from Belle to the approaching horse and rider. "Stranger's acomin'."

Belle sobered in the blink of an eye and was on her feet before Mother Reed could draw a decent breath. Shading her eyes with one hand, she examined the interloper but couldn't identify him. He rode a pinto that reminded her of Queenie. He was tall for his age, but he was no more than thirteen or fourteen. A boy. An Indian boy with straight black hair hanging in twin pigtails with feathers stuck in them.

"Who goes there?" Belle asked, wishing for her shotgun.

He reined the horse a yard from them but made no move to dismount. His eyes were dove gray, triggering a snatch of conversation in Belle's memory about an Indian with light eyes.

"Are you one of the Starr boys?" she asked.

He nodded.

"What do you want? Jimmy's not here. He's off somewhere with his brothers Sol and Scott."

The Indian boy shook his head.

Belle stepped in front of Mother Reed and Pearl in a purely instinctive gesture of maternal protection.

"Can't you talk, boy?"

"I can." His voice was a pleasingly deep baritone, unusual in a boy of his age. Boys in their teens usually squeaked like stuck pigs.

"So, talk!"

"I come here to take you to James Reed."

Belle glanced over the Indian's buckskin breeches, fringed jacket, and scuffed boots. The pony was lathered. He'd ridden a long ways.

"Where's Jim?" She reached back and grabbed one of Mother Reed's hands. "Is he dead?"

"No, he lives at the place of my family."

"Why didn't Jimmy come here himself? Why did he send you?"

"Too dangerous to come here."

Belle sighed and looked back at Mother Reed, releasing the older woman's cold hand. "What do you make of this?"

"He's a savage," Mother Reed whispered, her eyes large with fear. "Don't you dare go off with a heathen like that one!"

"Fiddlesticks," Belle scoffed. "He's just a boy in pigtails."

"You pack bag and bring baby," the Indian said.

Belle moved closer, drawn by his proud bearing and silvery eyes. "What's your name, boy?"

"I am named Sam."

Belle pointed toward the watering trough. "You rest your horse and give him a drink while I pack that bag."

"You're not going off with him, are you?" Mother Reed wailed.

"I sure as hell am. Jimmy wants us with him, and we're going."

"That Indian might be lying!"

"No," Belle said, exchanging a long look with the young Indian. "He's not lying. Dress Pearl in traveling clothes and have one of the boys saddle Dazzle for me."

"But this Indian might cut your throat or scalp you," Mother Reed whispered loudly, following along behind Belle like a scared puppy. "No telling what he's up to."

"Jimmy sent him, so he's okay. Besides, I've always wanted

to see Youngers Bend and meet the notorious Tom Starr. This here is my chance and I'm not about to pass it up."

"Belle Reed!"

Belle and Mother Reed both turned toward the Indian, who was still astride his pinto. He brought the horse up closer to them, looking down from his height advantage.

"Yes, what is it?" Belle asked.

"James Reed sends message to you and other Reeds."

Pearl chose that moment to issue a hunger wail, and Belle took the baby from Mother Reed. She bounced Pearl against her shoulder, trying to pacify her until she could get inside and feed her.

"What's the message? I'm not standing here all day while this baby cries in my ear!"

"Jim Reed says Scott Reed is dead."

Mother Reed screamed like a banshee, but Belle took the news like a woman who'd come to expect death as others expect the sun to rise each morning.

"Amanda! Sarah!" Belle called to her two sisters-in-law. "Come here and see to your mama. She's had an awful shock." She headed for the house again but paused long enough to glare at the impassive Indian.

"You need to learn some tact, boy. It's a wonder you didn't kill that old woman with news like that."

Chapter Twelve

YOUNGERS BEND was a naturally constructed fortress. Located in the great elbow of the South Canadian River, the land was buttressed by mountains and foothills. Faces of sheer cliffs rose up on either side of the trail, leading to the heart of the Starr Ranch and providing excellent lookout points. No one could enter this bountiful land without being eyeballed or ambushed.

The primitive beauty touched a chord in Belle. She had dreamed of owning a ranch like this where she'd raise horses and rule a large family in a house fit for a queen. The dream came back to her in all its glory, making her yearn again for better days. . . . She imagined Cole riding along this narrow trail ribboned by wildflowers and budding trees. They had spent their youth defending a land that no longer existed.

But this place—this place of verdant forests, swift streams, and even a rushing river—this place reminded Belle of those shattered dreams, giving her a sense of hope for the future. This was God's country and anything seemed possible.

Youngers Bend was a kingdom unto itself, with old Tom

Starr ruling it with an iron fist and thumbing his nose at white man's law and edicts. Indian land, beyond the jurisdiction of U.S. Grant and his Yankee laws. Oh, to be autonomous, Belle thought with a wishful smile as her yearning intensified. To pull these great cliffs close around you in a sheltering embrace. No wonder Cole had made this crook of the wild Canadian his second home.

"How come you ride in that saddle?" Sam Starr asked, surprising Belle with the first complete sentence he'd spoken since leaving the Reed ranch.

"Sidesaddle, you mean?" she asked, and he nodded once in a grave, stoic way. "It's more comfortable for me. I'm used to it." She shrugged. "I don't know. I've always liked sidesaddle. I guess it's a holdover from the days when I was a Southern lady." She laughed to herself and shifted Pearl from one arm to the other. "That was a long, long time ago."

"You not old."

"No, but I'm not young like you either."

"I not so young."

Belle glanced at his unlined face. "From here, you are. You're a boy. I've got brothers older than you."

"How come you didn't bawl like that old Reed woman when I tell of Scott dying?"

Belle drew a deep breath and released it in a nonchalant sigh. "I guess I'm saving my tears for big tragedies. Was Scott stealing horses when he was plugged?"

"Don't think so. Someone else's bullet got him. Jim will tell you."

"How many Starrs are there?"

He measured her with a glance. "Many."

She sighed. "How many brothers and sisters do you have?"

"Nine, but there are many more blood kin around Youngers Bend."

"I'll bet." Belle looked around at the thick brush and wild vegetation. "I like it here. It feels safe."

"Safe for friends, not enemies."

"Yes. That's why I like it." She smiled, enjoying the sense of omnipotence. "I can understand why Cole loves to stay here."

"Cole Younger?"

"Yes. You know him, don't you?"

Sam nodded, but his gaze sharpened as he studied the unusual light that appeared in her eyes. That name was magic medicine for Belle.

The Starr house was surrounded by a stand of young pine and plume-shaped sycamores. It was larger than the Reed's, although probably not as well built. The log cabin was in the shape of a U and had a porch running around three sides. Chickens and geese sat in the porch swing and nested in rocking chairs. Four baying hounds skidded around one side of the house and came loping toward Belle and Sam. Sam issued a high-pitched whistle and the hounds wagged their tails. Their ferocious growling became over-joyed whining.

Indian boys, pigtails flying, wrestled and romped in the yard. They paused long enough to greet their returning brother and eye the white woman and baby with him.

"Belle!" Jim Reed emerged from the house and flew off the porch and across the dirt yard. "Oh, honey, it's good to see you."

"Jimmy, help me down. Here, take Rosie." Belle transferred Pearl to Jim's waiting arms, then slipped from the saddle. She hooked an arm around her husband's neck and pulled him sideways for a smacking kiss. "Sam told me about Scott. What happened, hon?"

"How's Ma taking it?"

"How do you think? She's crying her eyes out."

193

Jim looked at the fussy baby in his arms. "Poor Rosie Lee. I bet she's all tuckered out."

"She's hungry."

"Come inside." Jim looked past Belle to Sam. "Thanks, partner. I owe you one."

Sam lifted a hand in response, then grabbed Dazzle's reins and led the horses toward the barn and water trough.

"Tom's not here right now," Jim said as he ushered Belle inside. "You can go into his room and close the door while you feed Rosie."

He went with her and perched on a trunk while Belle sat on the bed and nursed Pearl.

"So tell me about Scott," Belle urged.

"He just got caught in a crossfire between some warring families. By the time I got there—"

"Where?"

"Fort Smith."

"Where's his body?"

"Buried in a field outside of Fort Smith."

Belle sighed and rolled her eyes in exasperation. "Did you mark it at least?"

"We put a big rock on it and carved his initials in it," Jim said, then spread out his hands. "I couldn't haul him back to Rich Hill! Not with the law on my butt!"

"The law's on your butt? You mean you're a wanted man now?" She took note of the nervous waver in Jim's eyes and tick at the left side of his mouth. He was running scared. "Tell me, Jimmy."

"Trumped-up charges," he blurted out. "They say I brought liquor into the Territory. If Tom hadn't taken me in, I'd be in jail right now."

"Then we'll stay here with Tom for a while?"

"No, we can't. Tom's generosity is limited." He gestured wildly. "Hell, the law's all over the place looking for me!

Tom don't like it any more than I do, but it's not his trouble. It's mine, and I'm bringing too many lawmen down this way." His voice broke and he made a concerted effort for composure. "Belle, we've got to get going. I was thinking of California—"

"California?" She shook her head, slinging her thoughts into order. "Where in the hell would we go to in California? We've got no folks there or friends—"

"Wrong. We've got friends there." Jim's eyes sparkled as he hit on a right fine idea. "We could go to that sanitarium owned by Jesse and Frank's uncle. They say that it's a regular stronghold. Once you're in, nobody can come inside and get you. Everything will be fine if Jesse lets us stay there."

"Don't worry about Jesse," Belle said with confidence. "If he's at his uncle's, he'll have to let us stay."

"Why's that?" Jim asked, rocking his head to one side like a curious hound.

"Just because," Belle answered vaguely. "He can't turn us away, that's all."

"We'll be safe there until this all blows over."

"Until what blows over? Just what have you been doing while I've been stuck at Rich Hill like a bump on a log?"

"You know what I've been doing." He stood up, turning his back on her. He moved restlessly around the dark, windowless room. "I've been taking horses and running whiskey. I've been providing for you and Rosie. Been giving you a life of easy living."

"Easy living," Belle mused, thinking of putting up with Mother Reed's sly remarks about Pearl's sire, the daylight hours of endless chores, and the nighttime hours when Belle's punishing imagination wove scenes of Jim with other women.

"That's right. A fella's got to make a living when he's got a family."

"Jimmy, if you'd set your mind to making a go of the stud farm, we'd have plenty of money. You and your brothers know more about good horseflesh than anyone I've ever known. It's even rubbed off on me! I used to be a sorry judge of horses, but now I can look at one and tell whether it's an investment or a hardship."

"It's a little too late to be telling me you want a husband who lives by the straight and narrow," Jim said, casting a sour look her way. "You knew what I was doing and you took the money and kept your mouth shut about it."

"And if I'd asked you to stay home with me?" she argued, angry to be blamed for his lack of honest ambition. If he was going to be an outlaw, why didn't he just come out and say that was the way he wanted it? She'd never heard Jesse or Cole blaming their way of life on women or children.

"Ever since I met you, I've tried to keep you out of saloons and on the farm. What good has it done?" She plucked her tender nipple from Pearl's mouth and laid the baby on the pillows against the carved headboard. She buttoned her dress, her fingers trembling from aggravation and exhaustion. "I give up. I'm sick and tired of keeping you out of trouble." She walked across the room and stood before him, her hands on her hips, the expression in her eyes an open challenge.

"Keeping me out of trouble? Is that what you've been doing?" He thrust his face close to hers, half rising from the trunk. "Where I come from they call it nagging. Nag, nag, nag! I can't take a piss without you telling me how to hold it and where to point it!"

"It's a piss poor job that doesn't pay well, but somebody's got to do it!"

Jim rose to his feet like a shot. His furious expression suddenly gave way to a face-splitting grin, and before Belle could react to his mood change, he splayed his hands at the sides of her head and gave her a hard, blunt kiss. Examining her shocked expression, he laughed and kissed her again, more gently this time.

"We're a fine pair, ain't we?" he asked softly, brushing his lips and mustache across her cheek and threading his fingers through her dark hair. "I need you beside me through this. I know I haven't been a good husband lately, but I'll change. Go to California with me. I'll be so blamed lonely without my Belle and my Rosie Lee."

"Oh, Jimmy," Belle moaned, melting under his familiar kisses and boyish grin. "What am I going to do with you?"

"You have to ask?" he murmured. "Make love to me here and now. I've been walking funny for weeks thinking of you."

"Honey, you walk funny anyways," she said, laughing and tugging at his belt. "So I reckon nobody paid much notice."

His mouth slanted across hers with uncharacteristic passion. Belle's breath came in little gasps as Jim lifted her up and carried her toward the bed. She wound her arms around his neck, pressing her face into the warm cavity above his shoulder, and a feeling of sweet nostalgia swept over her, when suddenly the door rattled on its hinges.

"You got your wife in there, James Reed?" The voice was deep-throated and it vibrated in the rafters. The door burst open, slamming against the wall. A massive man filled the doorway. "This her? Bring her into the light. Let me see her. I want to see the crazy woman who married a lop-eared skunk like you."

Pearl's little face wrinkled into fret lines as the voice jarred her from sleep, and Belle laid a comforting hand on the baby's chest. Pearl immediately drifted back to sleep, calmed by her mother's touch.

"Lower your voice," Belle whispered as she hurried from the room with Jim at her heels. She elbowed Jim out of the way and closed the door on her sleeping child. "If you keep yelling like that my baby will never get to sleep."

"My house, my rules, woman," the big Indian said. "If that baby don't like it, I'll throw her out to the chickens and let them peck at her."

Belle turned on him, hands clenched into fists at her sides and the veins standing out in her long, slender neck.

"You do, and I'll pluck out your eyes and stuff them down your throat till you gag to death. Hear me, Injun?"

"Belle, Belle!" Jim's fingers closed at her elbows and he pulled her back against him and away from the iron-eyed Indian. "Hush your mouth. This is Tom Starr. *Tom Starr.*" Jim said the name the same way he would "Lucifer, the Beast." "She don't mean nothing by that, Tom. She's only—"

"I did mean it," Belle argued.

"Belle, honey, Tom was only fooling."

"I'm not fooling. I've got a good sense of humor, but I don't see anything funny about threats made against my child. I want that straight up front." She swung her shoulders, twisting them from Jim's clutching fingers. "Quit squeezing me like I'm a ripe melon!"

Jim laughed nervously. Tom Starr sized up Belle with iron-gray eyes. Belle returned the favor, studying him with eyes as black as coal.

He was no raving beauty, but he wasn't downright ugly either. The best that could be said for him was that he was successful at cultivating the image he wanted—that of a dangerously evil character.

His black-and-gray hair was straight, glossy, and shoulder-length, covered by a felt hat that had seen better days. At six feet six inches, he was imposing in his long, hand-fashioned coat of many colored squares with fur at the neck and cuffs. His long legs were encased in fringed buckskin and his boot tops stopped just above his knees. His face was unlined, although he was in his fifties, and his eyes were deep-socketed and piercing. At first Belle couldn't guess why his eyes were so disturbing; then it hit her. He had no eyelashes. She didn't know if it was a freak of nature or if he plucked them to make himself look all the more menacing.

Tom liked to get his bluff in early on people and keep it that way. He wanted everybody to tremble in their boots around him and jump when he said "rabbit." Belle wasn't in the mood for trembling or jumping.

"Are you going to just stand there with your bare face hanging out or are you going to offer your guest some refreshment? I rode all the way from Missouri and I'm as dry as a bone."

She heard Jim's mewling moan behind her, but she knew that she'd gone up a notch in Tom Starr's estimation. He grunted and clapped his hands. A rotund, moon-faced Indian woman dressed in a pair of pants and a flour-sack shirt sprinted into the room from outside.

"Whiskey," Tom said, and the woman leaped for the cabinets. Tom sat down at the table in the center of the room and pointed to the others. "Sit."

Belle and Jim sat down on either side of him. The Indian woman, presumably Tom's wife, set the whiskey bottle and three glasses on the table. Tom poured. His wife disappeared out the back door. Belle could see the woman's bent knees when she sat down wearily on an upended barrel just outside the door. A bucket of green pods sat beside her and she reached in to grab some for shelling.

"You," Tom said after he'd taken a healthy swig of the fiery liquid, "got much backbone for a woman."

"Belle's never been one to back down," Jim said, laughing with an edge of hysteria.

"You brave or just crazy?" Tom asked, ignoring Jim altogether.

Belle arched a brow, realizing that Tom Starr was enthralled with her.

"Sometimes they're the same thing," she answered after a few moments of speculation. "I want to thank you for hiding out my husband."

"He's always welcome here." Tom poured Belle another shot of whiskey. "You, too."

"Thanks."

"You knew Quantrill?"

"Sure. I spied for him when I was a kid."

"He like another son to me," Tom said. "Quantrill, Jesse and Frank, Cole Younger. They my spirit sons. Sons brought to me through the war."

"The war," Belle said, thinking that it had divided her life into halves. She took a deep breath and threw the measure of whiskey to the back of her throat. It burned like hell, but she fought off the tears and coughing bout that threatened her tough façade.

"They good soldiers," Tom said, still back in the war. "We all good soldiers."

"We? You, too?" Bell asked.

"Of course!" Tom jabbed a thumb into his chest. "I hot-blooded Rebel. I spit on Yankee scum!" He called up some phlegm and spat it out to illustrate his point. "President Davis surrendered, but not me. Never me!"

"Damn right!" Righteous anger straightened her spine and burned through her veins. Belle knew that her eyes were shining with it and that her cheeks were rosy. She felt alive, and she was grateful to Tom Starr for making her feel this way again. "I'm so tired of being part of the losing side and being treated poorly. I'm sick of it! I didn't sign that damned treaty!" She pounded the table with her fist. "I didn't sign it, so I don't acknowledge it." She was aware that the two men were staring at her with some alarm. She blushed and looked down at her clenched fists on the table. "I'm sorry. I just—"

"No apologies," Tom said. "You're right to speak out. More should speak out instead of accepting the Yankee law." He sat back and a faraway look came into his metallic eyes. "You were a scout for Quantrill? I was scout for General Stand Watie's Indian Brigade. Watie was my father's brother. We fought the Pin Indians. They'd fallen in with the Federals." He smiled and laced his hands across his stomach. "We had good fights. Good battles. The Confederacy was strong here."

"Did you fight with white troops sometimes?" Belle asked, her interest piqued.

"That's how I met Jesse and Cole and the others. We fought side by side many times. Near the end we made our mark just north of the Arkansas River. We dug down banks, cut out trees, rolled wagons and artillery up hill and down by hand." He examined his own massive hands and the scars on them. "Fourteen days. We march fourteen days and cover some four hundred miles. We kill ninety-seven, take over a hundred prisoners, and burn six thousand tons of hay and all the reapers and mowers with them." He brought his gray eyes around to her. "All that in just fourteen days."

"And Cole and Jesse were there?" Belle interrupted.

"They were there. Cool and brave as ever. A man could

trust them boys. Especially Cole. I would walk through fire for that one."

Belle nodded, thinking that she would, too. Through fire, raging waters, twisting winds. Anything. Oh, she'd give anything to see him just one more time.

"If we'd had more men like the Youngers and the Jameses we would not have surrendered," Tom said, then sighed away the tattered dreams.

"Indians fought Indians?" Belle asked.

"Always that way. Before the war, it was so," Tom said, his expression taking on more intensity. "We came to this place some thirty years ago. We come on our own. No one forces us. My father was one who signed Removal Treaty and came here to start new life away from white man's laws. But some Indians wouldn't leave. They stand still and must be run off the land like cattle." His expressive eyes grew as cold and hard as steel. "Indians like John Ross." He said the name as if it were a bitter oath.

"There's a troublemaker," Jim chimed in. "He's not fit to kill, that one."

"Oh, he's fit," Tom said with a wicked smile. "Ross sent thirty-two men to kill my father." His smile took on a hard edge. "I killed all thirty-two over a dozen years. Ross will be the next to die."

"Why did he want your father dead?" Belle asked.

"Because my father was leader of those who wanted to leave Georgia and other states spoiled by white men, and Ross was leader of those who were forced into the Territory by white soldiers." He waved a dismissing hand. "Ross wants to rule all red men, but he'll never rule the Starrs. I rule the Starrs."

"With a vengeance, no doubt," Belle murmured to herself, but the big Indian heard her.

"You can sit at my table and share my roof as long as you never double-cross me or any of my kin—spirit kin or kin of the flesh," Tom warned her, then fished under his shirt collar for the strip of rawhide he always wore around his neck. "See this? You know what these are?"

Belle leaned closer to examine the bits of dried meat.

"The earlobes of my enemies."

The whiskey climbed back up her throat, scalding it, but Belle clamped her lips together and sent the sour stuff back down to her belly. Her gaze sought Jim's across the table and he managed a weak smile.

"Anyone who crosses me or my blood, I kill," Tom explained, stroking the necklace of savagery. "And I take a piece of them to carry with me always." He smiled and Belle was reminded of the skull and crossbones on bottles of poison. "My enemies would rather embrace the devil than look me in the face."

Tom was testing her, and since Jim seemed incapable of anything besides a watered-down smile and a nervous chuckle, Belle knew she'd have to take on the Indian herself. She set her empty whiskey glass on the table with a mild thump and faced Tom Starr, pug nose to hooked nose.

"Same here." She narrowed her eyes to the meanest slits she could muster. "I guess that makes me and you about the orneriest polecats that ever drew a breath."

Jim dropped his face in his hands. Belle held her breath. Tom Starr stretched the moment into a dozen before throwing back his head and raising the roof with his belly laughter. Belle released her pent-up breath and glanced toward the open door leading outside. Sam stood there, a shy grin lighting his silver eyes and curving his full lips. In the blink of an eye, he was gone, making Belle wonder if she'd only imagined she'd seen him standing in the doorway.

"I like you, woman!" Tom announced, then clapped Jim on the back. "You done good with this one, James Reed. You should keep this one."

"I think I will," Jim said, winking at Belle as the color flooded back into his pale face. "I think she's the best thing I ever stole."

"Honey, you didn't steal me," Belle said with a tight smile. "I reckon I'm the only thing you ever came by honestly."

PART THREE

California
1869

Chapter Thirteen

J ESSE LAY SPRAWLED in a striped hammock. A frosted glass of orange juice and tequila rode his stomach, held steady by his silver-and-turquoise bejeweled fingers. He opened one eye and grinned.

"*Siesta* time. My favorite part of the day."

Belle sat in the wicker chair nearest him, lazily waving a straw fan, back and forth. Back and forth. She parted her knees to let a breeze run up her skirt and cool her damp thighs. "Where's Doc?"

"Checking on his patients, I guess." Jesse's voice was as lazy as the drone of bees.

"How are you feeling today?"

"Much better." He laid a hand on his right side, just under his ribs where a bullet had ripped through him four months ago. "Guess I'm going to live after all."

While Jesse's eyes were closed, Belle compared him to the younger version she'd met during the war. He'd aged, but like Cole, he'd aged well. He sported a neatly trimmed beard and mustache of glossy sable, the mustache tipping up at the ends and held in place with dabs of wax. He had a

long face, sharp nose, and sultry mouth with a thin upper
lip and full lower one. His voice was deep and honeyed. He
was a rover, a Romeo. A family man who rarely saw his
family. Belle figured he hardly thought of them, either—
except for his mother. Like all good Southern boys, Jesse
always thought of Mama first and his wife and children last.

Belle leaned her head back. Her eyes traveled from the
supine Jesse to the sprawling grounds of the sanitarium.
Paso Robles was near the Mission San Miguel and only
twenty miles from the Pacific. Belle and the other guests of
Dr. Drury Woodson James stayed in the short end of an
L-shaped adobe building. The longer part housed the sanitarium where poor souls suffered from mysterious diseases
of the lungs and kidneys and where many soaked their
arthritic joints in the bubbling sulfur springs. None of the
inmates were really crazy. No crazier than Doc's invited
guests. A wry smile played on her lips. Frank James was
probably the only true lunatic on the property.

"Frank's getting restless. Guess we'll head out soon."

Belle jumped slightly. Had he read her mind? She smiled
at him. "Where to?" she asked, putting aside the useless fan.

"Back home, I reckon."

"Missouri? I thought you two were wanted there."

"Naw, not really." He shrugged in a bored way. "Nobody's fingered us for nothing. No hard evidence."

"Except those bullet wounds," Belle pointed out.

"I came here to shake a virus and recuperate from war
wounds," Jesse recited dutifully. "I don't know anything
about any bank robberies or killings."

"Sure, tell that to the judge."

"I will, if I'm asked, which I won't be." Jesse stretched
lazily and the hammock swung back and forth. "Did Frank
and Jim leave just now?"

"Yes." Belle closed her eyes and clamped her teeth together for a moment. "God! I wish Jimmy would stay here and out of trouble. Frank is a bad influence on him." She winced, thinking that she sounded just like Mother Reed.

"That's a good one, Maybelle," Jesse said, laughing as he lifted his head for a sip of the liquor and juice. "Frank's a bad influence on James Reed. Yeah, that's right funny."

Belle threw the fan at him, hitting him squarely between the eyes. He broke up again, kicking his bare feet in the air.

"It's not funny," Belle declared, crossing her arms and sending Jesse a smoldering glance. "It's nice here. A good place for Pearl. Jimmy's going to ruin it for sure."

"You might as well settle down with the facts, sweet pea." Jesse propped himself on one elbow to stare at her levelly. "You married a hairy-legged, wild-eyed Rebel and he's not about to change. Chances are you'll end up a widow."

"Don't say that!" Belle shot up from the chair, propelled by fear and desperation. She stood over a shocked Jesse, who was rocking ever so gently in the hammock, his head cradled in his hands, his ankles crossed. "Me and Jimmy don't have a pot to piss in nor a window to throw it out of, so don't wish death on Jimmy. I'd be left destitute. Don't wish that on me and my Pearl!"

"I'm not. I'm trying to make you see Jim for what he is instead of what you wish he was."

"And don't lecture me about my husband," she added. "Hell, don't you think I know him? I know him better than anybody."

"He's dancing on a borderline, Maybelle. He doesn't feel alive unless he's gambling with the devil. Others might make excuses for us by saying that we're sticking it to the Yankees or trying to live by the straight and narrow while the Yankee courts force us into outlawing, but we know better." He smiled, showing off his incredibly beautiful teeth. "We know that we like it. We like the danger, the drama, the duplicity. The difference between me and you and Frank and Jim is that we've got brains and Frank and Jim don't."

Belle turned away from him, running her fingers over her hair to check her neat chignon as she mulled over Jesse's words.

"Jim was doing good while you planned his horse stealing," Jesse pressed on. "He got in trouble when he started thinking for himself. Jim's a follower. You're a leader."

"Just what are you getting at?" she asked, whirling to face him again as she planted her fists just above the swell of her hips.

"All I'm saying is that if you don't want to be a poor widow, you'd better take part in Jim's life instead of ignoring it. He's going to rob and steal and cheat at cards as surely as the sun's going to set in the west. He'll live longer if you do his thinking for him."

"Why can't he raise horses or farm?" she asked, although part of her knew the answer because part of her hated that way of life, too. "Why can't he be satisfied with a good life with me and Pearl?"

"Why can't mules sprout wings and fly?" Jesse rejoined, then swung out of the hammock and set his empty glass on a low table. He paced lightly to the hedge surrounding the secluded patio. "Somebody's coming. Two riders. I hope it's not that goddamned sheriff from Los Angeles. That pesky son-of-a-bitch is going to . . . Well, I'll be damned."

"What?" Belle stood behind him and looked over his shoulder. "Who is it? Jimmy and Frank?"

"No." Jesse grinned and glanced back at her, his sparkling eyes speaking fathoms. "It's your knight in shining armor, Maybelle. Thomas Coleman Younger and his brother John. Looks like this is your lucky day."

"In a pig's eye," Belle sassed. "What I don't need is two

more reckless Rebs to stuff Jimmy with more lawless tales and make him itch to raise some hell."

Jesse chuckled and stepped barefoot from the patio to the open courtyard, going to greet his old compadres.

Belle patted her hair down with her hands, tucking a few wayward strands back into her chignon. She ran her hands down her cotton dress and then touched the cameo pinned at her throat. How would she look to him? Since Pearl's birth, her hips were an inch wider. Her breasts fuller. Would he notice? Would it bother him? If she saw a hint of disappointment on Cole's face, her self-confidence would collapse like a house of cards.

Jesse and John led the horses off to the stables while Cole walked straight to Belle. He swept off his floppy brimmed hat, revealing the golden glory of his hair, and whacked it against his black leather chaps. Dust rose in clouds and settled across his double-breasted, mustard-colored shirt. He'd gained some weight, most of it muscle. He was tanned, the skin around his eyes creased to make tiny white lines. He'd shaved off his facial hair, but a day's growth of whiskers shadowed his cheeks and chin. If anything, he was better looking than the last time she'd seen him. There should be a law against it. Belle marveled at the sight of him.

He unnerved her by stopping a few feet away and letting his gaze roam over her face and figure.

"Stop that," she said after a few tingling moments. "I don't like being inspected as if I were a cow at auction." She smiled, one corner of her mouth tipping up. "How have you been? You're looking good. I'm surprised to see you way out here. You're not in trouble, are you? You can hide here—everybody here is hiding from something or other. Is John the only one traveling with you? Are you hungry? How about a—"

"Whoa there." He held up his hands, warding off her barrage. "One question at a time." His eyes shone with amusement. "I've been fine and I'm not in trouble. Me and John just rode out here to check on Jesse. We were worried about him. Heard he'd been under the weather."

"Under the weather, my ass." Belle laughed harshly. "He was shot during a holdup, which you know all about since you were there. A little place called Russellville, remember?"

"I remember," he said. "And I remember that you told us it was a bad job."

"Do you also remember that I was right?"

"No, but I remember that we made off with a nice bankroll and that my share bought me some land outside Scyene and a few head of cattle."

"You're living in Texas?"

"Sure am. I see your folks now and again. Me and your daddy go hunting and fishing together every so often. They're all fine and send you their love."

"How's your mother doing?"

His mouth twisted sadly and he screwed up one eye in that way she found so endearing. For a moment she wanted nothing so much as to rip off his clothes and make his hurting go away.

"Not so good. She's ailing lately." He walked his fingers around the oily brim of his hat and stared down at his hands, avoiding Belle's all-too-intense gaze. "You're a mother now."

"I am." Belle wet her dry lips and stepped closer to him, pretending to be drawn by the blooming rosebushes along one side of the patio instead of her blooming feelings.

"Your daddy said you named her Rosie Lee," Cole said, still staring at the hat he held in his hands.

"We did." Belle leaned over to smell one of the white roses. She felt Cole's piercing eyes boring into her back.

"But she's my pearl." Belle turned around to face him fully. "And that's what I call her. Pearl."

He swallowed and his Adam's apple bobbed in his tanned throat. His blue eyes misted.

"Pearl . . . Reed."

"Yes, that's right." Belle went back to the roses, unable to watch Cole's inner struggle. "Pearl Reed. She's a beautiful baby."

"Would you let me see her? I know I've no right to ask, but I was hoping—"

"Of course you can see her." Belle swung back to him, pleased that he'd showed paternal interest. She motioned for him to follow her. "Come on, but be quiet. She's napping."

"I won't wake her," he promised, tiptoeing along behind.

Cole moved silently to the cradle and leaned over the sleeping baby. Wonder spread over his face. He bent nearer to the child and touched one of her fists with his forefinger. Pearl stirred and closed her fingers around his. Cole sucked in his breath and tugged his finger loose from the baby's fist. He touched Pearl's button nose and then gently stroked her cap of reddish gold hair.

"My, oh, my," he whispered, his voice no more than a wisp of sound. "She is a pearl, Belle. A delicate, white-skinned pearl. Look at that hair!" He ran his hand over her head again and glanced up at Belle. "Strawberry blond, isn't it?"

"I get a lot of questions about her hair," Belle said, wondering if he were dense or just trying to be a gentleman. "Folks ask where it came from since me and Jimmy don't have any redheads in our families."

"But the Youngers do," Cole tacked on, affording her a long, knowing look before he grinned again. He shook his head in amused irony as he returned his attention to the babe. "Lord have mercy, she's a pretty thing! What color are her eyes?"

"Sky blue like yours. Just like yours." Belle's throat tightened and she felt her lips tremble. She couldn't keep back the flow of emotions any longer. The unsheathed truth came spilling out of her in a voice that was punctuated by sobs. "Oh, Cole! Every time I look at her I see you, and I thank God I've got her to hold and kiss and love."

"Belle." He said her name in a choked voice and looked helpless in the face of her tears. He muttered an oath, tossed aside his hat, and gathered Belle into his arms. He kissed her love-soft mouth and then her small, pink ear. "I've missed you. I've wondered about our child, but I told myself that you wouldn't want me to see her."

"How have you been? Really. No fooling." She leaned back and ran her fingers through his thick hair. "Is the law leaving you be after Russellville?"

"Russellville didn't give me any problems. I wasn't identified. I've been fine and dandy, just like I said." He massaged her temples with his thumbs and a smile rode his mouth. "We're all in Scyene and living upstanding lives, mainly for Mama. We don't want to upset the apple cart because an upset could do her in." He smoothed wisps of hair off her forehead. "You look good to my eyes, Myra Maybelle. As usual, I can't keep my hands off you."

His smile covered hers. He lifted his lips away, looked for and found pleasure in her eyes, and kissed her again more thoroughly. Belle accepted his advances as a starving woman accepts a crust of bread. She offered herself up to him, grinding her mouth against his and adding more friction to the heat he created.

His hands knew her, knew every curve and dip and how to draw responses from her. Wanting consumed Belle like flood waters cresting and banking and spilling over. It was never like this with Jimmy, she thought. With Jimmy it was a trickle that sometimes built into a bubbling stream. With Cole it was a flash flood that gave her no time to shield herself. All she could do was take a deep breath and let him take her around the bend and back again.

Pearl's cries reminded Belle of her misplaced, misguided loyalties. Belle wriggled from Cole's arms and clung to the side of the cradle, gazing down at her daughter as she struggled for equilibrium.

"Belle," Cole whispered behind her, his hands riding the tops of her shoulders. "What's wrong?"

"I'm married with a child and you're not my husband. *That's* what's wrong." She sniffed and swiped at her tearing eyes and stuffy nose; then she set to changing Pearl's diaper. "You could have had me and this baby if you'd wanted, but you didn't."

"I told you that I was willing to try."

"I didn't need an 'iffy' proposition." She shook off his hands. "I needed security."

"You sound as if you're mad at me."

"I am!" She whirled to face him, furious at him and his foggy brain. "I'm mad as hell at you!"

"Why?" He held his arms out at his sides in an elongated shrug. "I thought we settled this. I offered to try, and you decided to stay with Jim."

"Cole, this thing will never be settled. What makes me mad is that you think you can waltz through my life every so often and whirl me around the floor and then drop me." She sighed and gazed at the ceiling as if it held solutions to life's problems. "Sometimes I think that men are like tumbleweeds. They roll where the wind blows and never put down roots. Women do that. Women put down roots because they've got to give their children something to hold on to. My mama loves boys best, but for the life of me I don't know why. Females have a lot more sense and you can depend on them. Males—most of them anyways—aren't worth killing."

"Belle, that doesn't sound like you," Cole admonished gently, smiling a little as if he were trying to get her into a better mood.

"How would you know how I sound?" Belle challenged. "You're never around me more than a few hours at a time—just long enough to satisfy your hankering and then you're gone."

"You make me sound as low as a snake's belly," Cole said, anger raising his voice.

"If the skin fits . . ."

"Hold up a goddamned minute!" He grabbed her by her upper arms and jerked her around to face his outraged squint. "Don't go acting like the victim here, Belle. It doesn't fit. You came to me with both eyes open. I never promised you a damned thing, and you never asked for anything. Now that doesn't make me a saint, but it doesn't make me a dirty son-of-a-bitch either." He let go of her and turned aside. His chest rose and fell in a choppy sigh. "The way I've got it figured, you're chewing a bone that's got nothing to do with me, but I'm getting growled at anyway because I'm the closest one to you." He looked askance at her. "You want to tell me about it or do you want to keep growling and spitting and getting nowhere fast?"

Belle handed Pearl a colorfully painted gourd. The child clutched its skinny end and gurgled, swinging the clattering gourd for all she was worth. Belle smiled with a mother's pride; then she sat in the rocker beside the cradle.

Cole dropped to his haunches before her and placed his hands on the armrests, imprisoning her as if he were afraid she'd bolt and run. "You're still holding a grudge against me for asking Jim to ride with us into Russellville?"

"Sort of."

"That had nothing to do with you and me. It was business. You and me are private, personal."

"Business." Belle laughed shortly and without humor. "That's a highfalutin' way to put it. Is robbing your business now, Cole?"

"It's a sideline. Let's talk about you. Where's Jim?"

"Taking care of business, I reckon." She tried on her lopsided smirk and laughed again. "He's at work, Cole. Gambling, stealing, passing homemade money. Busy, busy, busy."

"I'm sorry, Belle." Cole hung his head. "I know you came out here because Jim ran into a little trouble."

"He didn't run into it, he went looking for it. Jimmy goes out of his way to land in every puddle of trouble he can find."

"It'll blow over and you can come home soon."

"In about a year," she agreed. "But where's home? Texas? Missouri? I don't have a home and never have had since I married. I'm a boarder."

"Your pa will give you and Jim a corner of his land. I'll set y'all up with breeding stock. Me and Judge Shirley have talked about it. He wants to give you some land. He knows the family hasn't done right by you." He tucked two fingers under her chin, forcing her to look at him. "Next year isn't too far off. By next year the law will have cooled off about Jim running whiskey."

"Why am I whining to you?" she asked with a bittersweet smile. "Doesn't do any good. Like Mama says, 'It's my baby and I've got to rock it.'"

"My baby, too," Cole reminded her. "Jim doesn't know about that or suspect anything?"

"No, but he's the only one. I think everybody else knows that Pearl isn't a Reed."

"I don't think Frank's got any inkling of it."

"Sometimes I wish Jimmy would get wise so I wouldn't have to pretend."

"Tell him."

"Tell him?" she repeated with an incredulous laugh.

"That's right." Cole nodded, deadly serious. "Everybody knows and he'll find out eventually. Tell him and get it over with. I'll help you through it."

"No." She shook her head. "This is between me and Jimmy. I don't want your help."

"She's my baby and I—"

"No!" Belle banged her fists on the arms of the rocking chair. "Cole, Pearl is mine. You hear me? All mine." She almost touched her nose to his. "You gave up claim to her when you called her a ball and chain."

"Oh, hell!" He wrenched from her and bolted to his feet. "You're going to beat me with that stick until I'm senseless, aren't you?"

"I'll forgive you for everything except that," she said calmly and succinctly. "I needed you then. God, how I needed you!" Tears blurred her vision and she fought them off. "I was carrying your child and all I needed was just a hint of pride or joy from you . . . God, that would have meant the world to me."

"Belle, I was—"

"No, don't make excuses for being honest." She stood up and went to the narrow windows, keeping her back to him so that he couldn't see the anguish on her face. "You broke my heart, Cole, but I take comfort in knowing that I've got the best part of you." She lifted her chin, straining to keep her tears from rolling and her voice from breaking. "I've got my Pearl."

She could see his reflection in the window pane and she was stunned when his mouth twisted out of shape and tears spilled onto his lean, weather-worn cheeks. Before she could turn to him with open arms, he'd wrenched open the door and stalked from the room. Belle stared after him in speechless remorse, realizing for the first time how deeply she could wound him. Hers wasn't the only heart broken.

It was well past midnight when Belle slipped out of the house and out to the stables. Thunder galloped across the skies, riding ahead of the rain. Belle glanced back at the adobe building. All was dark and quiet. It seemed that everyone could sleep except for her.

She went from stall to stall, looking in on the horses and dreaming of having her own stables and raising her own stock. Would Papa really give her a piece of land? She knew Cole would give her breeding stock.

Belle sat down in a mound of fresh hay, thinking back on the past week. She'd spent most of her time in her bedroom with Pearl, avoiding Cole. The men had spent the week in a jolly reunion. When Cole and John announced at dinner that evening that they'd be riding back to Texas at first light, Belle had broken down and joined in the farewell party of dancing and drinking and retelling of war adventures.

John and Frank had played some old songs on their guitars, and Belle had danced with Jimmy, Jesse, and Cole. She shivered and hugged herself, thinking of being in Cole's arms. Belle stood up and brushed hay off her nightdress, trying to brush her feelings aside, too. She'd be glad to see Cole's back come morning. Being near him was too painful . . . too damned tempting.

"Belle."

She spun around at the sound of her husband's voice. He stood just outside the stables, lightning flashing behind him.

He'd hardly been a model husband of late, nightly passing out in the hammock on the patio.

"Jimmy, I thought you were asleep. Did the thunder
wake you?" She waited for him to answer, and when he
didn't, she shrugged and looked past him to the dark sil-
houettes of the trees bending to the will of the wind. "Storm's
coming."

"Storm's already here."

She squinted into the night, trying to see his face clearly
because she sure didn't like the timbre of his voice. Rain
began to fall in a steady sheet, cooling the oppressive air.
Jim moved inside the stable. The horses stamped restlessly.
One kicked its stall door as Jim passed by. Belle nearly
jumped out of her skin, but Jim didn't acknowledge the
commotion.

"You meeting someone out here?" he asked.

"No." She laughed softly. "Who would I be meeting?" He
came closer. She could see the hateful glint in his eyes. She
stopped laughing.

"Rosie's father, maybe?"

"That's you." Belle instinctively crossed her arms in front
of her.

"Yeah, I reckon that's right." His smile packed cold shiv-
ers. "When she's Rosie Lee, she's mine. When she's Pearl,
she's Cole's. Ain't that about the size of it?"

For a fleeting moment she thought of lying to him, but
she could see by the dark cast of his face that it would be
futile.

"That's about the size of it," she said in a clipped, tense
way.

"Everybody knew but me. I figured it out tonight while I
watched you dance with him. You made love to him with
your eyes. You ain't never looked at me that way. And that's
when I knew. You've loved him all along and bore him a

child. All the time you've been married to me, you've been sleeping with Cole Younger. I hate the son-of-a-bitch, but I hate you more." His laughter was like sand scraping across Belle's nerves. "I guess I've been the butt of a lot of jokes between you two, huh?"

"No, Jimmy. It's not like that."

"Not like that, huh? Well, the last joke's on you." He flexed his fingers; his arms hung limply at his sides. "I don't think you'll be laughing this time, Belle."

"Jimmy, what are you talking about?" She stepped back, holding up one hand in a pitiful attempt to stop him. "Let's talk about this. Whiskey has made you dream up most of this."

"No!" His voice cracked like a rifle retort. His hand shot out and grabbed a quirt off a peg beside him. He looped the leather strap around his fingers and brandished the short whip, making it sing as it sliced through the air. "Time for talking is done past. Now's the time for squaring things . . . making everything equal."

"Wh-what are you talking about?" Frantically, she looked past him at the torrential rain and knew escape was impossible. The quirt kept singing. Belle flinched. Jimmy grabbed her elbow with his free hand and brought her up against his body.

"Jimmy, please, don't."

"He got a daughter off you," Jim said, his face thrust close to hers. "Now I'm going to get me a son. Once you give me my boy, I'll be through with you. Until then, you'd better stay away from Younger or, I swear to you, I'll cut his throat from ear to ear." His upper lip lifted and his breath washed over her face like spilled whiskey. "And don't you never call that redheaded little bitch you bore a Reed again or I'll cut out your tongue. Hear me, woman?"

The quirt made a wide arc and swept down across the

back of her nightdress. It cut through the fabric and stung the back of her legs. She bit down on her lower lip to keep from screaming.

"Y-yes." Belle released a hiccuping sob. She'd never been scared of James Reed until now. His hands locked at her waist and threatened to crush her bones to dust. He stepped back, raising the quirt high over his head. Belle cowered.

She wrapped her arms around her head and waited for the stinging kiss of leather. She dropped to her knees, trembling and quaking.

Jimmy grinned sadistically, tossing the whip to the ground. "Good girl," he said as if to a pet dog. "Good, good girl."

He reached out, almost nonchalantly, lifting her off her feet, forcing her to face him. He grabbed the collar of her nightdress and gave a good yank. It ripped from collarbone to navel. When she opened her mouth, he plastered one of his big hands across the lower half of her face.

"Don't you scream," he warned. "Don't you even make a squeak or I'll pick up that whip and beat the living shit out of you. Now lay down nice and quiet, spread your legs, and give me what's rightfully mine."

She thought of fighting him, but liquor had made him meaner, and nature had made him stronger. Guilt and humiliation made Belle passively lie down on the hay-strewn ground and Jim Reed mounted her.

Chapter Fourteen

HE CAME RIDING UP at dusk. A dark silhouette against the indigo Texas sky.

Belle set her porch rocker into motion, listening to the rumble of hooves mingle with the squeaking chair. He reined his horse beside the water trough, swung out of the saddle, tethered his mount, and came to her with long, graceful strides. He was dressed like a field hand. Baggy tan trousers held up by black suspenders. A sheer cotton shirt. Scuffed shoes without laces. Ratty straw hat. A red kerchief around his neck. He was beautiful and brought a lump to her throat.

"I should be mad at you," Cole Younger said as he folded his muscled arms on top of the porch railing and rested his square chin on them. His eyes were brilliant blue like the California ocean.

"I saw your daddy yesterday and he told me that you'd been back since March. I couldn't believe it! You've been here for two months and you didn't send word to me?" He studied her passive expression and frowned. "How long's it been since we parted company?"

"Two years," Belle answered. "I wasn't sure I wanted to see you again. That's why I didn't tell you I was back."

"Why didn't you want to see me?" he asked, rubbing the fringe of his reddish blond mustache across his forearm. "We parted friendly, didn't we?" He was clearly hurt.

Belle leaned her head back against the rocker and closed her eyes. There wasn't a simple answer. Her feelings for him had never been simple. How could she talk sensibly when he was looking at her like a scolded child? She could take almost any kind of pain, but she couldn't stand seeing him hurt and being the cause of it.

"You're not talking?" he persisted.

"I'm glad to see you." She opened her eyes and the sight of him made her heart gallop. When he smiled at her the world tipped on its axis. "Really glad." She noticed the pinched skin at the corners of his mouth and the tightness at the bridge of his nose. "You didn't just come out here to rag at me. You're bringing news I don't want to hear, aren't you?"

He chuckled and removed his low-crowned hat. "You can see right through me, woman. That's right. I'm bringing sad tidings. When I heard about you being here, I had to laugh. I couldn't help but think that God Almighty must get a kick out of moving me and you around like checker pieces on a big old board."

"You're leaving." Belle's chest tightened, squeezing her racing heart. "That's what you've come to tell me."

"Yes, but that's not the only reason I came. I wanted to see you." He glanced around. "Where's Jim?"

"Who knows?" She smiled sadly. "Who cares?" She looked over the flat land, her gaze moving slowly over to the garden patch she'd worked in all day. "Didn't Daddy tell you about me and Jimmy?"

"No, the Judge is usually quiet about your personal affairs."

"We left California on the run. The law was after Jimmy, as usual. We came back here right after Eddie was born." She glanced at Cole and tossed off a smile. "I've got me another baby."

"That's what I heard. You name him after your brother?"

"Yes. James Edwin." She sighed and shifted onto the side of her hip in the big rocker. "Daddy gave me this piece of land, and he and Shug built this house for me and my children. Jimmy's long gone. I think he's at Youngers Bend, but I'm not sure."

"You mean he left you? He hasn't even sent money to you?"

She shook her head.

"That dirty bastard." Cole slammed a fist against the railing. "You give him a son, and he heads for the hills!"

"I don't want to see him." Belle lifted one shoulder in a half shrug. "Well, maybe I'd like to see him one more time to tell him what I think of him, but that's it. I'm through being Mrs. Reed." Her gaze slid to his and her smile was sadly sweet. "And you're leaving. When?"

"Tomorrow." His voice dipped lower along with his spirits. "Mama doesn't like Texas. She wants to die in Missouri, so me and my brothers are taking her back."

"That's it?" Belle asked. "Your leaving doesn't have anything to do with a couple of your brothers getting into some hot water with the law around here?"

"W-e-l-l . . ." He chuckled, grabbed the support post with one hand, and swung around the corner of the porch to the steps. "That has a little to do with us high-stepping it out of Texas." He bounded up onto the porch and looked inside the house. "Not bad. Are the children asleep?"

"Yes, I just put them down." Belle stood up from the rocker. She placed her hands at the small of her back and swayed side to side to release the tautness around her spine. "Have you eaten?"

"Yes, but I'd be grateful for a cup of coffee about now."

"I can manage that. I've got some left over from supper." She moved ahead of him into the dark interior. "Light the lantern and I'll get you a cup of it."

Lantern light pushed dusk from the room, revealing a roughly hewn table and four chairs, a trunk with brass fittings, a butter churn, a big fireplace full of glowing embers, and a sideboard and dry sink. *Meager* was the word that came to Cole's mind. He glanced at the closed door as he hung his hat on a peg and realized that behind that door was her bedroom where two children were sleeping. Their daughter, her son.

"Could I look in on her? I'll be quiet."

Belle nodded. "Have a look. She's growing like a spring flower."

He opened the door and moved quietly into the room, dodging bulking shadows until he'd reached the narrow cot. He bent over to study her serene face, her Cupid's bow mouth, her rosy cheeks, her mass of red curls. Beautiful. A vision. His Pearl.

"Well, what do you think?" Belle asked when he'd come back into the main room, closing the bedroom door with infinite care.

"I think she's an angel. How could we have created such a pretty thing? I mean, she's so perfect."

"You should hear her when she chatters like a chipmunk. You wouldn't think she was perfect then."

"You don't fool me. You think she's heaven-sent. Admit it."

"I admit it."

She handed him the cup of coffee and he took it with him to the open door. He stood on the threshold, his back to

Belle and his eyes focused on the sliver of moon sailing low in the sky. Fireflies were so thick that it looked as if the stars had dropped down for a visit.

"Pretty night," he murmured, then turned to Belle, so fragile looking in her pale pink pinafore dress. "Being a mother of two becomes you. I do believe that you're more beautiful now than you were at sixteen when you stole my heart." He sipped the coffee, his eyes flirting with hers. "Why don't you let me give you some stock?"

"What would I do with cattle?" she asked, sitting down at the table. "It's all I can do to tend my garden and my children. Daddy and Shug are taking up the slack for Jimmy."

"I left some of my best calves with Judge Shirley. They're yours, but he's going to tend them for you." He held up a hand when she started to protest. "Done done it, so don't fuss with me about it." He looked around the small room and frowned. "Why struggle out here? Go back to your folks. They'll take you in."

"No. I'm not going back there with my tail between my legs and my children dragging behind me. Besides, I couldn't stand living with Mama. We don't get along."

"Because of Pearl?"

Belle nodded.

"That's what I figured. Mrs. Shirley's never been friendly toward me since that baby was born. I've brought you hardship, haven't I?"

Belle lifted her gaze to his again. Starlight outlined him, making him seem unreal . . . larger than life.

"You've brought me heaven." She glanced toward the other door, then back to him. "You're my hero," she said, smiling as a weight lifted from her heart. It was good to speak truthfully, to tell him exactly how she felt about him. "Jesse calls you my knight in shining armor."

"Does he?" Cole laughed and finished his coffee, then ran a forefinger over his damp mustache. "How romantic. I never knew old Jesse had a romantic bone in his body."

"I tried and tried to convince myself that you were a scoundrel with no pride nor honor, but it didn't matter. I still loved you, still worshiped you. Just when I think I'm all grown up with my feet planted firmly on the ground, you turn up and I'm a kid again." She studied her clasped hands on the table top. "There are times, Cole Younger, when I hate myself for loving you so relentlessly."

"I know the feeling. I've got no willpower around you. No sense." He glanced toward the bedroom. "You sleep in there with your children?"

"Most nights I sleep on a pallet in here so I can hear if anybody rides up."

He set the cup on the table with a thump. "You shouldn't be out here alone with those babies. What's Jim thinking about leaving—"

"Don't talk about him. I don't want him mentioned tonight." She stood up and closed the distance between them to place her fingertips against his lips and soft mustache. "You *are* staying the night, aren't you?"

"Am I?"

"Yesterday is for our elders," she said. Rising on tiptoe, she wound her arms around his neck and kissed his full lips. "Tomorrow belongs to our children. But tonight is ours. You're staying."

"I'm staying," he said, taking one of her hands and pressing a kiss in her palm. He folded her fingers over it, then let go so that she could slip her thumbs under his suspenders and bring them down off his shoulders. He lifted his arms out of them.

"Have you been working in the fields?" she asked, then gasped when he held up his hands to show her his red and callused palms. "Lord, you have been! Who would believe that Cole Younger's been farming and ranching?"

"Not the law, that's for sure. Every sheriff in the country thinks I'm robbing banks and stage coaches day in and day out." He slipped his roughened hands behind her to unbutton her dress. "But I've been living clean for Mama."

"And what about after she's gone?"

He bowed his head in a show of momentary remorse. "Who knows? If I get an itch, I'll have to scratch." He gathered her hands and held them to his mouth.

"My hands are as rough as corncobs," Belle complained. "Not like a lady's at all."

"Oh, hush." He kissed them, then her lips. "I like you just the way you are. You can rub those hands over me any time you please."

She laughed and stepped out of his loose embrace. She pulled pins from her hair, letting him watch the dark strands tumble down her back.

"You pretty thing," he said. "Now I'll put on a show for you."

He unbuttoned his shirt, letting it hang open, and kicked out of his shoes. She tossed the pins onto the table, then shimmied out of the dress to stand before him in her muslin petticoat and pantaloons. His gaze lowered to her bare breasts and he smiled.

"You win. You put on a better show than I do." He came to her, bending low to take one of her rosy nipples into his warm mouth. Goose bumps erupted all over her. She threaded her fingers through his silky hair, scraping her fingernails on his scalp.

"You're lucky I'm not a lady," she whispered, her voice trembling as Cole's tongue washed her sensitive nipple. "A lady would send you packing. Married women aren't supposed to take up with single men."

He lifted his head and smacked his lips. "Your milk is awful sweet. I bet Eddie loves it."

She slapped his shoulder. "You rascal! You're not my baby."

"I want to be." He pushed his fingers through the sides of her hair. "I want to be your baby, your man, your lover, your knight in shining armor. I want to be everything to you."

"You are," she assured him.

She unbuttoned his trousers and reached in for him. He moaned and closed his eyes as her fingers closed around him. She dropped to her knees and pulled the baggy britches down his legs so that he could step out of them. His long, sinewy muscles flexed. His legs were covered with auburn hair.

"Magnificent," she said. "Look how dark it is at the shaft. I can feel the power pulsing through it. I love you." She leaned forward and pressed her mouth just above the outgrowth of chestnut hair. Her lips moved upward and her tongue circled his navel. "I love you, love you, love you."

He groaned and came down on his knees. He tipped her head back. His open lips captured hers, his tongue sucking her sweet juices, playing hot games. His arms came around her, pulling her up and into him. She reached out, her hand closing on a folded quilt on top of the trunk.

"Spread this on the floor," she said, then stood up to remove the rest of her clothes.

He took off his shirt and tossed it aside, then arranged the patchwork quilt on the floor before the big fireplace. He paused, looking at his trembling hands. How long had it been since he'd been so shaken by a woman? What kind of magic did Belle possess? She came up behind him, her arms snaking up his hairy chest, her hips gyrating against his buttocks. She kissed his shoulder blade, then ran the tip of her tongue along his backbone. He shivered uncontrollably and covered her hands with his.

"Nobody loves me like you do," he said in a yearning way. "Nobody ever could."

He pulled her around in front of him and framed her lovely face in his hands. Her eyes were enormous and as black as night. Her lips were parted, pink and pinker inside. He outlined her mouth with his tongue, painting it with slick strokes.

"Each time I'm with you, it's like the first time," he confessed, feeling that adolescent surge within him. "Like I've never done it before with anyone else." He nibbled her lower lip, then her flushed cheeks and her pug nose. "You taste good, sugar."

She lowered herself to the quilt. Folding her arms behind her head, she lay back and waited for him, a smile curving her lips.

"All for me?" he asked, dropping to one knee beside her.

"All for you." She curved a hand behind his neck and pulled him across her.

"You're beautiful."

"I'm not. I've gained some weight since Eddie."

"It looks good on you." He slid his body alongside hers in a silken caress of skin upon skin. Propping his head up in one hand, he used his other hand to draw grapevines around her navel and up between her breasts. His fingertips played upon her skin for a while before moving lower to the dampness between her legs.

"I'm melting for want of you." Belle closed her eyes. His fingers slid back and forth over her swollen petals. She arched and lifted, crying out from his slick fingers' circular energy. Tension coiled inside her, tightening her muscles and making her quiver like a plucked fiddle string. Cole's lips smoothed down the curve of her neck to her shoulder. He nipped and nuzzled all the way down to the inside of her elbow then across her stomach. His lips replaced his fingers and he sipped her as he would from a chalice. She exploded inside, crying out his name. Cole answered by covering her mouth with his. He tasted juicy and sexual.

She twined her arms behind his neck and pulled his body over hers. He slipped inside her like a sword into a sheath.

"My God!" She sucked in a deep breath that cleared her head for a moment. "I wish I could keep you here forever . . . inside me where you belong."

He was making her feel whole and womanly. She ran her hands up and down his back, glorying in the writhing of muscles beneath his damp skin and the earthy smell of him. His tongue swept into her mouth, delving and delighting. She bit it lightly and made him laugh.

They moved together, rising and falling, pushing and pulling in the age-old undulation of loving. His kisses drugged her. His hands bewitched her. Even the animal utterances he made enthralled her.

"My Belle," he whispered fervently as his body shuddered into hers in sweet release. "Mine. Always mine."

"Always," she agreed, taking his face in her hands and raining kisses over it.

"What God has joined together, let no man put asunder," he recited with a naughty grin.

She laughed with him, hugging him close and feeling his beating heart.

"Such a lovely dream. What would we do without our dreams, Cole?"

His eyes misted and he rested his cheek upon her breasts and didn't answer. He rolled onto his side, pulling her with him, still inside her. He held her face very tightly, gazing into her eyes with such rapture that she felt a swoon coming on.

"Don't move," he whispered urgently. "Not a muscle. Don't even blink. Just be still. Can you feel me?"

She gasped with pleasure, sensing the stirring inside her. "Yes!" She laughed huskily. "Can't get enough, can you?"

A tear escaped from the corner of his eye. Touched, Belle lapped it up with the tip of her tongue.

He left an hour before sunrise.

Belle looked up at him, sitting tall in the saddle. "Take care of yourself," she said, thinking that he was taking her heart back with him to Missouri.

"I want you to take these." He removed the pearl-handled six-shooters from his holster and handed them down to her. "Take them, love."

"No. I've got a shotgun somewhere inside the house."

He jiggled the guns impatiently in front of her nose until she accepted them. Then on second thought he unstrapped his holster and gave it to her as well.

"I'll feel better if I know you've got some proper firearms. You being out here defenseless while Jim runs wild."

"But you'll need these."

"I've got others." Cole smiled down at her adoringly. He ran his hand over her head. "It's not a romantic present, but—"

"I'll treasure them."

He chuckled and gave her a wink. "Just be sure to use them if anybody lays a finger on you or those sweet babies of yours."

She hugged the six-shooters in their hand-tooled leather holster to her breast as he rode off into the morning mist.

*   *   *

Youngers Bend was beautiful, covered in ice crystals that made a tinkling music when stirred by the winter wind.

Belle looked at the stalwart Indian riding beside her and laughed. He threw her a wary glance.

"Sorry, Sam," she apologized. "I was just thinking how stupid it is for me to come here to see Jimmy."

"Why silly? He your husband."

"Not anymore." She shook her head adamantly. "I haven't seen his cowardly face for . . . let's see. It's been more than three years since I've seen him. Some husband, huh?"

"He been in trouble."

"Don't make excuses for that bastard." She wrinkled her nose at the youngster. "Sorry again. I shouldn't be tongue-lashing you. It's just that I've been holding all this anger in for too long." She looked ahead through the snowy trees. "Aren't we almost there?"

"Yes. You can see house now."

Smoke rolled from the twin chimneys of Tom Starr's cabin, and Belle knew it would be warm and cozy inside. Sam helped her dismount, taking her weight easily and making Belle aware that he wasn't a boy any longer. He was a young buck who probably had doe-eyed girls falling all over him.

Belle sighed, remembering when she'd known the spark of youth. She was only twenty-five, but she felt old beside the broad-shouldered, amber-skinned Cherokee. She edged past Sam and hurried inside the cabin.

Jim sat before the roaring fireplace with Tom Starr. In contrast to Tom's robust figure, Jim resembled an old elf. His shoulders were hunched, his back rounded. He huddled close to the warmth of the flames and shivered under an Indian blanket. His brown eyes were lackluster as they focused on Belle. His wrinkled lips parted in a weak smile. He coughed and his lungs rattled.

"What the hell's wrong with you?" Belle asked, sniffing the air and recognizing the stench of sickness.

"I caught a cold," Jim said, standing up from the chair. He wore faded red longhandles under the blanket. "It's good to see you, honey bunch."

Belle coughed as if she were choked. "Now you're making *me* sick. Stay away from me." She waved a hand, shooing him as he stepped closer. "I mean it. Stay away."

"Awww, honey."

Belle coughed again. "You smell like sour mash. Is whiskey your medicine or your illness?"

"Medicine." He looked at Tom. "You remember Tom, don't you?"

"Sure." Belle held out her hand to shake Tom's. "Good to see you again."

"You hang your wet cloak and hat on rack." Tom nodded past her to the coatrack on the wall, then he lifted his arms above his head and his fingertips touched the rafters. "I hunt for meat. You talk to James Reed. You stay for supper." He shrugged into his multicolored coat, pulled a red hat low over his hawk eyes, and took down his double-barreled shotgun from the rack over the fireplace. "You bring children?"

"No, I left them with my brother and sister-in-law."

"Good."

"So don't bother about supper. I can't stay. I've got to get back to my children."

He frowned and strode outside, slamming the door behind him.

"How you been?" Jim asked after a minute of tense silence.

"You've got your nerve to ask me that." Belle pulled off

her wool cloak and felt hat and hung them on the rack, then went to stand before the fireplace to warm herself.

"I can't come home for a long, long time," Jim said, almost whining as he dropped back into the chair. "I got some money. You can take it. Tell Mama I'm okay, will you?"

"You tell her."

"I can't go to Rich Hill either. I'm in a mess of trouble."

"No shit." Belle looked away from him, bored with his whining and mewling. "You think I haven't heard about your shenanigans?"

"I've done what I could for you."

Her eyes widened in disbelief. "You haven't done a damned thing for me in years! I've been practically living off my folks, and you know I don't like that. One thing I've learned though, is that I can get along without you."

"Belle, you've always been on my mind. I just couldn't get in touch because—"

"Because you've been busy riding with the Youngers and the James Brothers. I know. I've heard about it. Y'all been robbing banks and stage coaches and having a rip-roaring time of it."

"I've been with Jesse, but not Cole. Never Cole. I don't trust that bastard."

"Oh? Since when did you ever know a friend from a foe?" She laughed at the notion, then gave him a piercing glare. "What do you want from me?"

"Nothing." He slipped down into the blanket, looking for all the world like a saggy-skinned turtle shrinking into a gaily painted shell. "I sent for you because Tom wanted me to. He wouldn't hide me no longer until I done right by you."

Tom Starr had blackmailed her husband into doing right

by her? Maybe there were a few good men left in the world, after all.

"Give me the money and I'll be on my way," she said, holding out her hand, palm up.

"Tom wants you to stay the night."

"I've got children back in Texas. I can't be cooling my heels here." She wiggled her fingers impatiently. "Gimme."

"You sound like a whore wanting her money before she takes off her pantaloons." He batted her hand aside.

"I am what you made me that night in the stables at Paso Robles."

"You were a whore before that. You had Cole's bitch and passed her off as mine. I hope your precious Pearl grows up to be just like you—a ball-crushing slut!"

Fury, black and deep-rooted, ruled her and she reacted on pure instinct. She grabbed a handful of Jim's thinning hair and yanked back his head, then drew out one of the six-shooters strapped around her waist and pressed the tip of it between Jim's crusty eyes. She shoved one knee into his stomach and leaned in closer as she pulled back the hammer. Jim whimpered and sweat broke out across his forehead.

"Christ! Where'd you get them guns?"

"From a friend."

"You shouldn't play with them like this."

"Who's playing?"

Jim closed his eyes and moaned.

"What's wrong, big man?" Belle taunted. "Did you think I'd still love you after all this time? I'm sick of you, and I don't want to see you or hear from you ever again." She gave his hair a good yank. "Hear me? Don't make me blow a hole through you."

"Belle, please ..." It was a whine, not a sound that should come from a grown man.

The light changed in the room and Belle looked up to see

that Tom Starr had come back, dead rabbits in one hand and his shotgun in the other. Sam stood behind him, his silver eyes shining with curiosity. Tom arched his white brows and waited for an explanation.

Belle smiled and let the hammer slide back into place harmlessly. Jim released a long, shuddering breath as Belle holstered her six-gun and let go of his hair. She straightened to her full five feet three inches.

"Back so soon, Tom? Me and Jim were discussing big-game hunting, and I was showing him the only sure way to kill a two-legged skunk."

Tom's leathery face creased into wrinkles as he slung the rabbits onto the table and let out a spate of whooping laughter.

Chapter Fifteen

SOMEBODY COMING." Pearl pointed a chubby finger toward the dirt road cutting through the fields.

Belle straightened from the potato patch, hoe in hand, and recognized the rider. She raised a hand in greeting, but checked the response when a shiver ran down her spine. Sam Starr never came without jarring news.

"Stay here and watch your little brother," Belle told Pearl as she stuck the hoe into the ground and strode forward to speak to the Cherokee. "Jimmy's dead, isn't he?"

Sam nodded, swung his leg over, and slid off the big black stallion.

"Who appointed you my messenger?" Belle asked, flattening her hand to her stomach. She felt a momentary pang of regret, a twinge of loss, then nothing at all. "When? How? Who did him in?"

"Bounty hunter James Reed thought was friend," Sam said. "He was put to rest in Paris."

"He was buried in Paris, Texas?"

"Yes." Sam crossed his arms and leaned back against the stallion. The horse stamped its front hooves but didn't move away. "Your children growing."

"Yes." Belle looked back at them playing in the vegetable garden. "I don't rightly know what to do. Does Jimmy's mother know?"

"Solly rode off to tell her three days ago."

Belle sighed and glanced up at the unrelenting August sun. "Well, I should mourn, but I don't have it in me. How about a cool drink? Come on inside the house." She turned and motioned for her children. "Pearl! Bring Eddie and y'all come on inside for your supper!" She looked back at Sam. "You'll stay for supper?"

He nodded.

"Thanks for riding all this way to tell me about Jimmy."

"You take bad news good."

"Do I?" Belle chuckled to herself and started for the house. "I guess that's because I've gotten my share of it. Of course, Jimmy's death doesn't come as any shock. In fact, I've felt like a widow for years."

"He treat you bad."

She glanced at the young man and nodded. "So how's life treating you? How's your father?"

"He send me to you. He say you should know you are free."

"Free?" She paused going up the porch steps to throw him a startled look. "With two little children and a farm to work by myself? That's some freedom, boy."

He frowned at her. "No boy. I man."

She examined him, realizing that he was a foot taller than she and as broad as a sturdy oak. "My mistake. You are a man, after all." She reached down and pulled Eddie up into her arms. The toddler pressed his face into the curve of her neck and sniveled. "Hush, baby. This here *man* isn't here to harm us."

Sam and Pearl followed her inside. Belle put Eddie in a high chair while Pearl scrambled up into one of the four regular chairs around the drop-leaf table. Belle set a pan of cornbread and a pitcher of milk in the center of it. She wiped her hands down her apron in a nervous gesture.

Her guest was so damned self-possessed, it unraveled her. She arched a brow at him, standing in the middle of the room like he was planted there. She nodded with jerky impatience toward an empty chair. He sat down and looked from the meager offerings to Belle.

"Here are the bowls," she said, handing them around. "Dig in."

Sam watched Pearl grab a wedge of the yellow bread and crumble it into her bowl, then pour milk into it. Belle helped Eddie prepare his mash of bread and milk, then did the same for herself.

"This all for supper?" Sam asked when the others began to eat with gusto.

"This is it. I'll stew some vegetables for dinner tonight. What's wrong? Are you used to a bigger feast than this?" She sent him an apologetic smile in between bites. "Sorry, but we're poor folks."

"No meat?"

She shook her head and spooned the cornbread and milk into her mouth. "Not now. I haven't had time to go hunting."

"You need husband."

Belle sent him a wry smile. "No, thanks. I've had one of them. Me and my children are doing fine. Just fine." She stopped eating for a moment as a thought struck her. "I wonder if Jimmy left any money?"

"The law is looking for money he took. The law will come question you, my father says."

"That's all I need." She rolled her eyes and sighed. "Aren't you going to eat?"

"No." He pushed aside the bowl. "Not hungry."

"Liar." She smiled to show him that she was joshing him.

"You just hate to take food from a widow and her fatherless children."

"What's he come for?" Pearl asked, wiping drops of milk from her chin with the back of her hand.

"He came to tell me that Jimmy is dead." Belle spread a dish towel across Pearl's lap. "Be a lady and wipe your mouth with this."

"Jim Papa's dead?"

Belle pinned her daughter with a cool glare. "I told you that he's not your papa."

"He's dead?"

"Yes." Belle glanced at Sam. He didn't seem surprised by her personal tidbit. "Dead and buried. You want some more cornbread?"

"No." Pearl slid off the chair. "All full. Going outside."

"Stay in front of the house!" Belle scooped Eddie from the high chair and into her lap. She noticed Sam's watchfulness. Did he stare at everyone like that? "You got a girl, Sam?"

He shook his head. His inky black hair brushed the tops of his shoulders.

"It's about time you got yourself one, don't you think?"

He nodded and folded his arms across the front of his buckskin shirt.

"Got your eye on one?"

He nodded again.

"Hope she likes her men quiet." Belle sighed again and felt awkward. How did one entertain a silent young buck? She didn't feel like company, and she admitted to herself that the news of her widow status had shaken her more than she'd thought possible. She eyed Sam Starr, wishing he'd quit staring at her and be on his way back to Youngers Bend.

"Well, you best be on your way," she spoke up. "I've got

that garden out there to tend and I know you've got better things to do than wagging your head at me." She stood up, propping Eddie on one jutting hip. "Thanks for bringing me the news of Jimmy's death. Give my regards to Tom."

Sam got to his feet slowly, his eyes never wavering from her face. Without a word he left the house, sprang onto his horse, and sent it along the road at a gallop. Belle watched him from the doorway, wondering what had been going on behind his silver eyes.

"That there's one weird boy," she told Eddie, then let the toddler slide down her body to the porch. "You play with your sister, baby. Mama's got to get back to working the garden."

She looked toward the road again and wished she could go back to Youngers Bend with Sam. Her gaze tracked over the flat land given to her by her father. A restlessness blew through her like a fond memory.

"Free," she murmured. "Free."

Belle removed her wedding band and dropped it into her apron pocket. She went inside to pack her trunk. There were relatives in Missouri and friends in Arkansas. No need to spend time in the garden under the hot sun when she had people who would be more than happy to comfort a grieving widow and her poor children!

"Pearl! Eddie!" she called over her shoulder as she threw things into the trunk. "Get in here! We're going on a trip."

Pearl raced into the house, her blue eyes wide with excitement. "Where we going?"

"Lots of places, honey. Go get your clothes out of the bureau drawers."

"Will we be gone long, Mama?" Pearl asked.

"There's no telling, sweetie. There's just no telling. Now run and get your things. Bring Eddie's, too."

*   *   *

"Don't you think this skirt is a mite too short?" Emmalou Jones asked Belle as she turned around and around to see the brown skirt in the general store's tall mirror.

"This is eighteen seventy-six, not the dark ages," Belle said, throwing up her hands in exasperation. "Live a little. What if it does come up to your shoe tops? You can't see anything. Nothing to be ashamed of, anyway."

"You're bolder than me, Belle," Emmalou said, but Belle could tell that she liked the skirt and would buy it. "Does it make me look fat? The color . . . does it wash me out?"

"Buy it, buy it!" Belle sat in a chair near the potbelly stove that was cold on this August day. She looked out the window at Fort Smith's busy main street and pondered her recent state of irritability. Maybe it was time to move on. But where to this time? Back to Rich Hill or to Texas? Neither held any appeal to her. Home was just a word, not a place anymore.

She knew better than to remain still for long periods, because it always set her to thinking and wondering. Thinking about her poor papa, dead two months now, and her mama living alone in Scyene. Wondering about Eddie, who was staying with the Reeds in Rich Hill, and about Pearl, whom she'd left with a married friend in Conway. Mostly she thought about Cole and ached to contact him. Hadn't he heard about her being widowed? Why hadn't he come looking for her? Robbing banks and cattle rustling couldn't take up all his time!

"Belle. Belle!"

"What?" Belle snapped from her thoughts and stared blindly at her friend. "I'm sorry, Emmalou. What did you say?"

"I said that I've purchased the skirt so we can leave now. You ready?"

"Yes." Belle stood up and walked beside Emmalou out into the summery afternoon. "I was just thinking about my people all scattered to the four winds. Guess I should start rounding up my loved ones."

"What's the hurry?"

"The hurry?" Belle scoffed. "Emmalou, I've been bouncing from one place to another for a couple of years now."

"I know, but I've had so much fun these past few months with you being in Fort Smith. You've got so many men in love with you, Belle Reed, it's a downright sin! Why, every available gentleman in town is at your beck and call."

"And a sorry lot they are." Belle sniffed with contempt. "There's not one among them worth my trouble. Where are all the real men?" She looked at the ones around her—some in business suits, others in field clothes—and didn't see one that could hold a candle to Cole or Jesse. "This town is so tame, it's boring."

"Law and order is what Fort Smith's all about these days," Emmalou said as she drew on her gloves. "Judge Parker doesn't cotton to outlaws and renegades. I like it. Makes me feel safe."

"Feeling safe is like being dead." A jolt of awareness zipped through her. She sounded like Jim. Like Jesse. Like Cole. Life was too predictable for her and she was longing for excitement. She wanted to dance on that borderline between right and wrong again. "I think I'll head back to Dallas tomorrow. I'll collect Pearl on the way, but I'll leave Eddie at Rich Hill. Mother Reed dotes on him."

"Don't leave!" Emmalou turned huge green eyes on Belle. "What about the party next week?"

"I've had all the parties I want for a while—at least in Fort

Smith. I hear that Dallas has some honest-to-goodness barn burners. That's more to my liking."

"You always were a bit wild," Emmalou said, pouting. "Back in Carthage you and Bud rode up and down main street like a couple of wild Indians. "Lawdy mercy!"

Belle stopped in her tracks and looked back at Emmalou, who was staring in horror at the wooden stand outside the Fort Smith newspaper.

"What's wrong?" Belle asked, coming back to Emmalou.

"Look there. See what I mean? Law and order isn't just in Fort Smith. It's all over the country."

Belle stared at the black block letters marching across the top of the newspaper. She grabbed up one of the editions and held it closer to her face. Cole's name blurred before her eyes. Her hands began to tremble.

"Northfield, Minnesota," she read aloud. "What the hell were they doing in Minnesota? Oh, my God!"

"What?" Emmalou pressed against her, trying to see the article.

"It says that Jesse and Frank got away, but the Youngers were caught. They've been wounded. Cole . . . Cole . . ." She ran her eyes down the gray column of type as doom pushed up against her heart until she gasped with pain. The awful truth swam before her eyes and she had to force herself to keep upright and not pass out on the street. "He's been s-shot . . . eleven times!"

She closed her eyes and the paper slipped from her fingers. Emmalou gripped her shoulders and shook her.

"Belle! Don't you faint on me! Myra Maybelle, you hear me!"

"Y-yes."

"You paying for this paper?" a man asked, coming out of the newspaper office and retrieving the fallen edition.

246

"Hello, Mr. Perkins." Emmalou smiled sweetly. "Yes, we'll take that paper." She handed him his money. "We were taken aback by your front-page story."

"One for our side," Perkins said, chuckling as he tucked his forefingers into his vest pockets. "It's a shame they let the James scum get away, but they'll get their just reward sooner or later. Mark my words. Those outlaws will all swing before the year's out."

A vision of Cole and Jesse twisting in the breeze burned against Belle's eyelids. Her throat tightened around a moan. Cole . . . shot eleven times . . . facing a hanging judge!

"W-when did this robbery happen?" she asked, forcing the words past her dry lips.

"Three days ago. They caught the Youngers and brought them back to town yesterday," Perkins answered. "If they were facing Judge Parker, they'd be as good as dead."

"Let's go, Emmalou." Belle clutched her friend's sleeve. "I'm feeling sick."

"Oh? Well, in that case, let me see if we can get a ride from Mr. and Mrs. Duncan." Emmalou stepped off the boardwalk and hailed a passing buggy. She spoke to the middle-aged couple in it, then turned back to Belle. "Come on, hon. They'll give us a ride back to my place."

Belle gathered her senses and followed her friend. She looked at Emmalou's worried expression after she'd climbed into the back seat with her.

"I'm fine, Emmalou, but I've got some powerful planning to do."

The buggy jostled past the old fort that was now Judge Parker's territory. He'd turned the officers' quarters into his courtroom and had taken up private residence in the commissary building.

"I hate this town," Belle said, fired by indignation.

"You don't," Emmalou insisted. "You're just upset."

"I hate all this iron-fisted law and order."

"Oh, Belle," Emmalou said with a laugh. "You don't mean that. Everybody likes law and order. We've got to protect ourselves."

"Against what?"

"Well, against bank robbers like those Youngers."

"What's so wrong about some Rebs stealing Yankee money?"

"Hon, the war is over." Emmalou stared straight into Belle's dark eyes and repeated slowly, "Over."

"For some. For others it keeps popping up. Some of our boys were forced into lives of crime, Emmalou."

"Do you believe that? Belle, do you?"

"I not only believe it, I've lived it!" Belle faced her, nose to nose. "I've seen it with my own two eyes. Men like Cole and Jesse were never given a chance."

"They were offered the same chance as anybody," Emmalou said in a whisper, glancing toward the man and woman seated up front. "Nobody is forced to rob a bank, for heaven's sake!"

The buggy came to a stop in front of the schoolhouse where Emmalou taught. Behind the white building was a small cottage belonging to the schoolteacher who had been Belle's friend since Carthage. Emmalou had married after the war and moved to Arkansas, only to be widowed three years later.

Emmalou gripped one of Belle's elbows as the two women moved briskly along the boardwalk toward the modest dwelling.

"What are you planning, Belle?"

"I've got to go to him."

"Go? Where? Who's him?" Emmalou asked, pulling off her gloves and perky green hat as she entered the house.

"Minnesota. Cole Younger."

"Cole Younger?" Emmalou's fingers bit into Belle's forearms. "You know Cole Younger that well?"

Belle nodded.

"What are you planning to do once you get to Minnesota?"

"Hire him a lawyer. A good one."

"With what?"

"Money." Belle looked away from Emmalou, anticipating the next question. "That's part of the plans I've got to make. I've got to raise money and raise it quick." She disengaged herself from Emmalou's firm grip and went to sit at the kitchen table. Dropping her head into her hands, she closed her eyes and tried to think.

Cole . . . Cole. Eleven bullet wounds. God, he might be dead already! Please, God. Not Cole, Belle prayed. You've taken every man that ever meant spit to me except for Cole and Jesse. Don't take them, too!

Emmalou put on a kettle of water for tea while Belle forced herself not to panic, but to think clearly, constructively. What did she have worth any money?

"My land that Daddy gave me." She winced, hating to give up the only thing she had left of her father's loving generosity.

"Don't sell your land," Emmalou begged. "You'll regret it. Land is important, Belle. You need a place for your children. Your daddy wouldn't want you to sell."

"Pearl and Eddie can stay put for now."

"Yes, but later—"

"I can't think of later. I've got to think of now. I've got to think of Cole. He's bleeding, maybe on his deathbed, in a place called Northfield. I've got to get to him and help him, Emmalou!"

The teapot released a column of steam and Emmalou set it off the fire and brewed the tea. She set two cups and saucers on the table, then gave Belle a long, measured look as she sat primly in one of the carved chairs, a calculating smile on her pouty mouth. She patted her blond hair as she often did just before she said something catty.

"So it's true that he's Pearl's daddy?"

Belle sipped the tea, wondering if she should lie or not. Why lie? Emmalou had her figured.

"Cole is Pearl's daddy. He's also the only man I've ever loved with a passion so divine that . . . well, I can't speak about it."

"My, my!" Emmalou giggled. "He must be something to make *you* speechless."

"He's something. Something special. I'd sell my soul to get him a chance at freedom." Belle laughed at herself. "Regrettably, my soul is worth about as much as Confederate money. All I've got is my land, my stock that Cole gave to me, and a little money I've put back for Pearl's schooling. That'll have to do."

"You think a lawyer can get the Youngers off free and clear?"

"I don't know." Belle reached for the newspaper again. "Let me read this story again. Sounds bad. What in hell were they thinking of, robbing a bank in Minnesota of all places!" She read the article, shaking her head in confounded fury. "Says here that folks think Frank and Jesse got away without nary a scratch while Cole, Bob, and Jim were shot so many times you could see daylight through them." Belle's lips trembled. "It's a wonder any of them are still alive."

"What else does the article say?" Emmalou leaned closer when Belle made a little squeak in her throat and pressed her knuckles against her lips. "What, honey?" The sheen of love in Belle's eyes brought a lump to Emmalou's throat. "Tell me."

"It says here that . . ." Belle paused to bat away a tear

from the corner of her eye. "It says that when the sheriff brought the Youngers back to town in the back of a wagon, a big crowd was waiting to see them. Cole . . ." She paused again to smile through her tears. "He stood up and doffed his hat to the ladies. The damn fool." Her voice broke and she waited a few seconds to compose herself. "Shot eleven times, but he bows to the ladies."

"A true Southern gentleman," Emmalou said, clasping one of Belle's hands. "I've never seen you so wrapped up in a man. I always thought you were immune to real love."

"No." Belle smiled sadly. "Not immune, just unlucky."

"Honey, I think you shouldn't do anything rash. Give yourself a few days to think—"

"No." Belle squared her shoulders with firm resolve. "In a way, I'm glad this happened. I've been moving around like a cloud in the sky, restless and rootless for too long."

"Who could blame you?" Emmalou reached across the table to grasp one of Belle's hands. "Your husband is murdered, then your daddy dies suddenly, then your mama sells the family farm and moves to Scyene. Everything changed so fast for you!"

"It's been two years since Jimmy died," Belle said, finding it hard to believe herself. "I need to make a new life myself instead of leaving my children with others and pretending I'm sixteen and single."

"That's right," Emmalou agreed, squeezing Belle's hand affectionately. "And that's why you shouldn't go to Minnesota. How will that settle you down? It'll only make you worse."

"Oh, no." Belle shook her head slowly and smiled. "Seeing Cole again will make me whole . . . it'll heal me up inside. I've been dreaming that he'd send for me . . . or, at least, send word to me." She grew misty-eyed again and her smile was strained. "I thought he'd come riding up like a modern-day knight in shining armor. We'd marry and raise Pearl and Eddie together." Belle sighed and drank some of the spicy tea. "Well, some townsfolk in Northfield shot holes through my dreams, but Cole needs me, and I'm going to him."

"Hon, there's nothing you can do. He's too far gone. He's a bad man and—"

"No!" Belle snatched her hand away as if Emmalou's touch burned her. "Don't ever call him bad! He's the best man I've ever known." She narrowed her eyes to slits of anger and watched as the color drained from Emmalou's face. "Are you going to help me or hinder me? Tell me now. I've got to know."

Emmalou studied her for a long minute before she lowered her golden lashes in a sign of surrender.

"I'll help. I see the devotion in your eyes. There's no denying it, so I'll help."

"Thanks, Emmalou." Belle smiled warmly at her friend. "I knew I could count on you."

"What will you do first?"

"Go to Texas and sell my land." Belle glanced upward with a twinge of guilt. "Daddy gave me that land so I'd have something to fall back on if my luck ran bad, but I think he'd understand my selling it for Cole. He always thought Cole hung the sun and the moon."

Chapter Sixteen

THE COURTROOM IN NORTHFIELD was packed with spectators and reporters. Belle sat between Bruce Younger, Cole's cousin, and Henrietta Younger, Cole's sister. She paid little attention to either. Her attention was riveted on Cole, who stood at the front of the courtroom, surrounded by reporters.

Under the advice of the high-priced attorney Belle had hired, Cole and his brothers had admitted their guilt. Minnesota law called for prison terms for those pleading guilty. For those professing their innocence and found not to be so, there were the gallows.

"He looks drawn," Henrietta said beside Belle. "Doesn't he look sickly?"

"He is," Belle whispered back, never taking her eyes off Cole. "He's weak from the bullet wounds." Weak of spirit, too, she thought to herself. The past few weeks had been a strain on everyone.

Cole and his brothers had spent their time in jail. Crowds were allowed to pass through and talk to the outlaws. Cole's attorney had urged him to use this to his advantage by playing on the sympathy of those citizens.

Glancing around her at the stern faces in the courtroom, Belle wondered if the grandstanding had done any good. How long would he be sent away from her? Five years? Ten? Fifteen would be too cruel. Fifteen years without Cole Younger! Belle swallowed hard and sent up a prayer that Cole's sentence be no longer than ten years. She'd sold everything she had of value to come here and hire the best attorney in the state. Her sacrifices would pay off, she told herself. Cole would serve time and be back in her arms within a decade. That would give her time to buy another piece of land and a house for him. It would be perfect. Ten years wasn't that long. It would pass quickly.

The reporters dispersed by order of Cole's attorney, and Cole moved around the long table toward the chair he would occupy beside his brothers. His gaze found Belle's and he froze, not moving a muscle, as if the very sight of her sent him into a trance.

Belle shifted uneasily on the hard wooden bench. Cole's thickly lashed eyes looked sad, forlorn. One corner of his mouth twitched, then lifted ever so slowly in a hollow smile. He lifted his shackled hands, crooked one finger, and Belle rose as if she were tied to that curling forefinger by an invisible cord.

She came to the low banister that acted as a barricade, and Cole stepped closer so that he could whisper and be heard by her.

"It's almost time, sugar."

She nodded, her throat so tight with emotion that she couldn't speak.

"I wanted to thank you for coming here like you did." His hands moved up to the left side of his rib cage in an unconscious gesture. He flattened his palm against the place where three bullets had been extracted only weeks ago. "Just like a knight in shining armor."

She smiled and her eyes filled with tears.

"None of that." He looked away from her and his mouth thinned into a straight, stern line. "I can't stand seeing you cry."

"It'll be okay," she said, finally managing to speak. "We'll be together soon."

"Oh, Belle." He sighed and looked down at the dusty toes of his boots. "I don't think so, honey. I think me and the boys have fallen into a mess of misery this time."

"No, Cole. Your attorney is the best that money can buy."

He lifted his hands and the chains jangled from his wrists as he smoothed his forefingers down Belle's damp cheeks.

"But money can't buy miracles, sweet Belle." He looked to his left and right, then leaned over the banister and kissed the tip of her nose. "I love you."

She felt her eyes grow enormous as her heart took wing. He chuckled softly at her reaction, then stiffened when he heard the door behind the judge's bench open and close.

"All rise!" the bailiff intoned. Cole stared into Belle's eyes another moment before he turned his back on her and faced the bench.

Belle made her way to Henrietta and Bruce. They sat down, side by side like ducks in a row, and held hands as the judge glared at the three men before him.

"Cole Younger," the judge began when the courtroom became as silent as a church. "You are guilty of attempted robbery and murder. Bob and Jim Younger, you are guilty of attempted robbery and complicity in murder."

Belle drew a deep breath as Henrietta squeezed her hand. The judge motioned for the men to stand. Chains rattled as all three brothers stood, their feet and ankles held by iron cuffs and heavy balls of lead.

Staring at the back of Cole's head, Belle remembered running her fingers through the golden glory of his hair.

She trembled, wanting to hold him and feel his mouth on hers again. One more time, she prayed. I'd give my life for just one more kiss.

The judge cleared his throat and everyone in the courtroom seemed to take a collective breath and hold it.

"I sentence all three of you to life in prison. You'll be taken immediately to the prison in Stillwater, Minnesota, where you shall live out the remainder of your days. May God have mercy on your souls."

Bob and Jim slumped back into their chairs, leaving Cole to stand alone. The courtroom erupted into a fury of movement and shouting, but above it all, Cole heard a heart-wrenching wailing of his name. He turned and was stunned to see that the ululation was coming from Belle. An officer of the court grasped his shoulder to force him around and out of the room. He caught Belle's gaze, her dark eyes swimming with tears and strangely unfocused, and then she fainted in the arms of Bruce Younger.

Her cry of agony echoed in Cole's head as he was led from the courtroom and toward a destiny that had been born in the battlefields of his youth.

The room was so bright that it burned her eyes, so she closed them again, wondering where she was and who she heard moving so quietly near her. A painful memory tried to rear up in her mind, but her survival instincts blocked it out. Comforted by the false realization that nothing would hurt her, she opened her eyes again. The bright light was sunlight pouring into the room. Two masculine hands came into view to pull the lacy curtains together and diffuse the light.

"Who's that?" Belle asked and her voice sounded far off and weak.

"It's only me."

Blue eyes sent a healing power over her bruised spirit. She touched the man's face with trembling fingers. Cole?

"Bruce. Bruce Younger."

Younger? her mind repeated.

"Cole's cousin."

Cole?

"Don't you remember?"

"Cole," she said.

"Yes, that's right. You remember, don't you? You remember me?"

"Bruce."

"That's right." His hand was gentle upon her forehead. "You fainted dead away and I brought you here."

"Here?"

"My hotel room. I had a doctor look at you and he said you'd had a bad shock and to let you rest. You've been asleep for hours." He pushed her hair back from her face. "Henrietta went on to Stillwater. She said to thank you for everything."

That hurtful memory tried to burst into her mind, but she steeled herself against it, sending it back to its dark corner.

"I didn't know what else to do." Bruce shrugged helplessly. "I hope your staying here doesn't ruin your reputation."

Belle laughed weakly at the notion.

"Are you hungry? Thirsty?"

"Yes." She glanced sideways at the pitcher on the table. "Is that water?"

"Yes. I'll pour you some."

She watched as he busied himself with the pitcher and glass. He was a handsome man in his early thirties. His hair was almost brown with streaks of blond through it. He wore it brushed straight back and it curled at his collar. His dark blond beard was a mass of tight curls and clipped close. His cheekbones were sharp, giving definition to his face. Wearing gray trousers and vest and a white shirt, he had a polished look about him. A monied look.

"What do you do for a living?" she asked, realizing that she knew nothing about him.

"Oh, a little of this and a little of that." He held the glass to her dry lips and let her drink from it.

She reached for his free hand and turned it over to examine his unblemished palm. Looking up at him through her dark lashes, she asked, "Are you a gambler or a thief?"

"Gambler," he confessed.

"Where do you practice your trade?"

"All over, but mostly in Missouri."

"Whereabouts?"

"Galena. You know it?"

"I've ridden through it a time or two. It's wild."

"And wonderful," he said, his expressive eyes taking on a glint of excitement. "Redhot Street has the prettiest dance-hall girls and the best poker players in Missouri, bar none."

"Is that where you'll go now?"

"Yes, I guess so." He glanced toward the lacy curtains that billowed outward. "I'm sure not staying here. I don't like Minnesota. It's full of cold weather and cold people."

"I'll second that." Belle glanced down at her wrinkled peach-colored dress and bare feet. "Where are my shoes and purse?"

"In the closet. Where are you going?"

She pushed herself up to a sitting position on the narrow bed, surprised by her own weakness. Looking around at the Spartan furniture, she felt disconnected and adrift in turbulent feelings she couldn't understand. "I don't know where I'll go from here."

"Why don't you come to Galena with me?"

His eyes reminded her of Cole. Temptation took hold of her senses and she couldn't think of any reason why she shouldn't go off with him. She didn't want to see anyone she knew. She didn't want their false sympathy or their hollow words of encouragement. Something dreadful had happened in her life ... something so terrible that she didn't want to face it. It was better to turn her back on it and head for unknown territory where no one knew her, where no one expected her to grieve or cry or fall to pieces.

"Why don't I?" she asked, lifting her chin at a jaunty angle.

"Why, sure!" He chuckled, standing beside her bed and tucking his thumbs in his vest pockets as he rocked slightly on the balls of his feet. "I told Henrietta that you were the kind of woman I'd like to have on my side. There's not many women like you."

"Thank God!" She smiled, realizing that she hadn't lost her sense of humor. "You don't mind if I tag along after you?"

"Hell, no, lady! Be glad to have your company. There's a coach leaving in the morning. That'll give you time to collect yourself and regain your strength. You've had a bad setback, but you're not the type to hang your head and crawl on your belly for long."

"No, I'm not that type."

"He'd want it this way, Belle." Bruce set his handsome face in a stern scowl. "He wouldn't want you to pine away in this hellish place. He'd want you to get on with your life."

She didn't have the heart to argue or even to wonder if she were doing the right thing. The important thing, it seemed to her, was that his last name was Younger and that his eyes were a familiar shade of blue. Looking into them made her spirit rise from the ashes.

*   *   *

The whiskered, white-haired old gentleman crossed his arms on top of the upright piano and smiled toothlessly at the bittersweet song that Belle was playing.

"That's right pretty," he said as she finished. "I sure love to hear you play. How long you been working in here?"

"I'm not working," Belle said with a laugh. "I'm just passing time."

"This is a friendly establishment," the old geezer said, looking around the crowded saloon. "Galena is a friendly town. I've been here six months. How long you been living here?"

"Oh, not long." Belle looked squarely at the old miner, seeing him—seeing everything—crystal clear. "Me and Bruce have been living in the Four Star Hotel for two years," she said, more for her own information than for the old man's. Hadn't she talked to this old gent before? Many times before? Her head began to swim as her past rushed back at her. "Chester Tyler!"

"Yep." His dark blue eyes twinkled. "How's your little girl? She's a right pretty thing. Did she go back to Arkansas?"

"Pearl . . . yes, she's in Conway." Belle began playing a song she'd played for her daughter when she'd visited a few months ago. All of it had seemed like a dream until now. Two years! She'd been living in this mining town for two years. She was known as "Mrs. Younger" and her daughter had answered to "Pearl Younger." Belle smiled, thinking that it was time to call a spade a spade and a Younger a Younger. How many nights had she sat at this piano and played for hours on end while Bruce won and lost money at poker? How could weeks slip into years without her being aware of it?

"You okay, Mrs. Younger?" Chester asked, jarring Belle from her inner revelations.

"Yes. Why?"

"Well, you stopped playing right in the middle of that song."

"Oh." Belle looked at the piano keys. "I play this thing a lot, don't I?"

"Every night," Chester said. " 'Cepting for Sundays, and then I understand that you play the church organ."

"Yes, I do." Belle pressed her fingertips to her temples to ease the pounding there. She turned on the piano bench to look for Bruce.

Wagon wheels rimmed with lanterns were suspended from the ceiling. They shed light over the twenty round tables in the center of the saloon where poker games and serious drinking reigned supreme. The men were absorbed in their card games, barely paying any attention to the two or three saloon girls flitting from table to table. Glasses were refilled. Ashtrays were emptied. Money was thrown into the pot, then scooped up by winners as losers moaned and called for more whiskey and a kiss from Lady Luck.

The batwing doors flapped as new customers arrived and others staggered home. It was Saturday night and Redhot Street was heating up as miners came down from the hills looking to wash off the grime and grit of the work week. Smoke hung halfway down from the ceiling, barely stirred by the breeze that floated in from outside every so often.

Two rowdy cowboys, riding at breakneck speed, flashed past the saloon, guns blazing. Belle jumped and looked to the barkeep. He shrugged off the incident and his expression said, "Boys will be boys and men will be men."

Men get away with murder, Belle thought, then straightened as if someone had put the tip of a knife to her back. No, that's not right, an inner voice told her—a voice that hadn't spoken to her in a long, long time. Men don't always get away with murder. Some of them go to prison for life—for life, Belle!

She stood up just as Bruce Younger came forward. He slipped his arms around her and whirled her toward the back of the saloon. The shadows were thick beneath the stairs that led up to the rooms; four rooms where the bar girls plied their trade.

Bruce kissed her, his hands moving with familiarity, squeezing her waist and caressing her hips.

"I won a pile of money," he whispered in her ear. "It's my lucky night. See those two in overalls sitting by the window?"

Belle glanced in that direction and eyed the two surly-faced men in their dirty overalls and shirts. She nodded.

"They fell off the hay wagon," Bruce said, laughing as his mouth skimmed down Belle's neck. "They never suspected a thing but their own bad luck."

"In other words, you cheated."

He laughed lightly and kissed her pursed lips again. "I'm feeling my oats tonight, baby."

"Baby." Belle pushed back from him. "I think I'll send for Pearl and Eddie. I'm missing them ever so much."

"Since when?" Bruce frowned at her. "Pearl was just here a couple of months ago. Leave her where she is. As for Eddie, he's better off with the Reeds."

"Says who?"

"Baby, aren't we having fun? What kind of fun can we have with two kids hanging on to you?"

"They're my children. I should be with them."

Bruce backed away and straightened the striped silk cravat at his throat. The diamond stickpin sparkled in the dim light. His smile was forced as he ran the fingers of one hand lightly down her cheek.

"What happened? You seem so restless all of a sudden. So different."

She was fascinated for a moment by the comforting blue of his eyes, but she shook off the feeling.

"We've been here two years, Bruce. I . . . where has the time gone?" She flung out her arms to indicate her surroundings. "I've spent two years in this town and all I've seen of it is a saloon, a hotel room, and the insides of a church!"

"You've had a good time," Bruce said, taking one of her hands and lifting it to his lips. He looked at her from beneath his blond brows. "Admit it. You've had the time of your life, and I've been damn good for you. When I think of all the times we've laughed and loved and—"

"Loved?" She grew cold inside because she knew the difference between what she felt for Bruce and love. "Do you really love me, Bruce?"

He turned her hand over and kissed her palm. "I love being with you. You know how to have a good time and give a man his space."

Belle gently extracted her hand. His opinion of her rankled and made her ashamed of herself. Her head throbbed again and she laid a hand against her forehead.

"I've got a headache. Let's go to the hotel."

"Not now!" Bruce ran his hands down his cinnamon-colored jacket and tugged his vest into place. "I've been invited to join another game."

Belle looked toward the table he indicated. Three men were waiting patiently for a fourth.

"Go on then," she said, standing on tiptoe to kiss his jawline. "Have your fun."

"Play something lively on the piano," Bruce urged. "Not any more of your sad love songs."

"No, I'm going to the hotel."

He shrugged in an uncaring way that sent a pang through Belle. "Suit yourself. I . . . don't wait up for me."

Belle saw something akin to a shadow flit across his face. The change was subtle, but it was there. She followed his eye line to one of the saloon girls, then read his mind with the ease of a woman who had lived around men long enough to understand their short attention spans.

"I won't wait," Belle assured him. "See you around."

She swept from the saloon in a swirl of emerald-green satin. Bruce had bought the dress for her as he'd bought many things for her. She'd accepted them with abandon, seeing them as baubles that would bring money once she rolled out of Galena. That time was drawing near, she thought as she made her way along the dark street to the hotel.

Upstairs in the room she shared with Bruce, she looked around it as if she'd never seen it before. It was impersonal like the life she'd led in it for two years. Belle sat in the velvet-covered wing chair near the window and felt tears sting her eyes. What the hell had she been doing? Had she followed in her mother's footsteps and unhitched herself from reality? Had she been blinded by blue eyes and a last name she'd wanted to share?

A tapping at the door startled her. She ran her hands across her burning eyes and gathered her composure. Rising slowly from the chair, she glanced in the mirror at her shiny black eyes and upswept ebony hair before she crossed the room to open the door.

A tow-headed boy stood in the corridor. He turned big brown eyes up to her and his lower lip trembled.

"Jesse James sent me," the boy said, his chest rising and falling under his cotton shirt. "He sent me to get you. You're Belle Younger, ain'tcha?"

"I am." Belle examined him with a jaundiced eye. "Why

would Jesse send a boy like you to find me? Why didn't he come here himself?"

"He can't. He wants you to meet him outside of town. You know the old Chambers' place? The one with the barn half-falling down?"

"I know it."

"He's there."

Belle smiled and ruffled the boy's straw hair. "Do I look like a fool? I'm not going anywhere."

The boy looked panicked for a moment. He gave off the distinctive odor of sweaty children.

"He said you wouldn't come unless you was told that you can't refuse him. You promised to always help him if he needed you."

Belle went to the bureau and came back with a silver dollar, which she dropped into the boy's shirt pocket.

"The Chambers' old barn, did you say?"

"Yes'm."

"Okay. You've delivered your message, now get."

She listened to his bare feet pounding against the wood floor and bouncing on the stairs. It had been more than a decade since she'd heard bare feet slapping down hotel hallways. Bud and Ed and Mannie and Shug. Her first boys—not her sons, but they'd been her boys. She'd raised them and they'd raised her. Maybe she'd mothered all she could. Maybe she was mothered out and had nothing left for her daughter and son. She felt empty like a pastry shell with nothing sweet inside it.

She closed the door on the shadowy past and went to her closet for an outfit suitable for meeting an outlaw by moonlight. As an afterthought she packed a satchel and even tucked inside it one of Bruce's shirts and a pair of his trousers.

She retrieved her horse from the livery and rode out of

town, heading for the dilapidated Chambers' barn. The property was for sale and long since abandoned, so there was nobody around to witness Belle's approach. She dismounted, removed her Winchester rifle from its sleeve, and approached the barn in silence.

"Jesse? It's Belle. Show yourself or I'm heading back to town. I'm in no mood to play hide-and-seek."

"Inside the barn," a voice instructed.

Belle drew a deep breath as her heart lurched and she forced herself to move past her initial qualms. The barn was empty and milky light slanted through the rafters and missing boards. Owls swooped overhead. Mice rustled hay. Someone breathed heavily over in a corner. Inside was black as pitch. Belle cocked the hammer on the rifle and it sounded like a cannon blast. The breathing stopped.

"Don't shoot me," Jesse said. "I've already been shot once today."

"Jesse?" She craned her head forward, testing her eyesight on the dark. "That you?"

"It's me." A match flared and behind it was Jesse's handsome face. "I knew you'd come even though you must be madder than a wet hen at me."

"Mad?"

"Because of Cole. I'm free as a bird, and he's in prison. Hell, he'll be an old man by the time he gets out. Damn shame, not to mention a waste of a good man."

"Cole." Belle said the name slowly.

"Cole should have listened to me," Jesse said, waving out the match to let darkness shroud him again. "If he'd gone off with me and the others, instead of staying with Bob, he'd be a free man today. But, no. He had to stay behind with Bob bleeding like a stuck pig. Hell, I would have sworn that Bob Younger would've been as dead as a doornail within an hour. Shocks me all to hell to hear that he's recovered and is in prison along with Cole and Jim."

"What are you saying?" Belle asked, her voice a monotone. But her insides were churning like a Texas twister. "You wanted Cole to leave Bob for dead? You should've known better! Would you have left Frank?"

"If he'd lost that much blood and was holding me back, you betcha!" Jesse chuckled to himself. "Hell, I would have left my sainted mother. That posse was so close we could smell them. Wasn't no time to be charitable, I'm here to tell you."

"Come into the moonlight where I can see you." Belle waited until he'd butt-walked into the feeble light. He was wearing a black hat and there was something black and sticky all along one side of his neck and down his shoulder and upper arm. "I wanted to be certain it was you. Now I am. No mistaking that sneer."

"It's me, honey. I've got a favor to ask of you."

Belle raised the rifle and cocked it. Jesse held up his hands in alarm.

"Hey, hey! What's going on here? Put that rifle down, woman. I told you, I've been shot once today and I'm not looking to get—"

"How can you ask a favor of me after what you've done? If it weren't for you, Cole and me would be together. I'm sending you to a place of torment just as you sent Cole to one."

"Quit kidding around, Belle." His laugh was anything but confident.

"Who's kidding?" She squinted one eye and took a bead on him. "I want to thank you for giving me a good kick in the seat of my pants. I'll be able to draw an honest breath once I pull this trigger."

"Belle, I mean it! Put that damn thing down!"

Her lips pulled back in a smiling grimace as she squeezed the trigger. The rifle's report sent the nesting owls into a frenzy overhead and feathers rained down from the rotting rafters, but they failed to catch Belle's attention. She was too immersed in watching the quick succession of disbelief, panic, fear, and shock on Jesse's lean face as the bullet tore cleanly through his hat, whipping it off his head and behind him. Sweat soaked Jesse within seconds and his skin was deadly pale and gleaming, his eyes enormous as he realized that he wasn't dead, but that Belle had cocked the rifle again.

"The next one should take off the top of your skull," she said in a cold, lifeless voice. "This is the price you pay for deserting your friends, Jesse. Since Cole can't settle the score, I'll do it for him."

"Cole wouldn't want this," Jesse said, finding his voice. "You know he wouldn't! He fights his own battles. He doesn't want women fighting them for him."

"Keep talking, but it won't do any good."

"He knew the risks, Belle. We all know them. Hell, by this time next year we might be in prison with him. Put the rifle down. Don't we have enough enemies without becoming that to each other?" He made a placating gesture and his smile was unusually gentle. "Put the rifle down, Belle. I'm sorry about Cole. I really am, honey, but what's done is done. Killing me won't spring him . . . or you from whatever prison you've put yourself in."

Tears stung her eyes. She fought them, but lost the struggle and then was glad of it, for they washed away the blackness from her soul and let in the light again so that she could see the folly of her recent past. She emerged from her dark, cottony place, blinking like a newborn baby. Jesse's worried expression floated before her. Fingers closed around her hands, pulling the rifle from her loosened grasp, then smoothed over her jet-black hair.

"Sit down, Belle," Jesse said, placing his hands on her shoulders and pushing her down onto the hay and dirt. "Are you thinking clear now? Want a drink? I've got some whiskey left. It's in my saddlebag, and I'll be happy to share it."

"No. Whiskey won't make me think clear." She pressed the back of one wrist to her sticky forehead. "I'm so tired, Jesse. I'm tired of being strong. I guess I'm tired of living."

"Don't say that. I'm tired, too, but living is better than dying. You've been living pretty good of late. Is it true what they've been saying about you and Bruce Younger?"

"What have they been saying?"

"That you and him have been shacked up in a hotel in Galena."

Bell winced at Jesse's description of her tawdry life. "I guess they're right." She closed her eyes for a moment, trying to look back on that relationship.

"He's a Younger," Jesse said with a sly grin, "but he's a sorry substitute for Cole."

"Don't I know it." Belle nodded, impressed by Jesse's wisdom. She shouldn't be surprised. Jesse had always been smart and seasoned.

"Where's Bruce now?" Jesse asked.

"Sleeping with a saloon girl, probably." She shrugged and laughed at herself and her situation. "If I don't come back, he'll breathe a sigh of relief." She sighed and closed her eyes for a moment to look inward. "You're right. He was my substitute; part of the nightmare I've been living since Cole went to prison." Her voice broke and she didn't resist when Jesse took her into his arms. She rested her cheek against his shirtfront and closed her eyes again. "I spent most of my money on the lawyer for him and his brothers, but there wasn't much anybody could do. What made you pick that Northfield bank in the first place?"

"Seemed like a bright idea at the time. Remember Gen. Benjamin Butler out of Massachusetts?"

"He's a bluebelly rascal, isn't he?"

"A damned Yankee of the worst sort. He and his son-in-law own the Northfield bank. Makes my blood run cold when I think of all the Yankees sitting behind their desks in those fancy banks. They made a killing off us Southerners."

"That's the gospel truth," Belle agreed, resting comfortably against Jesse. It was nice to be held by someone she knew and trusted. Never in a million years would she have imagined herself in Jesse's arms. Her life, it seemed, was chock-full of ironic surprises.

"The more we thought of Butler wearing his fancy suits and counting the money he made by foreclosing on Southerners, the madder we got," Jesse went on. "Problem was some of the boys started drinking and were woozy by the time we hit the bank."

"The older you get, the dumber you get. Just like Jimmy."

"Have some respect for the deceased," he cautioned, but he was teasing. "It was just one of those days when it didn't pay to crawl out of your bedroll. That town is full of heroes, I'm telling you. The townsfolk came out shooting, like they were all duly sworn deputies."

"Do you think somebody tipped them off?"

"No, I think they were a bunch of Yankees with more guts than sense and they got lucky that day. Damnedest thing I ever saw. The whole blamed town was armed to the teeth. They tried to plug us as many times as they could before we got out of town. Cole was shot up. Bob was as good as dead, and Jim wasn't that much better off."

"They all looked bad in court."

"Did you talk to them?"

"Just Cole, and then not much. We didn't have much to say to each other under the circumstances. I don't think he liked having me see him chained up like an animal. He's got a lot of pride."

"I know. Too damned much, if you ask me."

"Nobody did."

"Sorry to tarnish your knight's armor." He gave her a squeeze.

"What's this?" Belle sat up to touch the sticky places on his shirt, but it was her sense of smell that identified the goo. "Blood!"

"Sure is. I told you I'd been shot today."

"Where?" she asked, leaning back to have a better look.

"Here, right behind my ear. It's only a flesh wound."

Belle examined the place where Jesse's skin and hair were missing. "Looks like you were pretty lucky. If the bullet had gone in, they'd be measuring you for a burial suit."

"Don't I know it. For a minute, I thought I was dead, and a few minutes ago, I thought I was dead again. You scared ten years off my life, woman!" He picked up his hat, stuck his finger through the hole, and glared at Belle when she laughed at him.

"I swear, Jesse, you've got nine lives just like a cat."

"I know when to cut my losses and head for the hills. Besides, I'm too ornery to die."

"That's what Jimmy always said," she observed dryly. "So what happened? Another job gone awry?"

"You got it. But this time it's going to work to my advantage." He covered his wound with trembling fingers, wincing as a sharp pain careened through his skull. "Me and the boys have hatched a beautiful plan. Classic, in every sense." A vicious smirk twisted his lips. "Don't you see? It's perfect. I got shot today by a bounty hunter and left for dead. He rode off to tell the sheriff in Joplin. I'll let them think they killed me and that my men rode back and collected my body. I'm taking off for Mexico or the Territory. I'll send for my wife and kids later when things die down a little."

"Don't you think the law will be suspicious when they can't find a body?"

"There's a body." He grinned, showing off his straight teeth. "It just isn't mine. We've got a doctor to swear it's me, and we're shipping the poor fella to my mama's place for burial. The boys will swear I was killed and they'll fill Mama in on the farce. She'll go along. She'll love it!"

"Your mama thinks you can do no wrong. She makes the papers more than you do," Belle observed, thinking how different Jesse's mother was from her own. "Mine, on the other hand, always suspected that I was one step away from being a whore." She laughed without humor. "I guess these last couple of years I've proved her right. She's probably gloating."

"Quit feeling sorry for yourself and start counting your blessings," he snapped.

Belle covered her face with her hands as shame grabbed hold of her and gave her a good shaking.

"Lord, we're a mess. You're playing dead, and I've been sleepwalking through my life like some ghoul! We make a fine pair, don't we?"

"Two of a kind," Jesse agreed. "I remember that I thought you were trouble the minute I laid eyes on you. Then I looked real hard and realized that you were a soul mate."

"A what?" she asked, lifting her face from her hands.

"Soul mate." He flattened one hand against his chest as if that were the place where he kept his soul. "That's when you know somebody before you even know their name. Like you felt with Cole."

"Are you telling me that you love me?" Belle asked in a shocked whisper.

"In a way, I guess I do. You've got to love somebody a

little to trust her as completely as I trust you. I always knew that you were true blue."

"How do I fit into this classic scheme of yours?" Belle asked, growing uneasy with the turn of the conversation. She didn't mind having Jesse as a friend, but she didn't want him to get any other ideas. She'd awakened from one nightmare and she wasn't about to dive into another.

"I need you to spirit me to Youngers Bend. Folks won't think anything about you hitting the road. I want you to get yourself a wagon, load it up like you're heading for greener pastures, and come back here for me. I'll hide in the back of it and off we'll trot to old Tom Starr's place. I figure I can stay in Robbers' Cave awhile before I mosey on down to Mexico. Frank's going to meet me at the cave in a couple of days and—"

"Robbers' Cave? I never heard of that," Belle confessed.

"It's a cave not too far from Tom's place where Rebs used to meet during the war. Me and Cole met there oftentimes when we needed to talk out a job or make plans. It's a safe place. You'll bring the wagon for me, won't you?"

"Sure, but should we wait until tomorrow? That boy you sent to get me might squeal all—"

"No, he won't. He's my cousin. He won't tell a soul about me or you. Bring the wagon round about sunrise if you can. I'll be ready."

"Ooops! I clean forgot. You stay put," Belle said, snapping her fingers.

"Where are you going?" Jesse asked, sitting upright when she bounded to her feet.

"I've got something for you." Belle ran outside and returned with the satchel. She tossed the change of clothes at him. "I always come prepared. Change into those and bury the others. You won't look so conspicuous in clean clothes."

He examined the shirt and trousers and chuckled. "What else did you pack in there?"

"Some things for me. Guess I've lived on the run for so long that I'm always ready to take off at a moment's notice."

He unbuttoned his bloodstained shirt and wiggled out of it. "Do you forgive me for being here instead of Cole?"

Belle sat down again, watching as he buttoned the fresh shirt. "I guess. Of course, I would have never left him and his brothers. United we stand, remember?"

"What can I say?" Jesse asked, spreading out his hands with a shrug. "I'm a survivor, not a gentleman. Cole, on the other hand, is a true gentleman, stuffed full of honor. See where it got him?"

Belle waved aside the argument. "Forget it. At least Cole's alive. That's something to be thankful for."

"Maybe he'll escape from prison."

"Oh, sure," Belle said sarcastically. "And maybe you'll go to heaven." She turned aside while Jesse changed trousers, but faced him again when he was done. "It's been awhile since I was at Youngers Bend. Me and Bruce went there . . . I think . . . but I'm not sure when it was or how long we stayed."

Jesse watched her distress for a moment, then held out his arms wide to her. She hesitated only a moment before stepping into his gentling embrace. He ran one hand over her silky hair and let her cry softly against him as he slowly lowered himself and her down to the cold ground. He felt awkward at first because it wasn't in his nature to hold a woman for purposes of consoling, but Belle had always had the power to make him go against his own nature. She brought out feelings in him that he was ashamed to admit he had. His mother and wife would have been surprised to see how tenderly he held Belle and how downy soft his voice was as he spoke to her.

"Welcome back to the living, Belle. When I heard about you taking up with Bruce, I could hardly believe it. I should've known that something was wrong with you. Bruce is a hard-hearted cad. Not your type in the least."

"He was there. I was alone." She hid her face in his shirtfront, gathering the material in her tight fists. "I'm so ashamed."

"Don't be. We all handle things differently. Once we're at the Starrs, you'll be on the mend. That place rejuvenates better than a day in a mineral springs."

"You're right. It's a magic place." She lifted her eyes to his. "Thanks, Jesse. In a way, you've rescued me."

"Glad to do it. Now you can return the favor by showing up here bright and early with that wagon."

"I'll be here," she vowed, and Jesse knew he could bank on her word.

Chapter Seventeen

YOUNGERS BEND DID REJUVENATE HER, Belle thought as she rocked on the front porch and looked over Tom Starr's pastoral domain. The whole Starr bunch had gone into Briartown for the day, but Belle had insisted on staying behind. She craved peace and quiet, time to think of what she would do with herself from here on in, and time to get used to being without Cole Younger.

Ever since she was sixteen, she'd kept a candle burning for him in her heart, and the flame had remained constant because she'd known that their paths would cross from time to time. But a judge in Minnesota had dashed her feeble hopes of seeing him, living with him, and maybe even marrying him. A lifetime was too long to wait for any man. Cole was living in a dark place and so would she. They could share that, if nothing else.

She'd always love Cole, but she had to live without him and learn to like it.

The six or seven bird dogs the Starrs kept on the place raised a ruckus minutes before Belle heard the approaching horses. She stuck her hand in her skirt pocket and gripped the handle of one of the six-shooters Cole had given her. Being around the Starrs had made her more conscious of her own safety. The Starrs never went anywhere—not even to the outhouse—without a weapon, and Belle had begun to adopt their ever-ready attitude.

When she recognized the riders, she smiled and pulled out her empty hand from her pocket to wave at Jesse and Frank. They were dressed for traveling and their bedrolls were tied behind their saddles.

"Quiet, dogs," Belle commanded as she'd heard Tom do so often, and the yipping hounds were silenced. "You're leaving today?" Belle asked, anticipating Jesse's opening remark.

"That's right. Robbers' Cave is all yours again." He pulled his black hat down lower and glanced at Frank, who was staring straight ahead in a stubborn refusal to acknowledge Belle. Frank held on to the saddle horn, shoulders hunched, arms stiff to take his upper body weight. He looked like a big toad trying to climb up on a tiny mushroom. Jesse laughed, catching Belle's gaze to share the moment. "Frank's anxious to leave."

"Well, I'm anxious to see him leave," Belle retorted, laughing again when her remark made Frank's skin suffuse with angry red. "I always thought that Frank's best feature was his back."

"I'll miss you, little sister," Jesse said, turning sideways toward Belle and ignoring his sullen brother. "Thanks again for helping me out."

"Glad to do it." She looked around at the porch yard, grassless and dotted by homey articles such as butter churns, wooden tubs, tree swings, and farm implements. "You got me back here, and I so love it here at the Bend."

"I know I'm leaving you in good hands," Jesse said. "Tom

thinks you're the cat's meow and young Sam has been making calf eyes at you all week."

"Say what?" Belle's eyes narrowed with suspicion, then widened with alarm. "He's not sweet on me!"

"Oh, no?" Jesse chuckled and ran a hand over his grinning mouth. "Guess I need my eyes checked."

"Hell, Jesse, he's just a boy."

"Nope, you need *your* eyes checked."

Belle batted a hand at him. "I don't have time for such foolishness. Men aren't my priority and won't be until I know what I want and how to get it."

"Let me leave you with the advice my mama always gave the girls in our family," Jesse said, then leaned close and lowered his voice to a conspiratorial whisper. " 'Where cobwebs grow, comes no beau.' "

"I've heard that one," Belle said. "My mother says the same thing."

"Then use your heart for something more than pumping." He touched the brim of his hat and nudged his mount with his heels. "*Adios,* Myra Maybelle. Keep the wind at your back, girl."

"I'll do it." Belle watched as he and silent Frank reined their horses between trees and finally out of sight. Belle closed her eyes and thought back on her friendship with Jesse, amazed that it had lasted this long and had grown stronger over the years.

She thought of another saying her mother spouted, "You pick your friends, but not your relatives." Well, in this case, she hadn't picked Jesse as a friend. He'd picked her.

She dozed but was awakened an hour later by the excited whines of the dogs, which meant the Starrs had come home. So soon? They hadn't been gone more than a couple of hours. Belle sat up in the rocker to see Sam Starr come riding up, leading a flighty black mare with a blazed face.

"Where's everybody?" Belle asked when she realized he was alone.

"Still in town." He slid off his horse and coaxed the other animal toward the corral. "I buy this horse and bring her home."

"She's pretty." Belle stood up and stretched her arms over her head. She started to turn and go into the house, but something in the way Sam spoke to the mare—so gentle and lilting—gave her pause. Instead of going inside, she went to the corral and crossed her arms on the top rail to watch Sam gentle the new arrival. "She's not broke?"

"I will break her."

"She sure is a beaut." Belle admired the horse's sleek body and high-stepping hooves. "Lots of spirit."

"Good horse," Sam agreed. "She plenty smart. Make good trail horse."

"What's wrong with Warrior?" Belle asked, looking back at Sam's grazing palomino.

"Nothing." He laid a finger against his full lips, motioning her to be quiet while he worked with the nervous mare.

Belle obeyed, thinking of Jesse's teasing and sage advice. She switched her attention from the rearing mare to the boy . . . man. Yes, man, she thought. He was no longer a youngster. He was a full-grown man.

Not as tall as his father, Sam still stood over six feet and was as taut and supple as a bow string. He moved with a liquid grace, gliding across the corral with the ease of a panther. He was part civilized and part wild, part precocious and part wizened, part placid and part piquant. She felt her allegiance to Cole waver.

"Sam, how old are you?" she asked, shattering the silence she'd given him.

He threw her a confused glance. "Old? Twenty-three." His eyes twinkled. "And you?"

"Uh . . . twenty-seven," she lied, shaving five years off her actual age. Knowing she was almost ten years his senior sent a dread through her. She chided herself. Some men were born mature, and Sam was one of them.

"Why ask?"

"Uh . . . no reason." She shrugged and rested her chin on top of her clasped hands. "Go on with what you're doing. Sorry I bothered you."

"You are no bother." His silvery eyes sparkled in the sunlight and there was the barest hint of a smile on his lips.

Sam removed the halter but kept one hand buried in the horse's mane. The mare tried to dance sideways, but Sam spoke softly and she settled down.

"Whoa, little girl," he said, his voice rolling across the space to Belle. "Nobody will hurt you. Thatta way. Thatta way, pretty one."

He grabbed one of the mare's ears with his free hand and spoke in that velvety voice that seemed to flow like honey. Belle sighed and her eyelids grew heavy. She loved that voice, loved the way it wafted through her head like curls of smoke and warmed her insides like glowing embers.

The next thing she knew, Sam had released the mare, but she didn't bolt and run. The animal stood perfectly still as Sam ran his large brown hands down her neck, withers, and back. The mare trembled, her nostrils flared, and she stamped her front hooves.

Belle trembled, her stomach fluttered, she swayed her hips ever so slightly as a yearning poured through her.

Sam took off his shirt and dropped it to the ground. He squatted down and massaged the mare's legs. Muscles writhed in his back, just below his coppery skin. His backbone made a ridge, his ribs pushed out, then disappeared. His hands and arms were veined and corded. He stood up again, and Belle admired the length of his legs. He wore leather pants that defined his tight buttocks and thighs. Belle smiled, feeling flushed and breathless. She closed her eyes and pretended to be the horse. She felt Sam's stroking hands, massaging fingers, full lips against hers. His remembered voice seduced her.

"Thatta way, pretty one," he said in her head, and Belle released a long, whispery whimper.

The sun beat down on her upturned face, making her aware of her surroundings again. She opened her eyes slowly, then fully when she realized that the mare and Sam had moved closer to her. Sam looked at her over the horse's back. His eyes glittered like diamonds. His smile was full of certainty.

Belle started to deny the overt sexual awareness, but she knew it was too late for denials. He'd seen the evidence in her heightened color and heaving breasts. He'd heard her soft moan of yearning. She uncrossed her arms and stepped away from the corral fence, all the while holding Sam's riveting gaze.

"You've got quite a touch," she said, her voice so soft that Sam could barely hear her. "Quite a way with . . . animals."

"So everyone says."

She nodded, feeling her throat tighten with tension and something else—anticipation?

"Well, I'm going inside. It's hot out here."

"Very." He glanced up at the sun, finally releasing her from his rapt attention.

Belle seized the moment and raced across the yard and into the house, her heart fluttering in her breast like a captured bird. She laughed, putting a hand to her pounding heart.

"Well, Jesse, I'm using it for more than pumping," she whispered, laughing again at her excited state.

She pirouetted in the center of the room, then dropped

like a feather into a chair. It felt good to *feel* again. To feel something besides remorse and desolation and anger. She felt years younger and knew that Sam Starr was responsible.

Had he been making calf eyes at her and she'd been blind until now? Or was she imagining his interest because Jesse had planted the seed of it in her mind?

Guilt triggered a wince, then made her sit up straight in the kitchen chair. Cole, she thought with a dousing of sadness. How could she feel good about a man when her beloved Cole was rotting in a cell? It wasn't right! She couldn't just take up with another man as if Cole didn't exist!

"Belle?"

She jumped up from the chair as if she'd been shot and whirled around to find Sam standing on the threshold of the open back door. He filled the doorway as he filled her mind with thoughts that made her blush and feel girlish again.

"W-what?" she asked, then laughed at her reaction. "You snuck up on me."

"Bought you something in town."

"Oh?" She noticed that he was hiding something behind his back. "That's nice. Let's see it."

He whipped it forward, then out to her. It was a white hat, broad-brimmed with one side swept up and secured by a diamond-studded pin and three brightly colored ostrich feathers.

"My, oh my." Belle took the hat and looked it over. "Would you look at this?"

"You like?"

"It's the prettiest thing I ever did see." She smiled at the Southern flirtation in her voice. She hadn't used that lilt in so long, she was surprised she still had it in her. "I'll try it on in front of the mirror. Be right back."

She headed for Tom Starr's bedroom, which had the only

mirror in it. Standing before the full-length looking glass, she put on the hat. Her heart kicked against her ribs when she saw Sam's reflection appear behind her.

"What do you think?" she asked, holding his reflected gaze. He stood over her, his shoulder even with the top of her head. "I like it. It's not a bonnet, but it's not a man's hat either."

"It is Belle's hat."

"Yes." She smiled, liking the symbolism. "All mine."

Delight made his eyes turn to quicksilver. He lifted his hands to the tops of her shoulders.

"It's not too flashy?" she asked, not quite knowing what to say next.

"You don't need to dress like old widder woman."

"That's what I am," she said, her lashes sweeping down to dust the tops of her cheeks. Too old for you, she thought. You should be with a young, dark-skinned beauty like yourself.

"You are the morning dew," Sam said, capturing her attention and holding it easily. "You are the sunrise and the first buds of spring."

"Why, Sam Starr! I don't know what to make of you." She laughed, but it had a nervous, high-strung quality. She eased away from him, taking off the hat as she moved across the room and toward the safer territory of the main living room. "Jesse and Frank left a couple of hours ago. I guess they'll go on down to Mexico so Jesse can play dead awhile longer."

"But you stay."

"Yes, but I should be getting on, too. You know what they say about company. Fish and company smell after three days, and I've been here more than a week." She hung the hat on a peg near the door, then stood back to admire it.

"You belong here."

She shook her head. "No, I don't. This is Starr country."

"Could be your country." He moved around the table as if he were stalking her. "I know what you felt outside by the corral. I felt it, too. I have been feeling it for long, long time."

"Puppy love," she scoffed. "Rarely lasts."

"I hunger for you."

Belle swallowed hard and knew she couldn't speak if her life depended on it. Sam's gray eyes narrowed as he came to stand before her, towering over her and making her all the more aware of his masculinity. His chest was well-defined and as smooth as a baby's butt. Belle forced her gaze up, past the shelf of muscle and bone, to his square jaw and wavy lips.

"I have kept a dream of you in my head, but now I think I can share it without dishonoring you or me." He cupped his hand around her neck. Her skin was warm and vibrant; his touch, cajoling and magnetic. "You are without husband. I am without wife. There is no shame in us now."

Belle stared at him, alarmed at how loquacious he'd become. Usually he didn't have more than a dozen words to say, but suddenly he was a fount of poetry before her. Had lust loosed his tongue?

"What would Tom say about all this?" she asked, trying to make light of the seriousness she sensed in Sam.

"He thinks I should already have told you of my hankerings. He thinks I should take you to bed. Now." He nodded toward Tom's bedroom. "In there."

"W-what?" She backed up a step. "Hold on a minute. I'm not so sure a man is what I need. Men haven't been that good for me, you know."

"You've never had a man treat you good."

"Yes, I have." Belle shrugged off his look of disbelief. "Well, as well as can be expected. I'm no gem, you know."

"You are my jewel. I want a woman of grit, of flash, of many shining sides."

Belle edged past him to the open back door. Hens clucked busily in the yard. A rooster strutted his stuff among them. The black mare pranced and danced in the corral. Bird songs filled the air.

"I could stay at Youngers Bend," she murmured, not realizing she'd spoken until Sam came up behind her in one long stride. His hands closed on her shoulders.

"You stay. With me."

"Sam, listen to me." She turned around, pushing him from her so that she could look at him without tipping back her head. "I know what I'm talking about. You don't want to tie yourself down with an older woman like me; a woman who's had a husband, not to mention a couple of other men on the side. You're young. You deserve a young woman who can keep—"

"I want you, and I'll have you!"

His firm statement brooked no argument. Belle saw the granite determination in his iron eyes. He was a man to be reckoned with, and she reckoned she could handle him.

"We'll see," she said in a placating tone. "But don't rush me. You might have had this dream in your head a spell, but it's news to me. Just because I'm without a man, doesn't mean I'm taking up with you. Give me a little time to get used to you, then we'll see."

"You'll come to me," he said. Then he smiled, and Belle knew right then and there that he was right. In time, she'd come to him, because she couldn't resist that sensual smile and those silvery glances for long.

Belle and Sam rode side by side toward the southwest corner of the Cherokee Nation, where Sam had built a house for his new bride.

"That," Sam said, pointing to a jutting point of land, "Hi-Early Mountain. You can see it from our cabin."

Belle reached out and held his hand as the horses inched closer. The road grew narrow with the approach to the cabin located on the north side of the yellow-watered Canadian, a slip of a canyon that led from the river to the uplands. The cabin came into view. It was made of sturdy cedar logs and shingles and perched on a knoll facing south. The back door faced Hi-Early and the front door looked out over a meadow where any rider could be spotted easily. Belle examined the outside of the cabin carefully before she let Sam help her down off the black mare he'd given her as a wedding present.

"I'm going to name my horse Venus," Belle told him, laughing when he made a face. "It's perfect! I fell in love with her when I watched you tame her that day in the corral, and I fell in love with you right after that. Venus is the Goddess of Love."

"Your goddess, not mine." He gathered her up into his arms and carried her over the threshold and directly into the bedroom. He set her on her feet, then stepped back so that she could have a good look at his other surprise.

"Sam!" Belle gasped when she saw the rose petals strewn across the bed. Her eyes filled with tears. "You . . . you're too good to me."

He withdrew a small, square sheet of parchment from his jacket pocket and dropped it to the bed.

"All legal. You belong to me. Forever."

Belle picked up the document and read it aloud for her own benefit. "On this day the fifth of June, eighteen hundred and eighty, were joined Belle Reed and Sam Starr in matrimony by District Judge Abe Woodall." She laughed and folded the paper, then tucked it in the Bible beside the bed. "Yep, it's legal all right."

He ran a forefinger from the gathered material at her shoulder down the satin sleeve and across the back of her hand. His fingers laced through hers. Belle looked up from their interwoven fingers to the smoldering desire in his gray eyes.

"Oh, Sam. I love this cabin, this land, and you."

"I make you happy?"

"Oh, yes." She turned around and waited for him to understand and release the buttons down her back. He fumbled with the cloth-covered buttons, giving a sharp sigh of impatience midway down her back.

"Silly woman's clothes," he muttered.

"Here." Belle reached behind her, caught both sides of the fabric and pulled gently. The buttons slipped from the eyeholes, one by one.

"It's easy when you know how," she said, laughing at his look of chagrin. She shimmied her shoulders and the top part of the dress she'd made for this auspicious day slipped away to pool at her waist. "You look mighty handsome, honey." She reached out and untied the black and gold bandana at his throat. "Let me see what you look like under that black suit and clean white shirt."

The heat of their passion increased and their clothes melted away. Sam made the first decisive move by picking Belle up into his arms and depositing her upon the feather mattress. It took her weight, then his. The perfume of crushed rose petals filled their nostrils.

Sam made love to her with a one-mindedness that Belle responded to with equal gusto. His powerful, yet powdery soft hands were everywhere upon her overheated body, coaxing and seducing and gathering steam as they made their way to the hair that grew like an arrowhead between her thighs.

Belle found in him a source of strength and a solidity that

she cherished. She matched his ardent lovemaking with her own less hurried style, making him take it slow and easy, although he champed at the bit like a blooded stallion. She tamed his youthful zest with her seasoned know-how, creating a calm before the inevitable storm that made them both tremble on the brink of ecstasy.

The forces of nature whipped through them. Sam cried out her name, his voice sounding like a lone wolf's on a dark night. Belle watched the exquisite pleasure upon the bold plains of his face, and in them found the wellspring of her own satisfaction.

Sam's mouth moved whispery soft at first before growing more demanding. His tongue parried with hers, warm and wonderfully frenzied. His lips and tongue danced over her body and he began to swell again, nudging toward that place that joined him to her.

Belle's mind wandered and flitted and flirted with notions of how she would be received as Mrs. Sam Starr. She laughed against Sam's roving mouth.

"What makes you giggle?" he asked, smoothing her long hair back from her temples where it clung in wet curls.

"I was thinking of how my mother would take the news of my marriage to a Cherokee."

"She'll take it bad?" Sam asked.

"She'll faint dead away," Belle said with another hearty laugh.

"And what about you?" He kissed her eyelids and drew his thumbs along her arched brows. "Is it bad or good that you mix your race with mine?"

"Well, I can't speak for the Starrs," Belle said, her lips inching into a grin, "but it's sure to improve the Shirley bloodline. A little copper will do us good."

Chapter Eighteen

MAMA, ISN'T THIS the prettiest place you ever did see?" Pearl asked as she rolled onto her stomach to observe the sprawling meadow.

"It sure is, honey," Belle agreed. "You like it here, don't you?"

"It's the best home I ever had. I like it ever so much better than being with Auntie Emmalou or Auntie Connie. I can stay here, can't I?"

"Yes, honey. We're all going to stay here. We're family now."

Belle recalled her girlhood when she used to stand by her bedroom window at the hotel in Carthage and survey the town as if she ruled it. She'd imagined then that she would own property one day and reign over it in queenly fashion, and now her dream had finally come true. And what a magnificent kingdom it was!

"Mama, why does Grandma Reed dote on Eddie so? Sometimes she flat ignores me," Pearl complained, picking another dandelion to weave into her necklace of wildflowers.

Belle sighed and lay back on the horse blanket she'd

spread in the meadow. Bees buzzed somewhere near her head. Horses whinnied in the distance. A cow sent a moaning moo across pastureland.

"Mother Reed sees Jimmy when she looks on Eddie, that's why."

"What does she see when she looks on me? She usually clucks her tongue like some old hen when she eyes me."

"When she looks at you she sees my betrayal." Belle rolled onto her stomach and looked up into Pearl's oval face. "You're not Jim Papa's child. I told you that. Remember back in Galena when folks started calling you Pearl Younger?"

"That was because of Uncle Bruce being with us."

"Yes, but I let them call you that because that's what you are. You're really a Younger. Not a Reed or a Starr. A Younger." Belle smiled a mother's proud smile. She reached out a hand to smooth back her daughter's curly flame-gold hair and looked deeply into eyes as blue as Cole Younger's. "I was just a few years older than you when I met your daddy. I fell in love with him so fast that it made my head spin. I never knew what hit me until it was too late."

"He's in prison."

"Yes, baby. A lot of the Confederate's heroes are in prison." Belle propped her head in one hand. "Do you remember much about Jim Papa?"

"Not much," Pearl confessed as she worked diligently on her necklace. "I remember that he had a mustache and that he smelled like liquor a lot."

Belle winced. "Yes, he did. That's one good thing about Sam. He makes liquor, but he doesn't drink it."

"I like Sam." Pearl smiled brightly. "He likes me and Eddie the same. He doesn't love one over the other like Ma Shirley or Grandma Reed."

"Does Ma Shirley treat you bad?"

"Not bad. She snaps at me. Says I'm too much like you.

Grandma Reed is pretty good to me. It's just that Eddie gets whatever he wants when he wants it. The Reeds spoil him something fierce!"

"Let them." Belle ran a hand along the hem of Pearl's buckskin skirt, which she'd had made special. "I'll spoil you. You're my precious Pearl. Always will be." She laughed when Pearl planted a smacking kiss on her mouth. "That's sweet sugar, honey. You need one of our Canadian lilies to weave into your necklace."

"They're too delicate. The minute you pluck them, they wilt."

"You're my Canadian lily," Belle said, rubbing the back of her hand along Pearl's flawless cheek. "Your skin is as soft and white as the petals of those lilies. Mama loves you very much. Don't ever forget that. All I have to do is look at you and I'm happy all over."

Pearl finished the necklace and she held it out to her mother.

"It's for you, Mama. It'll look pretty around your neck."

Belle batted away sentimental tears as she allowed her daughter to string the greenery around her neck.

"Thanks, honey." She fingered the flower necklace and wiped her tearing eyes. "This reminds me of a time I spent with your daddy. I made a chain like this out of morning glories—blue and purple ones, I think—and he wore it. He rode off with that silly flower thing strung around his thick neck like it was fashioned out of gold and diamonds. That was a wonderful time. I hadn't married Jim Papa yet. I was so young and still living with Papa and Mama in Texas. Seems so very long ago."

"Does Eddie look like Jim Papa?"

"Some. Mostly he favors the Shirley side of the family. Don't you think that him and Uncle Shug look some alike?"

"Yes. He looks some like you too."

"But he's got Jimmy's ways. He struts instead of walking. He talks instead of thinking. Every Tom, Dick, and Harry he meets is his good buddy. Just like Jimmy. Lord help him."

"Mama . . ."

"Yes, Pearl?"

"Is it true that you were once the Queen of the Bandits?"

Anger pumped through her and she grabbed Pearl's arm, making the girl cry out.

"Where did you hear such rubbish?" Belle demanded.

"In school," Pearl said, puckering up to cry. "Mama, don't hit me. I didn't mean nothing."

"What else are they saying in school about me?"

"N-nothing."

"What else?" Belle repeated, shaking Pearl by the arm. "Tell me."

"Tha-that you and Sam make whiskey and . . . and take other people's belongings."

"Hell's bells." Belle stood up, brushing grass off her tan skirt and motioning for Pearl to shake a leg. "The whole town's talking about us. You know what that means, don't you?"

"No," Pearl said, sniffing as she folded up the horse blanket.

"It means that somebody's going to try to pin something on us if we're not right careful. Who's been talking?"

"Andy Crane. He says that John West told him that you took his pony."

"That gimpy little bastard," Belle seethed. "John West is blabbing around town on us, too, is he?"

"Are you going to jail, Mama? Like Cole Younger?"

"Hell, no. Not if I can help—" Belle broke off her sentence when she noticed the fear in Pearl's face. Pity quickly replaced her anger and she pulled Pearl into her arms.

"There, there, my pretty lily. Don't go getting fainthearted over nothing. We've got a good life here, don't we? And we're going to keep it that way." Over Pearl's head, Belle spotted Eddie making for the stables. "Eddie, is Sam out there?" she called, and Eddie nodded.

"He's in the hay barn," Eddie shouted back, pointing to the towering building. "I'm going to saddle Venus and ride into town."

"No, you're not, little man!" Belle patted Pearl's pale red hair lovingly and released her. She strode across the meadow toward her dark-eyed son. "Your horse is Rondo. You keep your gloves off Venus. She's all mine."

"But Rondo isn't as quick-footed as Venus," Eddie whined.

"He's quick enough." Belle shook a finger in Eddie's face. "Hear me, and hear me good. If I ever catch you riding Venus, I'll take a horsewhip to you and beat you senseless."

"Aw, Mama . . ." Eddie kicked angrily at the grass.

"That's right, Johnny Reb. Senseless." She left him in his frowning fit of fury and went to find Sam.

"Sam, we're in trouble," Belle said, locating Sam outside the hay barn. "Pearl says that we're the talk of the town."

Sam removed the red bandana knotted around his neck and swabbed his face with it. He took his time speaking like he always did.

"Talk in Briartown? What they saying?"

"They're saying that I took Crane's horse."

"You did."

"I know I did, but I didn't want everybody in town to know it. John West is spreading most of the gossip about us."

"No can be. West is Indian."

"I don't give a damn if he's the high chief, he's flapping his gums about me taking Andy's horse."

"I spoke in secret to West. He wouldn't betray a blood brother."

"Well, he's doing it. Pearl wouldn't fib about this. She knows I'd beat her black and blue if I found it out."

"I told you not to take that horse."

"Who would have thought that Andy Crane would make such a fuss over it? I offered to pay him thirty bucks if he'd drop it. Stupid kid."

"He is crippled. The horse is his wings. He would miss the horse." Sam leaned back against the side of the barn and tied the kerchief around his neck again. "I could go into Osage and see if I could get the horse back from the man I sold him to."

"That's good. What about West?"

Sam laid the back of his hand against Belle's upper arm and shoved her aside as he made his way toward the pump.

"West would not betray me. You and Pearl all wrong."

Belle glared holes into his straight back and cursed his stubborn Indian blood.

A twig lacerated Belle's left cheek as Venus sideswiped a tree. She buried her nose in the mare's black mane and glanced sideways at Sam, making sure he was still astride Warrior and all in one piece. The sour smell of the sweaty horse filled Belle's head. She wondered if it were only the horse she smelled. She felt sticky all over and knew she was wet to the skin with her own cold sweat.

Bullets whistled through the air, making the horses tense with fear.

"Go, go!" Belle whipped off her brown slouch hat and used it to slap against her mount's backside. "Yah! Yah-ha!"

Venus laid back her ears and stretched out, hellbent for leather. Trees and shrubs blurred past Belle and she squinted her eyes against the wall of wind she and Venus galloped through.

Behind her were three riders. How far behind, Belle had no true notion, but the irrational side of her imagined them to be no more than a few strides. She could feel them gaining on her and Sam, their bullets slamming home any second now, ripping through meat and lodging in bone. Fear clawed its way up Belle's spine and she looked to her husband for a way out of this black hell.

Sam was plastered against Warrior's side, hanging on with one hand while he aimed his pistol with the other. His head swiveled and he looked at the winding path, then back toward the three lawmen on their trail.

"Robbers' Cave!" Sam shouted over the thundering hooves. His silvery eyes found Belle's wide and black.

Belle forced herself to recognize her surroundings and determine how far she was from the cave hideaway. She was closer than she'd thought. A familiar outcropping of rock and boulder loomed ahead. Belle tugged back on the reins, hauled Venus's head to the right, then dug her heels into the mare's heaving sides. The mare answered the call, checking her speed, changing direction, then diving uphill toward a ledge that wasn't visible to the naked eye and a hole that was covered by vegetation.

Belle sensed Venus's moment of uncertainty, and she answered the animal by flapping the ends of the reins in a decisive flourish.

"On, Venus. On!"

The horse lunged forward in a display of blind faith. Belle yanked the blazed face sharply to the left and around the camouflage of brush and timber. Venus shuddered beneath Belle in startled confusion as her hooves slid upon smooth rock, clattering and finally tapping confidently as the big horse realized it was on solid ground and not plastered against the side of a hill.

"See? I'm not crazy," Belle said, running her hand along Venus's damp neck. "Move over and make some room for Sam and Warrior." Belle reined the horse to one side of the cool cave. The walls were moist and glittered like diamonds.

Sam burst into the cave astride his wild-eyed palomino. The honey-colored horse snorted, started to rear, then settled down when Sam laid a long-fingered hand between its ears. He slid off the horse, grabbing up the reins and pulling the horse farther inside the high-ceilinged cave. He put a finger to his lips, let go of the reins, and tiptoed to the cave opening to peer out at their pursuers.

It seemed like an eternity while Belle remained on her horse and listened to the pounding of hooves in the distance. Sam was a statue. Only his eyes moved from side to side as he watched the three men ride in circles. Voices rumbled, but words were lost by the time they floated up to the cave. Belle ran her fingers through Venus's midnight mane, calming the winded mare and praying that the horse would remain silent.

Finally, Sam turned from the cave opening and ran a hand over his forehead in an exaggerated gesture of relief.

"They're gone," he said, whispering to be on the safe side. "Confounded and bewildered. They think we have great magic and can disappear like smoke."

"Our magic is running out, Sam." Belle motioned for him to help her from the saddle. His hands circled her waist and he lifted her down to the ground. Belle brushed dried leaves and bits of twigs from her doeskin jacket, then swiped at a tickle on her cheek. Her hand came away bloody. "What's this?"

"You got cut." Sam took the kerchief from around his

neck, licked a spot on it, and wiped the blood from Belle's cheek. "Not bad cut. Better than bullet hole."

"Did you see who that was, Sam?" Belle asked, her voice taking on a decided edge.

He nodded.

"John West," Belle said, wanting it said aloud so there'd be no mistaking it. She planted her fists at her waist and leaned into Sam's impassive face. "John West, your blood brother who will never turn on you. He would have shot you full of holes if he could've got close enough!"

Sam turned away. He leaned against the cool rock wall and slid down to his haunches. His hands hung loosely between his knees. He breathed heavily as if he'd run the last ten miles instead of his horse. He tossed his kerchief to Belle, and she dabbed at her cheek.

"He's been bad-mouthing us, Sam. He's going to get us into trouble. I just know it."

"He can be handled."

"Like hell! He was lying in wait for us this morning. He saw us stealing those horses, Sam! He's not going to forget it just because your skin is red like his."

"It is only his word against ours. Nothing will come of it."

Belle barked a harsh laugh and sat down in front of her husband. Sometimes she wanted to slap him into reality and knock some of his pride down his throat.

"John West is an Indian marshal. He's the law out here, Sam. If he tells a judge and jury that he chased us after we tried to steal some horses, nobody's going to be interested in what we've got to say. That's the way the goddamned law works, honey, and you'd better understand it. West has been after us since I took that crippled kid's horse. He's not letting up. He's going to see us in court or die trying."

"Then he die!" Sam shot up to his feet, his fists slamming

back against the rock so hard that pebbles broke loose and rained to the ground. "I am not afraid."

"Nobody said you were." Belle got to her feet wearily. "Being afraid doesn't have a damn thing to do with it. Being guilty as sin does."

Sam went to the cave opening again. He walked outside, had a look around, then came back in.

"Mount up. We take the back way to my father's. West won't look there first. He'll go to our place first. My father will say we've been at his cabin overnight and have not left it."

Belle shook her head, realizing that Sam still didn't comprehend that lying was not a cure for what ailed them. She swung up into the sidesaddle and followed Sam and the big palomino from the cave and into the morning sunlight. The horses picked their way through the dense underbrush and among saplings and mighty oaks. Smoke curled from one of the chimneys poking up from the roof of Tom's house. The smell of frying bacon and freshly baked bread floated out to Belle as she dismounted and went up the steps to the porch. Sam didn't knock; he just popped open the front door with one hand and grunted a greeting to his father and mother, who sat at the kitchen table.

"West is chasing us," Sam said without preamble. He sat down, straddling the chair, and grabbed a wedge of hot bread. "You tell him that me and Belle been here all night."

Tom nodded. "West, you say? John West?"

"He turned on us like night into day. Bastard."

Tom looked to Belle and smiled as she sat beside Sam. Something in his metallic eyes sent a jolt of alarm through her. She studied his tense smile and saw that it was sympathetic, not friendly.

"What's wrong?" she asked, looking from him to his round-faced wife Catherine. "What's happened?"

Sam stopped chewing the bread he'd shoved into his mouth and looked from Belle to his father. He swallowed the bread with difficulty and waited for the news that was undoubtedly bad.

"We heard this morning," Tom said, shaking his head in a sad way. "One of the boys heard in town."

"Heard what?" Belle reached across the table and grasped Tom's hand. "Tell me, for Christ's sake!"

"Jesse James was shot and killed yesterday in his own home by a fella he befriended. Brought the man home for supper, and the rotten son-of-a-bitch shot Jesse in the back."

For a few moments she stared stupidly at Tom, the facts refusing to sink into her resisting mind. Then, like an ax slicing through a frozen pond, the truth cracked wide open inside her. She slumped forward. Sam was out of his chair and behind hers in a blink of an eye. He held on to her shoulders, keeping her from falling face forward onto the hard table. She felt as if a vise were squeezing her chest and any minute her heart would pop up into her mouth.

"Belle?" Sam's hands tightened and he pulled her back so that she could rest her head against his stomach. "You okay?"

She closed her eyes and the tears ran hot, burning the cut on her cheek.

"I'm not going to be able to take this bad news good," she said, her voice trembling and the tears making trails down her cheeks.

Sam laid one hand against her cheek to keep the salty tears from finding the angry scratch. He bent over and kissed her forehead, taking in her misery like a sponge takes in liquid.

"So sorry, Belle. I know he was like a brother to you."

"I hated to tell you," Tom said, "but I knew you'd want to know."

"Jesse . . . dead. Shot in the b-back." Belle pushed herself up from the table and stumbled toward the back door. She threw it open and took in gulping breaths of crisp morning air. The breeze dried her tears, but the hurt stayed put in her heart. "I can't believe it," she said to the world at large. "I never thought he'd turn his back on anyone but Frank. Frank! Lord, how will he get on without Jesse?" She thought for a moment about her departed friend. "You know, Sam, Jesse was the smartest of us all." She placed a hand to her stomach, feeling barren and hopeless.

"You sit. Have some milk and whiskey," Sam urged.

"No." She turned to face him. "Don't you see what this means, Sam? It changes everything."

"What do you say?" he asked, shaking his head until his shoulder-length hair swayed like a dark curtain around his neck.

"I'm saying that with Jesse's death comes the death of our way of life. We used to be respected, put up on high horses. People remembered the war and wanted revenge just like us. For every person that was agin us, there was one for us. But no more, Sam. People are changing just like the times. They've forgotten the Rebels and the Yankees. They're all trying to live peacefully."

"Not all," Tom argued. "Not in the Bend. We don't forget!"

"But you're not the king around here anymore," Belle said, then stood tall in the face of Tom's ire. "I know you don't like to hear this, but John West and his Indian marshals are closing in on us. If we don't stay on the straight and narrow we're going to end up like Jesse or the Youngers."

"Not us," Sam said, crossing his arms on his chest and jutting out his chin at a stubborn angle. "West can't touch us."

"Sam, listen to me!" Belle grabbed him by the forearms and gave him a shaking. "West will come with a warrant for our arrest. Hear me? We can lie like dogs and pound our chests and dig in our heels, but we'll have to go to court. This time we'll have to stand trial. He caught us red-handed stealing those horses!"

"Didn't catch us!" Sam shook off her hands. "We got away."

"Only for the time being. Only until he can get that warrant. They'll come for us and we'll have to go with them into Fort Smith."

"Never." Sam sat down at the table and reached for the platter of bacon. "Will never happen."

Belle went to the door again, needing the sense of wide-open spaces. She stared at the vista long and hard as she thought of Jesse, the Youngers, Quantrill, Ed, and Bud. Nobody wanted war heroes anymore. The men wearing the tin stars were the new heroes, and she, Sam, and the others left of their breed were the vermin that had to be put away or put under. What would it take to make Sam understand that?

Judge Parker, seated high and mighty on the bench in his Fort Smith, Arkansas, courtroom, looked through his dark eyebrows at the tall, silver-eyed Indian and the short, black-eyed white woman.

Notorious, both of them. It was a red-letter day. A day that would end up in history books. A day the judge had waited for ever since the trial began a week ago. Sentencing day.

He wetted his lips, folded his hands primly atop his notes, and placed a stern expression on his heavy face. "Sam Starr. Belle Starr."

Both attorneys twitched nervously, but the Starrs were granite still and taciturn. "You have entered a plea of 'not guilty' and the evidence on both sides has been presented before this court. The verdict went against you, so punishment must be meted out." He craned his head forward. "You understand what I've said so far, Sam?"

"He's not an idiot, just an Indian," Belle snapped, and faced off the judge glare for glare. She won that contest.

Judge Parker looked down at his clasped hands and cleared his throat.

"My client understands you, sir," the attorney for the Starrs piped up.

"Very good." Judge Parker looked at them again, then past them to where old Tom Starr and his brood sat like so many fenceposts; arms folded on their chests, knees spread apart, shoulders squared, eyes as still and penetrating as a cottonmouth's. "As I was saying, punishment is at hand. I have given this a good deal of thought and I'm going to be lenient this time around since it's your first convictions." He waited for a reaction and got none, so he forged ahead. "The jury deliberated one hour and found Mrs. Starr guilty on two counts of horse stealing and Sam Starr on one count of the same. I want to say that I agree completely with the verdict. The testimony of John West was most thorough and convincing."

The spectators in the courtroom murmured and shifted uneasily. Belle and Sam never batted an eyelash.

"I hope that you will spend your time incarcerated wisely and in pursuit of solid citizenry. Sam Starr, I do hereby sentence you to one year in the House of Correction in Detroit, Michigan. Belle Starr, I do hereby sentence you to two six-month terms in same said correctional institute. So be it." Parker slammed down the gavel.

Sam looked at Belle and shrugged.

"Shit," Belle said, then turned to the attorneys. "And that's what you'll get paid with. You can collect your loads of manure at my father-in-law's place. Tom, you'll take care of these dimwits, won't you?"

Tom smiled and his gray eyes clouded over with hatred. "My pleasure."

The attorneys never came around to collect their fees.

PART FOUR
Youngers Bend
1885

Chapter Nineteen

THE WIND HOWLED and whistled around the house, its voice penetrating the closed window. Belle listened intently to the sounds of Youngers Bend, taking nothing for granted anymore. She heard and saw and experienced every nuance of the land. She'd been out of prison for several years, but there wasn't a day that went by that she didn't think of her dingy cell and thank God to be out of it.

Sam began snoring softly beside her. Belle slid closer to him, resting her cheek against his smooth, muscled chest. A fat moon hung in the sky, visible through the window. Belle watched, fascinated, as a fleecy cloud clung to it and then sailed away. The moon wore a surprised expression. His mouth was a shocked O. Why surprised? Belle asked him silently. You ought to know by now that pretty things don't hang around too long. Got to enjoy them while they're around because there's no telling what the next minute holds.

It had been a time of adjustment since their release from prison. She and Sam had clung to each other and to Pearl and Eddie, forming a tight circle. Sometimes they went over to Tom's and saw other relatives, but the circle was never broken. She and Sam had agreed to keep to themselves.

Now as the night settled around her like a heavy blanket, Belle wondered if she shouldn't keep track of Sam's comings and goings. He was consumed with hatred for John West, and that worried Belle. Sam was on the warpath. Everything he did was aimed at getting under West's skin. Belle could certainly understand why Sam hated West with such a vengeance—his testimony, after all, had sent them to Detroit—but she didn't understand Sam's mounting fury. It was like a locomotive picking up steam, huffing and puffing, growing bigger and bigger until it overpowered and crushed everything in its path.

"My father's father was murdered," Sam had said yesterday evening after supper. "My father killed every man responsible. It is unwise to cross a Starr."

"I thought you wanted to be free from now on," Belle had reminded him, knowing that his conversation was turning toward his revenge against West.

"It's true."

"Do you really think that you can kill a sheriff and stay free as a bird? Sam, they'll hang your red ass so fast you won't have time to kiss it good-bye."

"But I'd be free. West being dead would free me."

"That's right. Don't think of me or the kids. You do what you want to do and leave us to scratch out a living."

"I'm not going to kill him. I make him suffer. I torment him. I make misery on him."

"You're tormenting yourself, you stubborn jackass. I thought we were going to keep to ourselves."

"We do."

"But you keep dragging West into our lives!"

"You tend your children and don't worry about West. He is my worry."

The baying of the dogs roused Belle from her thoughts and Sam from his sleep. Soundlessly, Sam slipped out of bed and into his trousers. He pulled his suspenders up over his shoulders and picked up his shotgun on the way to the back door. Belle was right behind him, belting her flannel robe as she went. She waved him out the back.

Someone stepped onto the front porch. The dogs were frantic, barking and yipping and waking the whole country-side. Belle grabbed the shotgun leaning against the fire-place, then she swung open the door with one hand and aimed the gun, hip high, with the other. Belle leaned side-ways to see the intruder, but the night hid his face from her.

"What's going on here?" Belle asked, remaining calm on the outside although her insides were beginning to roil.

"We want to ask you a few questions," John West said, stepping into the light with leggy ease. He thumbed his mustache and hid his smile behind his hand. "Your hus-band is in trouble again and I'm going to take him to Indian court this time. What do you think of that?"

"I think you've finally gone around the bend," Belle sassed, beginning to understand why West was a burr under Sam's saddle. The man's smile was like salt on a wound. Unbear-able. "State your business and get."

"We're here to get the truth out of you." He looked back at the two men behind him.

"What truth?" Belle faced him, lowering the shotgun. She heard Pearl and Eddie behind her. "Get back, babies. We got animals out here on the porch." She pushed Pearl and then Eddie back with her free hand. They sat down behind her to watch the show.

"Where's Sam?"

"I don't know. He went hunting with his papa and brothers a couple of days ago. I sure hope they bring home some bear meat."

"You expect us to believe that?" West asked, giving her a sweeping once-over with his beady eyes, then glancing back at his companions.

"I don't give a rat's ass what you believe," Belle shot back, and West's lips twisted into a grimacing sneer.

"Stand aside."

"Why should I?" she asked, keeping one eye on the two other lawmen behind him.

"Because I'm going to come in and look around."

Belle's hands closed around the rifle and she had it up to her shoulder and ready for business before the three lawmen could react. West stared at her as if she'd grown horns.

"What's this about?" he demanded. "Put that rifle down."

"You get away from my house," Belle ordered, forcing an iron will to her voice that contrasted with the fear that writhed through her like a nest of snakes. "You've got no right to bust in on us or search my home. You got an arrest order?" She caught the nervous bob of West's Adam's apple. "I thought not. You get on your horse and get the hell away from us, John West."

"You wouldn't shoot me," West said with a confident smile. "You're not that stupid."

"And you're not stupid enough to test that theory," Belle rejoined, and she saw the flicker of apprehension in his eyes. "The first one of you boys who goes for his gun will be the one to send West here to meet his Maker."

West stood motionless for several seconds while he debated with himself; then he shrugged.

"We're going," he said, keeping his hands up and out as he went to his horse, followed by the other two lawmen. He swung up into the saddle with a creak of leather. His smile was so stiff that it creaked too. "Won't do no good," he assured Belle. "I'll find Sam Starr sooner or later. He can't hide from me forever. The Indian court won't be as lenient as the white man's court. We won't put him in prison—we'll kill him!"

Belle kept the rifle pointed at West's heart and was ever so relieved when the sheriff finally turned his mount around and led his party away. When the sheriff's party was on the road back to Fort Smith, Belle's knees buckled and she sat heavily on the floor.

"Mama," Pearl said, scooting across to her. "Are you okay?"

"I'm okay now." Belle leaned the shotgun against the wall.

"You were so brave, Mama," Pearl said, draping an arm around Belle's shoulder and giving her a hug. "The way you stood up to those men! It made me and Eddie proud."

Belle smiled weakly.

"It's over now, Mama," Eddie assured her. "They're long gone. It's all over."

"How long will Sam be gone?" Pearl asked, sitting before her mother so that Belle could braid her long hair for bed.

"I don't know. He's been gone three days and I look for him to be gone a few more."

"John West wants his hide," Eddie said, stretching out on a pallet in the floor. "Ain't that right, Mama?"

"That's right. When will they leave us in peace?" Belle moaned, dropping her hands into her lap as a feeling of defeat wormed through her. "Are we the only people in this whole territory who've been known to take a horse now and then or sell off some corn whiskey? It's West, you know. It's that goddamned John West who's bringing all this woe down on our heads. No wonder Sam hates that man so much that he can't think on him without blowing his stack."

"You won't have to go to prison again, will you, Mama?" Pearl asked, turning around to look up into Belle's face.

"No, honey." Belle picked up the half-finished braid and her fingers began working through Pearl's strawberry-blond hair again. "I sure missed you two kids back then. I knew you'd get on fine without me, but I worried about you anyway. And I was half out of my mind with worry over Sam."

Belle swung around in the chair, alert and all atremble. She laid a forefinger to her lips to silence any noise from her children. Standing, she reached for the rifle over the mantel and moved resolutely to the door. She opened it, listening for the rustling of bushes that had warned her that lawmen were afoot.

Cryer, Sam's hunting dog, got the scent and lengthened his scrawny neck in a night-splintering howl. Cap'n followed suit with a baying Rebel yell.

"Damn dogs," came a whisper from the brush a few yards from the porch. "Heshyup, you fleabags!"

Belle settled the rifle butt against her shoulder and took a bead on the whispering bushes.

"You hush up and show yourselves before I send you straight to hell," she ordered, making her voice rock hard although her spirit was sagging and her stamina was that of a minute-old kitten. "I can hear y'alls teeth chattering and your knees bumping against each other, so you might as well step out from those bushes you think are hiding you. You're cowards, so you must have been sent by John West."

Two slumped-shouldered men stepped around the bushes, hands held out to their sides so that Belle could see they weren't after their holstered guns. One held a rifle in his hand, but he was holding it way up where it couldn't do any harm.

"Miz Starr," one said in a voice that was pretty near a whine.

"What is it, boy?" Belle asked, then cast her gaze down to his bony knees poking against his trousers. "It's a wonder y'all haven't worn your knees and elbows plumb out from crawling here on your bellies. Don't you know that I've got men posted all along Belle Starr Canyon just to take pot-shots at yellowbellies like you two?"

"Yes, ma'am, but we're here on official business," the other said, his voice a tad bit stronger. "We're here to take Sam Starr into custody. We believe he's in there with you."

"Well, you believe wrong. The only people inside are my son and daughter. I haven't seen Sam in days. For all I know, he might be dead. I know one thing for certain, he's not here. You two crawled all this way for nothing."

The moon sailed free of cloud cover and showed the men's faces to Belle. She'd seen them with West before.

"John West shot your husband clean off his horse earlier today," one of the men said. "Killed the horse dead away. Some of the Starrs held West off and Sam got away. We figured he came here. He's not at Tom's."

Belle forced herself not to show any surprise or pain. She kept the rifle steady.

"My husband was shot, you say? Well, you know more about him than I do. Like I said, I haven't seen Sam for days on end. He went hunting. That's all I know."

"Let's go," the taller of the two said. "I think she's telling the truth about him not being inside."

"I don't know." The other one stared past Belle at the open door where light and shadow flickered. "Okay, but we'll be back. I know he'll come here sooner or later and I'll be lying for him."

"You do that," Belle said, delivering a cold smile. "You've been mighty lucky up to this point, but no more. Next time you ride up my canyon you'll be so riddled with bullets that your own mother won't know you."

"Don't forget that you're speaking to an officer of the law," the shorter one said, puffing out his chest.

"And don't you forget that you're speaking to a woman at the end of her rope." She jerked the rifle in an impatient gesture. "Now go on. I'm tired of messing with you. Vamoose!"

They scrambled off into the night, rustling bushes and raising a ruckus. Jim July, one of Sam's distant cousins, oozed from the shadows at the side of the house and Belle realized he'd been there all the time, knife in one hand and a short rifle in the other.

"Sam's at his brother Tulsie's," July said, then looked toward the brush. "Want me to follow them and make sure they get off the property?"

"Yes, do that. I'm heading over to Tulsie's to see Sam. You keep an eye on Eddie and Pearl while I'm gone."

July nodded. "I'll stay until you get back."

"Thanks, Jim." Belle went back into the house, feeling jittery and panicked. How bad was it? Was Sam near death? "I'm heading over to your Uncle Tulsie's," she announced to her son and daughter. "You two stay here. I'll be back before sunrise. If anybody comes up, you run out back to the smokehouse and hide. Jim July will be outside somewhere guarding the house until I get back. You mind him."

"Yes, Mama," Pearl said.

"Is Sam hurt bad?" Eddie asked.

"I don't know, but I'll find out. Eddie, look after your sister." Belle put on her hat and kissed her son and daughter. "Mama and Sam will be home for good soon. That's a promise."

She slipped out into the cover of night. Jim July had brought around a horse for her. Belle settled herself on the sidesaddle and set off for Tulsie's place. The mare was unfamiliar to her and she missed her Venus. Sam had taken Venus with him the night West had come for him. Damn John West! Venus had been her partner, the best horse she'd ever ridden and a special gift from Sam. She'd never forgive West for killing Venus. Never!

Tulsie's house wasn't far away, but it was hard to get to since it was set way off the beaten path and in a densely wooded area. Belle slowed the horse to a high-stepping prance and guided her around trees and bushes that loomed black and foreboding in the night. The mare was fidgety and nervous, but Belle didn't blame her. The animal was probably picking up on Belle's own high-strung state. Horses were good at catching moods and making them their own.

The glow of lanterns in the distance excited the horse and she trotted the rest of the way, eager to find civilization again. Tulsie stepped onto the porch, rifle in hand.

"It's me," Belle reassured him. "I've come to see about Sam."

"Come in."

"How's Sam?"

"He resting good. Got hit in the side, but we got bullet out and he heals up fast. We got him down in the dugout."

"Right. Is there light down there?"

"You take this lantern." Tulsie pushed aside a low-backed sofa and opened a trapdoor in the floor. "Sam?"

"Huh?"

"Belle's here. She comes down to you." Tulsie steadied Belle with one large hand as she wrestled with her skirt and climbed down the ladder. He handed her the oil lantern. "You knock when you want up again." Tulsie closed the trapdoor.

"Sam?" Belle turned, holding the lantern aloft and peering through the dusty, musty interior of the cellar. Glass jars, lined up on shelves, reflected the lamplight. A cot was against one wall and that's where she found Sam, sprawled upon it and looking worse for the wear. "You're looking peaked. How are you faring, hon?"

He held out a hand to her and she crossed over to him and grasped it, letting him pull her down on the cot with him. He kissed her, but it was a weak facsimile. Belle studied him for a moment, sensing that he was physically strong but spiritually diminished.

"What is it, Sam?"

"He killed Venus. My fault. I should not have taken your mare that night, but she was in the corral and Warrior was out in the pasture."

"Sam, it's all—"

"You loved Venus. I failed you."

"Sam, Sam, listen to me." Belle framed his angular face in her hands and forced his silvery gaze to hers. "I'm glad it was Venus and not you. A horse I can replace, but I can't replace my man."

"You have never loved me."

"What?" She jerked back, wondering if he was crazy with fever. "Of course I love you. What kind of jibberish is this?"

"You love Younger. Always love Younger. But I love you, Belle. I loved you since I was boy and before I knew of how men please women. I told my papa, 'That Reed woman makes me twitch.' Father laugh much and tell me, 'Mebbe her man take off and you can make *her* twitch.' But I never make you twitch. Younger make you twitch."

"Sam, this is stupid. I told you that me and Bruce Younger were never—"

"Not that Younger. Cole Younger."

Her heart thudded dully, and her hands slipped from his face. His perception stunned her into pensive silence.

"He sired Pearl. He lives in your heart. There is no room in it for another man. I saw this when you were married to Reed. I suffered with the man, then I followed in his tracks like a fool."

"No, Sam. You aren't and never will be a fool." Belle looked down at her fingers as she worried with the fringe on the lightweight blanket that covered him. "You're right about me loving Cole, but you're wrong about me not loving you. I love you both, but in different ways."

"Tell me the ways."

"Sam, why are we talking about this now? I came here to see about you and help you get well so that—"

"Tell me the ways. Since our wedding, I have wondered about your heart and who is in it. It is time I knew."

She sighed her resignation. How could she refuse him when he'd made such a naked confession?

"Very well. I love Cole with the intensity of a first love," she said, speaking with hesitation as the words came slowly to her. "He was the first man to make me feel womanly. A woman loves her first lover best, but not always last. You understand?"

He nodded, his gray eyes glistening like wet stones, his full lips stretched into a grave line.

"I was fond of Jim. There were brief times when I loved him, but they were never to last long. I never respected Jimmy, and it's hard to love someone you don't respect." She glanced up from her busy fingers to catch the minute nod of Sam's head.

"But my love for you is mature and deeply rooted in respect and gratitude," she continued. "No man ever came through on the promises he made me before you. Jimmy was full of promises, but forgot them as quickly as they were made. Cole's promises were few and too late. Even my own daddy kept promising things that he couldn't make good on. But then Sam Starr stampeded into my life and showed me that promises weren't always hollow words made by dreamers." She glanced shyly at him and smiled. "You promised me my own home in the Bend and you gave that to me. You promised to love and protect me, and you've done that. Sam, I love you. Maybe not with the youthful passion with which I loved Cole Younger, but my heart is full of you."

"Why not marry Younger when you get his child?"

"Several reasons, but none of them are important anymore. Pearl loves you. You're her father, not Cole." She tipped back her head to watch dust motes dance gaily in the lantern light. "When you're older you might better understand my feelings for Cole. They're all wrapped up tight in my memories of youth. When Cole loved me I was young, untried, spirited, bold, curious, beautiful, and thirsting for adventure; so when I think of Cole I feel all those things I used to feel about myself. I liked myself back then, you see."

"You are those things now," Sam argued, one big hand closing over her restless ones on the blanket.

"No, not really." She laughed softly, sadly. "Time and circumstances have beaten me down."

The recent events culminated and Belle felt as limp as a rag doll. She removed her hat and boots and stretched out beside Sam on the narrow cot. He made room for her by pressing his rangy body back against the dirt wall and flinging one muscled arm along her waist to keep her from falling off the edge of the wood and beaver-skin cot.

"Are you satisfied about me and Cole? He's in prison, Sam. I'll never see Cole again."

"You can visit men in prison."

"Yes . . ." Belle examined the possibility and her pulse quickened, then steadied. "No. Prison is no place to spend time with an old friend. It would do us more harm than good. Cole and me are history." She angled herself up to look him in the face. "Sam, I'm going to ask something of you that you're not going to like, but I want you to consider my request before you refuse it."

His black brows met in a frown. "I don't like already."

"Don't be that way," Belle cajoled. "This is important to me, honey." She smoothed her hands across his chest. His skin felt warm and inviting. "Where did West plug you?"

"In my side." He reached a hand around to indicate the square of cotton cloth covering the wound. "I hit my head on rock, but it heals fast." He touched his forehead, then grinned when Belle kissed the purple bruise. "Feels good."

"Are you twitching down there?" Belle asked, rubbing her lower body against his.

"I twitch," Sam assured her.

"Well, before this twitching gets out of hand, I want you to hear me out. Okay, big man?"

"Okay, little woman." His hands cupped her buttocks and his fingers walked in place to gather her skirt, hiking it up to uncover her ankles, her calves, her thighs.

"Enough for now. Listen to me," Belle begged, and Sam's hands settled down on her backside. "I want you to turn yourself in to the U.S. marshal."

His fingers flexed spasmodically and his eyes narrowed.

"Now, Sam, listen." Belle crossed her arms on top of his chest and rested her chin on her hands as she gazed beseechingly at his stubborn scowl. "You're going to get caught. We both know that. You can't live in caves and other people's houses the rest of your days. Sooner or later, you're going to slip up and go to jail. You can choose how you go, or you can take devil's luck."

"I go to hell first before I go to West on my belly."

"That's what I'm getting at. You'll have a better chance in the white man's court, Sam. If West or one of his monkeys arrest you, you'll go to tribal court and they'll throw the book at you. Those old Choctaw chiefs hate you and your daddy. They blame you for all their ills. You won't stand a chance with them. They're itching to string you up."

"So is white man."

"Not so," Belle argued. "You've got one federal charge against you and that's for that post-office burglary awhile back when you were so blind with rage about West that you weren't thinking too clear. Parker's sentencing will be mild compared to what the Choctaw chiefs will do to you. They'll shoot you or burn you or beat you senseless. Parker will just throw you in prison for a year or maybe two."

"I die in prison. I not go."

"Maybe you won't have to go. If you surrender, you'll be protected by the government and John West and his Indian policemen won't be able to touch you. They'll have to quit bothering you and me. I'll get you free on bond. Hell, there's a chance that you'll never go to trial." She pumped excitement into her voice, hoping he'd catch it. "John West will be fit to be tied when he realizes that you're free as a bird and he can't hunt you anymore."

"Can't hunt me. Free as a bird." Sam mulled this over for a few moments and then smiled. "You could do this?"

"Sure, honey. Let's get all the trouble behind us and start fresh again."

"Start fresh," he repeated as if the very idea were ludicrous.

"We can do it. No more horse stealing or whiskey peddling—"

"How will we live?"

"Off the land like everybody else. We'll farm and raise

horses. We'll fish in the streams and hunt game in the winter. We'll be fine."

"We starve."

"No, we won't!" She gripped his shoulders and her expression begged him to share her dream. "Sam, we can do anything if we're a mind to. Say you'll go into town and surrender. Say you'll come back to me and stay with me. No more stealing and killing and getting shot off your horse. Say it, Sam. For me."

Witnessing the desperation in her voice and in the way she looked at him with her enormous doe eyes, Sam crumbled.

"I surrender," he promised, then laughed low in his throat when she flung her arms around his neck and kissed him soundly. "I twitch again."

"Twitch all you want, honey. Thank you, Sam. Thank you, thank you, thank you." She punctuated each with a kiss upon his warm lips. "Now all you've got to do is convince Tom to follow your example."

"Ha! He never surrender to law."

"He'd better, if he knows what's good for him." Belle shook her head when Sam started to argue. "Enough talk. I'm feeling all twitchy myself. What are you going to do about it?"

She squealed with delight when he deftly rolled her off him and the cot. She laughed, finding herself supine on the dirt floor with Sam straddling her. He dispensed with her layers of clothing in record time, flinging them every which way until she was nothing but satiny skin and flowing ebony hair.

"I miss you," he murmured as he draped her legs over his brown shoulders and made ready to enter her. "I tell Tulsie that I must live and get strong to join my body with yours one more time."

"More than once," Belle corrected. "Once isn't enough for us. It never is."

Sam drove into her, and she released a little scream and her eyes rolled back in her head. She held to his corded forearms as he guided her body back and forth to match the surging of his. In her mind she saw California's ocean again, crashing against the rocky land and then moving away. Crashing and retreating, crashing and retreating. Sam was the mighty ocean and she was the thirsting, rocky coastline. He kept crashing into her, chipping away at her rational thought until there was nothing left of it.

It was good not to think, but only to feel. Good to unfurl gossamer sails and ride the crest of Sam's raging ocean. So good to drown in the bronze sea of him and leave not a drop of thought for tomorrow.

On a crisp October morning in 1886 Sam Starr rode into Fort Smith, as fiercely proud and as breathtakingly handsome as an eagle on the wing. Wearing black breeches, black shirt, and gray suede vest, knee-high black boots, and a strip of white leather tying back his shoulder-length, blue-black hair, he was a fine-looking specimen. He rode right up to the federal court with a deputy at his side. Belle Starr rode behind her husband, revolvers strapped around her narrow waist and wearing her flamboyantly feathered hat and an off-center, saucy smile.

The good folks of Fort Smith stopped in their tracks to watch the procession. Jaws dropped like eggs from tall chickens.

Sam Starr surrendered to the federal court. Bond arrangements had been made by Belle before Sam had ridden into town. He was freed on the recognizance of two land-holding relatives of Belle's. He and Belle celebrated his freedom by attending the annual state fair being held in Fort Smith that week.

The wheels of justice turned slowly for Sam and he was not required to appear before the court and face his charges until February of the next year.

The wheels turned faster for Tom Starr. He was apprehended during the first week in November and charged with bringing liquor into the Territory. Belle's lawyer could do nothing since Tom had stubbornly insisted on pleading guilty as charged. Judge Parker didn't argue with Tom about it. He sentenced the old Indian to a year and a half in an Illinois prison. Tom left the Bend and was delivered to the prison by Thanksgiving, swearing that he would add Judge Parker's earlobes to his necklace.

Sam swore that he would fashion his own neck chain with only John West's earlobes as ornaments.

Chapter Twenty

I T'S A TERRIBLE NIGHT for a party," Belle observed, pulling her shawl up over her head as drizzle wet her head. "But I'm glad you decided to come ahead. It wouldn't be right to miss Aunt Lucy's Christmas hoedown."

Belle noted Sam's stern expression and glanced to the back of the wagon with a frown of worry at Pearl and Eddie. They both shrugged, reading her mind and agreeing that it was anybody's guess whether or not Sam Starr would leave his thirst for vengeance behind and enjoy himself. He was hellbent on being mad at the world.

Tom's imprisonment had brought Sam's ire toward John West to an all-time high. His promise to Belle of starting fresh and leading a straight-arrow life had been broken. The past few weeks had been spent in a shroud of doom and gloom, and Belle and her children had literally begged Sam to take them out to Aunt Lucy Surratt's Christmas dance. His thunderous mood was getting on their nerves and they needed a break from it.

Music floated through the trees, and Pearl and Eddie stood up in the wagon to see the brightly lighted barn up ahead. The party was in full swing, having started hours ago. The roads were rutted and muddy, making the trip take twice as long as usual. Eddie and Pearl were out of the wagon before it had come to a full stop. They raced ahead and disappeared inside the crowded barn.

Belle turned sideways to look at Sam. She adjusted the string tie at his throat and kissed his lean cheek.

"You look awful handsome tonight, honey," she told him and managed to coax a smile from him. "I sure will be proud to walk in there on your arm."

"Still love me?"

"Of course. What a silly question." She wrinkled her nose but felt a nagging doubt. Loving Sam wasn't easy of late. Most of the time she wanted to kick his ass. "How do I look?"

His dove-gray eyes swept over her full-skirted, buttercup yellow dress with a scooped neckline that tantalized the male eye.

"Good." His response was more of a grunt than an actual word.

"I guess I'll do." Belle arched a brow at him. "Are you going to help me down from the wagon like a gentleman?"

"I'm not one." He swung down to the ground and grinned up at her as he held out his hands. "But I guess I'll do."

Gratitude washed over her. Thank God, he was hanging up his guns tonight! She rested her hands on his broad shoulders and let him swing her to the ground.

"Sam, let's have fun. Let's forget our troubles and our enemies and let ourselves go. It's Christmas, sweetheart. Can't we just think of that this evening?"

"I will try." His lips brushed her forehead. "You have fun. I watch."

Belle poked an elbow into his stomach, making him double over with a chuckle.

"You stubborn mule, you!" she complained, laughing under her breath. "Let's go inside where it's warm. This drizzle has soaked me to the skin!"

They made a mad dash across the muddy ground to the barn. Folks cleared a path for them, some calling out their names in greeting. The fiddler on the stage motioned for Belle to sit at the pedal organ and help him grind out a few favorites. Never one to pass up a chance to show off her musical skills, Belle consented and took her rightful place on the stage. Sam pulled up a chair and sat right behind the organ, arms crossed, feet planted apart, frown firmly in place. Belle wanted to slap him into next week, but she ignored him instead.

She caught occasional glimpses of Pearl and Eddie as they danced with one partner after another, and she was ever so grateful for their smiling faces. At least *they* were having fun.

During a break in the songs, Sam stood up and leaned over the organ. "I am cold. I go outside by fire." He pointed to a bonfire outside where a circle of men stood and spit tobacco juice at the dancing flames.

Belle nodded. "You do that, honey. Trade stories, tell some lies, talk about how good I am in the sack. Go on, shoo!" She waved her hand at him. He shot her a dubious glare. "I mean it, Sam. It would please me to no end if you'd loosen up and think of something besides settling scores."

"I go tell them how good *I* am in sack and how you moan beneath me like old lumber."

"Get going, you jackass." Belle pursed her lips, sipped a kiss from Sam, then went back to playing the organ. She glanced up briefly to see his wedge of shoulder, edging through the crush of dancers. Handsome son-of-a-gun— and he's all mine.

Her fingers moved automatically across the keyboard and she pumped out a beat with her feet. The fiddler winked at her, and she smiled back at him, sharing the joy that music can bring to the soul.

She heard the gunshots echo in the night. She felt the bullet tear through her own heart. She leaped to her feet and stared over the heads of the others.

"John West and Sam Starr have plugged each other! Both of 'em took it through the heart. They're dead as fire kindling!"

She didn't remember bashing through the stunned crowd. She only knew that, in the next moment, she was kneeling in the mud by the fire. Sam's head was in her lap. His eyes were closed. A trickle of blood ran from the corner of his mouth. Belle felt him. Finding the sticky patch, she tore open his shirt and pressed her hand over the hole to keep the blood from pouring out of him.

"Sam, Sam," she sobbed, bending over him. Her cheek pressed against his and her lips were close to his ear. "I'm scared, honey. I don't know what to do now. I didn't want us to end this way. I wanted us to go on living at the Bend, growing old together and bouncing Pearl's and Eddie's babies on our knees. What am I going to do without you, Sam? I don't want to be a widow again. I'm afraid I'll go crazy like Mama. Don't let me drift again, Sam. Keep me here, safe like you always keep me."

"Ma, he's gone." Eddie squatted beside her and gripped her shoulders, trying to pull her away from the corpse. "Come in out of the rain."

"No!" Belle's eyes flashed wildly. "I'm not leaving him out here alone! He's all wet and cold. He needs me."

She touched the ripped place in his shirt. "Look what you did to your shirt. You looked awful pretty tonight, honey. Why'd you go and mess yourself up like this?"

"Ma, please," Eddie begged, his voice breaking. "Don't do this. Sam's dead, damn it! He done went and challenged West to a draw and got killed. At least he took West out with him. But it's all done. Sam has crossed over."

"He hasn't." Belle wept hysterically, twisting out of Eddie's hands and bending over Sam again to kiss his cool lips. "He promised to take care of me. Protect me for always and always."

"Mama?" Pearl dropped to her haunches in front of Belle. She reached out and smoothed a wayward lock of Sam's hair. "Let's take Sam inside where it's dry and warm. Let go of him, so these men can pick him up and carry him inside. Please, Mama. Let go."

Belle looked into Pearl's calm blue eyes and then at the white, grief-stricken faces around her. She kissed Sam once more on the mouth before letting the men carry him inside Aunt Lucy's house.

Belle and Pearl sat beside Sam's body all night. Belle uttered not one sound, but her head was full of noise. She relived her precious moments with Sam, her furious fights with him, and she said farewell to him with big, glistening teardrops that rolled, one by one, down her cheeks, off her chin, and onto her muddy, bloody hands.

Eddie and Tulsie brought a buckboard for him at daybreak.

"Is she going to be okay?" Eddie asked Pearl, glancing with worry at his mother's dull eyes and pallid skin.

"Yes, in time," Pearl assured him.

"She's fine in the head, isn't she?" Eddie asked.

"Edwin," Pearl said with an exasperated sigh, "Mama just lost her husband. Let her grieve over him a sufficient time before you start wondering if she's crazy, will you?"

"Okay, okay!"

They were halfway home when Belle suddenly spoke up.

"We'll bury him in the Starr cemetery near Tom's house. You know the place, Eddie?"

"Y-yes, Ma." Eddie turned wide, red-rimmed eyes on Pearl, getting a lifting of blond brows from her. Tulsie sat on the tailgate of the buckboard, guarding his brother's sheet-wrapped body, and paid no attention to them.

"Well, then take this other road," Belle said, motioning to the right of the forked trail.

"But I thought you'd want to go home—"

"No, not until Sam is resting comfortably."

"Ma?" Eddie said, leaning forward to look into his mother's face.

"Yes?" Belle retorted, giving him her full attention.

"You okay?"

"Other than being pissed off at having my children talk about me as if I'm deaf, yes."

"Mama, we didn't mean anything by that," Pearl hastened to explain. "We were just worried about you since you haven't talked since last night."

Belle shrugged off her behavior. "Sam isn't the first man I've buried. My life has been full of dead men. This time it was . . ." She paused and swallowed hard as her eyes filled with tears. "This time was the worst. Worse than when I buried sweet Bud." Belle blinked away her tears and drew a deep breath, filling her lungs with damp air. "It'll be a blue Christmas, children, but we'll survive. I always seem to survive."

Belle glanced upward at a sky that was as gray as Sam's eyes had been the last time she'd seen them. She wondered if there was a God up there and if anybody she'd buried had ever made it to heaven.

Chapter Twenty-One

BELLE SAT STIFFLY in the hardwood chair and looked around her at the four bare, whitewashed walls. The floor beneath her feet was a black-and-white checkerboard pattern, scratched and broken. Above her hung a rusty lantern. High up in one corner of the tiny room was a window. Sunlight fell in bands through the bars. She could hear a bird singing, bragging of its freedom. It was a cruel, cruel song.

Folding her hands over the beaded purse in her lap, Belle sat straight and prim in her gray velvet jacket, long black skirt, pearly pink blouse, and smart, narrow-brimmed bonnet. She'd retired the white plumed hat along with her life as Mrs. Sam Starr.

"Why am I being put in solitary confinement? I didn't do nothing."

The voice was so achingly familiar that Belle had to press her lips together to keep from sobbing with joy. Her body trembled with sweet memories.

"This ain't solitary," a stranger's voice informed. "You got a visitor."

"In here?"

A key scraped around in a lock and then the heavy door swung open. Belle strained her eyes, cursing the halo of light that obscured the man's face. The guard gave him a push and he stumbled inside.

"Thirty minutes, ma'am, and I'll be right outside. Them's my orders." The door closed with a hollow boom.

The shadowy form shuffled closer until a bar of sunlight fell across his whiskered face. It was a gaunt face with sunken cheeks and dry lips. His carriage was stooped. His hair stuck out this way and that like straw. His clothes, dingy white and gray, hung on his thin frame. Only his eyes held yesterday in them. Pastel blue. Like Pearl's.

He blinked, then rubbed his eyes in an endearing way that made Belle think of a little boy awakening from a fantastic dream. He clutched a black leather Bible in one hand.

"It's me," she assured him.

"Myra Maybelle?" he asked, still unsure.

Belle smiled. "It's been a long time since anyone's called me that. Sounds good to me, though. If I'm Myra Maybelle, then you must be Thomas Coleman, but you sure don't look much like him." She touched the gray at her temples, knowing exactly where it was. "Of course, I don't look sixteen anymore myself."

"What in hell are you doing here?" he asked, flinging out his arms to indicate the dank cell.

"Visiting an old flame, I reckon."

"B-but how did you . . . I mean, we're alone in here and I . . . what about the warden?"

Belle stood up, grabbed his wrists, and guided him over to the cot in the corner. She pushed him down on it and sat beside him.

"Comfy?" she asked. "Good. You ought to know by now that when I set my mind to something, I get my way."

"But visitors are taken to the visitation room where they speak to us through—"

"No, no." Belle shook her head. "There's no way I would see you like that. No way. That's why I never visited you while you were in jail back in Northfield. I couldn't bear the thought of seeing you behind iron bars."

"Belle . . ." His voice trailed off and he hung his head. "You shouldn't have come here."

"I wanted to. I sold my piano and came here to flash that money under the warden's nose. Seeing as how I'm the famous Outlaw Queen and I was talking cold, hard cash, he decided to grant me thirty minutes alone with you with no bars to separate us."

"You did that?" He wagged his head in amazement. "Why? What's happened to make you want to see me so bad?"

"We don't have time for me to tell you all that's happened to me since I saw you last. I'm a widow. You should know that."

"Jim died. I heard about that."

"No . . . I mean, yes. Jim died. But I married Sam Starr after that. He died five months ago. He was shot by a marshal."

"Sam Starr . . . one of Tom's boys?"

"Yes. His oldest."

"I'm sorry you lost another husband." He shrugged helplessly as if he didn't know what was expected of him. "How's Pearl?"

"Pretty and all grown up! Young men are swarming all over her. It takes all my time just to keep swatting them away. You'd be so proud of her, Cole. She looks so much like you. She's got your hair and eyes and sweet nature."

"Sweet nature?" His smile was full of irony. "I don't think a sweet nature landed me in this pit."

"Don't argue with me." She turned sideways so that she could face him squarely, but he avoided her direct gaze. Was he angry with her for waiting so long before visiting him? Was that why he was keeping his distance from her?

"Cole, I should have come before now, but I didn't think you'd want to see me. My heart broke when they sent you to this place. I was foolish enough to believe that you'd maybe get only a year or two behind bars."

He placed the Bible off to one side of the cot. "Me, too. I used to live on hope, but no more." His hands were laced and hung between his bent knees. He lifted his head to stare at the window set high above him. "Hope dies in darkness. It's always dark in here."

She knew his frame of mind because she had once felt the same sense of damnation. Kneeling in front of him, she reached up to take his bearded face in her hands.

"Cole, I came here to tell you that I'll wait for you."

He blinked his beautiful eyes in confusion.

"I'll wait for you," Belle repeated. "I've never been able to forget you. Even though I loved Sam, I thought of you so often that Sam even knew you still had a hold on me."

"I'm not a saint!" His voice rose alarmingly as if signaling the inner fury that seethed under his docile surface. "I never was! You always treated me as if I were beyond reproach . . . as if I could do no wrong. I was always in the right, no matter if I cheated or lied or robbed or murdered. You always made excuses for me."

"You did what you did because you had no choice! The Yankees—"

"Had nothing to do with it." He sighed and fell back to rest his shoulders against the wall. "Oh, maybe at first, they did. I was bitter, just like every Confederate soldier. Losing

336

isn't a pleasure. Later, I could have turned myself over to the federal government, served a short sentence, and have been released, but I decided not to do that. Instead, I kept right on looting and robbing and ruining people's lives like I had a right." His gaze caught hers and held fast. "I had no right. Neither did Jesse or Frank or Quantrill—or you."

Belle stood up, shaking with anger. "What have they done to you in here? What mental trash have they been shoving at you? Why, you act as if the South was to blame for the North being so all-mighty uppity! We didn't ask them into our lives. They barged in with guns and cannons ablazing! Have you forgotten that, Cole Younger? Have you forgotten that the Yankees killed your papa?"

"The war is over, Belle. Has been for years now."

"You're a hero," she said, pointing a shaking finger at him.

"I'm a convict." His tone didn't change, and his expression matched it. Bland, bored, uncaring. "I'm in here for life because I robbed a bank and killed a man. It was an accident—the murder—but I did it. Those are the facts, Belle. Why can't you face them?"

"Those are your facts, not mine. Why should you have gone to prison for being a true son of the Confederacy? As for the bank robbery, you needed that money to set up your brothers and you in a new place, didn't you?"

"What if I did? That gave me no right to go into a bank and steal it!" He wrapped his arms around his head and stamped his feet in a burst of frustration. Glancing at her and seeing her bewilderment, he reached out his hands and clawed the air as he released a playful grimace and growl. Belle couldn't help but smile at his speechless exasperation with her.

"You just refuse to give up your pretty picture of me, don't you?"

Looking into the eyes that had held her spellbound for so many years, she felt young again and completely rejuvenated. He was, above all else, her fountain of youth.

"You're all I have, Cole. I can't give you up. That's why I came all this way. I had to tell you that you're still my hero and I'll be waiting for you at Youngers Bend. When you get out—"

"*If* I get out, I'll be an old man. At least sixty. In fact, I don't imagine I'll leave this place alive."

Belle knelt in front of him again and pressed her fingers against his lips.

"No, no. Don't say that. You'll walk out of this place, believe me. You'll come straight to me and I'll love you back to your former self. Cole. Say you will." She took his hands in hers and lifted them to her lips, kissing each. "We both need something to look forward to. Let's look forward to each other."

He smiled, warming her heart, and then began to chuckle. His eyes filled with tears of mirth and then he started to laugh until the tears spilled onto his cheeks.

Belle stared at him, watching him double over with belly laughter. She giggled, glad to see him laughing, but not understanding what had tickled him so.

Cole drew her up from her knees to sit beside him on the hard cot, his arm around her shoulders, his laughter mingling with hers and bouncing off the walls.

"Cole," she said when she could talk amid her giggles, "what are we laughing about? This isn't funny!"

"Y-yes, it is." He flung back his head and released another howl. "It's goddamned hilarious!"

Belle glanced toward the door and saw the guard's face stuck up against the barred window set in it. He was frowning at her.

"Cole, hush up! The guard thinks we're crazy." Belle

elbowed Cole in the ribs, but she couldn't keep herself from laughing again with him. She struggled for composure, lost it, caught it, lost it, then grabbed on and held fast. "Cole, stop laughing," she begged, grabbing his shirtfront and shaking him.

His cheeks were wet with tears. His eyes were bright blue as if they'd been cleansed of their earlier despair. His lips were no longer dry, but moist and inviting. His chuckles died away, but his smile remained.

"I'm sorry, but I got tickled thinking about the two of us. We're a pair, you know that? Two romantic fools, making poetry out of carnage. We're a couple of dunces." He angled a glance at her. "So you've been up to no good, have you?"

"Some good. I still have my Pearl and Eddie. From here on in I want to make them proud of me. I don't want them to be ashamed of their mother. I'm going to live quietly at Youngers Bend and not give the law any reason to even glance my way."

"That'll be the day."

She punched him in the shoulder. "I mean it!" Her glance fell on the Bible and she picked it up. "Look at you. You're carrying this Bible around with you and telling me how you made a choice to rob and murder and now you're sorry for it. You're singing a different tune, so why can't I?"

He took the Bible from her and laid it in his lap. His fingers moved lovingly over the gold letter *B*.

"Thinking of becoming a preacher once you're out of here?" Belle asked, trying to make him grin again. She loved his smile. Loved to feel it in her heart.

"This book has given me a measure of peace when I've needed it," he admitted. "When I've seen my darkest hours, I've opened this book and found a little ray of light." He opened it and the pages fell naturally to a center page.

Belle smiled, thinking of Cole sitting in his lonely cell and opening the Good Book for some encouragement. She looked down at it and her smile trembled on her lips. Cole lifted the Bible so that she could see the chain of dried flowers lying upon a page bearing Psalm 69.

"Remember this?" he asked, touching the faded morning glories with the tip of his forefinger. "You gave it to me after you'd given me the last minutes of your girlhood. The sweetest gifts I ever got." He seemed surprised when she burst into tears. "What's wrong?"

She flung her arms around his neck and cried on his shoulder. His arms circled her waist and his lips moved hesitantly against her forehead and temple.

"Cole, I never kn-knew you'd k-kept those." She'd waited so long for a sign from him—a clear sign that he truly loved her as much as she loved him. "You do love me, don't you?"

"Yes, Belle." His hands moved up to frame her face and his fingertips edged into her hairline where time had frosted some strands. "I love you. I've sinned so many times I can't count them all, but my blackest sin was in not sharing your joy about having my child. If I had only put aside my own selfish needs and taken you in my arms right then. If I'd only—"

"Hush," Belle urged, silencing him with her lips upon his. "We can't change any of that. Let's think about our future, not our past. We've still got time, Cole. With luck, we'll both live to be one hundred and that'll give us forty years together. That'll be enough, don't you think?"

"That'll be just fine," he agreed; then his mouth melted over hers in a perfect fit.

His kiss put to shame all those that had gone before it. She kissed him back, sliding her tongue into his mouth and memorizing his taste and texture. The memory would have to last many, many years.

The guard unlocked the door and stepped inside. "Time."

Belle nodded and turned back to Cole. She closed the Bible upon her flowers and placed the book in his work-roughened hands.

"Hold on," she whispered, and he gave her a smile to take back with her to Youngers Bend.

Epilogue

ON FEBRUARY 2, 1889, three days before her forty-first birthday, Belle Starr was ambushed by an unknown assailant. She'd been out visiting friends and was riding back to her home in Youngers Bend when she was shot off her horse.

Pearl arrived in time to share her mother's last moments. Legend has it that Belle revealed the name of her murderer. But if so, Pearl kept it to herself and no one was ever arrested. There were any number of suspects, including Belle's son, Eddie.

Belle was buried near her house on February 6, the day after her birthday. Her pearl-handled revolvers were buried with her, but her grave was looted and the guns were taken. Her tombstone, designed by Pearl and etched by a local stonecutter, still stands at Youngers Bend in Oklahoma. Carved into the granite are pictures of a horse, a bell, and a star. Beneath Belle's name, place of birth, date of birth, and date of death are these words:

Shed not for her the bitter tear,
Nor give the heart to vain regret.
Tis but the casket that lies here,
The gem that filled it sparkles yet.

Cole Younger was granted a parole in 1901. He died fifteen years later on a farm in Lee's Summit, Missouri, at the age of seventy-two.

He never married.